SALVAGE RAT

Larry N. Martin

SALVAGE RAT

CHAPTER ONE

GUNSHOTS WENT WITH the territory, no matter how much Wyatt intended to avoid trouble. But here and now? This was not part of the plan.

Space salvage was not for the timid or those with a tender conscience. Wyatt was neither. When the first shot sizzled past his shoulder, he had nearly pried out the last of the electronic panels he had come for, panels that were worth more for the rare metals in their components than for their long-outdated tech.

He dove for cover at the next junction in the corridor and wondered how anyone knew he was on the old, abandoned mining colony. No one else was supposed to be there, let alone be shooting at him. He had scanned the place thoroughly. They must have come in after he'd already entered the mining base.

Then he realized that for once, the shooters weren't after him.

They were shooting at a woman who appeared to be running for her life. She tore past him without a glance, and he noticed her civilian jumpsuit and lack of weapons.

In that split-second, Wyatt's battle instincts kicked in, just as a pack of six security men in gray uniforms raced down the corridor with guns drawn. Part of him knew he should stay out of it, that it wasn't his fight, let alone a fair fight. He knew it, but he leaned around the corner, aimed, and shot anyhow.

"Dammit! She's got back-up!" one of the Grays swore as Wyatt's shots clipped three of them before they got a bead on where he was. Outside, those would have been kill shots, since "winging" someone in a pressure suit was as good as putting a bullet through their head. But he had coaxed the old mine's main gravity and air recycler to working again. With only emergency lighting operational, the corridors had deep shadows.

"Requesting more men," the Gray spoke into his link as the others opened fire from where they'd taken positions at the next cross-corridor. One of the shots barely missed Wyatt's ear.

"Screw that," Wyatt muttered, getting in a couple more shots to pin down the Grays and then running like hell as he followed the path the woman had taken. He took the next right and headed down a long hallway with doors on both sides. *Probably the offices for the old mining colony,* he thought. Wyatt picked a door and dove into the darkness seconds before he heard the Grays clear the corner. The security guards thundered past, and he leaned back against the wall and let out a deep breath.

Definitely not one of my smarter moves. Damn.

"Who the hell are you?" It was a woman's voice.

Wyatt blinked in the dim glow of the emergency low-level lighting. He wondered briefly if he should feel grateful or cursed that fates had him choose the same hiding spot as the woman. He took a moment to check out his surroundings. The room looked as if the mining bosses had just walked out and left everything behind—furniture, files, even the pictures on the wall. *Very likely since it would have cost more than the stuff was worth to ship it home again,* Wyatt thought. Which was what brought him to the mine in the first place.

Most of the time, salvage meant boarding derelict ships and recovering anything useful or saleable. But when space stations and colonies started being built, occupied for a short time, and then abandoned and left to rot, the laws were expanded. Even a hundred years out of date, usable stuff in good condition brought good money piecemeal, especially with the homesteaders out on the hardscrabble moons and the Fringe. Enough to keep Wyatt in fuel and supplies for a while.

Vandals and thieves had been picking at the place for a while, though it was off the main trading routes. Wyatt had a map and blueprints he'd picked up from a trader on Gascon—the great-grandson of someone who had worked in the mine's construction crew. This job was supposed to be an easy in-and-out. Not anymore.

"You're welcome," Wyatt said to the figure in the deep shadows. "For shooting at those Grays back there."

She snorted. "They'll think we're together. So instead of just shooting me, they'll shoot both of us."

Wyatt could only make out her silhouette, but it looked as if she had a weapon trained on him. He pondered for a moment as he clearly remembered her hands were empty when he saw her pass.

"You didn't come in with us, and no one else is supposed to be here," she whispered. "So what are you doing here?"

"Freelance salvage," Wyatt replied. "This site just crossed into 'fair use' status. It's been abandoned for a century, so I've got a right to be here." *Take that. I know my salvage laws, even if I bend them now and again.*

"Kalok Enterprises," she said. "We founded this colony. And you're wrong. It's ours for another three months. The clock starts from the Stellar Commission's license date, not the Interplanetary Mining Guild acquisition date."

"Details, details," Wyatt replied. *She came here with the people trying to shoot her? So maybe I've got what she needs—a way off this rock.* Wyatt slowly stepped closer. He kept his left hand away from the gun on his hip and kept the gun in his right hand pointed at the floor.

"That's close enough. Who are you?"

"Wyatt William McCoy, salvage reclamation specialist. And you are?"

"None of your business."

"Remember, I have a ship, and you don't," Wyatt said. "Want to reconsider?"

She was silent for a moment; her weapon still pointed at his chest. "Oh, what the hell. I'm in deep shit now anyway," she said finally. "Elizabeth Parker—Beth. I'm with the Space Archeology Department at the University of Ceritan Four, doing a special project for Kalok. Or at least I was," she added. "Since they're shooting at me, it probably means I've lost the job."

Wyatt held back the laugh and inched farther to the right while they talked, and whether Beth was aware of it, she mirrored his movement. That meant the emergency light was no longer behind her, and Wyatt could see her better. Short, petite, attractive, with dark hair cut chin-length, perfect for a helmet, late twenties or early thirties, he guessed. Wyatt also got a better look at the "weapon" in her hand.

"If you promise not to shoot me with that statue, I promise not to shoot you with my gun."

Beth rolled her eyes and lowered her arm. "It worked all right in the dark," she muttered.

"We need to get out of here. They'll be back. So—why are they shooting at you? Make it quick." He moved back to the door and put his ear close to listen. He considered calling Nellie to get some recon, but that might alert the Grays to her presence, which was something he definitely wanted to avoid.

Beth glared at him. "How's this? I found out Kalok engineered the explosion that killed the miners, then let the clean-up crew die rather than pay for transport out of here. Cheaper for the company that way. Not just here, but on lots of mines and colonies. People died. Kalok covered up. *They* found out that *I* found out, and now I think they mean to kill me to keep me from talking."

Damn. Wyatt thought, turning back to look at her. Given his own experiences and what he knew about the mine, Beth's story had a good chance of being true. The Comstock mining colony had run out of *platitite* ore a hundred years ago. The Yellow Jacket mine was the real motherlode in its time but ran its course, and the Yellow Jacket's end wasn't a good one. Right about the time the ore veins were running dry, there was a big accident—no one seemed to agree on exactly what happened—and all the miners died. The corporation shut the place down and flew away.

I've heard plenty of speculation and rumors about Kalok out in the Rim, but no one ever had proof, Wyatt thought. *If she's telling the truth—if she's got the goods—this could be huge. We'd just have to live long enough to tell the tale.*

"How do you expect to get out of here?" he asked.

"I didn't think the Kalok people would figure out I was onto them this soon," she said. "But there's an old ship near the mag-rail. If it was closed down properly, it might still fly."

Wyatt raised an eyebrow. "That's at least two klicks north. If the ship still works and if you could fly it. The odds are not in your favor."

"My dad was a pilot. He taught me. I can fly it," Beth replied.

"My ship's closer and it hasn't been left to rot for a hundred years. Let's go."

"When did this become your business?"

"When they started shooting at me. Besides, you've got an important story to tell—and you don't have a gun." Wyatt knew from the look on Beth's face that she disliked the situation, but there wasn't much room to argue. He also wondered again if he should trust fate because this was either an incredible coincidence or a trap.

"Go where?"

"For now, anywhere besides here," Wyatt replied, checking the charge on his weapon and the readings on his armored pressure suit, which was deactivated for the moment. "Your boss doesn't have a way to deactivate your atmo suit, does he? Company property and all that?"

Beth shook her head. "Give me a break. I thought ahead enough to hack the IOT connection, so it isn't recording, and I removed the tracker and beacon, so it isn't telling tales."

He gripped her arm as she moved toward the door and turned her, so she was facing him. "Be clear on this. Kalok is playing for keeps. You're a threat. So they'll shoot to kill—and so will I. If you can't handle that say so now and I'll leave you on your own." Wyatt paused. "And if you're good with it, once we're out of here, I want the whole story."

Something hard glittered in Beth's eyes. "Just keep the corpses to a minimum. Let's go."

I don't make promises I can't keep, Wyatt thought as eased out of the door, looking in both directions. It was clear, so he signaled for Beth to follow. He had already disabled the mine complex's internal surveillance cameras along the route back to his ship, just in case.

They'd only made it a short distance when they came to a "T" in the hall. He did a quick check; the Grays were waiting at the next corridor.

Wyatt shot first. The Grays returned fire. One of the blasts almost hit Wyatt in the shoulder. Wyatt's shot didn't miss. He may have been a pilot first, but years in combat had ingrained his training, so it was second nature. Wyatt picked off a second Gray, so focused on his target that he didn't notice the big hole in the wall from the shot that just missed his head. He knew the sound of gunfire would bring more guards, even if they hadn't already called for backup, but for the moment, the way was clear.

"Come on," he said in a low voice. Wyatt grabbed the dead Grays' guns and shoved one into Beth's hands, then checking charges, slung the other over his shoulder. He glanced at Beth, surprised to see she held the blaster like she knew how to use it.

They ducked down a side corridor, around a couple of corners, and through two large rooms that opened between hallways. "How do you know this place so well?" Beth whispered, just barely audible.

"Old construction blueprints," Wyatt returned. He found the stairs—no chance of taking a lift where they could be trapped—and he hoped the colony hadn't renovated. The dark, utilitarian stairs weren't really meant for regular use once the station was put into operation. He listened at the exit door and then carefully opened it, checking the corridor. "Clear."

Wyatt led through several more corridors, and stopped at what appeared to be a dead end and stared at the blank wall. "There's supposed to be a door here."

"Are you sure we're in the right place?"

Wyatt had downloaded his scan of the old map. He pulled up the hologram which glowed brightly in the dim lighting, he held out his forearm, aligning his position and checked again. "Yeah. We're in the right place."

"Maybe someone remodeled," she replied.

He tapped on the wall. Once upon a time, this section housed offices for the brass, so it looked nicer than some of the other sections. That meant the "walls" weren't the real outer skin; they had a thin plasti-sheet over them for looks. "Maybe you're right," Wyatt murmured.

"Close up your suit, the air may not be good in the maintenance tunnels," he said and activated his portable helmet. It wouldn't work in all conditions, but this was supposed to be a simple salvage. The helmet telescoped out of his collar and locked into place. He double checked the seals and transferred the holo to the internal screen. Wyatt pulled a plasma torch out of his bag, one with enough power to cut through thick metal, and sliced easily through the thin, plasti-skin wall covering to find the door behind.

"Come on," Wyatt muttered as he wrestled with the lock. The metal door was mechanical, not computerized because the computers weren't online when the place was built. The only concession was the control lock added later, and he just happened to have an old passkey that had come with the map. To Wyatt's relief, the door wasn't locked, and he didn't need it. The heavy metal door stuck from years of disuse, but when he and Beth both put their shoulders into the effort, it opened with a shriek of protest.

Wyatt entered first with his weapon drawn, checking the corridor in both directions before moving forward. There was no emergency lighting here, so he had to use the lamp on his armor suit. Wyatt hated using the suit's L.E.D.s; he always thought it made him too easy a target.

His assessment of the corridor was instinctive: *No cobwebs or rats to worry about, no dripping water or mold. A fine covering of dust meant no one had come this way for quite a while.* These tunnels should have been pressurized and had breathable air, but he wasn't about to trust that was still the case. Beth had suited up, and her light added to his. Wyatt gave a momentary scowl as he realized that her civilian-issue suit had no armor, and minimal protection. The helmet was no more than a force field bubble. He shook his head. *Worthless piece of crap.*

"What about the door?" Beth asked with a jerk of her head. Wyatt pulled out the passkey and hoped it fit the lock. It did. There was a faint click.

"There. If the Grays find it, it'll be locked, and they'll probably figure we gave up and went elsewhere," Wyatt said.

"Or they'll blow the lock off and come after us."

"Then let's be far away from here by the time they do."

"Where are we going?" Beth stuck right behind Wyatt as they wound their way through the service tubes. The tunnel was pressurized, but his suit readouts confirmed that the air was bad. He kept his gun out. The legend and info he found on the data stream held that construction workers saw some strange things building the Comstock complex, and Wyatt wasn't taking any chances.

"My ship," Wyatt said. "Parked it near one of the old equipment depots. No one's used that area since they finished construction."

That's when he realized Beth had stopped still a few paces behind him. "We're not alone down here," she said.

Wyatt leveled his gun at the darkness ahead. He wasn't picking up readings, hadn't heard anything, hadn't seen anything… "Grays?"

"No. Ghosts."

Wyatt turned an "are-you-crazy" look at Beth, who glared right back. Even through the distortion of her atmo helmet, he could see her expression. "I found a piece of alien tech from an abandoned trading colony on Ribus Nine," she said. "And when it activated, I got more than I bargained for. It picks up out-of-phase energies trapped in time and space. What most people call 'ghosts.' That's part of how I figured out that Kalok was lying."

A prickly tingle went down Wyatt's spine. "And?"

Beth tilted her head as if she were listening to a transmission on a glitchy headset. Maybe she was, in a way. "I'm getting jumbled images. Kind of like watching a holofilm with bits and pieces missing. There's something big, scary, and dangerous down here. People disappeared."

"What is it?" Wyatt asked, wondering first if his new companion was batshit crazy, then wondering whether a monster from way back when could still be active. *Hell of a long time between meals. Then again, we don't know squat about most of the planets we build on. Just enough to slide the plans past the right approval boards along with the bribes. So it wouldn't be the first time that an "uninhabited" planet really wasn't.*

"I can't get a good look at it," she replied. "But from what I see, looks like it killed a bunch of maintenance workers and a few hardlucks." She meant stragglers, people with nowhere else to go. Mines were a last-resort employer for people who were already down on their luck, so if something pushed them over the edge, they gravitated toward places like the tunnels.

"We sure as hell can't go back," Wyatt said. "So we're going to have to go forward."

Wyatt watched the map, and Beth watched the ghosts. The Comstock was a big place, and its underside was just as big. Its builders dug tunnels under the mining colony to run wiring and conduits, and to bring in supplies from the landing pads. From what showed on the old map, Comstock took up almost as much room underneath the ground as it did above, not counting the mine itself.

Old piles of tattered clothing, blankets, and rucksacks littered the tunnel. Whoever had sought refuge down here was dead and gone a century ago, along with the doomed miners and shut-down crew.

Something rattled against Wyatt's boot. He looked down and saw a crushed bone. "More of them up here," Beth said. The tunnel floor was littered with old bones, human bones. Some of the smaller bones were intact, but the big ones had all been snapped, sometimes more than once.

"Whatever did this; it's coming our way!" She grabbed hold of Wyatt's arm, and as soon as she touched him, he could see the images as if someone had turned on a holograph projector in his brain. Glowing images overlaid reality. Ghosts surrounded them. Old men with hard-bitten features watched the corridor balefully. A few younger men stared glassy-eyed. Ragged women glanced fearfully down the dark tunnel and then ran right through Beth and Wyatt.

A muffled thud from behind them told Wyatt that the Grays had blown open the door. Ghosts and monsters ahead, men with guns behind, and still some distance to cover to get to the ship.

Ahead, a shadow moved, close to the floor, just at the edge of their lights. Thick around as a man's torso, but long, undulating and graceful, the shadow was fast and nearly silent. "Can it hurt us?" Wyatt asked as he tried to figure out if it was real or part of the shared vision.

"I don't know," she replied. "And you've got to be touching me to see what I see. The tech has a very limited range."

"Let's run for it," Wyatt said. "Worst case, we die. If we break contact, just make sure to tell me where to go—or not go." Wyatt and Beth ran toward the shadow beast. Its black body coiled and stretched, long enough that its tail was lost in the shadows, thick enough that it could have certainly preyed on humans. Maybe it was native, or maybe one of the miners or vagabonds had smuggled it in long ago. For a time, it could have fed on the hard-lucks. Odds were that when they all died, it died, too. The image flickered for Wyatt as they separated, and he tried to stay close enough to Beth to keep contact.

"Keep all the way to the right," Beth called as she sprinted, trying to pull Wyatt along with her.

The shadow beast's toothy mouth opened wide, its jaw unhinging, blocking the corridor. It looked like a cross between a snake and a centipede, and its huge mouth was full of teeth. Beth led them right toward the maw of the monster before they stepped to the right. For an instant, bone-chilling cold passed through Wyatt, through his skin and the marrow of his bones. And then they were clear, on the other side.

"Think the Grays will be able to see it?" he asked as they kept on running.

"Don't know," Beth answered. "I'm new at this ghost stuff. Could you see it when we weren't touching?"

"No, but I could feel it."

Wyatt's leg brushed against something, and he leveled his gun to shoot until he realized what he was looking at—the perfectly-preserved mummy of the biggest snake-monster he had ever seen, the beast whose ghost they had run through. He shivered in spite of himself, glad he had only seen the creature after it was dead.

The tunnel led upward toward ground level. Wyatt and Beth climbed over piles of bones and debris to get through the rest of the tunnel and reach the maintenance exit. Wyatt found the manual wheel to open the airlock just as shouts echoed behind them. With a lurch, the airlock wheel gave under Wyatt's efforts, and the first door opened. They ran inside and secured the door behind them. Wyatt swore under his breath as he put his full weight into tugging the wheel on the second door free. Beth turned to face the first airlock door, gun raised.

"Here we go, hold on," Wyatt said, as the balky wheel turned. The door opened, and Wyatt blinked in the blinding daylight as the pressurized air behind them rushed toward the opening like a brief gale-force wind.

They sprinted the short distance to Wyatt's ship, which was right where he left it, hidden by old metal shipping crates and storage buildings that were almost as large as it was. "There she is, the *Nellie B*," Wyatt said with a note of pride. "And she's all mine." To anyone who'd served, they'd immediately see the Star Force gunship she used to be. Even with the modifications, odd repair patches, and additions Wyatt had made, there was no missing the menacing profile or the signature anti-reflective black finish.

Wyatt opened his com-link. "Open her up for me, Nellie."

"Please confirm," the female voice echoed in his ear.

"It's me baby, Wyatt William McCoy. Oh, and I'm bringing on a passenger."

The ship looked out of place near all the scrap and ruins. While not the sleekest or prettiest, she was imposing. A bright white light illuminated around the ramp seam in the otherwise mat-black surface. It slowly extended to the ground before a louder *woosh* sounded with the opening of the outer airlock. Wyatt quickly made his way to the ramp and indicated for Beth to proceed him. He kept his gun drawn and watched the mine facility exit until Beth was up the ramp and he could follow. Wyatt backed up the ramp and once inside the outer lock, put his hand to the panel and closed the hatch. The ship's outer hatch slid into place with a loud metallic thud and Wyatt could hear the locks engaging.

"Nellie, begin startup procedures. Engage anti-personnel guns and shields."

Beth turned to him with a questioning look.

Wyatt shrugged as jets of air and a disinfectant spray filled the airlock. The light over the inner door illuminated green and the heavily armored hatch slid open. Wyatt hit the release for his helmet and took a deep breath as it slid back into his suit.

"Make yourself at home, Ms. Parker. Watch your step. I didn't really worry about passengers when I made additions. Nellie, pull in the ramp and prepare for take-off. Oh, and Nellie. This is Beth Parker; she'll be traveling with us for a bit. Be nice to her. Beth, meet Nellie."

"Thanks for hosting me, Nellie," Beth said to the open air,

Wyatt made his way to the bridge, stepping over and around equipment haphazardly bolted to the dark gray supports and low-hanging wiring conduits a few times before passing through the heavy hatchway to the bridge. Wyatt dropped into the pilot's seat as Beth looked around at the plethora of displays and controls at the bridge's workstations. He pulled the harness into position, hit the release, and let the seat and harness conform to his body. Images from the external cameras popped up on his screens. He saw the mine door blow open and then Grays in pressure suits stormed out of the utility tunnels and opened fire. The shots sounded like small pings inside the ship.

"Can they damage the hull?" Beth asked.

"They don't have anything Nellie's shields can't handle." Wyatt grinned as he heard Nellie's responding fire and he angled the thrusters.

"Nellie, engage and assume a low orbit while we plot a destination."

"Unable to comply. Ms. Parker is not secure."

"Where?" Beth asked as she looked around the bridge.

"Pick a seat, any seat, and buckle up. We need to get out of here."

Beth sat in the co-pilot's chair and pulled on the harness. It quickly tightened around her, and she gave Wyatt an apologetic shrug. "Got distracted."

"Engaging now," Nellie responded. Wyatt watched the monitors as the engines kicked a cloud of dust in the guards' faces, throwing them back toward the airlock.

"Where to?" Beth asked as she looked again at the various consoles.

"I'm thinking Rum Row," Wyatt replied. His hands flew across the input panels, bringing up star charts and streams of information. "Yeah, that should work," he muttered. "Nellie, I've entered the destination. Plot and set course." Rum Row was the ring of appropriated old space stations, hijacked satellites, questionable space liners, and disreputable docking platforms just outside government-patrolled space. It was also a jumping-off point to most of the settled planets. "I need more fuel. And you'll be able to find a ship to anywhere you want to go."

"Why would I want to do that?" Beth asked, stretching out her long legs. "There's nowhere I can run that Kalok and its partners can't find me—nowhere legitimate. I can't go back to the university; it's the first place Kalok will look. I still have a copy of my data. But if I show up on any colony Interplan controls, I'll disappear before I can do anything with the information."

"So what's your plan?"

"The way I figure it, I can be an asset to you," Beth said, giving him a pleading look as excitement glittered in her eyes. "I'm an archeologist with more knowledge of languages and native cultures than you've even heard of. I know all about old colonies and ruins. You're a salvage rat. You loot those places."

"Please," Wyatt protested with exaggerated pain. "The term is 're-claim.'" Wyatt's eyes narrowed. He glanced down at the display and quickly confirmed Nellie's course and calculations. "Now would be a good time to explain more about these 'ghosts' of yours—and why we just left an abandoned mine with people shooting at us."

Beth sighed and took a long pause before speaking. "Space archeology is all about going to abandoned colonies, outposts, space stations, mines, and other places that provided stepping stones to the colonization of the quadrant. They're part of quadrant history, but in their day, no one thinks they're important—until later, when it's up to people like me to reconstruct the sequence of events and save it for the archives."

"And since Kalok and the Interplanetary Mining Guild—Interplan—bankroll a lot of those settlements, the history of the settlements is also the history of the company and the guild," Wyatt supplied.

Beth nodded. "Exactly. Kalok has a big anniversary coming up, and they hired me to write their story. It was supposed to be prestigious for both of us as well as the guild. I'm pretty well known in academic and space archeology circles, which legitimized them, and Kalok was an opportunity for me to get some visibility and earn some good credit. And then it all went wrong."

Wyatt nodded, then turned as an alarm sounded.

"A ship is taking off and appears to be in pursuit," Nellie stated.

"Evasive maneuvers. Course is set. Jump when we're clear," Wyatt said before turning back to Beth. "Might want to brace yourself. It's a short jump, and we don't have time for jump packs. Sorry."

They both waited, steeling themselves for the jump reaction. Nellie gave a countdown, and Wyatt closed his eyes. He kept his breathing steady as the wave of nausea and disorientation hit him hard. He counted, using the calming techniques he'd been taught at the academy. He hoped Beth could handle it. Most humans didn't do jumps without help from drugs or hiding themselves in a cryo stasis tube for the duration. He opened his eyes, knowing his senses wouldn't work quite right in the dark, the in-between of the wormhole. The few minutes seemed like an eternity, but the feeling gradually receded, and Wyatt glanced over at his passenger who was now coming into focus again. Beth wasn't looking so good.

"Damn, I hate jumps," Beth muttered.

"The drugs help, but then you're out of it for several minutes or longer. That's real bad if you've got hostiles waiting for you on the other side of the tube. I try not to use jump packs unless I have to."

"You're either crazy, or you have an impressive constitution. Just give me a minute."

"You've got time. We're still a ways out; it's not safe to jump in closer to Rum Row. Too much space junk and way too much traffic. And out here on the frontier, we don't have all those helpful navigation satellites and beacons to set our course."

Wyatt occupied himself with checking Nellie's reports. The company ship hadn't cleared the compound before they jumped—a small bit of comfort. A few more minutes passed before he heard Beth take a deep breath.

"Don't think I'll ever get used to that."

"You do up to a point, but it takes a good many jumps, and it still isn't fun. Even the most seasoned jumpers heave their guts more often than not. You ready to finish?"

"Yeah… Did you ever hear about the 'shadows' the old nuclear bombs cast when they exploded?" she asked.

Wyatt frowned, surprised at the change in topic and not sure where she was going. "You mean the permanent shadows of people caught in the blast because the light of the explosion is so bright?"

"Yeah," Beth replied. "Well, the piece of alien tech I found homes in on something like those shadows, only it's seeing left-behind energy, not silhouettes. Not really 'ghosts.' That word suggests sentience. These are more like stone tape recordings, emotional and physical energy so intense it made a molecular imprint on the space around it. A few people, 'sensitives,' have always picked up on that energy. The alien tech I found can translate that imprint into sound and light; the moving, audible versions of those nuclear blast shadows." She rolled up her sleeve and held out her arm turning it palm up.

"Impressive." Wyatt had seen tech implants before, but not like hers. He had a sub-dermal bio communicator, they were standard issue in Space Corps, but he'd had his replaced and upgraded. He'd also seen a number of weapons interfaces implanted, the military's solution to not losing valuable equipment. But the geometric, metallic tattoo embedded in Beth's forearm looked alien.

"Kalok found several pieces of alien tech in our search, and they asked me to translate the markings. Wanted me to determine if they were valuable or should go into their exhibit. Most were just native jewelry, or worthless, then I started on what I thought was a fancy gauntlet," Beth said, and rolled her eyes. "But I got careless. I took it out of the clamps and slid my arm under it to brace it as I cleaned some of the markings. I ran my fingers over it, and yes, I was wearing gloves. Didn't matter—the symbols lit up, and it attached to me. I searched for a catch, some way to open it and get it off my arm. The entire gauntlet began to glow, and within an hour it had embedded itself under my skin. Then the visions started," she said as she pulled down her sleeve, covering the strange markings.

"They didn't say anything, examine you?"

"I was alone when it happened—and I'm not stupid," Beth glared at him. "I kept it to myself as much as I could and planned on getting someone I could trust to check it out when I returned. One of the assistants was with me the first time it activated. That's how I knew the range. But I haven't been back to Ceritan Four, and now," she said with a shrug, "here we are."

"You think the assistant ratted you out?"

"No. Because if he had, they'd be trying to capture me, not kill me. And he didn't see the tech, just shared the vision. Probably thinks I'm some kind of mutant or psychic."

"Those visions are how you figured out that the official histories were fake?" Wyatt asked as the enormity of the situation began to sink in. He eyed Beth with curiosity and maybe a little more respect. He wouldn't have pegged her for an academic by appearance. She had fire in her green eyes and carried herself like she was ready to challenge anyone who got in her way. He liked that fire, and the way her silky, dark brown hair framed and softened her face. *Damn, this might have been a mistake.*

"Yeah," Beth said. She sounded bone-weary. "Like what happened a month ago, out on the old Corrigon mine site, I was along to gather mine records and some of the personal items miners left behind for our museum. You ever heard of Corrigon?"

Wyatt had salvaged it two months ago but saw no need to tell Beth that. "Un-huh," he replied. "I've heard of it. Rare metals, stuff they use in spaceship electronics. The place has been shut down for a long while."

She nodded. "Except all the people didn't leave, the way the official record says they did. This tech," she held up her arm, "picked up images of miners, office workers, even some of the camp followers."

Mining colonies were lonely places. Space had its vagabonds, people who went from place to place, making that loneliness a little more bearable. Sex workers, bootleggers, shady merchants, even traveling performers made the "circuit," staying at remote colonies and homestead planets for a few months at a time. Plenty of people just passing through, people no one considered important.

"And?"

"The official records said everyone had been lifted off, and the documents I'd seen listed lower casualties than usual during the mine's run," Beth replied. "But with the alien tech, I picked up something completely different. I saw people dying when the last of the oxygen and atmosphere finally gave out."

Wyatt felt a prickle on the back of his neck. He had heard rumors about Kalok and Interplanetary Mining Guild leaving people behind, covering up mining disasters, eliminating witnesses. Plenty of scuttle-butt, never any proof.

"How sure are you the alien tech is right?"

"Because when I knew what to look for, I found enough things that didn't make sense, places the records were changed or missing, numbers that didn't add up," Beth replied. "The mine had a lot of more deaths than Kalok admitted. As soon as I started digging around, I saw there were two sets of records. What the alien tech showed me was right. I found the files to prove it."

She took a deep breath before continuing. "It was the same at Comstock. Higher than usual deaths, faked records, proof they were skimming the maintenance budget. And an explosion that looks more like Kalok sabotaged their own mine. But the other thing that I found, because the ghost images led me to it, was a problem with the life support systems. Someone fudged the maintenance records on that, too. And it was pretty clear, when I put it all together, that the mine foremen didn't fix things, although they billed for the repairs, and they never sent a ship back for the shut-down crew." She paused. "Given how much trouble our guys had getting some of the systems to work when we landed, I can believe it. How did you manage to get the life-support systems up and running? I heard the guys talking; they fully expected them to be off-line. They said they hadn't just been turned off way back when—they had failed."

Wyatt turned around to stare at her. "You mean they left the shut-down crew to die? Well…damn. I guess I was just lucky."

Beth met his gaze. "Yeah. You were and probably means the sys-tem was likely to go down again at any time. I'm betting someone pocketed the money that would have been spent on the last run. Or figured it was cheaper to settle a lawsuit or two than pay to get them out."

Kalok Enterprises was one of the major players. It controlled half of the mining colonies and a lot of the interstellar cargo shipping. So if murder was business as usual, the possibilities were mind-boggling. Especially if people up the chain knew and looked the other way. Wyatt also knew from personal experience that Kalok had many governments and Space Corps in their back pocket.

Holy Mother of Space, what a big honkin' mess. And I've stepped right into it.

"I documented, photographed, and downloaded all the evidence, encrypted it, and transmitted everything via a private channel to my personal research cloud until I could figure out what to do about it." Beth sighed. "The same kind of thing happened on the last three runs. Too many ghosts, faked records, and all of it with sign-off, payoff, or 'plausible deniability' right to the top."

Damn. The top of Kalok Enterprises went pretty far up, with treaties and contracts with the major planetary governments. *Had to be a hero, huh?* He mocked himself. *Had to come to the rescue. This is why heroes aren't always the brightest stars in the galaxy.*

"Let me guess," Wyatt said. "You started poking around, pulling old documents, and asking questions. So they hacked your data cloud?"

Beth made a face. "Apparently," she replied wryly. "I suspected but didn't know for sure until now. Kalok said they were coming out here to the Comstock to clear out their intellectual property before they razed the site for a new trade outpost." She snorted. "As if any IP that old would be worth stealing. And there are no plans filed anywhere for an outpost here."

"A set-up?" Wyatt asked, taking her measure a little more carefully. Anyone willing to consider going up against an outfit like Kalok deserved some outlaw respect.

Beth shrugged. "I'm guessing they really did want to take a look for files or old prototypes that shouldn't fall into competitors' hands. Maybe they're here to cover up or destroy what I stumbled into. Getting to me was just a bonus, I imagine."

"They tried before the shooting started?" I asked.

She nodded. "There was a guy on the ship who was trying to look like one of the crew, but he reeked of HQ. Too chatty. I didn't give him anything, but that's when I started watching my back. Took precautions."

Smart lady. Quicker on the uptake than a lot of people, especially if no one had made a big move.

"I'm pretty sure someone went through my flight bag," Beth continued. "One of my data crystals was missing. But I'd already copied everything to a secure account on RimNet. There wasn't anything notable on the one they took."

That she'd already dealt with the black market to get a RimNet account said she wasn't too stuck on the letter of the law. That boded well for them working together. "If what you say is true, they've probably put a bounty on your head," Wyatt said, watching Beth for a reaction.

"Probably," she replied. "But with my background in archeology, plus what the alien tech 'ghosts' can show us, we can make a lot more money working together." She gave Wyatt a level look. "And somehow, I have the feeling you're not a big admirer of Interplan—or Kalok."

"Do you understand what's at stake?" Wyatt was aghast as he thought through the ramifications. "Kalok's not going to stop looking for you. I'm not sure there's anywhere to run that they can't find us. The data you found could bring down Kalok—and make things really uncomfortable for Interplan…turn the Rim economy inside-out…give the Fringe worlds the excuse they want for a war to get rid of the corporate colonies."

Beth nodded soberly. "Yes. And probably other stuff we haven't even thought of." The corner of her mouth quirked upward. "So do we have a deal?"

"We?"

"Partners," she said, extending a hand. "Fifty-fifty."

"Sixty-forty," Wyatt bartered. "I've got the ship."

"Fifty-fifty," Beth countered, a note of steel coming into her voice.

"And I'll split the money with you when I sell my Kalok data to the highest bidder."

"Deal." Wyatt hoped this wasn't the biggest mistake of his life.

Beth grinned. "Deal," she repeated. "Guess we've got business to do out on Rum Row."

"Yup, you ready for the grand tour? You get your own cabin. It's small but private; we've got a great gym to keep in shape and the latest replicator in our galley."

"Sort of…um…big for one guy to handle." Beth said.

"Yeah, that's why I've got Nellie," Wyatt said with a smile.

Chapter Two

ONCE AGAIN, WYATT was running for his life, and people he didn't know were shooting at him.

This kind of thing happened way too often.

"I thought we were supposed to be meeting your contact." Beth squeezed off a shot that winged one of their pursuers in the shoulder.

Wyatt shot a second pursuer in the knee. The man went down cursing and bleeding. That left two still chasing them. Wyatt and Beth kept running.

Maybe elsewhere their little dust-up might have caused a stir. But this was Rum Row, and shots fired were just part of another day in paradise. The corridors of the illicit space station cleared with the first shot, except for one old man who swore at both of them and their pursuers, waved his cane threateningly, and hitched his way down the corridor without even looking up as shots flew past.

"We are," Wyatt answered Beth as they ran down another corridor. "We just have to make it to the meeting place."

"And you know how to get there?"

"Sort of." *Gimme a break.* Rum Row was a linked-together patchwork quilt of metal, with an old decommissioned station as the hub and hundreds of smaller ships that docked and provided products and services out of rented storefronts—until the day those ships zipped off into the void and others took their spot. That meant nothing was ever in the same place for long, and it was easy to get lost. There were no maps, no signs, and no helpful A.I.s to guide them. Under normal circumstances, wandering around the wrong part of the station could get a person blackjacked and robbed, or worse. It was likely to get them killed unless Wyatt could get his bearings soon.

"Welcome to the Sonovan Quadrant's best place for purloined goods, illegal substances, unlawful services, and people who change names more often than most people change underwear," Wyatt added, sounding a little breathless.

"You think those goons are Interplan or Kalok?" Beth asked as they swung around a corner to find a bazaar that stretched the entire length of the next expansive corridor. Beth and Wyatt dove into the shoulder-to-shoulder crowd. Wyatt threw money at one pushcart vendor to buy a shawl for Beth and a jacket and hat for himself, barely slowing down long enough to grab the stuff. Wyatt figured that he probably paid double what the goods were worth, but now was not the time to haggle. Beth threw the shawl over her head and shoulders. Wyatt stuffed his dark wavy hair under his cap, pulled the jacket on and made sure they were in front of a really big man who hid them from view.

"I don't have a clue, but most likely Kalok. I'm not sure they want the guild to know too much about their troubles," Wyatt said under his breath. "Besides, they're trying to kill you, not me. You're the one who made them mad."

The bazaar was one of Wyatt's favorite spots in Rum Row. Traders from dozens of planets offered their wares. The aroma of foods from a score of star systems hung in the recirculated air, warring with the body odor of several species of travelers who had gone too long without a trip to a cleansing unit.

"How's the food?" Beth asked, stepping around a pile of garbage.

"Most folks don't die," Wyatt replied with a shrug. "It varies by species, of course, but I wouldn't recommend being adventurous."

He saw Beth eye him as if she wanted to believe he was kidding, and then a look of shock spread across her face.

"We came to Rum Row because it's that kind of place," Wyatt said. "Take the seediest bar you've ever seen, the most disreputable street you've ever been on, and the city with the highest murder rate and mix them all together—you'd have something like Rum Row, but tamer."

Rum Row was a place where a person could get hired, drunk, laid, lucky, and dead all in one cycle. Their sim parlors were some of the busiest in the Rim. Plenty of business went on there; most of it illegal, or at as least dodgy as hell. Deals were done, contracts signed, people made promises and told lies, and money changed hands. Most of the time, people kept their word on those business ventures, because as big and empty as space could be, reputations stuck, and yet, the station was not big enough to run away from someone who really wanted revenge.

"Is that really a TU-936 over there?" Beth nudged Wyatt so she did not have to point.

He looked at the battered old ship through the viewport and frowned. "I'd have said it was a 938, but I could be wrong."

"I can't believe one of those is still flying," Beth replied, awestruck. "Or half the ships hooked up here, come to think of it."

Given Rum Row's reason for existence, old beat-up ships were not a big surprise. Rum Row's hub was a declassified Potocnik-wheel space station, which had been built by a government or corporation that decided, after a while, that they didn't need it anymore when the Sonovan Waystation closed. Someone had figured out how to add a lot more docking ports, and Rum Row was born. Traders of every description and port of origin docked their ships, opened shop, and stayed until they sold their cargo or the people they stole it from caught up with them. The station also got a fair number of ore traders, independent asteroid prospectors, small cargo ships, salvagers, mercenaries, thieves, vagabonds, traveling performers, and old-fashioned sex workers. They were the respectable visitors, coming for a little rest and relaxation, or to do some business, or a little of both.

"So where's Miss Liddy and how do we find her?" Beth asked as Wyatt navigated through the crowd at the bazaar.

"We don't," Wyatt replied. "She finds us—if she wants to. We're supposed to be at Rummy's Bar at oh-eight-hundred. Which is in ten minutes."

"And you're sure she won't sell us out to Kalok?" Beth pressed.

Wyatt laughed. "That, I'm sure of. Mostly." He glanced at her. "Are you getting any tips from your 'friends?'"

"I can see them," she said while they moved through the crowd. "Holy shit, there are a lot of dead people around here! But I'm not seeing anything that looks helpful. I haven't figured out how to turn the visions on or off. So far, the tech seems to have a mind of its own and shows me images when it wants. Sometimes, like now, it's just flashes and other times the vision is more like a news vid."

No one knew how many people actually lived in Rum Row, and no one would be counting how many died, either. The folks who made their living on the station weren't much for filling out forms or answering the census. In its heyday, the old space station housed several thousand people, and Wyatt guessed that with all the ships that were docked, that about as many lived there now. Most of those visitors would stay a few days and move on, leaving a skeleton crew of shopkeepers and maintenance workers. The majority were just passing through. Some never left, either by choice or by death.

"Go left," Wyatt directed, and Beth let him lead. They walked down another crowded side corridor, and then down a back hallway. In the distance, Wyatt heard a ruckus. It looked like some of the locals were taking an exception to the company guards.

They made their way past the fight and found Rummy's Bar, pretty classy for a Rum Row tavern. Ralph, the barkeeper, looked up as they entered. "Hey, Wyatt. How's business?"

He shrugged. "Enough to keep me in fuel, food, and a little fun," Wyatt replied, plunking down some chits to buy a beer. Respectable places elsewhere took credit, but Rum Row was strictly cash. Harder to trace. No one here wanted to leave a trail.

Ralph eyed Beth. "Is she the fun?"

"No," Wyatt replied with more force than intended. "She's my new business partner."

Ralph slid two beers across the counter. "Suit yourself," he said. He nodded toward an empty table in the back. "A mutual friend reserved a seat for you."

Wyatt left a tip and headed for the table Ralph indicated, squeezing through the crowd, making sure Beth was following. Some of the patrons played cards or bet at dice, while others hunched over their tables, faces hidden, doing business. In the corner, three musicians tried to make themselves heard over the loud conversation. A couple of sex workers circulated, looking for customers. He wondered briefly if there were any patrons with that kind of wealth. With the sim parlors so readily available, living, breathing comfort was either extremely expensive or extremely risky.

"Picking up anything else?" Wyatt asked, taking a seat with his back to the wall and leaning back to watch the door.

Wyatt sipped his beer and let out a satisfied sigh. Rum Row brewed and distilled its own alcohol, and did a mighty fine job of it. Of course, since the station was located in the no-man's land between territories, none of the alcohol or other substances were taxed or permitted, which meant the whole enterprise broke dozens of laws in scores of star systems. Someday, maybe one of those systems might be foolhardy enough to try to crack down, but given how heavily armed the station's patrons and their ships were, it would be a colossally bad idea.

"In a place like this? Plenty. But still just flashes and short clips." Beth glanced around the crowded room, absently pulling her sleeve down to hide the glow. "Couple of guys with nasty gunshot wounds, over by the door. A lady who got her throat slit, by the stairs. About five people at the bar don't look like they died violently—maybe they didn't have anywhere else to go."

I guess when your luck runs out, you could do worse than being a barfly at Rummy's, Wyatt thought.

"Anything helpful?"

Beth frowned as if listening to something she could barely hear, and her eyes lost focus. After a few moments, she roused. "A few were killed by Interplan people gauging by the uniforms of the shooters. So I'd assume they and Kalok may both have people on Rum Row. I can't tell how long ago," she said, dropping her voice.

"Ralph is all right. He doesn't sell out his customers. Miss Liddy doesn't like bounty hunters, so we're probably safe with her," Wyatt said.

"I heard you were looking for me."

Wyatt and Beth looked up, to see Miss Liddy standing beside the table. She looked to be in her late forties, skinny as a rail with ropey arms and calloused hands from hard work. Her dark hair was shaved on the sides and short on top.

"We've got some special merchandise," Wyatt replied, sitting up and putting his empty glass on the table. His hand slipped beneath the table to the gun in his holster, just in case. Beth shifted so she could reach her own weapon if things went badly.

"Let's go somewhere quiet and talk about it." Wyatt and Beth followed Miss Liddy out through the back of the bar. They cut through the kitchen and went down a short corridor to a comfortable office.

"Ralph and I have an arrangement," Liddy said looking at Beth. "He lets me come and go as I need to, and gives me a front room for business. I make sure my boys bring him hard-to-get supplies. I help him, he helps me." Two large men had taken up places by the door. They carried themselves like soldiers, and Wyatt guessed that they were some of Miss Liddy's "boys." Miss Liddy ran the biggest organized crime syndicate on the Rim, and her large extended family formed the inside circle of the Liddy Pack. Fortunately she seemed to like him.

She sat behind her desk and motioned for them to sit as well. "So what did you step in this time, McCoy?" she asked in an amused voice that sounded like she had ignored the safety warnings about tobacco and alcohol. "Keep telling you, Handsome, if you're not careful someone's gonna come along and mess up that pretty face."

"It's not Wyatt. It's me," Beth interrupted. "I have evidence that Kalok Enterprises—and Interplan—are leaving colonists and miners to die when they close down a mine because it's cheaper than picking them up. It's happened several times and has been covered up. But I can prove it." They had agreed to leave mention of the alien tech out of it.

Miss Liddy's eyes widened, just for a second, then went flat again. "Well, well, well," she said, and leaned back, regarding them as if Beth had suddenly changed into two-headed chaffer fish. "Now that's mighty interesting." She looked at Wyatt. "And you decided to drop this hot mess of shit in my lap why?"

"You ever hear of something called the Coalition?" Wyatt asked.

Liddy did a slow blink. "Rumors. Why?"

"People say the Coalition wants to bring Interplan and Kalok to account for all the deaths," Beth said.

"People say a lot of things," Liddy replied. "Doesn't mean they're all true."

"C'mon, Liddy. You've got connections," Wyatt said. "You've also got no love for either Kalok or Interplan. They're never going to leave us alone now, data crystals or not, because of what we know and might tell someone. So the best we can do is make sure that information gets passed to someone who can strike back at the big guys and make it hurt."

"We? You mean her. Why's this your problem, McCoy?"

"I helped her escape. We're partners for now, and while I don't know for sure, it's possible they picked up the *Nellie B*'s signature."

Liddy snorted. "Yeah, right." Liddy pulled out an elaborately carved stone pipe, lit the tobacco, then gave a few puffs. "I can't take your data crystal," she said finally. "Wouldn't know what to do with it." She held up a hand before Wyatt could protest. "But I know someone who can—and might know some of the people you want to reach."

"Oh?"

Liddy gave a deep, rich laugh. "Don't be so cautious, Wyatt. It's too much of a change for you." She reached out and ran a finger along Wyatt's square jaw.

Wyatt saw Beth give him a questioning look as he shivered at Liddy's way-too-familiar gesture.

"Right now two of the biggest corporations in the quadrant are trying to kill us," Wyatt retorted, trying to ignore both Liddy's actions and Beth's response. "We've pissed off a better grade of enemy than usual."

"You've come at a good time," Liddy replied, growing serious. "There've been rumors about Kalok and Interplan for a while now— about exactly the kind of thing you say you can prove. Other rumors, too. Manned cargo ships mysteriously exploding if the price of the ore they're carrying drops too low to be profitable. Miners being wooed to off-planet colonies with promises of big bonuses and getting slaved instead." She shook her head. "Bad stuff."

"How does that make it a 'good' time?" Beth asked.

Liddy leaned forward. "Because Wyatt is right. People, and groups like the Coalition, are starting to take action against the Corporations. Spacers are getting nervous and angry. I know someone involved."

"You think anything is going to stop Interplan or Kalok from doing what they want to do?" Wyatt challenged.

Liddy shot them a cold smile. "Eventually, they run their course. They're not the first to do this kind of shit; they won't be the last. But sooner or later, all those groups take a fall. And I think what's afoot just might make that happen—even faster, if your information is as good as you say."

"I'll meet with him." Beth's voice didn't leave room for debate. She looked at Wyatt. "You can leave me here, Wyatt. You've done your part. Go on. They won't follow you without me."

Liddy's stare practically bored a hole through him. "Forget it," Wyatt said. "We made a deal. Partners. We haven't even started on the sites you're going to show me." He sighed. "If we get killed, I guess that means I won't have to pay my bar bill."

Liddy gave a deep guffaw of approval. "That's more like it. That's the Wyatt I know. You're too good for salvage work, kid. Gonna be the death of you." She gestured, and one of her "boys" came over immediately. "I need a diversion," she said, with a smile that promised mayhem. "Keep the deaths to a minimum, don't damage the station. Gotta cover us for about half an hour." She fixed the very large man with a deadly glare. "Don't fail me."

The bodyguard bowed. "Consider it done."

Liddy looked to the second guard. "Get us ready to go. We're probably going to have to make a fast exit." He nodded, made the same little bow, and then headed out.

"Come with me." Liddy edged around the desk. She eyed Beth and Wyatt's guns, gave a grunt of disappointment, and opened a long drawer. "Take these." She shoved the biggest two blasters at them that Wyatt had ever seen.

I'm pretty sure they're illegal in just about every civilized star system. And they are absolutely beautiful, Wyatt thought remembering his old Space Corps days.

"Quit looking at them like they're naked virgins, Wyatt. It's just a gun," Liddy said with a laugh. She glanced at Beth, and they seemed to have an understanding. "Men," she muttered.

"Let's go meet some troublemakers," Liddy said, grabbing a small bag and throwing it over her shoulder. "Guard our asses," she barked at the bodyguard as he dropped into step behind them.

Alarms shrieked as they left Liddy's "office." Ralph gave them a nod as they slipped out one of the back doors behind him, and yelled that the next round was on the house, which led to a run on the bar that jammed the place. No one would be following them through there.

Liddy knew Rum Row like a street rat knew the city. She led them down passageways that even the vagrants hadn't found, and over catwalks across air ducts where only the maintenance crew ever went. It seemed to Wyatt as if the whole space station stretched beneath them, and he decided not to look down. A few times they had to use the guide rails and grips as gravity waxed and waned crossing between sections. They picked their way among wiring and conduits, Wyatt tried not to think about what might happen if they pulled something loose.

Liddy led them to what appeared to be a deserted section of Rum Row. Most of the station had been reclaimed when it was towed to its present location, but this area was obviously left untouched for a long time. It was crowded with dusty crates and bins that had not been opened in years. Wyatt sneezed, and both Liddy and Beth glared. Alien vermin, bugs, and rodent-like creatures scuttled out of their way.

They came to a dead stop after rounding another corner. "Knock, knock," Liddy said.

"Why are you here?" a man's voice sounded from behind a large stack of crates.

"We've got something you'll want to see," Liddy replied. "Something important enough to bring me down to this godsforsaken hole."

A door that Wyatt hadn't noticed slid open behind the crates, and a thin man appeared, peering out around the crates, holding a gun trained on them. He had curly brown hair and light brown skin, with worried dark eyes. "It's not safe. You shouldn't be here. Someone might follow you."

Liddy produced a handful of food bars from her bag. They were the bane of space travelers everywhere, edible and enough to sustain life, but most people thought the wrapper tasted better than the contents. Still, the man's eyes lit up. "I've got more than this for you, Worm, if you hear us out."

"All right." He conceded, holstering his gun and stepping back.

Liddy spoke quietly to her bodyguard before he took up position behind the crates.

Worm waved them into the room, pulling the door closed behind them, throwing a bolt and putting a steel bar across it. The space had probably once been assigned to the captain of the watch, or a night guard. It still had power and plumbing, since no one had thought to turn them off. The furnishings were sparse: a cot, table, chair, a few possessions, and a standard spacer duffle bag, along with a collection of tablets and computers.

"This is Worm," Liddy said. The worried little man nodded in acknowledgment.

"It's the name I go by these days. You know, like 'worm in the apple?'" he added with a shrug. "Small creature, working from inside, big damage."

"We don't need names," Wyatt replied. "In fact, I'd be glad if you didn't remember anything about us. But if you don't care for Kalok Enterprises and Interplan, we might be able to help."

Worm squinted at them as if spending too long in the dim light of the abandoned sector had harmed his eyesight. "What do you have for me?"

Beth glanced at Liddy, who nodded approval. "I've got proof Kalok permitted colonists and miners to die rather than spend the money to pick up the shut-down crews on closed colonies," Beth said.

"What kind of proof?"

"It's all on a data crystal. Documents, photos, names, dates."

Worm licked his lips. "Show me."

Beth held up the crystal. "It's here. Common readable. Clean scan. You won't have any trouble retrieving what you need."

"Is it the only copy?"

Beth gave him a look. "I want the goons off my tail. Why would I give them reasons to keep looking for me?"

Wyatt kept his poker face, wondering if Beth was telling the truth, while seriously doubting it.

Worm's eyes narrowed. "What do you want for it?"

Wyatt named a price.

Worm laughed. "Be serious. Insurrection doesn't pay well." He gestured to his meager quarters. "Do I look like I'm in this for the money?"

"What can you pay us? There are competitors that would probably love to have this for blackmail."

Worm shrugged. "So, sell it to them. Why waste my time?"

Beth and Wyatt had argued about this the whole way to Rum Row. He wanted to see Kalok get what was coming to them, but thought they should make a profit for their trouble. Beth argued there was benefit enough in taking out one of the most ruthless players in the game, possibly two if the guild fell as well.

Liddy gave Worm a hard stare. "I don't work for free, Worm, and neither do they. Compensation for risk. Cough it up."

Worm glared at Liddy, and then grumbled as he went back to the table and picked up one of the devices. It was apparent he was communicating with someone given the back and forth. He ignored them for several minutes before returning with a scowl. Worm lifted the mattress, pulled out a small box, and retrieved several chits.

"Here," he said, thrusting a handful toward Beth.

Wyatt checked them and put them up to his comm scanner. He steeled his face as the reader told him they held more than double the credits he'd make from a really good haul of salvage.

"Fair enough," Wyatt said and handed one of the chits to Liddy to cover her percentage. She nodded her thanks and Wyatt looked back at Worm. "Why are you in this?" he asked. "I don't trust people who want to save the world unless they figure there's something in it for them."

Worm blinked at him. "My dad was on one of those clean-up crews for a Kalok mine. He never came back. When my mother made a fuss, she died in an accident. I want to bring Kalok down, and so do the folks I work with. What you've given us," Worm held up the crystal, "just proves what I always suspected."

Wyatt decided he could believe in personal revenge much better than do-goodery. "How do you get money? And if you've got money, why are you down here?"

"Friends, patrons," Worm said, a little more guarded. "Kalok and

Interplan have made a lot of enemies. And really—who's going to look for something like we're doing in a place like this?"

Wyatt heard an alarm chirp then turned to look at Liddy, who was scowling.

"We've got company headed this way," she barked. "Worm, grab what you can't leave behind and go! I'll meet you where I found you! We'll hold them off, now get!" Liddy grabbed Wyatt by the arm as Worm opened a second door out of the room. "Beth, go with Worm. Wyatt, help me hold off these bastards to give them some time." Liddy unbarred and unlocked the door, pulling Wyatt into the corridor behind the crates before he could argue.

Liddy's guard had taken up position on the other side as the first shots were fired.

Wyatt fired back, catching one of their pursuers in the thigh. The man went down with most of his leg missing, forcing the guy behind him to hesitate, just long enough for Liddy's guard to put a plate-sized hole right through his torso. The big blasters she handed out did not mess around. Blood splattered the walls of the corridor, and Wyatt got in another shot that creased the dark, steel wall as the dead men's companions fell back.

Liddy, Wyatt, and her guard moved down the corridor after Beth and Worm were gone, passing the door they'd used for their escape. The Corporation men were close behind. They stepped over their fallen comrades and came running. Wyatt and team used a leapfrog maneuver; the guard fired first giving Wyatt and Liddy time to get to the next bend before he joined and they took up the offensive. They moved quickly, zigzagging crazily to avoid the energy bolts, taking turns to give cover fire. One grazed Wyatt's shoulder, giving off a strong burnt smell and causing him to yelp in surprise, but he kept going.

"This way!" Liddy hissed, and Wyatt followed. They skidded around a corner into another small hallway, Liddy's guard opened a hatch. Darkness loomed on the other side.

"What about Beth?"

"They'll catch up with us. In you go!" Liddy said, clipping something to Wyatt's belt before giving him a shove. He fell feet-first into the shaft. Liddy climbed in behind him, followed by the guard. Wyatt heard a mechanical *click* and a *hiss* before she shot the door mechanism.

A pitch-black cylinder enclosed them as they fell, and Wyatt had a pretty good idea where it went. Rum Row's shops and living areas were located in the ring portion of the station, with the visiting spaceships docked off the hub. The center hub was the mechanical heart of the station, which housed the computers and the systems making the station habitable. Like spokes of a wheel, service shafts connected the outer ring to the hub. Some moved people and cargo from the hub to the rim, and others were for maintenance and systems. Depending on the station's rotation, the spokes could be up, down, or horizontal. And gravity was iffy. Just their luck, when they needed one of the shafts, it was more of a pit.

Wyatt felt a tug on his belt as they slowed. Liddy clicked on a light, revealing ladders on the inside of the spoke, stretching down into shadows. They descended at a steady pace, and Wyatt could hear the hum of a winch motor above them.

"Swing!" Liddy commanded when they stopped, using their momentum to move Wyatt closer to the ladder. The rungs were just out of reach. On the next swing, Wyatt caught the rung and realized that Liddy had clipped a cable to his belt and that they both hung from maintenance tethers. The guard had done the same and was just below them on the ladder.

"I thought we were going to die," Wyatt said. Liddy chuckled.

"Yeah. I figured as much. Did you really think I'd kill myself rather than fight it out with those goons?"

Wyatt rolled his eyes, realizing he should have known better. Surrender was not in Liddy's vocabulary.

"Not many people have the spoke door codes, but I made sure I got them as soon as I found out about them," Liddy said as they climbed down the long, long ladder. They had fallen or floated nearly to the ring side of the spoke, which did not seem so far away now that

Liddy's light illuminated the workspace. "Since most people don't even think about the maintenance spokes, they make for a good getaway now and again."

"Ma'am, they've got the ship secured," the bodyguard said.

Liddy opened the hatch to the hub. They had their guns ready as they peered through the hatchway, into an empty corridor.

"Aren't they going to expect us to go back to your ship?" Wyatt asked, as they made their way to the main passageways and ducked into the crowd.

"Yep," Liddy replied. "Which is why we're heading back to Rummy's first. That way I can have my boys plow the road for us." Liddy turned to the guard. "Find them and meet us at the bar."

"You sure you don't want me to stay with you?" the guard asked.

"I'm good, Jace. Thanks, but I can handle myself. You need to get the others moving," Liddy replied. The guard gave a nod and took off in the other direction.

Wyatt and Liddy took one of the regular pedestrian spoke-corridors back to the outer ring and emerged in a side corridor that supplied Rum Row's busiest stretch of stores, sim parlors, and bars. Customers packed the area shoulder to shoulder, although with some of the species, Wyatt found it difficult to tell where the shoulders actually were.

The smell was strong enough to wilt steel. Ore miners and cargo haulers got iffy about regular cleansing. Chem showers and even the expensive steam baths were a big draw on Rum Row. Most ships did not have the resources to waste water. But the stench was more than body odor. The chemicals secreted by some of the aliens could make a person's eyes water, mingled with the food spices and hygiene products of dozens of star systems.

They surfaced in the middle of a rough crowd. Wyatt had seen prison colony riots that didn't look as tough as this bunch. Miners, prospectors, haulers, and explorers, this group was well armed, but many looked like they'd be able to rip someone to pieces with bare hands if need be. Liddy and her boys fit in perfectly. Wyatt was well trained in weapons and hand-to-hand, but he knew when he was outclassed. He had no desire to step on any toes or tentacles.

Liddy wove through the crowd without looking up, and whether they recognized her or just sensed her presence, they got out of her way. Wyatt followed in her wake. Both he and Liddy gripped their guns, keeping the weapons low and out of sight.

"There they are!" A man's voice shouted over the crowd and fired a warning shot above their heads. Kalok's men didn't have to wear the gray uniforms to stand out.

That was the wrong thing to do in this crowd. Curses and grunts filled the air as the hard-bitten spacers turned to see who the pursuers were. Most of the crowd had a warrant or two out for them from the Stellar Federation, maybe even bounties on their heads.

"It's Stellar Fed!" Wyatt shouted. "It's a raid!" Stellar Fed was the strong-arm brother of the Interstellar Patrol and the bane of anyone who operated on the Fringe. The Feds didn't even pretend to play fair or abide by their own laws. Everyone knew they were corrupt and owned by the most powerful guilds and corporations.

In a heartbeat, the crowd bristled with lethal weapons, and a tide of angry spacers rushed toward where the shots had been fired. Wyatt heard more shots, then answering fire, and a roar of shouts as the crowd turned on their attackers.

He bit back a curse as two guys nearly squashed him between them, then yelped in pain as a huge boot caught him in the shin as the crowd tried to move in the opposite direction. Wyatt realized that he and Liddy were more in danger of being trampled than shot, but at least the corporate goons weren't going to be catching up soon.

Shouted curses turned into ugly taunts, and within minutes, Wyatt and Liddy were in the middle of a brawl. The fight was a free-for-all since the people getting thumped on weren't the ones doing the original shooting. No one seemed to care, so long as they had someone to hit.

A big hairy fist caught Wyatt in the jaw. He swung; and the satisfying smack of knuckles to face nearly made up for the pain that radiated through his hand. Wyatt ducked the next blow, and the hairy-fisted guy hit the miner behind him.

A knee nearly got Wyatt in the groin, and he kicked back, landing a solid hit to someone's thigh. The colossal guy to Wyatt's left picked up his opponent, threw him overhead down the corridor and into the battling mob.

A Scorcian with red skin and a dark black mane rounded on the big man and let out a roar like a wounded bull. His punch not only broke the man's nose, it pushed in the whole front of his face, and the big guy would have fallen down dead if there had been room to drop.

More shots rang out from every direction. Sirens clanged, summoning Rum Row's bouncers, but they had no chance of fighting their way through the mob. Knives glinted in the stark overhead light, and the man next to Wyatt got opened up like a fish. A tall, skinny man in front of Liddy shouted insults above the roar of the crowd, then went suddenly quiet, his head hanging at an odd angle, severed by a sharp knife that left only the spine attached. Too much blood spray filled the air to tell whether Liddy was the one to cut him.

Between the butt of Wyatt's blaster and his knuckledusters, he pummeled his way through the mob, squeezing between unwashed bodies, spacesuits stained with substances he didn't want to dwell on, and species he could not identify. The air smelled of blood, sweat, and alcohol, a potent mixture ripe for combustion. Blood soaked his suit, and while most of it was not his own, he wanted to keep it that way. Then they moved forward once more, step by step, he and Liddy fighting through the press.

The man next to Wyatt swung a punch, and Wyatt elbowed him hard in the gut. The punch missed but his vomit did not.

Glass shattered as the fight spilled into the storefronts along the corridor. Display items in the windows turned into missiles, hurled into the crowd. Shouts and curses, along with more breaking glass, led to more unidentified flying objects hurled with extreme prejudice. Something caught Wyatt in the back, and he staggered forward into a hulking creature with a face that looked like a boar. The alien let out an unfriendly squeal and snapped at him with his tusks, recoiling when

Wyatt landed a hit with his knuckles right to the snout.

Liddy and Wyatt snaked through the crush, and he caught sight of Rummy's. Most of the customers had emptied out into the corridor, not wanting to waste a good fight. Ralph barely looked up when they came in, but he gave them a nearly imperceptible head jerk in the direction of Liddy's office. Bloodied and bruised, covered in unmentionable effluent, they staggered past the bar toward Liddy's office just as three sodden corporate guys burst through the door of the bar.

"Get them!" the lead agent shouted, pointing at Liddy and Wyatt, and he had the drop on them. At this range, they weren't going to miss.

Later, Wyatt realized that there were three separate shots, but they sounded at the same instant, like a single blast. Worm swung around the corner, opening fire on Agent Number One, blowing his head off his body.

Beth stood in the doorway. She angled her shot over Wyatt's shoulder so close his skin burned from the blast, and blew a hole through Agent Number Two's ribs. Ralph stayed behind the bar, a blaster in hand, powering down from the shot that cut Agent Number Three in half.

"Get out of here," Ralph said matter-of-factly, replacing the gun where it came from beneath the bar and going back to drying tankards. "I'll put it on your tab," he added with a glance in Liddy's direction.

Before any more corporate guys could show up, Worm, Beth, and Wyatt followed Liddy down another maintenance corridor, through a secured, private spoke to the hub. Four dead corporate agents floated in the zero-G near the airlock, proof that Liddy's boys had been busy. The airlock slammed shut behind them, and with a click and the rumble of engines, they were on their way. Wyatt stared at Rum Row falling away from them through the viewscreen, and turned on Liddy in panic.

"What about my ship?" he yelled, imagining the Kalok goons impounding the *Nellie B.* Getting rid of evil corporations was a sideline. Salvage was his business, and for that, he needed his ship. He stared at the receding space station and clutched his chest, feeling heart palpitations coming on.

"Relax," Liddy admonished.

"Relax? Are you crazy? What am I going to do without my ship?" Wyatt demanded as he tried to remember what potentially incriminating evidence might be aboard, and which star systems might use it to come after him. It had taken him too long, too many risky runs and way too much work to see the *Nellie B* slip out of his fingers.

"It's been stolen," Liddy said, and Wyatt collapsed into one of the chairs on the bridge of her ship as if he had been shot.

"Stolen?" He echoed. *How is that even possible*, he wondered.

Beth and Liddy were chuckling, but Wyatt didn't see the humor. "What?"

"We stole it," The big guy Liddy had tasked with getting ready to leave said, trying to hide a smirk. "We figured things were going to get dicey, and so we stole your ship. It'll be waiting for us at the rendezvous point."

"Who's flying the *Nellie B*?" Wyatt looked to Liddy. "Well?"

She rolled her eyes. "My boys drew straws. The loser got to risk his life. Seriously, Wyatt, now that you've got a partner, shouldn't you tone down that A.I. of yours?"

"Liddy, what did you do to Nellie?"

"Don't worry, just took her off-line. She'll be fine. But, a military A.I.? Haven't you moved on?"

"Never," he swore. "The *Nellie B* is my ship, and Nellie is family. I'm sticking with her." He took a deep breath. It was unlikely they could actually hurt the A.I., and while they thought they'd taken her off-line, that wasn't so easy. More probable was that Nellie let them take the ship and was waiting for orders from him.

"What about Worm?" Everyone turned to look at Beth, who had asked the question. Wyatt had forgotten, in his panic about the *Nellie B*, that Worm was with them.

Wyatt thought of Worm as a scrawny computer guy, a scruffy agitator who spent his time lurking on the dark eddies of the data stream.

In the stark light of Liddy's ship, he got a better look and changed his mind. Worm shot a corporate agent cool as could be, and although he was covered with blood and looked like he had been roughed up, he had a matter-of-fact calm that told Wyatt this wasn't his first close call. Wyatt knew Worm was smart. Now, he realized Worm was dangerous.

"We'll get Worm to a safe harbor," Liddy said with a shrug. "He's got work to do. I've got some skin in this game too, you know, as an independent operator."

Wyatt coughed rather than laughed because Liddy's description fell so far from encompassing her illicit organization's scope it was like calling a moon a pebble.

"You could always join the Network," Worm said, glancing at Wyatt off-handedly. "If you're serious about wanting to see Kalok and Interplan get what's coming to them, that is. You've got a fast ship, and you're in and out of a lot of places. Perfect for a spy—or a courier."

Wyatt opened his mouth to object, but Beth beat him to a response. "It's not like they're going to quit looking for us, Wyatt," she said, and he could see that she had accepted the truth of that statement. "They'll issue warrants, maybe place bounties. We'll have to watch our backs everywhere we go, and every port we dock in increases the chances of being spotted. So maybe we can repay those headaches by causing a few of our own for the Corporation."

Wyatt was good at causing trouble, though most of the time he tried to avoid conflict if possible. But maybe it would feel different if he did it for a good cause. "Consider us freelancers," he told Worm. "Independent operators," he said, with a nod to Liddy. "I've got a salvage business to run, but if, in the process, we turn up information that might be useful we'll let you know."

"I suspect we'll be in and out of some old Kalok colonies," Beth added. "Odds are good we'll get more dirt on them, maybe even find others with stuff to hide." With her alien tech, getting new intel was almost a sure thing.

Worm nodded. "We're grateful for the help. I'll show you how to leave a message and set up a drop. Anything you can give us is one more nail in the Kalok coffin."

"Think we'll ever be able to go back to Rum Row?" Beth asked.

Liddy and Wyatt chuckled. "Sure," Liddy said. "Nobody on Rum Row has any love for the corporations. Give it a few weeks and the chance for there to be a couple bigger, better brawls, and no one will even remember."

Wyatt knew he would not be completely happy until he was back on the *Nellie B* heading for the next salvage site. While he was slowly getting used to having Beth as a business partner; having two of the biggest powers in space out for his blood made him long for being off the grid. It might take a while to get comfortable with the thought of being part of Worm's "Network;" that was a little more connected than he liked to be.

"Just get me back to my ship," Wyatt said, growing aware of every bruise and wound now that the adrenaline rush was fading. "We need to put some space between us and Rum Row."

CHAPTER THREE

"DID WE LOSE them?" Beth stared anxiously at the screens on Wyatt's panel.

Wyatt did not answer right away. He eyed the view screens and watched the sensors, wary of a trap. After a few minutes, he nodded and let out a long breath. "Yeah. At least, I think so." He slumped into his seat, feeling the adrenaline crash after two hours of playing a desperate cat-and-mouse game with Kalok patrols. His muscles were sore, but that was more likely from how he'd been pushing himself. His daily workout routines had gotten longer and more intense the more time he spent around his new partner.

Beth frowned. "What were Kalok ships doing this far into the Near-Fringe?"

"No idea," Wyatt replied, scanning his screens and sensors once more before easing the *Nellie B* out of the umbra of a small moon. "Nothing this far out belongs to them, or to Interplan. At least, not officially."

"Meaning what?" Beth asked, leaning forward, obviously watching his screens again.

Wyatt laid in a course and set the scanners to maximum range. "Nellie, verify and chart course and headings."

Wyatt looked at the screen and the readouts from Nellie's scans before hitting "confirm." He swiveled his chair, letting Nellie do the flying for the moment. "Kalok's never straightforward about anything. By the time they announce a new colony or the opening of a new mine, you can bet it's been a couple of years in the works, making sure no one else is going to challenge their claim. They've already staked their territory and paid off all the right people," he added bitterly. "So just because nothing's been in the news about Kalok expanding into the Fringe doesn't mean they aren't laying the groundwork."

"Or they could just be looking for us."

Wyatt nodded. "Yeah. Or that." He checked the readouts once more, a little paranoid that Nellie's automated scanners might miss something. "Looks clear out there—for now."

"Do you think they'll come after us again?"

"None of the Kalok ships that were chasing us were long-range craft with jump capability," Wyatt replied. "They need to refuel from a base or a carrier ship. So I don't think they can go much farther than where we lost them."

"Unless Kalok has a secret base," Beth supplied.

Wyatt grimaced. "Possible—but it wouldn't stay secret for too long with ships coming and going. What they might do is hire mercs to do their dirty work for them. False registration, illegal engine upgrades, pirated weapons—"

"Sounds like someone I know," Beth noted with a wry glance in his direction lifting her hand to indicate the ship around her.

"Takes one to know one," Wyatt muttered.

"I think you're right," Beth said, leaning back and putting her feet up. "I don't think the Kalok ships that chased us out of Rum Row will keep following us—they'll hand it off to paid hunters. And the problem there is—"

"How do we know who's working for Kalok when none of them are flying company ships?" Wyatt finished her sentence. "Shit." He thought for a moment and then shrugged. "So we figure that everyone we can't personally vouch for is out to get us. It's pretty much what I do anyhow."

"Okay," Beth said. "I can live with that. Wyatt…after what happened with the *Nellie B* and Liddy—Is there anything I should know about the A.I.? What if you get hurt or can't give orders?"

Wyatt turned and gave a serious look at his new partner. *Good question,* he thought then considered the options and risks.

"Nellie, please open security protocol alpha."

"Opened," Nellie responded.

"List Beth Parker as second in command and register voice and DNA for authorization," Wyatt said.

"DNA required," Nellie responded.

Wyatt unstrapped and went to one of the panels removing a med kit. He handed a swab to Beth and watched as she used it and handed it back. Wyatt returned to one of the other stations, swiped a reader slide and inserted it.

"DNA captured. Any change to primary orders?" Nellie asked.

"No, Nellie. Close security protocol alpha." Wyatt turned back to Beth as he buckled back in. "There you go, now an official crew member. Nellie already has your voice profile and palm scan so she'll accept your commands if I'm not available—as long as you don't order her to do anything that would harm me or the ship."

"Thanks."

Wyatt gave a nod. Neither of them spoke for a while. The view screens gave the sense that the blackness of space and the glow of the stars were almost within reach, just outside the window. Beth stared at the vast expanse and shivered.

"Please don't tell me you're getting space-sick," Wyatt said.

Beth wrapped her arms around herself, running her hands up and down her biceps. "No. Not space-sick. Just…realizing how big it is out there—and how little we are."

Wyatt turned to look at Beth. Her jumpsuit was stained and ripped, the knuckles on her right fist looked bruised and cut, and black goop stiffened a lock of hair on one side of her head. Long practice made him scan for injuries, but to Wyatt's relief, he did not see any burns or punctures, and no bloodstains that looked like they might be her own.

"You think it's bad in the *Nellie B*, spend time out here in a Viper Class fighter. That'll really make you question your sanity."

"I'm all right," Beth said.

Wyatt shrugged. "Inconvenient if you die on me. Can't show up at the next station with a stiff. I'd have to put you out an airlock." He shifted his chair. "I mean, not that it would be the first time, but I'd rather not."

"Thank you," she replied. "For checking on me."

Wyatt kept his gaze fixed on the stars as if there were a likelihood they might run into something if he looked away. "You did pretty well in a fight. Kept your head, shot straight. Lots of people don't under fire. I've seen many a battle veteran totally lose it and freeze."

Beth regarded him, and Wyatt fought the urge to squirm under the scrutiny. "You were in the war." She didn't make it a question.

"Yeah."

"Pilot?"

Wyatt looked away. "Does that surprise you?"

Beth shook her head. "No. Everything about you, the way you move, the build, your focus, screams military. What made you take up salvage?"

Wyatt stared into the black void. "Didn't have much patience left for following orders," he replied. "Out here, it can be simple. Do a run, sell it off, celebrate a little, resupply, and do it again. No bigger purpose except just getting to the next job, no politics, and no bull-shit."

"I've screwed up 'simple' for you. Sorry."

Wyatt shrugged again. "Don't be. It was bound to happen sooner or later. My luck works like that."

"And how did you manage to get a Space Corps' gunship?"

"A long story, and one I'd rather not get into right now. Maybe when things ease up," Wyatt said. "And I get really drunk."

"So where do we go now?" Beth stretched.

Wyatt did his best not to notice that even a jumpsuit couldn't completely hide the trim curves of her body. *Damn, it had been too long.* He shook his head to bring back his focus. "Resupply colony." Wyatt relaxed a bit as the conversation shifted away from his past. "Got a friend there who'll take care of us."

"Someone you can trust? Kalok'll be asking around."

Wyatt nodded. "Oh, hell yeah. Hendrick's got no love for the corporations, or Interplan. That's why he's out here, running the resupply."

"Which I'm guessing might lack proper licensing?" Beth speculated.

Wyatt chuckled. "Hendrick might have forgotten to file a permit or two along the way."

"So we're going off the grid."

"Yep. I try to stay off the grid as much as possible. We'll lay in supplies and buy ourselves some time."

"Kalok's not going to forget about us," Beth said quietly.

"No, they're not. But we're not gonna run blind. Need supplies, need fuel, and intel. Hendrick has all three." He grinned. "Well, the intel is hit or miss. Codger never met a conspiracy theory he didn't love."

"Codger?"

"His call sign. When he wasn't suited up, he wandered around in this old ratty sweater that looked like it should have belonged to someone's grandfather. So—Codger."

"What was your call sign?" Beth asked.

"Burner. 'Cause I was just that hot," he replied with a wink and a cocky grin.

"Uh huh," Beth replied, unconvinced. "Set something on fire?"

"Plenty," Wyatt said, his grin fading. "But there was this one time…it was rather spectacular. In a grim and deadly sort of way."

"Can't wait to meet him," Beth said. "Should be good for some stories."

Wyatt cleared his throat. "Um, about that. Codger—his real name is Hendrick Turner—doesn't like to talk about the war unless he served with you. He's a mite touchy about it—been known to clear out a bar just because someone said the wrong thing. So follow my lead. Please." He saw Beth's skeptical expression and grimaced. "He's a good guy. Just a little roughed up by life, that's all."

Beth looked like she wanted to say something and then reconsidered. "I 'll hold you to that," she said.

CODGER'S RESUPPLY POST lay three day's flight into Near-Fringe space, off the direct routes favored by the trading convoys.

"How does anyone find this place?" Beth asked as the ship set down on the landing pad.

"If you're welcome, you know where it is. If you aren't, you don't need to know," Wyatt replied.

Beth raised an eyebrow but said nothing. She reached for her atmo collar.

"You won't need that. The air's thin, but breathable. We need to see if we can get you a real pressure suit with decent mag boots while we're here."

Beth followed Wyatt out of the ship and looked around. "Not much to see," she remarked.

"Apparently this was an astronomy 'listening post' long before the Rim pushed out this far," Wyatt replied. "Bunch of die-hard academic types took a one-way trip out here to be the first to document this part of space close-up." He turned to look at Beth. "Back then, this was really far from the edge of settled space. It took them years to get here, with no expectation of ever going back."

"What happened to them?" Beth fell into step with Wyatt as they walked toward a cluster of round bunkers weathered by time. Patchy grass struggled up from ashy dirt. Near the bunkers, Wyatt made out several greenhouses of metal frame and polymer sheeting, as well as a few open-air gardens. Four spring houses dotted the encampment, as well as more modern water distillation equipment.

"Eventually, they died." Wyatt shaded his eyes against the glare of the sun. The dry air made his eyes sting, and fine dust put an itch in the back of his throat that made him swallow too often. "They knew that was the deal when they came out here. They brought everything they needed with them. Real pioneers." He paused for a moment. "All to get a good look at the stars from a different rock."

"And their data? Did it make a difference?" The earnest tone in Beth's voice made Wyatt give her a considered look.

"Don't know. I imagine they sent it back, though it would have taken time to reach their home base. You're the university type. Figured you'd know that kind of thing." He looked out over the harsh landscape. "They called the place 'Pointer's Landing' after the lead researcher." Wyatt barked a laugh. "Now we call it 'Codger's Corner.'"

As they trekked in from the landing pad, Wyatt got a better look at the ring of bunkers. A few had been damaged since his previous visit. A wind turbine spun lazily in the breeze, and as they neared the camp, Wyatt caught a glimpse of laundry fluttering on a wash line behind one of the domed buildings.

"How many people live here?" Beth asked, looking around at the silent base.

"Last time I was here, it was just Codger. He likes his privacy. Does business when he feels like it; refuses to answer when he doesn't. That's his place over there," Wyatt said, pointing to the second building on the left. "He lives in one of the domes, uses the rest for storage."

Before they could reach the building, they heard footsteps behind them and the whine of a blaster shifting from standby to ready.

"You didn't tell me you were bringing a stranger."

Wyatt and Beth turned slowly, hands raised. The man behind them was a little older than Wyatt, somewhere in his early thirties. He had dark blond hair and a hard set to his mouth. Sunglasses hid his eyes. Nothing about his military stance looked welcoming.

"I can explain," Wyatt said calmly.

"I don't like surprises." Codger did not lower his weapon.

Wyatt licked his lips. "I can vouch for her," he said. "You know I wouldn't bring someone here I didn't trust."

"Hell, Burner, I don't hardly trust you, let alone someone you vouch for," Codger replied. For another moment, he kept the gun leveled at them, and then he grinned and holstered his weapon.

"We good?" Wyatt asked, not moving.

Codger strode toward them, and Wyatt braced, expecting him to take a swing. Instead, Codger clapped a hand down on Wyatt's shoulder before pulling him into a rough hug. "Fuck, yeah. C'mon in."

Beth glanced at Wyatt, looking for direction. Wyatt shrugged, then followed Codger into the dome.

The inside of the old bunker had changed little. Its original occupants had probably slept three or four to a building. Codger had repurposed the space, making the front room into an office. Computer equipment and holographic readers covered a large desk, and Wyatt was not surprised that they were the newest models available. A rack of weapons hung on the wall behind the desk.

Shelves held books, star charts, and a variety of data storage media. A reinforced window looked out on the empty open space between the domes. Wires ran along the walls like a spider's web, and Wyatt guessed they connected to Codger's extensive security system.

"Business been good?" Wyatt asked, mentally tallying up how much the computer equipment must have cost.

"Brisk, actually." Codger glanced from Wyatt to Beth. "You ever gonna introduce your friend?"

"This is Beth," Wyatt replied. "She's going to be flying with me for a while."

"Not like you to pick up passengers, Burner."

Wyatt shrugged. "She's got a line on some good salvage, and it's a competitive business. Gotta take the breaks you get. Thought maybe it was time for a business partner."

Codger gave Beth an appraising look. "Huh. Don't let her get you killed."

"Not planning on it," Wyatt replied. "She's pretty good with a gun, fast on her feet."

Codger sighed. "If you already know that, then there's trouble right behind you. I should have known."

"No one followed us," Wyatt said. "I made sure."

Codger's expression made it clear he was unconvinced, but he waved them through the front room into a sitting room. Comfortably shabby furniture provided barely enough seating, making it clear Codger did not often host visitors. He went into another room and came back with a carafe of clear liquid and three glasses. Before he even poured, Wyatt could smell the alcohol.

"Am I supposed to drink that or fuel up the *Nellie B* with it?" Wyatt raised his eyebrows.

Codger scowled. "If you're gonna be like that, I'll keep it for myself. That'll teach me to be neighborly. Besides, if you upgraded that scow of yours, you wouldn't have to spend half your time refueling."

"Show some respect. You of anyone know she's a damn fine ship," Wyatt said with a glare.

"Yeah, but I love gettin' ya worked up," Codger laughed.

Beth reached out and poured a few fingers of the home-brewed alcohol into her glass. "To your health," she said, raising the glass in a toast, before knocking back most of the drink in one shot. Codger and Wyatt watched in amazement.

"You okay?" Wyatt ventured.

Beth grinned. "Never better." Her voice was raspier than usual, and a flush crept up to her cheeks, but she appeared otherwise unaffected.

Codger looked over to Wyatt. "She's good. Don't know why she's hanging around the likes of you."

Wyatt gave an exaggerated sigh. "You've always underestimated me."

Codger snorted. "Hardly. I was there when they named you, Burner. I remember."

Wyatt looked away. "That was a long time ago," He muttered. Unwilling to be shown up, he poured himself a double and took a sip. "Shit, Codger! You tryin' to kill someone?"

Codger filled his own glass and took a swallow as if it were water. "Nope. Just my liver. But they got pills for that now." He looked at Wyatt, and his eyes narrowed. "Don't figure this is a social call. What do you need, Burner, and who's after you?"

Wyatt took another sip and enjoyed the heat as the liquor scorched down his throat. He relaxed a bit, and sat back, knowing that they were safer here with Codger's paranoid protections than nearly anywhere outside the Fringe. "I can't just stop in on a Regiment buddy for old times?"

Codger gave him a withering look. "It would be the first time. Usually, you're hauling ass and someone's gunning for your tail feathers."

"We pissed off some goons on Rum Row," Beth said, unfazed by Codger's liquor. "Figured we'd do some runs in the Deep Fringe for a while, let them cool off."

Codger glanced at Wyatt. "That true?"

Wyatt caught his breath after another sip. "Yeah. Turns out some of my cargo was hotter than I knew."

"So who's chasing you? Dodson's gang? The Crawlers again?"

"Kalok," Beth replied. Wyatt shot her a warning glance, and she gave him a smile that said she knew exactly what she was doing.

"Shit. You don't do things by halves," Codger replied. "Whose ass did you light on fire?"

"We were in the wrong place at the wrong time," Beth said, "with the wrong people. So we want to stay off the grid for a while. And for that, we need supplies."

Codger nodded. His eyes told Wyatt that their host knew they were not sharing the whole story, but he did not press and probably didn't really want to know. Safer that way. "Okay. I've got what you need. And Kalok's nothing you want to fool with. They don't forgive—or forget."

"Figured that," Wyatt replied, still nursing his drink. "But if we lay in supplies, between what we can salvage and what we can barter, we can go a long while out in the Fringe, and maybe come back with a pocketful of credits, too."

"You always were an overly optimistic son of a bitch," Codger grumbled. "Only you would figure this is your lucky break." He refilled his glass. "Give me your list. I can probably make some suggestions, too."

He regarded Beth for a moment. "Hope you know what you're doing, Miss Beth. Known this boy a long time, and he may be pretty, but he's a handful."

"That's not news," Beth's tone remained pleasant, but it held an edge, and Wyatt hoped Codger didn't decide to dispense unwelcome advice. "We make a good team."

"You ever been to the Fringe?"

"I've never been past Rum Row before this." Beth met Codger's gaze without blinking.

"Ain't no luxury hotels, barely enough food, air, and water, and the folks you'll meet make me look positively refined," Codger warned.

Beth's smile vanished. "I grew up on a hardscrabble farming planet. We battled the elements and the raiders for everything we had. Shot my first man when I was twelve, some no-account thief stopped by to take what he didn't pay for—or have a right to. Shot a few more on Rum Row. Going Fringe doesn't scare me."

Wyatt felt an unexpected burst of pride at Beth's comeback. He slid a glance toward Codger for the reaction.

"Well then, if you're accustomed to thieves and brigands, you and Burner should do well together. He's a lot of things—not all of them good—but if he says he's got your back, he'll keep his word."

"Why Codger, I didn't think—"

"Shut up, Burner. Don't ruin it." Codger swallowed down more of his moonshine. "Guess since you're here, I ought to feed you, since you're a paying customer, and Regiment besides." He cocked an eyebrow at Wyatt. "You *are* paying, aren't you?"

Wyatt nodded, feeling the liquor warm his bones. "Of course we are."

"He has the money," Beth supplied.

"I don't need you to—"

"Obviously, you do."

Wyatt scowled, but he reached into his pocket and withdrew a pouch of chits, the untraceable currency preferred by many beyond the Rim. Even encrypted transactions could be hacked or traced. The chits were forgery-proof and widely accepted. "Happy?"

Codger grinned. "Yep. Now get your ass off my couch and help me gather what you need, and then we'll see about some food."

A FEW HOURS later, once supplies were loaded onto the *Nellie B*, Wyatt, Beth, and Codger sat down to dinner. Wyatt noticed Codger had upgraded the chicken coops since his last visit and expanded the corral with a few pigs, some goats, and a couple of animals Wyatt couldn't identify. One of those chickens now graced a serving platter in the middle of the table.

"I've added variety to my livestock since you were here last," Codger said. "Been taking chickens and other critters in trade ever since. Not rightly sure whether I can eat those blue things you saw, but they give mighty fine milk, and I ain't died of it yet."

"This looks fine," Wyatt said, and his mouth watered at the thought of a fresh meal not out of the replicator.

"Who taught you to cook?" Beth asked.

"Nobody, but I didn't feel like starving, and I got tired of ration packs long ago." Codger made a point to serve Beth first and blushed at her thanks. "He tell you we served together?"

"He did," Beth said and took a bite of the roasted chicken. She turned to look at Wyatt raising an eyebrow.

"I warned her that you didn't like talking about it," Wyatt said.

"I don't mind telling stories about you…"

"You mentioned the Regiment. Was that your unit?" Beth asked.

Codger slathered butter onto a thick loaf of homemade bread.

"We were the three-oh-first," he replied. "Best fucking bunch of Star Corps pilots in the whole damn inner Rim. Maybe the whole fucking galaxy."

Beth took him in stride, and Wyatt hid a smile. "Rim War?"

"Yes, ma'am."

"I'm curious," Beth continued and paused to finish another bite. "The Rim War was supposedly about stopping anarchists who threatened the Allied Worlds' colonization drive just beyond the Rim—"

"Supposedly?" Codger's voice had gone cold and gravelly.

Wyatt cleared his throat. "What she means—"

"I'm quite able to say what I mean, thank you, Wyatt," Beth replied without ever letting her smile slip or her voice lose its conversational tone. "It's been a few years since the war," she explained. "And in some circles, there've been questions raised about whether those 'anarchists' might not have just been protecting what was theirs against big corporations with the power to take what they wanted."

"And your friends in these 'circles,' were they there? Did they fight? Lose any of their friends out in the Dark?" Codger's hands tightened around his fork and knife.

"I said I was curious," Beth replied evenly. "If I thought I knew the answer, I wouldn't have asked the question."

"Don't matter what you or your friends think," Codger growled. "We did what we believed was right, based on what the commanders we trusted told us was true. Now if you want to go rewriting that long after the vapor clears, be my guest. Don't fix nothin', don't bring nobody back from the dead."

"My apologies," Beth murmured, looking down at her plate. "I didn't mean to give offense."

"You think I care what you 'meant' to do?"

Beth raised her head and met Codger's gaze without flinching. "I think that if what I said actually offended you, you wouldn't be off the grid, holed up in your own private fortress," she said without heat. She slid her chair back. "Been a long day, and I appreciate the meal, but I'd better turn in," Beth added, her posture making it clear that she wasn't backing down in the slightest.

Codger waited until she had headed back to the ship before he let loose a string of invective. Wyatt waited him out, pouring them both more moonshine.

"You done yet?" Wyatt asked. He leaned back, took a sip, and gave Codger a measured glance.

Codger glared at him. "Where'd you pick her up, anyhow?"

"Old Comstock mine," Wyatt replied. "Running from some Grays."

"And that was your problem why? I mean, she's a fine looker, but—"

"Don't." Wyatt's words came out sharp. "It's not like that."

"Really? Old dogs don't change their ways. You tell her why we called you 'Burner?'"

"A little."

"Yeah, I bet. Did you forget to mention about all those hook-ups in all those ports?"

Wyatt rolled his eyes. "Old news, Codger. Beth's a business partner. Nothing else."

"What's she got that you want? There has to be something because with a mouth like that she's gonna get you in some deep shit."

Wyatt weighed his options. He trusted Codger as much as he trusted anyone, which said volumes. Still, he was Regiment, and that counted. "For one thing, she's a space archeologist. It's actually Dr. Elizabeth Parker. She's smart and has a line on some good salvage. And for another, Kalok thinks she's a threat."

"Then either let her out at the next station or kiss your ass goodbye," Codger replied. "Kalok gets what Kalok wants. Don't we both know that the hard way? You just can't resist being the damn hero."

"Sorry about her stirring stuff up." Wyatt toyed with his glass. "You and I both know we got played, back in the war. Along with all the other poor dumb sons of bitches we flew with."

"Don't mean I like to think about it," Codger said, taking a gulp that should have sent him sputtering.

"Nah, you just drink about it, like we all do." Wyatt took a gulp of his own, unapologetically coughing as it burned.

"Never thought I'd regret winning."

"I don't regret winning—I just regret which side we fought on."

Codger held his glass up and stared at it as if it held the secrets of the universe. "Now that's the truth," he replied quietly.

"What do you hear, from the others?" Wyatt had told Beth the truth when he said the Regiment was all three-oh-first members, but it was so much more. They had flown and bled together, crashed and cheered and cried together, and they had the scars to prove it. For most of them, the Regiment was all the family they had left, closer than kin. No one who hadn't seen what they saw understood the marks it left.

"You know how it is," Codger said, setting his glass down with a quiet thud. "Hard to get news about men who don't want to be found. But I hear, now and again. Stretch got himself killed about six months ago, some kind of bar fight. No surprise, considering how he was."

"Yeah, I remember."

"Mouse got caught smuggling over in the Rellian system. He's either locked up or dead."

"He was never any good at anything but going in full-fire," Wyatt replied. "Not surprised he got that gigantic ass of his caught."

Codger shrugged, not meeting his gaze. "Nothing of note about any of the others. They come through now and again, most of the time they leave me a way to get in touch, just in case."

"Regiment rules," Wyatt said with a sad smile. Some habits never died. *Always have backup, and always let your squadron know where you were.* It was one of the first things the sergeant had drilled into their heads when they came in as recruits, and it sunk in to the bone.

"This thing that's got the goons on your tail, you stepped in some deep shit, didn't you, Burner?"

Wyatt paused and then nodded. "Big enough to cause Kalok some serious discomfort, Interplan, too."

"Damn. So that's why you couldn't walk away."

"That's why we need to go off the grid for a while; fuck, maybe forever. 'Cause this thing—we had to do something with it. But Kalok can't afford for her to get away, and they'll never give up. We need to lie low to figure out next steps or disappear so far into the Dark no one will ever find us."

"Which one you gonna pick?"

Wyatt's finger traced the rim of his glass. "Lie low, probably. How do you cope, Codger? Cause I sure haven't figured it out… Do you remember Red Rocks?"

"Wish I didn't, but I do. Dream about it sometimes. The way the smoke came up."

"Yeah, so do I. Supposed to be an 'anarchist base' only it was also a farming community. Incinerated the lot of them—women, kids, old folks—and the Corps told us it was 'bad intel.'"

"Like the 'bad intel' we got about Hinder's Point and Wasser Station, and that convoy ship—"

Wyatt gave a bitter chuckle. "The *Armistice.* Which was supposed to be on a munitions run and turned out to be full of passengers instead. It still gives me nightmares…"

"It's long over, Burner. Picking the scabs off don't serve no purpose."

"You mean it scabbed over for you? 'Cause it sure as fuck didn't for me. Bleeds fresh every goddamned night when I dream. How can you forget it?"

"Why you think I brew my 'shine?"

"We got played, Codger. Got *used* to do the corporation's killing for them, or whoever else bribed or twisted the arms of the big guys in Space Corps," Wyatt said in a tight voice. "We were good little soldiers, and they made murderers of us—sold our services to the highest bidder."

"Soldiers kill, Burner."

"Not civilians, Codger." He swallowed hard. "Not innocents. Those weren't *mistakes.* They were *targets,* and the people who sent us knew who was going to be killed, even if we didn't. I can't—I won't forget *or* forgive. I've tried to move on, I really have…but it still comes back."

"So you're going to get yourself killed over it *now?*"

"Not if I can help it," Wyatt replied. "If I intended to suicide over the guilt, I'd have done it long before now. Don't think it never crossed my mind. This…this is a chance to take those bastards down."

"Ya know, it may not help…" There was a long pause before Codger's eyes turned back to him with a spark of interest. "This thing you've got a line on—it's that big? Because you've got to know that a lot of money will be interested in shutting you up permanently."

"We already turned over what we found, but Beth thinks we'll find more. That's why we've got to run for now. I'm not looking to lead an army. Fuck, I don't even care whether I get to do the shooting. Get the information to the right people, let things take their course."

"Those anarchists we shot down probably thought the same thing," Codger mused. "And there'll be another squadron of bright-eyed fools like we were, waiting to do it again. You know how this ends."

Wyatt felt his temper rise. "No, I know how *that* ended. So what— no one ever does anything, just lets it go on and on? And what happens when Kalok gets grabby again—and they will—and they push out past the Rim? Or into the Fringe?"

"There's a whole lot of space out there," Codger replied. "A man could run into the Dark for a long, long time."

"No one can run forever—or hide," Wyatt said, with a pointed glance at the nearly empty container of moonshine.

"You might be surprised how far a man can run when it comes down to the wire."

"You think the Regiment—"

"You go to the Regiment; you go as Burner, not on some damn fool mission, you understand me? Don't you drag them into it! Gods know, they've got scars aplenty as it is. Let them have what peace they've found. If they want to sign on, they'll do it on their own."

"So you're telling me to stay away?" Wyatt's fist clenched on his lap.

"Gods, were you always this stupid?" Codger's hand slapped the table, so forcefully his drink sloshed. "No, that's not what I'm saying, Burner. I'm just saying that I'm not ready to go flying off to war, and you shouldn't ask that of them, either. Something comes of this thing of yours, if it really is as big as you think it is, they'll find you. Shit, you don't think they wouldn't all like to expose the corruption and bring down Kalok and Interplan if they could?"

Wyatt took a deep breath, willing himself to calm down. "No, you're right. We don't have all the pieces. But Beth and I are going to do our damnedest to get to the bottom of it. Don't have a choice—Kalok's already gunning for us. Might as well look for all the dirt we can find."

"Then keep your head down, do what you've got to do, and enjoy the fact that every day you stay alive, you're pissing them off even more," Codger said, raising a toast.

Wyatt clinked his chipped glass against Codger's. "I'll drink to that."

CHAPTER FOUR

"YOU HAVE ANY idea what that freighter was carrying, or are we just going in blind?" Beth watched as Wyatt did a fly-by of the derelict ship and drummed her fingers. Wyatt's idea of "research" was completely different from hers.

"It's a general-purpose cargo ship, Tevro registry. That means probably human," Wyatt replied, not taking his eyes off his instruments. "Whatever it's got we can fence. Can't go wrong on something like this."

The *Perseverance* hung motionless. Its lights were dark, save for a few flickers of the emergency power supply. Three months after disappearing from its flight plan, the ship's hull remained intact, though scarred with pockmarks from passing debris.

"Doesn't look like anyone else's found it," Wyatt said. "Then again, it's way off its course. Wonder if it drifted, or if they diverted for some reason?"

Beth shook her head. "Do we care how it ended up abandoned? Are you even sure it *is* abandoned?"

"The sensors aren't picking up any life forms—human or otherwise. As for how it ended up abandoned, don't care as long as it's not a plague ship, and the sensor sweep hasn't flagged any dangerous organisms."

"Nellie, please scan the *Perseverance* one more time for any life forms," Wyatt said.

"Results are negative," Nellie responded.

"That it recognizes," Beth supplied.

"I am programmed to recognize all life forms that have been registered with the Interstellar Commission for preserving and protecting sentient lifeforms," Nellie responded.

Beth rolled her eyes. Nellie had never been outright disrespectful, but she noticed the ship's A.I. took a different tone with her than it did Wyatt.

"Best we can do," Wyatt said.

"Humor me," Beth said. "See if Nellie or your scanners can tell us why it's just floating dead out here with no crew. If it wasn't a plague, then what happened? We'd see blast marks if they'd been beset by pirates, and if the engines blew up, we'd pick up a radiation trail, not to mention a damn big hole in the hull."

"Both life pods are missing," Nellie reported.

Wyatt read the scans Nellie sent to his screen. "So, odds are, something went wrong with the life support system, and the crew bailed." He looked into the vast expanse of the dark. "Hope they were closer than this to a settled system or had cryo tubes. If not, they likely drifted longer than their air held out."

"So what's the plan?" Only a few weeks had passed since they fled the Comstock mine, and most of that time had been spent running, first to Rum Row, then into the Near-Fringe. Now that Codger's base was several days behind them; they were starting to settle back into Wyatt's salvaging routine.

"Go in, get the goods, get gone," Wyatt replied, bringing the *Nellie*

B into position to dock with the *Perseverance.*

"How long have you been doing this?" Beth asked.

Wyatt shot her a blinding grin. "Years. And I'm still alive. So I must know what I'm doing, right?"

"Or it's true what they say about fools and blind luck," she muttered.

"Nellie, can you determine if any systems are operational or running currently?"

"Emergency generators, life support, and artificial gravity are functioning."

"Functioning…doesn't mean the air is good or that they're working well," Wyatt said, reading the sensor display at the airlock terminal.

"If this were a holovid, ominous music would be warning us that there's some new kind of really contagious virus that killed the crew," Beth said, crossing her arms.

"One more reason I don't watch holovids," Wyatt said. But just in case, he engaged his helmet, which rose out of the collar of his suit.

Beth struggled trying to figure out how the helmet on the new suit was activated, damned if she'd admit she didn't know how to turn it on.

"Here, the switch is on the side. Pull it forward and then down. It will lock into place."

The helmet rose out of the collar and sealed with a hiss as the air equalized in her suit. The new spacesuit wasn't a perfect fit, but it had basic armor plates and would keep out most of the contaminates they were likely to encounter.

Wyatt fussed with the fastenings, triple-checking them. Beth hid a smile. She appreciated that Wyatt expected her to be competent and treated her like an equal. Still, Beth had to admit it was sort of nice having him show a protective side. It took effort to keep things strictly professional between them. Wyatt was good looking in a bad boy kind of way, and she couldn't deny the attraction, which seemed mutual. *Been a long time,* she reminded herself. The last relationship hadn't ended well and made the thought of shipping out on the Kalok project seem like a good idea. *Be careful.* She glanced up to see he was staring at her.

"You good?" Wyatt's voice sounded somewhat metallic coming through the speaker.

"Yeah. Most places I've gone the atmo collar was all I needed."

"Welcome to the other side, Dr. Parker. We have no idea what's on that ship, and an atmo collar won't keep toxins from getting through a civilian jumpsuit. And it sure as hell won't stop a blaster or vibro blade. Nellie's showing the *Perseverance* has gravity, but power up the mag boots if it goes out."

Mag boots? Beth took a deep breath and reminded herself she could do this. None of the places she had gone with Kalok had required magnetic boots, and the archeology projects on-world now seemed tame compared to the kind of places Wyatt viewed as "all in a day's work." *Okay so maybe my prior space exploration wasn't typical for salvage, but I grew up making do.* She summoned her bravado and gave Wyatt a nod.

Wyatt released the outer airlock, which opened with a metallic clang as the locking bolts released and the hatch slid into the bulkhead. They waited a moment for the atmosphere to equalize between them and the *Perseverance.* Wyatt maneuvered an empty hover cart through the airlock, to help carry out anything they decided to salvage. They stepped through the docking bridge onto the receiving platform, and Wyatt held up his scanner. "Appears clear, but oxygen levels are a little low."

"Should we risk it until we know there's not a plague or alien virus waiting to turn us into green sludge?" Beth asked.

"If you want to be boring and safe."

"Either that or you open your suit, and I'll just watch and wait to see if you're all right."

"Very funny."

"I wasn't joking."

Beth pulled out her blaster and flipped on her light, walking backward as Wyatt moved forward across the hold. Nothing moved. She concentrated, listening for the muted hum of the life support systems, an essential background noise on any ship or space station that faded into the background. The faint sound reassured her, and she wondered how long the ship could remain adrift and still be habitable.

"Here we go," Wyatt murmured and opened the door from the receiving platform into the corridor.

Only the emergency lighting lit the corridor, making Beth glad she had her suit lamp. "This way," Wyatt said, giving a jerk of his head to the right.

Beth followed, facing forward, though she made sure to check behind them every few steps, just in case. Even in the suit, she was aware that the ship felt cooler than most, and she wondered if that was due to the system beginning to fail, or an emergency grid conserving power. A strange smell lingered in the air, growing stronger as they moved away from the docking platform. It had to be pretty potent to get through the suit's filters.

"Do you know where we're heading?" she whispered.

Wyatt waved his right arm, indicating a schematic of the *Perseverance* that hovered above his wrist unit. "Got it all right here."

Beth fought the urge to smack him. "Cocky, damn fool, know-it-all son of a bitch," she muttered.

"Flatter me all you want, I'm not raising your percentage of the take," Wyatt responded.

Beth huffed but chose not to say anything more. In the time since they fled the Comstock mine, she had spent much of that time assessing her new partner. She had proposed their business partnership on the spur of the moment, based on a gut feeling. She didn't regret that; Wyatt had willingly taken on enormous risks to get her away from Kalok's people, not just on at the Comstock, but on Rum Row and afterward. She did not doubt that he enjoyed the thrills and the chance to give Kalok a one-finger salute.

The military training was painfully evident the more time she spent around him. He was like a loaded weapon, ready to go off at the slightest sign of trouble. But at the same time, she saw how he interacted with his "friends," calm and caring, and he certainly seemed to watch over her. She'd watched him work out a few times in the small ship gym. Out of sight, of course. No denying the man had a beautiful, ripped body that wasn't just the gift of genetics or his athletic build. Sure, everyone who spent time in space had to exercise or pay the price. But Wyatt took it to an almost obsession. He confused her because the pieces didn't add up. She wondered about the cocky bastard façade.

She had glimpsed something during their brief stay with Codger that made her question appearances. The two men had stayed up, drinking and talking, well into the night. She had resisted the temptation to eavesdrop, yet she could not help picking up a pervasive sense of melancholy, which made her suspect that there was far more about the Regiment and Wyatt's military service than he had shared.

Codger had given her access to his secure, encrypted data connection, and she had looked up Wyatt's service record. He had been a captain, decorated for bravery, served on more than eighty missions. Honorably discharged. The accounts made him out to be a military hero. Yet a deep bitterness and anger lingered just below the surface when Wyatt had spoken of his part in the Rim Wars. Their current situation put him somewhat at odds with his former reputation—and the entities in whose name he had fought. She knew something of that bitterness now, feeling betrayed by those she had looked up to.

Where did it go wrong? I got off that rock I grew up on, made something of myself, a reputation, a career, working for the most powerful firms in the Allied Worlds…

"Hey! Don't get distracted," Wyatt snapped. "We're almost there."

Wyatt turned a corner and stopped abruptly, holding his arm up in a silent signal for Beth to halt. The odd smell had become an overwhelming stench. She wondered if the filters in her suit were bad. It took Beth a moment to figure out that the heap in the middle of the corridor was what remained of one of the *Perseverance's* crew.

"Cover me." Wyatt went down on one knee for a better look, while Beth kept her weapon up and scanned for danger. She heard the low whine of his scanner, and then he stood, lips set in a grim line.

"Been dead about as long as the ship's been missing," he reported. "No sign of weapons' fire. Scanner says natural causes—intestinal rupture."

"Just spontaneous like that?" Beth raised an eyebrow. "How can you stand the smell?"

"Smell? I'm not getting anything. You may have a bad filter. We'll need to get it checked next time we're on a station. As for what happened…" Wyatt shrugged. "Maybe there was some kind of accident. He could have gotten hurt. But yeah, I don't like it. Let's get what we came for and go."

Just like that, the banter vanished. As they moved forward, Beth saw nothing of the reckless salvage pilot she encountered at Comstock. Wyatt's entire manner had changed, from the tilt of his head to the predatory way he moved. This was Captain McCoy, every bit a seasoned soldier.

They found two more bodies in the next corridor, on their way to the cargo hold. But the corpse they discovered at the doorway to one of the medical labs made Wyatt pause once more.

"Shit," he muttered. "You see that?" Wyatt gestured with his gun. "He's fresher than the others, and someone damn near blew his head clean off."

"Pirates?"

Wyatt shook his head. "Don't think so. No sign of forced entry; can't see that anyone but us has come calling."

"Sabotage?"

"Maybe—or mutiny. Whatever it was obviously didn't go well since nobody won. We'll do one load since we're here, and get going."

He started to move forward when Beth laid a hand on his shoulder. "Listen," she cautioned.

Above the constant drone of the life support system, they could hear a faint *clink*. She couldn't tell where the sound came from, but it made her hackles rise. "Ventilation system? Or maintenance crawlways?"

"Could be anything," he said, though the dangerous glint in his eyes suggested he was unwilling to write off the threat. "Maybe they've got robots doing routine updates."

"They sure aren't cleaning," she replied with a look of disgust at the decaying remains.

It didn't take much longer to reach the cargo hold. Wyatt hacked into the lock easily, and they both readied their guns as the large doors slid open.

The dim reserve lighting left much of the cavernous hold in shadow. Beth glanced up; only one out of every three overhead fixtures glowed. Crates and boxes stretched in long rows, and from what she could see, their markings indicated origin or delivery on more than a dozen far-flung worlds.

"Watch my back." Wyatt moved to a computer console and hummed to himself as he worked the data entry pad. "Got it," he muttered.

"What?"

"Cargo manifest. Now we don't have to pry them all open to get the good stuff."

Beth heard a clinking sound overhead and froze. The look on Wyatt's face indicated that he heard it, too. "Over here," he said, leading the way with the hover cart.

"What are we grabbing?" Beth asked.

"Cases of Numarian whiskey," Wyatt said, lifting down several stamped and marked boxes. He gestured for her to follow as he strode down the aisle, consulting the numbered guide he had downloaded to his bio communicator. His armor suit's wrist unit synched and displayed a holo image.

"A box of Coltoran spices—they'll pay a fortune for these out on the Fringe," he said, and placed another case on the cart.

"Dried ears from the moon-raptor of Eratola 5."

"Ears?"

Wyatt spared a smirk. "They're famous in certain circles for their…um…enhancement properties."

"Spare me."

"Almost done," he promised, moving over to another row.

"I don't like this, Wyatt. We need to go." She went to follow him, but a sudden burning sensation in her forearm left her gasping in pain. Beth knew that the alien implant glowed beneath her skin, and suddenly she saw the hold as it had been before the *Perseverance* met its fate. An image overlaid her vision, the well-lit area bustled with busy crew members, she counted five of the forty Wyatt had said were onboard.

Nothing seemed awry, just a normal day on a well-run ship. Then one of the men sagged against the bulkhead, arms wrapped around his belly, obviously in pain. His crewmates ran to him, and while Beth couldn't hear their conversation in the stone tape echo, she could tell that they were trying to convince the man to get help.

Before medics could arrive, two more of the workers slumped to the floor, writhing in pain. Beth stared as they tore at the skin over their abdomens, trying to claw away the pain. Seizures wracked them, and then each of the three stricken crew went still.

Beth blinked, and she knew that time in her vision had passed. A different shift staffed the cargo hold, and for a moment, everything again appeared to be normal. Then the door opened, and three men lunged inside, tackling the nearest crew members and fighting with a feral, inhuman savagery. Two of the crew drew their weapons and shot at their attackers, and that was when Beth got a good look and recognized the same three people who had fallen sick in the first portion of her vision.

"Beth!" Wyatt's tone suggested he had been calling her name without response.

She startled, and the vision vanished. "A vision. We've got to leave. Something happened to the crew. I saw them. Wyatt, it looked like a contagion—virus, plague, something that spread."

"All right." Wyatt agreed far faster than Beth had expected. "This place is giving me the creeps, and we've got a full load. Let's go."

Beth tried not to flinch when she passed the spot where she had seen the initial three crew members fall. She looked away and noticed dark spatters on the bulkhead and more stains on the floor panels. Wyatt also saw them, and his shoulders tensed. "Tell me about it later," he said. "Getting any more warnings?"

She still felt the heat from her forearm, but no additional visions forced their way into her mind. "Nothing yet. You'll be the first to know."

They were about halfway back to the *Nellie B* when Beth pulled her arm to her chest and cried out in surprise, falling to her knees in the corridor. She'd had a flash of vision that startled her, and the alien implant was warm under her skin. The clunking sound seemed closer, along with scrabbling, scratching sounds. Wyatt looked up, toward the overhead vents.

The deck plating in front of them shook and then tilted up as arms pushed it out of the way.

Beth wondered why Wyatt held his shot as she tried to get her focus back. Then she saw them; five men and two women climbed from the access passage under their feet, wearing the ragged, filthy remnants of uniforms. *How could they have not registered on Nellie's scan?*

"Who are you?" Wyatt called.

The only response came when the two men in front rushed them.

Wyatt did not miss. His shot took the first man through the chest, dropping him in his tracks.

The other man rushed toward where she was kneeling. His face was stained with dark blood, eyes wild. A deep growl rumbled from his throat, and he reached toward her with hands clenched like claws. Beth pulled her blaster and shot, the force of the blast threw him backward, spraying the corridor with dark ichor. He didn't move or try to get up.

The blaster fire made the others back up a pace, and Wyatt stepped to the side protectively to grab Beth and drag her close to him and away from the man that attacked her. He kept his gun trained on the things that used to be the crew of the *Perseverance*.

Beth got a better look at the creatures. They had the mien of prison camp survivors, gaunt and sallow, eyes sunken, barely more than skin and skeleton. Wild-eyed and feral. Blood and other substances stained their clothing, and by the smell, they had forgotten any sort of hygiene. She would have called them "animals," but that wasn't fair to the furry kind of creature. They looked like the zombies in old holovid horror shows.

"Got a theory?" Wyatt asked quietly.

"About what made them like this? Nope. About what happened to the ship? I think we've got a partial answer to that one."

"Who are you?" Wyatt asked, keeping his gun trained on the others.

The things that used to be people exchanged glances and guttural barks, not quite a language but enough perhaps for them to convey meaning. They turned back to face them, apparently unintimidated.

Beth forced herself up the wall until she could stand. Her arm still tingled, but it wasn't nearly so distracting.

"Get another vision?"

Beth shook her head. "Not exactly. Flashes, bits and pieces of what happened here. I saw them change…"

"Fuck," Wyatt muttered. "Can you shoot? Because I don't think they want to talk."

"Yeah, if I have to. Think they'll let us just back away slowly?" Beth asked.

Moving carefully, they tried to step away. The crew snarled and lunged forward a step. "So, that won't work. Got another idea?"

Before Beth could answer, the remaining creatures moved in unison like a pack on a hunt. Beth tried to see past the visions and ignore the heat of the implant under her skin. She aimed. There were too many of them, too close for anything but kill shots, and Beth steeled herself as she pulled the trigger.

She and Wyatt stood shoulder to shoulder as the pack lunged toward them. Their shots dropped the attackers in mid-motion. Seconds later, it was over, and bodies and gore littered the corridor.

"Damn," Beth murmured, caught between giddy relief over being alive and revulsion at having shot the crew-zombies. She fought the urge to retch, knowing Wyatt would never let her live it down, but when she stole a glance at her partner, Wyatt looked rattled too.

"Let's get out of here," Wyatt said, turning toward the hover cart.

"Wait." Beth grimaced as she wiped blood spatter off her gloves. "We need to figure out what happened here. Make sure it's not contagious."

She saw horror dawn in Wyatt's eyes. "Shit," he muttered. "The bio scanners didn't pick up anything. We ran it twice—I never take chances with ghost ships."

"More of a zombie ship, this time," Beth replied. "And it's great that you scan, but instruments can only pick up what they're calibrated to detect. Maybe undead doesn't count on Nellie's list of registered sentients."

"So how are we going to find out what turned them all into flesh-eating freaks? They don't look like the journal-keeping type."

"Check out the logs on the bridge and in sickbay. Unless this was truly an instantaneous infection, odds are someone noticed something going wrong."

Beth tried not to look nervous, but part of her wondered whether they would read their own death sentence in the logs. She stole a glance toward Wyatt, but his face was unreadable. She didn't know him well enough to call his bluff. *If it comes to that, I'd rather eat my gun than become one of those things. Maybe we just shoot each other. Fast. Clean.*

"Since those things didn't show up on our scanners, we have to assume there could be more. Keep your weapon ready and eyes sharp. Cover me while I check the schematics." Wyatt turned his wrist and pulled up a holo of the plans to look for the fastest path. It was possible this ship had been modified from the standard configuration, but it was unlikely.

"So we try to be extra careful," she admitted, following as he headed off down the corridor.

"Here's the deal," he replied. "Let's get the cart back to the airlock. It's not a lot, but we grabbed enough to make a pretty profitable haul. Then we go play detective. If we don't start gnawing on each other, we take the loot we've already got and get out of here. It's not worth going back for more."

"That works." Beth covered them while Wyatt maneuvered the cart. She strained her ears for any sound that might suggest more of the crew-creatures, but heard nothing except for the hum of the support systems.

"I've got a theory about why the crew-zombies didn't register on your scan," she said as Wyatt mapped out the way to the bridge. "They might not have been alive enough—by the system's standards—to count as 'life forms.'"

Wyatt gave her a "no shit" look. "They still seemed pretty lively when they were trying to eat us."

"No argument there. Let's see what we can find."

After unloading their haul, they reached the bridge of the *Perseverance* without incident. Wyatt kept his gun trained on the door while Beth sat down to hack into the computer. She had gained a lot of illicit IT skills just to navigate the crazy bureaucracy of academia, finding it easier to break into a system and beg forgiveness than to fill out forms in triplicate to ask permission. Once she realized how hot the information she had acquired on Kalok was, she had gotten a crash course in even more illegal skills from a few of her shadier friends. *Never know when what you learn is going to come in handy,* she thought.

"Okay, the logs aren't encrypted—probably so someone can access them if things go wrong," she said. She leaned forward, scanning the screen. "The last few days of entries look pretty normal. They picked up some cargo, no indication of any problems. No new crew members, no mention of any mass outbreak. A couple of equipment problems, but maintenance said nothing major and they were being fixed."

Beth skimmed through the entries. "When it hit, it hit fast. Outbreaks everywhere, all at once."

"When?"

She squinted, trying to read the screen that had dimmed on emergency power. "Middle of the night," she reported. "The night shift went down first, and then it looked like the morning detail had it under control, but by mid-afternoon, almost everyone was affected."

"And up here? When did it hit them?" Wyatt asked. Beth looked around, noting the blood stains and a few rotting corpses.

"Looks like they were the last to go," she said. "They sealed themselves in, figured they'd probably starve to death, because no one had anything except the sandwiches someone brought up for lunch. Once that was gone—"

"Doesn't look like they starved," Wyatt replied. "And we still don't know how it's transmitted. Let's go to sickbay."

"Just a second. I want to change the beacon." With a few keystrokes, Beth set the automatic transmitter to the universal quarantine signal.

"They never sent a distress call," she noted, checking the communication logs. "Looks like more than one system acted up before the shit hit the fan."

"At least with that plague pulse going out, we're not likely to get company," Wyatt muttered.

The trek down to sickbay took them through eerily silent corridors. Bodies lay in their path, none of them looking like they had met a peaceful end. Wyatt opened the door and took up his sentry position as Beth worked on the computers.

"The doctor was looking for transmissions vectors almost immediately," she reported. "He didn't have a lot of time to work, but he noticed that the crew showed symptoms within six hours of eating."

"Sabotage?" Wyatt asked. "Think they had a poisoner among them?"

Beth shook her head, frantically trying to remember what she had seen that connected to the doctor's log…there was something, something important… Her fingers flew across the pad, tapping back into the bridge log.

"Meals," she said after a few moments. "That's it."

"I've never heard of spoiled food turning someone into a zombie."

"There wasn't anything wrong with the food—at least, not originally," she said, feeling a growing chill as her suspicions gelled into certainty. "The meal prep equipment had been malfunctioning," she said. "That's what I saw in the bridge log. They'd gotten new units installed when they went into their last port." Beth ran more queries.

"So they pulled into a legit station to get maintenance done, and from what the engineering logs say, the company that owns the cargo fleet—NuHorizons Shipping—had issued orders for an upgrade on the food prep units on all their ships. Captain was pretty excited—the equipment was supposed to offer more choices, better quality…"

She let her voice drift off as she studied the information. "Seems like they started to have problems not long after they left the repair bay." She checked the date. "The units failed, and then came back up again. Their diagnostics looked okay, so Maintenance cleared the equipment for use. That was three months ago." Beth looked up to meet Wyatt's gaze. "The same day the outbreak started."

"So you think that there was something in the food prep units that did this to them?"

"That's what the doctor suspected, only he ran out of time to validate his theory," Beth replied.

"What brand of equipment were the units?"

Beth consulted the logs. "BestStellar. I've heard of them. They do food prep equipment for space stations, cruise liners, outposts—they're a pretty big concern."

Wyatt sighed. "Download any info you want to take with us since I don't figure you're going to let this go. Then let's get out of here. I don't want some well-meaning patrol to come along and decide to blow up the ship now that you've helpfully told everyone it's a hazard."

"You didn't stop me."

"Yeah, well. Lesson learned."

Beth and Wyatt made it back to the *Nellie B* without encountering any more of the crew-zombies. They worked in silence, sobered by what they had seen on the *Perseverance*. Just in case, they ran the airlock through two decontamination cycles. She watched as Wyatt detached from the docking link and set a course for the Near-Fringe. When they were on their way, she saw him turn and give her a questioning look.

"You're quiet. That makes me worry. What's up?"

Beth hunched over her screen. "I logged into the data stream—don't worry, no one can trace me. Put in a query about 'zombies' and food prep malfunctions. And got a hit."

"What?" Wyatt confirmed the route and destination with Nellie, then he stood and walked around to lean over Beth's shoulder as she pulled up the information for him.

"From what people are saying, the roll-out of the new equipment had all kinds of problems. Production got delayed, so BestStellar was behind on their installation, and NuHorizons isn't the kind of outfit to look kindly on hold-ups that keep their ships out of service."

"So BestStellar rushed the production," Wyatt guessed. "Wouldn't be the first time a company like that puts out crap that doesn't work and figures they'll do recalls or deal with it as it breaks."

"Yeah," Beth replied, only half-listening. "Except that reports started coming in a few weeks after the first installs that the units kept breaking down. And then—some of the ships that got new units went missing."

"Missing?"

Beth nodded. "Never made their delivery, stopped responding, didn't file reports. Just…vanished, but no emergency signals, either. No debris reported on their flight path. Just…gone."

"Space is a big place if you go even a little ways out of the shipping lanes," Wyatt replied. "Little ships like these, if they're not transmitting, would be hard to find."

"Ghost ships," Beth murmured. "Drifting dead."

"That doesn't make sense," Wyatt argued. "If the units were bad, why didn't BestStellar do something about it?"

Beth clicked through several more pages of results. "Damn," she said quietly. Wyatt waited her out. She looked up and pointed to the screen.

"There's an anonymous post by someone who claims to have been part of the BestStellar R&D team. Says that the engineers noticed irregularities in the synthesis program—which was brand new—and the project was behind schedule, so no one wanted to listen. They installed the units anyhow. He says that when he pushed, worried that the problems might make the crews sick, he was told that it was cheaper to handle a few lawsuits than to get hit with penalties for delivering late or have to pay for replacing the equipment." She paused, then looked up at Wyatt.

"It figures. Look at this: BestStellar and NuHorizons are both subsidiaries of Kalok Enterprises."

Chapter Five

After the job on the *Perseverance*, Beth doubled down on research any time she could get a decent, untraceable RimNet signal, and Wyatt got quiet.

Beth wondered if Wyatt's dreams were as disturbing as her own, after seeing the crew of the cargo ship reduced to monsters. She knew she'd never be able to watch another zombie holovid again. Finding out that their deaths weren't due to an unknown virus picked up in the far reaches of space, that it was a manufacturing problem abetted by Kalok's greed, made it even worse.

Beth studied Wyatt in the cockpit, trying to get a read on him. She doubted the gore of the battle aboard the *Perseverance* had been anything he hadn't seen in the war. Then again, Wyatt was a pilot, not ground troops, and maybe all the blood and death had been at a safe distance, like a simulator game. If she had to bet, she'd put her money on the Kalok connection, the cold calculation that could have prevented the crew's death and didn't. As for herself, both aspects made her sick enough that days passed before her appetite returned.

"We need to do another salvage run and sell off the cargo," Wyatt announced, after flying for hours in silence. "Gonna need to replenish the credits so when we go deeper into the Fringe, we can pay cash. Harder to trace."

"Okay," Beth replied. "Can we look for a wreck over by the Orvidian System?"

Wyatt frowned. "Why there?"

"Ever heard of Keller Station?"

"No, should I? Do they have dancing girls? Beer?"

Beth sighed. "Neither. Forget I asked. It's an academic research outpost. Daniel Rostaven was my advisor at the university until he took leave to head up the outpost."

"And I should care, why?"

"Because Daniel was singularly good at keeping his ear to the ground," Beth replied. "And he always had a rebellious streak. Think of him as my version of Codger."

Wyatt gave a skeptical snort. "Having trouble imagining that. You want to swing by and say hello or something?"

Beth found her patience growing short. "How about this—you drop me off at Keller Station while you sell the cargo, and pick me up in a day or two."

"And what if this advisor of yours decides to turn you in for the bounty? I heard teaching doesn't pay well."

Beth chuckled. "He won't. Steller Fed has a bigger data file on Daniel than they probably do on you. He was a vocal opponent of the Rim War, said it was nothing but old-fashioned colonialism and that a bunch of young men and women were dying to pad corporate pockets."

She wondered whether that would get a rise out of Wyatt, but instead of anger, she saw sadness in his eyes. "Good for him. Some of us figured that out the hard way."

She knew from the set of his jaw he had no interest in discussing the topic further. "So you'll drop me off—and pick me up?"

Wyatt nodded. "You sure you want me to come get you? I mean, a bunch of university types in one place, sounds like your kind of thing."

"It used to be. Before I became a wanted criminal," Beth drawled. "And honestly, I think being on the run suits me. Yes, you idiot. Sooner or later, someone who looks hard enough will connect me to Daniel, and I don't want to be on the station when they do. Just a quick in-and-out. Sounds like your kind of thing."

Wyatt gave her a wicked glance. "Oh, that's where you're wrong. I always take my time."

He laughed, even when she slugged him in the shoulder.

"I'LL BE BACK in about a week," Wyatt said as he landed the *Nellie B* on Keller Station. "There's another derelict ship I want to check out— it's between here and the station where I was going to fence the cargo, so I might as well see if there's anything left."

Beth frowned. "You could wait until I could go with you—have your back," she offered, thinking about what had happened on board the *Perseverance*.

Wyatt gave her a bemused look. "You do realize that I've been salvaging on my own for a few years now? I like having back-up, and you're good, but I didn't suddenly lose my touch." He sobered. "Look, thanks for the offer. But I'll be fine."

She smiled. "All right. But do try to come back in one piece. I turned down Daniel's offer to be part of the staff for Keller when he came out here. Too much staying in one place, not enough good ruins to keep me interested." She grabbed the duffel she'd packed and left it in the corridor by the airlock.

"Oh yeah?" Wyatt's eyes narrowed. "Something goin' on between you and the Prof?"

Beth glared at him. "Just professional admiration."

"In other words, he had it bad for you, and you didn't notice."

"No! Wyatt—really, it wasn't like that—"

He chuckled and extended the ramp before opening the heavy outer door. Outside on the landing pad, a tall man in his early forties waved. "That's Daniel?"

Beth waved back. "Yeah. He's grayer than he used to be."

"Too old for you. It'd never work." Wyatt said with a scowl as Beth stepped through.

"See you in a week." Beth adjusted the duffel on her shoulder and walked down the ramp without looking back. That way Wyatt wouldn't see the smile. *I think he might be jealous… Damn it, Beth, get a grip. It's all business.*

"I'M SO PLEASED your travels brought you out this way," Daniel said as they walked toward the station's hub. "Even if you're only passing through."

Beth smiled, enjoying the comfortable camaraderie. It brought back memories of simpler times. Back when she still harbored a few illusions about how the universe worked. "Figured I'd take the opportunity when it came along," she replied. They paused as the sound of the *Nellie B* lifting off became almost deafening. Daniel led her into their compound and away from the noise.

"You didn't say what brought you out this way." Daniel nodded and smiled to members of the base's staff as they passed in the corridor, casting curious glances at the stranger.

"I guess you don't get a lot of visitors," Beth observed, dodging the question. "Your staff is looking at me like I've got two heads."

Daniel laughed. "You haven't grown a second head—no worries about that. And no, we're a bit off the most traveled routes, so other than supply deliveries, we don't see many new faces. Once in a while someone rotates off, and we get a replacement, but that hasn't happened in, oh, two years?" He shrugged. "Out here, it's about as close to pure academic study as you're going to get. No university politics, no pressure to publish or lecture, just the work, and plenty of it. People either love it or hate it. Fortunately, most of the people I shipped out with love it."

"Lucky you," Beth remarked, surprised to hear a touch of bitterness in her voice. Then again, thanks to the alien implant in her arm and what it had revealed, her once-promising academic career had ended abruptly, along with her lucrative corporate consulting contract. *None of that would have happened if I'd taken Daniel up on his offer back when they staffed the station,* she thought. *I'd have a career path, instead of a bounty on my head.*

"These are your quarters, for as long as you want to visit," Daniel said, stopping by a door. "It's not luxurious, but better than the dormitories back at the university and a bit more elbow room than on a ship. Once you've had a chance to freshen up, I'll show you around. You'll have a chance to meet everyone at dinner tonight."

An unwelcome thought occurred to Beth. "You haven't had your food prep equipment updated recently, have you?"

Daniel gave her an odd look. "No. Why?"

Beth shook her head. "Just heard something about recalls."

"Well, we've been doing just fine with it for years, and no one's complained," Daniel replied. "And given what we have to work with out here, the food is remarkably good." He grinned ruefully. "Or maybe I'm just used to it."

With a promise to meet in an hour, Beth closed the door and sagged against the wall. Before Wyatt's comments, it had never occurred to her that Daniel might have harbored interests that were anything but professional. Now, she wondered. *Come on. He's out here with two dozen people on a rock in the middle of space. He's probably so happy for news and conversation that he fawns all over the delivery pilots.* Somehow, she doubted that.

She had come so far since her time at the university, and even farther since she'd packed everything she owned into one duffle and left the hardscrabble farming colony for dreams of glory. Or, in her case, the allure of getting an education, a degree, and the chance to be part of something important. Her parents and the other colonists had their own dreams once, but those had blown away with the dust. Beth had been tired of struggling, sick of doing without, and was ready to start over. And for a while, those dreams seemed to be almost in her grasp. Until it all unraveled.

You can leave home, but home never leaves you. She'd been so eager to get away, only to give up everything she worked for to protect the people she left behind. Because of all the people who got hurt by Kalok and Interplan, the ones who had it the worst were the ones at the bottom of the heap: the miners, the haulers, and the farmers who supplied the manufacturing colonies. And now she could prove it and maybe, just maybe, do something to make it stop.

Her quarters were utilitarian, but comfortable, with a bed, nightstand, desk, and work chair, and another, more comfortable, reading chair. Beth dropped her duffel on the bed, dug out her kit bag, and headed to the bathroom. A quick shower made her feel much better. Beth paused as she combed out her hair. Since she had fled Comstock, fussing over her appearance beyond basic hygiene had been the last thing on her mind. When she had packed her duffel, she had intended to dress to mingle with professional colleagues. But the functional jumpsuits she had seen on the station's crew made her question that choice, as did Wyatt's teasing comments about Daniel. Deciding to sidestep any drama, Beth pulled on a clean jumpsuit, brushed her hair back and decided she would dress for the field and the others could deal with it.

Before she left to find Daniel, Beth paused and looked around the room. She had struggled with whether to bring her data with her or to leave it on the *Nellie B.* In the end; she had done both. She had also thought to wrap gauze over the implant in her arm and to keep her sleeves pulled down. Now, she debated hiding her data crystal, just in case.

Suddenly, nothing in the small room seemed suitably secure. With a sigh, Beth removed the data crystal and tucked it into her bra. *The age-old repository of last resort*, she thought.

Beth slipped out of her quarters and headed down the empty corridor. Keller Station had the tidy appearance of a well-run, if spartan, institutional facility. Despite everything that had happened, she still felt a thrill of excitement thinking about the chance to get a look at the ruins Daniel had finagled funding to study. Saying no to his original invitation had been hard.

"You must be Beth—I mean, Dr. Parker."

The voice startled her, and she turned to find a young man with sandy brown hair and a pleasant smile. "I'm Jeremy. Daniel sprung the big surprise about your arrival just a few hours ago. We're all curious, to say the least."

"Nice to meet you, Jeremy. And 'Beth' is fine," she said, a little unnerved about being recognized by a stranger and wondering why Daniel had kept her arrival a secret when she had contacted him more than a day earlier. She'd never made a big fuss about the title; and with everything that had happened, the whole "Doctor" thing made her uncomfortable. Too much of a reminder of what she'd lost.

"We don't get a lot of visitors—none, unless you count the delivery ships—so this is kind of exciting," Jeremy said. He reminded her of some of the graduate assistants she had back at the university, and she wondered what could have possibly wooed a young man with potential out to this godforsaken rock in the armpit of space.

"I'm looking forward to seeing the excavation," Beth said, falling in step. "Daniel promised me a tour before dinner."

Jeremy laughed, and he sounded so open and uncontrived that Beth found herself relaxing, just a bit. "Oh, you can be sure Daniel won't waste a minute. He's terribly proud of the dig; we all are."

While Jeremy guided her through the corridors, Beth tried to get her bearings so she could find her way around unaided, if need be. "…gotten down one full level since we started," he was saying when she came back to herself. "Found some interesting artifacts and things we think might have been utensils. Or maybe tools." He shrugged. "Sometimes, it's hard to tell."

Beth's hand went out of habit to cover her left forearm, as she remembered blundering into having a piece of alien technology permanently embedded under her skin.

"I trust you're taking precautions," she said, willing herself not to keep touching her arm. "There's no telling whether anything they left behind might still have a bit of life in it."

"You think it's possible?" Jeremy's face lit up. "That would be like hitting the mother lode, wouldn't it? We'd go down in the history books for sure."

Be careful what you wish for, Beth thought. "Yeah, that would be pretty exciting," she replied, with less enthusiasm than her guide. She decided to shift subjects. "There were a lot of researchers and scientists who decided to come out to the Fringe about the same time Daniel got this group together. Do you hear from any of them? I'd think you might keep in touch, being pioneers of a sort out here?"

Jeremy's smile faded, and his eyes grew shuttered. "I don't really know," he said, looking away. All of the excitement from moments ago had vanished. "That would be something to ask Daniel. I think we might trade findings now and again, but really, I'm here to dig and document."

His sudden discomfort gave Beth pause, and she filed it away for later. "So I'm guessing you all have gotten to be pretty close, way out here. How many of you came out on the original transport with Daniel?"

She thought Jeremy winced, but he covered quickly. "All of us," he said. "It was quite an honor to be asked." Something in his voice didn't ring true. "We knew when we came out here that we probably weren't ever going home."

Beth frowned. She didn't remember that caveat from Daniel's long-ago pitch for her to join them. "Did you know each other, before?"

He shrugged. "Some of us. Hard to remember when we weren't all in each other's back pocket. We worked with the three honchos: Daniel, Peter, and Tom." He blushed. "Well, back then we were more formal, but that's all past."

Beth tried to remember the two other head researchers. *Peter Johnson and Thomas Carpenter. They were all pretty big names in the archeology and history field,* Beth recalled. *Outspoken, mavericks. Must have left quite a hole in the university's faculty.*

"Here we are," Jeremy said, and Beth realized her mind had wandered once more. "The Workshop. Daniel's waiting."

"Thanks for helping me find my way," Beth said, noting that Jeremy seemed anxious to duck out. She did not have time to ponder, as Daniel hailed her.

"You found it! I hope Jeremy's been a proper host," he added, and Beth wondered if she imagined a touch of concern in Daniel's voice.

"Oh, he was the perfect guide, reminds me of one of my graduate assistants."

Daniel gave a wistful smile. "Actually, he was one of my teaching assistants. All the researchers I brought with me had worked on several of my projects before."

"Peter and Thomas, Dr. Johnson and Dr. Carpenter, they're here somewhere as well?"

"Thomas is puttering around the dig, as usual. Peter…" He took a deep breath. "We lost Peter our first year out. An accident out on the site. Scaffolding gave way."

"I'm so sorry," Beth said. They were silent as they left the building and headed into the dry, hot air.

"We knew the risks," Daniel murmured, almost to himself. Then he brightened. "Let me show you our star attraction," he said, as they climbed a small rise and the valley spread out beneath them.

Beth gasped as the dig sprawled across the arid land, almost to the horizon. "It's magnificent," she said in awe.

Daniel's grin was broad and genuine. "Right? I mean, it's the dig of a lifetime and just what our research told us we'd find."

"I'm surprised that you don't get more visits from some of the other research outposts and science observatories," Beth said as they slip-slid their way down the hillside in the powdery dirt. "I'd think they'd have complimentary projects to tie in. Unless you're keeping it hushed up for a big publication?"

Daniel's jaw tightened. "You've seen what the distances are like out here. Not like crossing the campus to have a look at something. And everyone's got their own projects. Maybe a little professional jealousy, too."

Beth let his deflection slide as they walked among the ruins. Only a portion of the site had been uncovered, and the sheer scope and audacity of the project boggled her mind. The foundations that remained showed a mix of early Interplan Guild style architecture with something "other."

"This was one of the very first outposts when the ships initially ventured into the near-Fringe," Daniel said. "Communications weren't what they are today, so the home worlds got no word back from the pioneers for a long time, but historians always wondered whether something got left out of the reports." He swept his arm to indicate the ruins. "And we were right. They must have found either an alien culture already on this world or alien colonists who came shortly after they did. And they obviously, clearly, collaborated. You can see it in the building styles, in the artifacts we've dug up, in the mixed technology. It's just—breathtaking."

"Are there other sites on the planet?"

"We don't have the resources to properly excavate *this* site. Don't know that anyone's spent the time or money to check for more," Daniel said.

Beth felt a pang of pure academic jealousy and pushed it away. That part of her life was definitely over. Daniel kept talking, pointing to half-buried walls and the remnants of stairways or terraces. Beth found that the further into the ruins they walked, the harder it became to concentrate on what he was saying. Her arm started to feel warm.

The scene in front of her wavered like a heat mirage, and Beth saw a city street take shape. The ghostly images of long-dead residents bustled around her, passing through her without breaking stride. She could hear the voices, multiple languages, most of which she couldn't understand. Beth spotted humans among the passersby, as well as humanoids—beings that definitely weren't from the allied home worlds.

The implant in her forearm ached, and Beth tugged at her sleeve unconsciously to hide the glow beneath her skin.

She turned slowly, taking in everything. The buildings had a familiar functionality and an aesthetic that was, truly, otherworldly. What she could see where they stood appeared new, well-maintained, and prosperous. The people walking around them showed no signs of hostility or that they noted or cared about the planet of origin of their fellow pedestrians. A clear sky and bright sun shone overhead, a perfect morning.

The scene shifted in a rain of fire and a suffocating cloud of ash. Screams echoed from the buildings. People—human and humanoid—ran for their lives, burned and bleeding. Loud explosions were almost deafening. Bodies littered the streets, and buildings went up in flames or toppled under the assault that came from the skies. In moments, everything was gone.

"Beth? Beth!" Daniel grabbed her by the forearms, shaking her lightly, concern and panic clear in his voice. Beth slumped and let him guide her to a low section of stone wall to sit.

"They never had a chance," she murmured, still lost between the vision and reality.

Daniel pulled a flask from inside his jacket and pressed it to her lips. "Drink. It's our own home brew," he added. "A little raw, but it does the trick."

Beth took a swallow and coughed, but clarity returned.

Daniel eyed her warily. "What did you mean, that 'they never had a chance?'"

Beth's mind raced, searching for a convenient lie, and came up with nothing. "I'll tell you—later. Just, let's get through dinner and then—"

"But if you can tell me something about the dig… If you know something, Beth. Please, this is my life's work."

"I need to process first. Please, Daniel, just give me some time."

"You promise you'll tell me later?" Daniel asked giving her a curious look.

"Yeah." Beth insisted on seeing more of the dig, and Daniel gradually regained his enthusiasm. He introduced her to staff at work excavating, cleaning, and tagging the site, regaling her with forced cheer about some of the more amusing moments and pranks. Beth tried hard to listen, but she zoned in and out, catching glimpses of how things had once looked every time she turned her head.

It felt as if she saw two realities overlapped; the current ruins and the long-ago city on its final day, and the firestorm that obliterated it. Beth forced herself to take deep, even breaths, and Daniel slowed his pace, solicitously guiding her by the elbow as if he feared she might swoon. *And maybe he's not wrong.* Her hands shook, and her mouth was dry. Polite conversation failed her.

"Are you unwell?" Daniel asked. "I think I need to get you out of this heat. It takes some getting used to. The air isn't what you're accustomed to and we all needed time to adjust." His eyes put the lie to the polite fiction.

"I'd like to lie down before dinner," Beth said. "I want to meet your staff, and if you don't get many visitors, you're probably starved for news. It's the least I can do to repay your hospitality."

"Oh, they'll have plenty of questions," Daniel replied with a rueful chuckle. "And afterward, we can do cocktails on the 'veranda' and get caught up."

That sounded ominous. Beth pushed it out of her thoughts as Daniel escorted her to her quarters. "Will all your people be able to join us tonight?" She asked.

"All but one," he replied. "Marcus Pratt took sick right after you reached out to me. He's been unconscious since then."

"Something he caught in the ruins?"

Daniel shook his head. "No. He has…fits. Old brain injury, our doc thinks. Nothing to do but wait for him to come out of it."

"Sorry to hear," she said, surprised Daniel seemed unconcerned.

"I'm sure the others will fill him in," Daniel replied. "I'll see you in a bit."

Beth tensed as she re-entered the room, and she realized that she had almost expected to find her things trashed, evidence someone had gone looking for something. She scolded herself for her paranoia and sank into the upholstered chair, leaning back and closing her eyes.

The images from the visions looped in her mind. Who had attacked the outpost, and why? What purpose was served by destroying the city and then making no move to claim the planet or its resources? There weren't enough habitable planets, so each one discovered was considered priceless and fit for colonization. The attack had been unexpected; the reactions she observed gave her no doubt. None of the people she glimpsed on the ruined city's streets had the panic of residents under siege. No one had been rushing to shelters, clutching children and possessions. No, it had been just another day, and a beautiful one at that. Then death fell from the skies.

Beth rubbed her temples. Whoever attacked the planet obviously had spacefaring technology, and given the age of the ruins, that narrowed the possibilities for known attackers. Of course, perhaps the ships had been enemies of the unnamed humanoids, an old grudge by a mysterious foe. *Because the only entity with armed ships that could travel this deep past the Rim back then belonged to the mining companies. But that didn't make any sense… Exploit a world, yes. Destroy resources, no.*

Beth woke and checked the time. She splashed water on her face, blinked away unquiet dreams, and put on her best game face to meet the station's staff. Then she squared her shoulders and followed the path she remembered from earlier in the day to the station's dining room, where she was sure to be the main attraction.

THREE HOURS LATER, Beth had regaled the twenty-three residents of Keller Station with all the news, gossip, and celebrity tidbits she could recall. They had quizzed her about old friends and colleagues at the university, and she had talked as much as she dared about her work. She played up the cachet of chronicling defunct stations, spent mines, and decommissioned ships, piecing together a history of exploration by backfilling information from the people who had colonized the rough worlds and distant moons, and sidestepped the fact that she had been on Kalok's payroll to do it.

The station's crew plied her with questions until Daniel finally noticed her flagging energy and shooed them off, promising time to regroup at lunch the next day. Nothing about the researchers made Beth think they were anything except what they appeared, although she still questioned the dedication that brought them this far out without plans to return.

"That's the most excitement we've had in years," Daniel said, going to a cabinet and pouring them both cocktails. He set one in front of Beth. "You've earned it."

"What's going on, Daniel?" Beth might be tired, but she had no intention of leaving without answers.

"I don't know what you mean." His gaze slid sideways; a sure tell he was evading the truth.

"Why are you *really* here? How come no one expects to go home? Why are there no other settlers? And why in the name of all that's holy haven't you heard from the other science outposts?"

Daniel stayed silent for so long; Beth began to wonder whether he would answer. "I haven't been entirely honest with you, Beth. About any of this."

She braced herself. *Was I wrong about trusting him? Has he called Stellar Fed to arrest me—and trap Wyatt?* "What do you mean?"

He let out a long breath. "You know that back during the Rim War I had quite the reputation as a rebel," he replied. "I got better at evading the spotlight, but I never quit poking at things that didn't seem right. And the more I poked, the more garbage I turned up. About the mining guild, Kalok, even the corruption in Stellar Fed. Eventually, people in high places noticed. They gave me a choice—come out here—permanently—and keep my reputation, or end up in one of their prisons...or worse, dead."

"On what charges?" Beth demanded.

Daniel shrugged. "Take your pick. Fomenting insurrection. Domestic terrorism. Espionage. None of those were true, but truth doesn't matter—it's what they leak to the news that counts. So I picked exile. For most of the crew, the choice was the same."

Beth frowned. "But you tried to recruit me—"

"I tried to protect you," Daniel replied. "I knew you'd turn up the wrong rocks sooner or later and get in the same jam I was. Thought I'd spare you the harassment, the surveillance. It wears on a person."

"The other outposts—they're prohibited from contacting you?"

"Officially? Yes. But we've been using RimNet since it was invented to communicate without being traced. What happened to us wasn't an isolated thing. It's going on throughout the allied home worlds, everywhere the big guys like Kalok and Interplanetary Mining Guild have influence. Historians and anthropologists get blackballed, losing their funding or their positions or they just go missing. Their crime? An article or a research project that contradicts the official histories."

Beth winced. *Kalok hired me to write those histories. Shit, I've been tied up in this and didn't even know it.*

"You said *most* of the crew came here as exile. Who didn't?"

"Peter," Daniel said. "He'd been a colleague of mine for twenty years and a dear friend from my college days. We raised a lot of hell together. All the things Stellar Fed has against me, Peter was with me when we did them. I didn't find out until after we got here that he was a mole for Kalok. Turned traitor to save his own reputation."

"So his death…"

"Wasn't completely accidental," Daniel admitted. "We found out that he was transmitting back to Stellar Fed. One of my staff is quite a hacker, and was working on a RimNet project for me when he stumbled across Peter's feed."

"Why did you kill him?"

Daniel stared off into the distance for a while before he answered, and took a sip of his drink. "We had agreed to make good use of our exile. The allied home worlds aren't the only game in town; there's value to the research that we're doing and that the other blacklisted scientists and academics are doing. Plenty of smaller worlds and the unaligned systems that can use the things we learn, do something good with it. Peter could have destroyed all of that and cost dozens, maybe hundreds, of lives. We couldn't let that happen. It was not a decision made easily." His eyes had a haunted look to them.

"And Marcus Pratt?"

Daniel chuckled. "Marcus was Kalok's back-up or Stellar Feds'. It's sometimes difficult to separate the two. We couldn't get rid of both of them, and Peter was the bigger threat. So our good doctor diagnosed Marcus with seizures, which strike at the most convenient times and leave him unconscious with some memory loss." Daniel managed to keep a straight face, and almost sounded convincing. "As soon as I heard from you, I drugged him. Didn't want him getting word off to Stellar Fed. I don't know what you've gotten into, Beth, but RimNet is buzzing about Comstock and Rum Row, and your name comes up in the damndest context."

Beth toyed with her drink and then nodded. "About that…" Daniel listened in silence as she told him most of the sordid story. "So here I am. Wyatt's going to pick me up, and we'll keep going."

"You saw something today, out at the ruins. What was it?"

Reluctantly, Beth pulled up her sleeve and peeled back the gauze. She held up her arm and turned it so Daniel could see the strange geometric pattern under the skin.

"What? How?" Daniel asked in a combination of shock and excited curiosity.

"I was charged with translating inscriptions…" Beth recounted the tale of how the alien tech came to be attached to her and the visions and experience it had shared so far.

"It lets me see things. Things that have happened in the past just like a holovid newscast. I saw those people die. It wasn't a natural disaster, and I doubt it was divine retribution. A warship obliterated them from orbit. So either your friendly aliens had enemies…"

"Or someone didn't like the idea of mining colonists teaming up with outsiders," Daniel finished her sentence.

"It fits with the kind of things I've documented at the other sites. Leaving the clean-up crews to die, not fixing the food synth units. It fits."

Daniel nodded. "Yes, it does. And you may have stumbled onto those revelations a little…unconventionally…but some of our exiled colleagues have been nurturing suspicions for a while. That's what got them sent off and why some other mighty fine researchers have gone missing, presumed dead. This goes beyond leaving miners colonists to die. There's evidence to suggest genocide."

Beth knew she should feel shock, but after everything she had seen, had experienced vicariously through the implant in her arm, she could only manage dismay and resignation. "When I think back about what I saw as a child, some of the things my father wouldn't discuss, the questions I got told not to ask, well… I was afraid of that. Damn."

"So what are you going to do about it?" Daniel challenged.

"Two outlaws in a fast ship can't take on Kalok and Interplan, or keep outrunning Stellar Fed forever," Beth said. "But we can get information to people who have more connections. Gather evidence. That's the plan—at least for now."

Daniel nodded. "Makes sense. This young man of yours…"

"Wyatt is *not* my 'young man,' and who says that kind of thing these days, anyhow?"

Daniel chuckled. "If he doesn't at least try to win you, he's a damn fool. Should have tried harder myself back in the day," he added, but his tone was fond.

"We can get you, or at least a few of your people, off Keller Station," Beth offered.

Daniel shook his head. "Thanks, but no. We've all made our peace with the situation, and we're safer here than we would be with Stellar Fed looking for us. They know where we are, so they largely ignore us. And in the meantime, we're feeding information to groups like the Coalition and the Regiment."

"The Regiment?" Beth echoed.

"You've heard of them?"

"I just thought they were a bunch of angry guys who saw too much in the war."

Daniel shrugged. "That's part of it. But some of them are out for blood. There are dozens, hundreds of groups out there with a cause. Gathering information. Looking for vulnerabilities. Waiting for the right moment. The mining corporations have made a lot of enemies. And there are outposts like Keller Station all over the Near-Fringe. When this all comes to a head—and it will—it's going to be big."

Pounding on the door made both Beth and Daniel jump. "Daniel!" Jeremy's frantic voice sounded through the door. "Ash picked up a Stellar Fed transmission. There's a ship headed this way, be here within half an hour."

Beth stared at Daniel, heart in her throat. *For all his pretty words, did he sell me out?*

Daniel met her gaze as if he guessed her thoughts. "I didn't betray you, Beth. But I'm guessing Marcus did manage to get off a message before I knocked him out. Maybe he intercepted your first contact. Shit."

"What now?"

He knocked back the remainder of his drink and stood. "When is your friend coming back?"

"Not for several more days. He had some business to handle."

Daniel nodded. "Good. It'll all be over by the time he gets back here if we're lucky. Come on; we've got to hide you."

"Where?"

He grinned. "We've added some features to the station that weren't on the original plans. Right this way."

Daniel and Beth jogged down the corridor and turned a corner, then Daniel shoved Beth ahead of him into a storage closet, glanced both ways, and followed her in, closing the door behind them.

"In here," he said, pulling up a section of the raised flooring. "Not easy to get in and out but it's secure. Marcus doesn't know about it." He got down on his hands and knees and pointed. "Slide the panel to the side. There's space on the other side to turn and slide it closed, should be a glow stick you can use just on the other side. You'll see a ladder that goes down into a decently sized cubby. There's fresh air and some emergency water and a food bar or two inside, in case you need them. Go. The others are stalling them, but I'll have to show up, and the sooner I do, the faster the Feds will go away."

Beth eased into the tight space under the raised flooring and slid through the panel, carefully sliding it closed as she saw Daniel replace the floor tile. The small room was dark, even with the glow stick, but she had enough space to stand or lie down. She wondered what the space was originally; it looked very utilitarian, and she could see two of the structural support pillars for the complex on either side. The ceiling, walls, and floor were lined with odd metallic tiles—even the back of the exit panel. A larger person might have had trouble getting in, but she wasn't going to complain.

Alone in the dark, Beth listened for any sounds that suggested her hiding place might be compromised. Her mind raced. *What if Wyatt comes back while Stellar Fed is here? What if they pretend to leave and set a trap for us or for Wyatt? If we get caught, will they send us to prison or just shoot us?*

Beth swore she could hear the pounding of her own heart. She took deep breaths, trying to slow the beat, afraid it might show on a scanner. *I can't let them catch me. Not after everything we've learned. What I saw out among the ruins here—it's one more piece of evidence. Damn! This goes beyond just embarrassing Kalok and Interplan. They've caused so much bloodshed. Maybe if we get the right information to the right people, someone can actually stop them. But only if I live long enough to pass along what I've learned.*

Beth heard faint footsteps, like a weak echo, approach and then move away, and she guessed their new "guests" had come near. Voices carried, too garbled to make out the words. Her chronometer showed the passing minutes, and as each went by, Beth felt unsure whether to believe herself to be farther out of danger, or closer to discovery.

Voices rose, loud, and angry. Beth could not tell who was involved in the argument and sincerely hoped Daniel could hold his own. *If it's true that they're really in exile, he doesn't have any bargaining power,* she thought. *Let's hope he's as good with a bluff as he's always been.*

She thought her heart would stop when she heard the door to the storage room open. It sounded as if more than one person walked overhead and the voices sounded closer but still muffled.

"Satisfied?" Daniel snapped. "Nothing but computer supplies and spare electrical components. I showed you the schematics. There's nothing you haven't seen."

A rattle sounded as if someone tried pulling on the metal shelving in the closet. Beth held her breath, hoping no one thought to look under the floor.

"We had a report that the fugitives were headed here," the stranger said, and he sounded aggrieved to leave without his prize.

"Goes to show the value of anonymous tips," Daniel replied. If the Stellar Fed agent knew Marcus had been the one to alert them, they dared not press the issue without revealing their mole. Beth leaned against the wall in the dark, still and silent. Just in case, her hand tightened around the grip of her knife. She'd never even considered bringing a blaster. *Damn it; I've got to stop thinking like an academic.*

"We'll be on our way. Sorry to have troubled you," the stranger replied in a tone that suggested he was anything but.

Beth listened for the click of the outside door and began to breathe normally, but she did not move, expecting a trick. She watched minutes become an hour, the third since Daniel hid her. After a long silence, she heard footsteps again. She drew her knife and moved into a corner away from the ladder, ready to spring if she found herself face to face with a Stellar Fed agent.

"Relax," Daniel called out quietly as he worked sliding the panel back above her. A faint light filled the space as Daniel set a lantern near the opening.

Beth blinked at the light. She did not take a truly deep breath until she climbed out of the secret room and found no one but Daniel in the storage closet. Only then did she realize how light-headed she felt from shallow breathing, how dry her mouth felt from fear. She wiped a thin sheen of sweat from her forehead. "Are they gone?"

Daniel nodded. "They weren't happy about leaving empty-handed, but there was nothing they could do about it." He chuckled. "The commander ranted about us being slow to finish the excavation and insinuated that we might not be taking adequate care of Marcus. But he's got nothing that'll stick. The dig is documented and following protocol, and my medical officer has Marcus's records lined up for a watertight diagnosis."

Beth sagged against the shelves, exhausted. "Thank you. At least Wyatt didn't show up while they were here."

Daniel rubbed the back of his neck. "About that—I happened to trigger the quarantine alarm 'accidentally' when the Feds showed up. Just turned it off before I came to get you. Wyatt looked like a clever fellow. I'm sure he'll figure it out."

Chapter Six

THE FREIGHTER DRIFTED in open space, out beyond the Rim, fair for salvage. Its engines were damaged beyond repair, and it had moved out of the main shipping lanes. *The crew must have abandoned the* Merchant Prince *when the engines blew*, Wyatt thought. The ship was a derelict hulk, but to Wyatt, it was a meal ticket.

"Now that's a beautiful sight," Wyatt commented to Nellie as he brought the ship to dock with the *Prince*.

"I detect no life form readings," Nellie reported.

"Yeah, that's what you said the last time. Look where that got me."

"Those were not life forms," Nellie said.

Wyatt couldn't help but smile. After their time together, he sometimes thought that the A.I. had taken on some interesting personality quirks. One being she did not like to be wrong.

He had several days before he needed to pick Beth up from her meeting on Keller Station, and if his luck held, this job would pay their expenses for weeks to come. He maneuvered the ship into position and tried not to think about how quiet it seemed. For the first time since he had been salvaging, he'd brought a partner on board, and now Beth's absence made the ship feel hollow.

You're getting soft, Wyatt, he chided himself. *Don't go making more of the arrangement than it is. Good company never lasts forever.* He forced his mind back to business.

Wyatt's best estimate, based on what Nellie's scans told him and what he had observed in his fly-by before docking, was that the *Prince* had been damaged six months before. Without the engines, and with no crew aboard to repair the damage, the ship still had minimal power from its emergency batteries. *Like keeping a body on life support after the brain is dead,* Wyatt thought.

The *Nellie B* was equipped to hijack the electrical system of a salvaged ship if possible, and to pry open the docking hatch. The *Prince* still had enough juice for the electronics to work, at least enough to open the hatch. Wyatt powered up his armored atmo suit and grabbed his gun. After the last run, no one could blame him for being a little paranoid.

A thorough scan had already told Wyatt what cargo remained on board and where the most valuable items were located. He had the hover cart to help him bring back what he could salvage.

Wyatt ducked through the airlock and moved cautiously into the freighter. From what he could see, the *Prince* hadn't been in great shape before its engines exploded. The ship was clean but hard-worn, and Wyatt noticed a number of jury-rigged patches made to the equipment and panels. That told him the crew of the *Prince* had been eking out a living at the margins, unable to afford proper repairs. Not uncommon for freighters that didn't have docking permits at the preferred space stations or the high traffic ports. But his scan had picked up supplies that the independent mining colonies and research outposts on the Fringe badly needed and would pay well to receive. Assuming no one else found the wreck, Wyatt might be able to make several trips, then finally strip the hulk of its wiring and reusable components. *Not a bad few day's work.*

Every wreck was haunted in its own way. Some were home to ghosts, spirits trapped where their lives ended, set free only when the dead hulk of the ship eventually succumbed to the gravitation pull and crashed or burned. Others became infested by the disembodied creatures found drifting among the stars, saprophytes that gave entropy a hand. Wyatt had even encountered squatters a time or two, though those were usually on old space stations or mining colonies.

The *Prince* was a drifting testimony to dreams gone wrong. Independent freighters had a hardscrabble existence. Closed out of big contracts that went to the corporation fleets, the indie ships took on odd lots, short runs, and questionable cargo, anything to make enough money to buy fuel, pay for supplies, and keep up with repairs. Most were either family-run ships or manned by a small, tight-knit crew. All the indies operated on the edge of legality. High on Wyatt's list of items to salvage were any weapons left behind in the evacuation. Freighter crews were usually well-armed.

The long corridor was dimly lit by emergency lighting. Artificial gravity was working, though the bounce in his step told Wyatt it wasn't quite up to standard. The backup batteries might last several months or even a few years, but they weren't enough to re-start life support. Power would gradually fade until the *Prince* was left dark and cold.

Wyatt navigated the map Nellie's scan had generated, heading for a cargo bay filled with medical supplies and dehydrated food that would go for a premium on the Fringe. As he looked at how things were left, the items scattered about, the valuable cargo abandoned, he decided it just didn't make sense.

So where did the crew go? Wyatt wondered. He had been so certain this was just a routine salvage run when he dropped Beth off. Now, he found himself wishing he could get her read on the situation, and see what the implant and her "ghost visions" told him about the *Prince's* last days.

He spotted scorch marks in the corridor and other places where something had raked against the steel walls with enough strength to leave gouges. Once or twice he spotted a single shoe or a piece of clothing. Other spots on the walls and deck were stained dark with blood.

Wyatt ran a scan again nervously, reassuring himself that there were no other life forms on the ship. He opened a service panel, quickly bypassed the lock on the cargo bay doors, and the hatch slid open. Some of the cargo had shifted, no doubt due to the shake-up during the engine's explosion and fluctuating gravity generators. Several large crates in the back had broken open and lay in pieces. Wyatt pushed the hover cart into the bay, deciding that he would get to the broken crates later if there was time.

Wyatt was used to silence. It reassured him since dead ships should be quiet. *You don't realize how much noise there is on a normal ship until it's gone,* he thought. *The engines, the air recirculator, the buzz and hum of equipment.*

Onboard the *Nellie B*, the ship seemed alive even when he was alone, with its constant status reports from Nellie, blinking lights, and the rumble of the engines. If he took his cargo to sell on any of the space stations near the Rim, Wyatt found himself cheek-to-jowl with beings from all over the quadrant, all packed into an enclosed space, each of them in a big hurry to be somewhere else. He much preferred to deal with the gray market of the Fringe worlds, where the crowds were smaller and the authorities farther away.

Wyatt was used to being alone. But despite what his sensors told him, his gut said that wasn't something wasn't right on the *Prince*.

He loaded up the hovercart with the most valuable items first and made sure it was secured. He guided it back to the *Nellie B* with no mishaps and unloaded, feeling a little better about things as he returned for a second load. A quick walk around the cargo bay let him prioritize the other crates. Some were full of parts that would go for a premium on the outer mining worlds, where homesteaders were sticking it out after the Interplanetary Mining Guild pulled up stakes and flew away. A couple of crates were filled with contraband substances that could get him a long jail sentence on some worlds, and make him a rich man on others.

He loaded up on the premium parts until the cart was full, and did a quick look around, realizing there was a lot more here that looked interesting than he'd expected. He guided the cart back and unloaded on the *Nellie B.*

See; you were worried about nothing, he told himself. *Just a standard job. That* Perseverance *shit got you spooked imagining monsters around every corner.*

He returned to the cargo bay and looked at the crates of contraband, debating with himself whether it was worth the risk. That's when he spotted the locked storage compartment. Wyatt smiled. *Oh yeah, locks protected valuables, and big locked closets usually hid expensive items.* He saw no easy way to circumvent the lock, so he blasted it instead. The metal door swung open after the lock and part of the door melted away.

Inside was a metal man.

Wyatt jumped back, gun drawn, but the robot did not move.

Well shit! Wasn't expecting that. Wyatt advanced warily, keeping his gun trained on the figure. The robot was dark, powered down. He scanned it. *Batteries are still good. Overall, in pretty good shape even though it's got some wear and it's an older model.* Battered or not, the bot would fetch a good price in the Fringe where such things were scarce.

So were you stolen or sold? Wyatt wondered. He wrestled the heavy robot out of its storage bin and did another scan. *No internal explosives, no built-in weapons. So far, so good.*

He looked the robot over for a clue to its past owner, hoping it wasn't either Kalok or Interplan. He let out a sigh of relief when he found no marks he could identify. The robot was proportioned like a man with a medium build. Its face had regular, humanoid features, and the markings on its metal backplate were in Standard Common, telling Wyatt it had been manufactured inside the Rim. Somewhere, the robot had acquired a fisherman's hat and a loosely-cut, floral shirt. *Someone's idea of a joke, I guess.*

He walked around the robot and pulled its shirt up to open an access panel in the back. The wiring was a little different from what he was used to, but he managed to dig around until he found the tracking device that was embedded in every mass-produced robot. The device was already disabled, damaged beyond repair.

Guess that answers whether you were stolen.

He found the power reset and pressed it. The robot woke up as Wyatt scrambled back out of reach. He kept his gun down, not wanting to start a fight, but his finger was on the trigger, just in case. The bot's mechanics made a low hum as he powered up. Then the robot turned to look at Wyatt.

"Mackillan mechanical assistant 31-48-2758," the robot said in Standard Common with a Hub Worlds accent. "But you can call me Mack."

"What are you doing here, Mack?"

"I don't know. Just woke up. Give me a clue?"

Despite himself, Wyatt had to smile. Whoever owned Mack last had programmed him for conversation, avoiding the default formality that made some bots annoyingly pretentious. "The crew is gone, and you were stuffed into a storage locker. Bring anything to mind?"

"No, sorry. The last thing I remember…" Mack's voice drifted off. "Funny, there isn't a last thing. Guess my previous owner wiped my memory banks."

Wyatt clapped him on the shoulder. "I use rum for that, personally. Just call me Captain." *I always wanted a reliable crew. And the less Mack knows about me, the less I have to wipe when we get to the Fringe. Wonder how Beth will feel about having a robot on board?*

Mack executed a snappy salute. "What now, Captain?"

"Lend me a hand with the hovercart," Wyatt directed. "We need to move some of this cargo over to my ship."

"Are you a merchant?" Mack asked as they readied the load.

"More of a salvage reclamation specialist."

"Ah," Mack replied. "So we're shady players."

Wyatt guffawed. "Most of the time. Got a problem with that?"

Mack gave a mechanical chuckle. Wyatt raised an eyebrow. It took sophisticated programming to recognize humor, and even more to initiate it. "I am programmed for adaptability. Whatever you say,

Captain."

"I like you already. Remind me to promote you."

With Mack's help, they loaded the cart quickly and got it to the ship. Wyatt eyed the remaining room in the hold of the *Nellie B* and decided to go for one more load. The creepy feeling had faded, and every little bit helped. "Let's go back for more."

Something felt different when he stepped back into the main corridor. Wyatt checked his scan. Still no other life forms. But he had learned long ago to trust his gut, and his intuition told him something was wrong. *Shit, back to jumping at shadows.*

"You have any special sensors that can see through walls or something?" Wyatt asked as they walked back to the cargo hold on the *Merchant Prince.*

"Unfortunately, no. Why?"

"Something doesn't feel right. Let's get this last load, and then we're out of here."

Mack paused and raised his face toward the ceiling as if listening to something only he could hear. "Movement," he said after a minute. "Two decks up."

"Living?" Wyatt wondered how that was possible. He sure didn't want to see more zombies.

Mack shook his head. "No. Mechanical."

"Size? Number?"

"Three that are moving. Smaller than I am, but very fast."

"I don't want to meet up with them," Wyatt said. "Come on. We're almost there."

Nothing rose to challenge them, and they reached the *Prince's* cargo hold without incident, but Wyatt's sense of foreboding did not ease. "Start stacking these crates on the hovercart," he instructed Mack. "I'm going to have another look around to see if there's anything else."

"I'm on it," Mack replied genially.

Wyatt looked back at him. "Do you have any idea what your core function is?" he asked, curious despite himself.

"Sure. I'm a bartender."

"Bartender?" That narrowed down the possibilities for Mack's origins. There were plenty of passenger liners that cruised between star systems, hosting their guests in varying levels of comfort depending on the price of their ticket. The shipping companies learned long ago that they could keep costs low and make more profit by substituting robots or the newer androids for as many crew positions as possible. Bartenders, waiters, entertainers, and stewards were easily automated, as were tour guides, maintenance specialists, and sex workers. Mack had probably been stolen off a damaged liner, which explained his odd attire.

"Best this side of Rum Row."

The sound of metal scratching on metal made them both stop in their tracks. "What was that?" Wyatt's scanner revealed nothing.

"No idea," Mack said. "But I agree that we should move quickly before we find out."

Wyatt made a quick circle around the hold, and this time, the damaged boxes in the back drew his attention. He got to the last row of cargo and stopped. Now that he was closer, he could see that the damaged crates had been ripped apart, not broken from falling. Large, tell-tale bloodstains marked the hold's deck, along with the mangled bodies of four men that had been hidden from view. Wyatt was grateful that his suit kept him from smelling anything. The *Prince's* life support system had been off for a while, and the bodies appeared to be mostly frozen. A powered-down maintenance bot sat next to the carnage as if it had come upon it and tried to clean up before the systems failed.

He bent down to retrieve a piece of a broken crate large enough to still bear most of the logo of its original sender. "Kalok Enterprises," Wyatt read aloud, feeling sick to his stomach. "Mack! We've got to get out of here!"

"Sure thing, Captain."

Overhead, the scrabbling noises were louder, closer. Wyatt glanced up and shuddered. "Come on. Let's see if we can get to the ship before those things figure out we're here."

Mack and Wyatt steered the hovercart out of the cargo hold. "What did you find back there?" Mack asked.

"Some of the crew or rather, what's left of them. The broken boxes didn't fall by themselves. My bet is the freighter stole them, and the owners activated the contents remotely."

"What was in the boxes?"

"That!" Wyatt answered as something the size of a large dog skittered across the corridor at the next junction.

"Got any ideas on how we get back to the ship?"

Wyatt drew his blaster. "I always say, when in doubt, shoot it out." He glanced at the robot. "How good are you with a weapon?"

Mack tilted his head. "Not part of my programming."

"If you're going to stick with me, we'll have to change that." Wyatt took his second blaster out of its holster and pushed it into Mack's hand.

"Here. Fire it by squeezing the trigger. It'll burn a hole right through a person, so it'll at least knock those things back a ways or fry their circuits. Don't shoot it at the bulkheads unless you want to be floating in space until your batteries run dry. It shouldn't make a hole but given the ship's condition let's not take chances."

"You've made your point."

Wyatt maneuvered the hovercart ahead of them and locked it on low power. It moved forward independently, while Wyatt and Mack flattened themselves against the bulkheads and waited, guns ready.

The hovercart hummed toward the intersection. As it reached the crossing, there was a blur of motion, and a multi-legged creature leaped through the air, pouncing on the hovercart and splaying ten articulated legs around its "prey" to pin it down.

"Fire!" Both Wyatt and Mack swung away from the bulkheads, aiming at the robotic creature. Their shots knocked the creature off the hovercart, but it took several crates with it, sending pieces of the smoking boxes and their contents scattering. The Kalok-bot managed to land on its metal legs and skittered off.

"I'm afraid the cargo is a loss," Mack said, with a realistic degree of regret programmed into his mechanical voice.

"Screw the cargo. I just want to avoid ending up like the crew. Come on." He and Mack peered out into the cross-corridor before stepping forward. "All clear."

"Watch out!" Mack yelled just as Wyatt began to move forward.

Something large and dark fell from the ceiling right in front of Wyatt. He fired his blaster without thinking, rocking the thing backward and giving him a few seconds to scramble clear.

The Kalok-bot was a little shorter than Wyatt's hips, with ten jointed legs that carried the oval metal body protected in their center, like a giant spider.

Before it recovered from the blast, Wyatt kicked the hovercart clear of debris. "Get on!" he yelled to Mack as he jammed the controls forward.

The hovercart lurched, then sped up. Its hum was a contrast to the metallic scratching of the Kalok-bot's many legs as the robotic creature regained its equilibrium and came after them.

"It's gaining on us!" Mack observed, conveying the panic Wyatt would have expected from a human.

"The hovercart was built for carrying loads, not joyriding," Wyatt snapped, fiddling with the controls to urge more speed from the dolly. The cart surged forward, pulling ahead. The Kalok-bot sped up.

"You drive. I'll shoot," Mack said. He shot the bot and caught it square in the body pod, sending it tumbling. He timed the next shot, so their attacker was underneath a beam, and aimed at the support. One end tore free, dropping the rest of it onto the Kalok-bot and pinning it to the deck.

"Go!" Mack urged. Wyatt gunned the hovercart.

"The good news is, we're putting distance between us and that thing," Wyatt reported. "The bad news is, we're moving away from my ship."

Wyatt slowed the hovercart once it became apparent the Kalok-bot was not on their tail. This section of the corridor looked like a battleground. Gouges scarred the bulkheads. Pipes and conduits had been torn down from overhead, leaving wires in a jumble. Splashes of dried blood were visible on the bulkheads, and bits of blackened, shriveled matter stuck to the deck, which Wyatt did not want to examine too closely.

"Here," he said, hefting a length of pipe and handing it to Mack. He grabbed one for himself. "Never know when it'll come in handy."

"Do you have a plan?"

Wyatt gave him a look. "I'm working on it."

Another Kalok-bot came at them from the opposite direction, charging down the corridor with its ten mechanical legs flying. Wyatt glanced around them. There were no access ladders or intersections in this stretch of corridor. The way behind them was blocked. He grabbed one of the lengths of pipe and jammed the controls to maximum speed, leveling the pipe like a lance.

"What are you doing?" Mack's vocal programming simulated fear very realistically.

"Clearing the way," Wyatt replied. "Hang on."

The Kalok-bot did not slow down. Neither did Wyatt. But as the distance closed, Wyatt eyed the enemy robot, trying to calculate its mass. The legs were deceptively slender, but the metal was sure to be stronger than it looked. The oval "body" was the vulnerability, housing the bot's sensors and control center.

"It's not going to veer."

Yards closed to mere feet. At the last minute, just before the hovercart came into range of those wickedly long legs, Wyatt pulled up on the controls. The hovercart's power system screeched, straining to rise higher than it was designed to go, wobbling dangerously.

The Kalok-bot thrashed, trying to snag them with the sharp, pointed ends of its metal legs, scratching the underside of the hovercart. Mack beat at the legs, smacking them with his length of pipe whenever they neared the edge of the cart. Wyatt urged the hovercart high enough to sail over top of the Kalok-bot without colliding.

The bottom of the hovercart scratched along the angular "joints" of the spider-bot's legs. Wyatt kept one hand on the controls and slammed his pipe-lance straight down, into the center of the robot's legs, straight into the "head."

The hovercart came crashing down on the other side, throwing Mack and Wyatt onto the deck. Behind them, Wyatt's improvised pike skewered the spider-bot's torso. The legs went out from under it, splayed in every direction, and the whole mechanical creature shook as the pipe short-circuited its innards.

Mack dove for his hat, which had flown off in the crash. "It's for luck," he said, pulling it down over his smooth metal head.

"Come on," Wyatt said. "We can't be sure either of them won't recover."

"And go where?"

"Down, then over and up," Wyatt replied, pointing at an access hatch. They left Mack's pipe behind reluctantly and were forced to secure their blasters as they climbed the ladder.

"How do we know they aren't wherever it is we're going?"

"We don't," Wyatt admitted. "But when I looked over the scan of the ship, the mechanical access tubes weren't much wider across than a man's shoulders. I'm wagering those things can't fit."

Wyatt paused at the bottom of the ladder and listened. He heard nothing and muttered a prayer to the gods as he cranked the wheel to open the hatch. "If something grabs me," he told Mack, "don't let go of my feet."

"That could go badly."

"Not as badly as it will if you let go," Wyatt replied, doing his best not to dwell on the savaged bodies of the crew he had seen in the cargo hold.

Nothing rushed at them as they crawled into the access tube. The emergency lighting was even dimmer here, and Wyatt was grateful he still fit with his armored atmo suit. They closed the hatch, and Wyatt let out a long breath, slouching against the tube's walls.

"What are those things?" Mack asked. "And why didn't your scans pick up on them? Why don't my scans identify them?"

Wyatt stretched, trying to lessen the tightness in his neck and shoulders. "Ever heard of Kalok Enterprises?"

Mack shrugged. "I have no record of it."

"Kalok is best known as a mining company," Wyatt replied, glad for a chance to catch his breath. "But, they also have a big investment in security technology. Officially, it's to protect their mines and colonies. But everyone who's dealt with them knows their security is as much to keep the miners and colonists under their control as it is to fend off attackers."

"Those bots down there belonged to Kalok?"

Wyatt nodded. "Yeah. How they got here is a mystery, except I'm sure someone stole them, not realizing who they were going up against. My bet is that Kalok realized the bots went missing and activated them remotely. I imagine whoever turned them on knew exactly what was likely to happen."

"They killed the crew?" Mack's tone was horrified even if his metal face showed no emotion.

"Very messily. For all I know, that's all those things are built to do. I can't imagine they have much other purpose. Probably use them to get rid of dangerous predators on colonized worlds, or patrol the perimeter of their mines. When they're not terrorizing the miners."

"You think Kalok knows where their bots are?"

"Someone destroyed your tracking mechanism," Wyatt said. "I don't think anyone got close enough to the Kalok-bots to do the same. So…maybe. If so, they haven't been in a hurry to retrieve them. Then again, if Kalok did set the bots on the freighter crew on purpose, they also know the bots will still be here whenever Kalok gets around to sending someone by to pick them up."

"What now?" Mack asked. "I don't want to get turned off again." He looked at Wyatt. "I bet I could get good at salvage with a little practice. Help you out. Lift heavy things. Do dangerous stuff. I can be useful." Mack almost sounded wistful.

Whoever programmed him to mimic emotions knew what they were doing. I bet he was damn good at slinging drinks and listening to sob stories. Wyatt grinned. "You make a good case. And you've done great so far—for a bartender. Maybe you *would* come in handy." He'd been thinking along the same lines before Mack brought up the possibility, impressed by how well the robot had adapted. "First, we have to make it back to the ship."

The access tube brought them out in a small compartment filled with equipment. Wyatt guessed it was a maintenance room. "We climbed back up a level in the tube, so we're on the same deck as the airlock to the ship," Wyatt said. "Now we just have to clear a path to get to it."

He started to move around the small compartment as he spoke, gathering odds and ends. Mack stood guard at the hatch, listening for signs of the Kalok-bots and making sure nothing opened the compartment before they were ready.

Wyatt found three boxy pieces of portable equipment and three industrial hovercarts, and began fastening the equipment to the carts. Then he rewired the controls. Mack eyed the contraptions suspiciously. Wyatt added a few more lengths of pipe to his pile to replace the ones they had lost and took several palm-sized gadgets out of his utility pouch.

"Nellie. I need a scan for active system frequencies. Disregard those you can tie to us or the *Prince*. What does that leave?"

Nellie responded by sending a series of numbers to Wyatt's comm display. He scanned them and turned to Mack. "What's your frequency?"

Mack, rattled off the numbers in response.

"Good. Then hopefully that means these are the bots and you're on a different frequency. This might actually work."

"What are those things?" Mack asked, staying by the hatch but craning for a better look.

"Frequency jammers," Wyatt answered. "And yes, they're frowned on, where they aren't outright illegal. Damn shame, since they're handy in plenty of situations. Once we open that hatch, my scan tells me we've got half a corridor to cover to get to the dock. We'll cross another corridor about ten feet outside this room. We've got to get to the ship without being torn apart."

"What did you strap to the hovercarts?"

"Laser welders. Hacked to send a wider arc. Make sure you stay behind them."

"I don't think I understand," Mack replied.

"There's enough atmosphere on emergency life support that the welders should work. We just need to be off the freighter before one of these babies hits an outer bulkhead. Or—" He made a whooshing noise and clapped his hands together sharply.

Mack flinched at the noise. "Let's avoid that."

"Definitely." Wyatt paused. "So we get the hovercarts to the intersection and head one in each direction except the way we're going. We use our guns to clear out anything in the passage to my ship and bash anything we can't shoot. I'll drop these," he held up the jammers, "across the corridor we're in. Their range is limited to a few feet, and they're not strong enough to hold off an army of those Kalok-bots, but they should disrupt the circuits of anything that tries to follow us enough to slow them down."

Mack adjusted his lucky hat and saluted. "Ready."

The Kalok-bots were waiting. One came barreling down the corridor to the left of the compartment doorway, ten jointed legs rising and falling with arachnid grace. They could hear others skittering toward the intersection.

"This better work," Wyatt muttered under his breath. He thumbed the controls on the first hovercart, and the laser welder came online with a hum. He sent it gliding toward the bot, welder arcing beyond the edge of the cart. Mack grabbed the second cart and ran toward the intersection, with Wyatt right behind. Two more bots headed for them, one from each direction. Mack pushed his cart to the right, while Wyatt sent his to the left.

"Go for it!" Wyatt yelled. They crossed into the corridor that led to the docking bay. Wyatt paused to set the jammer units across the opening and activate them. He heard nothing, but Mack gave a startled yelp.

"What's wrong?" Wyatt wheeled to look at the robot, who had staggered.

"Nothing," Mack replied, but his voice was thready. His hat slipped, covering one eye. "It's not my frequency—but I'm picking up distortion. I need to get out of here." He staggered, and Wyatt steadied him.

"We're almost out," Wyatt said, heading at a run for the docking bay door, with his gun in one hand and the length of pipe in the other.

"Nellie! Open the outer lock!" He yelled through the link in his helmet.

Too late, he heard skittering. He glanced wildly from side to side. Nothing was coming down the corridor. Then he looked up. A Kalok-bot headed straight for him, on the overhead, out of range of the jammers.

Mack barreled into him, knocking Wyatt through the now open hatch and into the *Nellie B* as the Kalok-bot dropped. Mack's hat tumbled from his head and onto the decking beside Wyatt. Mack slapped the control panel, closing and sealing the *Prince's* hatch door, and rammed the controls with the length of pipe in his hand.

Wyatt punched at the hatch controls from the other side, but the freighter-side door would not reopen. Through the reinforced glass, Wyatt saw everything.

The bot's razor-sharp legs punctured Mack's metal skin. Two more of the attack-bot's legs shredded Mack's floral shirt, then raked deep gouges into his chest. Mack did not make a sound. He shot the bot point-blank with Wyatt's spare gun, knocking the bot off of him, throwing it against the bulkhead.

Mack was almost to his feet when the bot recovered and pushed off from the bulkhead with enough speed to go airborne, landing with its sharp-clawed feet first and knocking Mack back to the deck.

Wyatt tried the controls again, punching at the keypad, but the hatch still refused to open. He beat on the window, trying to draw off the bot, but the space-tempered glass silenced his shouts. Wyatt turned to the control panel and brought the airlock surveillance cameras online. The screen lit up giving him another view of what was happening on the other side of the hatch.

Mack hit the Kalok-bot with the pipe, denting its body, tearing away two of the arachnid legs. The bot dug at him with its can-opener feet, peeling back the metal skin and tearing at the wires beneath.

Mack fired again, and this time the bot shuddered, then one leg stabbed deep into Mack's wrist, and his grip on the blaster went slack. Another leg of the bot kicked the gun out of reach. Mack twisted one of the long, jointed legs until it bent, yanking it out of its socket. The bot struck at Mack's face, opening a deep metal gouge across one cheek.

Mack's movements slowed. The bot was winning. Mack got out from under the bot, staggering to his feet. The bot swayed back and forth as if trying to anticipate his next move. Mack kicked at the bot, distracting it. Then he fell forward, putting his whole weight into driving the pipe down through the Kalok-bot's center. The bot shuddered and collapsed.

"Go, Mack!" Wyatt cheered, though Mack could not hear him through the glass. He kept turning his focus between the small glass window and the screen.

One leg of the dying bot thrust through Mack's body, impaling him, ripping through the tattered vacation shirt. Mack's whole form jerked, and for a moment, Wyatt thought the bartender would rally.

"Come on!" Wyatt yelled, pounding harder on the hatch. "Get up! Get up!"

Mack pushed himself up on one knee. His face was savaged, his chest torn open, and the arachnid's leg had penetrated his core processor. His legs shot sparks and twitched as he tried to stay up, but Mack turned his head toward where Wyatt was pressed against the hatch glass. His system was failing, and the power to his eyes made the light behind them blink erratically.

Mack raised his right arm and gave a shaky salute, then fell forward, onto the ruined Kalok-bot.

"No, dammit!" Wyatt yelled, but there was no one to hear him.

Two more bots appeared in the corridor, swarming over Mack's body and pulling him apart. How they got past the jammers, Wyatt didn't know, but he had no desire to find out whether they could pry the hatch door open.

"Prepare for launch! Uncouple the ship!" Wyatt yelled to Nellie. He secured the outer lock and ran the decontamination cycle. As he opened the inner lock and turned to leave, his foot kicked something soft.

Mack's fishing hat.

Wyatt jammed the hat on his head, wiping a tear from his eye and headed for the bridge. He dropped into the pilot's chair and grabbed the controls. "Detach, Nellie."

He swung the *Nellie B* away from the *Merchant Prince* as soon as the couplings had retracted. Wyatt pushed the ship to top speed, keeping manual control as a distraction and wanting nothing more than to put as much distance as possible between him and the ruined freighter.

"Would you like me to take over now, Wyatt?" Nellie asked. "Do you have a destination plotted?"

His eyes stung. *He was just a robot. Just a robot.* Wyatt rarely believed his own lies. This time was no different.

"Here ya go Nellie." Wyatt pulled up the coordinates for the station and plugged them in. "We have some cargo to sell before we pick up Beth. Warn me before we jump. I need a drink."

Chapter Seven

"I TAKE IT you had some trouble while I was gone?" Wyatt asked when they lifted off from the platform at Keller Station. Beth had been in a hurry, and for as friendly as Daniel had been, he also seemed relieved to see them gone.

"Yeah. Stellar Fed. It's a long story," Beth said, slumping in her chair. She eyed Wyatt for a moment. "What's with the hat?"

Wyatt looked away. "A friend gave it to me."

"Never saw you wear it before."

"Ran into him on the job."

Wyatt studiously avoided making eye contact. He still felt raw from Mack's "death" and the near-miss aboard the *Merchant Prince*, and it sounded like Beth had come close to disaster herself.

"Uh huh," Beth replied, but she let the matter rest. "You know Wyatt; I can smell the rum on your breath from here."

"Good. Means I did it right." Wyatt frowned; even getting drunk hadn't helped.

"Get anything good off the wreck?"

Wyatt nodded. "Yeah, but it wasn't worth it. Not even close."

"Tell me?"

"It was full of stolen Kalok-bots that activated and nearly blew up the ship and me with it. Barely made it off alive."

"And your friend…"

"Didn't."

"I'm so sorry."

Before Wyatt had to find a response, alarms blared, and Nellie's voice broke in. "Ships, incoming."

"Damn!" Wyatt said, adjusting the scanners and looking at Nellie's readouts she fed to his screen. "Unregistered vehicles, modified armaments. Bounty hunters."

"Shit. Want to bet they were tailing the Stellar Fed guys?"

"Just waiting for the prey to make a move when the Law moved on. Damn. We're not even out of planet's atmosphere yet." He fed power to the engines, and Beth felt the G-forces press her into the seat as they gained speed.

"Can you outrun them?"

"Nope. So I've got to out-think them."

"Then we're dead already."

Wyatt gave her a sidelong glare. "Nice you've got so much confidence in me. Hang on for the ride. Maybe if we can get past orbit and out of the gravity field, we can get by them." He looked back to the controls. "Nellie, prepare for evasive maneuvers and power up all weapons. Full shields."

The *Nellie B* might have been a little past her prime. And maybe she broke a lot of regulations and inspection standards, but for all her modifications and bastardized equipment, she was fast and maneuverable. *Once a gunship, always a gunship.* Wyatt reminded himself.

He watched his vid screens as the two bounty hunters tried to steer him back toward the surface. It could only go one way on the ground; badly.

"Hope you've got a strong stomach," Wyatt muttered, before pulling a hard turn and climb that sent the sensors screeching and made Wyatt and Beth momentarily weightless against their restraints.

"What are you doing?" Beth croaked, clearly torn between terror and nausea.

"Shaking our tail and getting off this rock."

Wyatt checked his instruments. The *Nellie B* was just clearing the outer atmosphere when a klaxon warned him that the bounty hunters had powered up their guns.

"Enemy is powering weapons," Nellie stated.

"Yeah, got that with the loud siren thing, Nellie."

Wyatt caught a glance of Beth turning a bit green out of the corner of his eye. He couldn't help but smile at the white-knuckled grip she had on her seat as Wyatt dove, rolled, and climbed, setting an erratic course that would have made any novice ill if they'd still been within the planet's gravity.

"What are you doing?" Beth yelped. "You're going to get someone killed!"

"I'm not the one doing the shooting. Yet," Wyatt replied, noting more ships coming into view. He fell back on his military training as he sent the ship through a series of precision maneuvers. The bounty hunters' ships were fast, but he was hoping the *Nellie B* was faster. Wyatt had no idea what armor or shielding they had, and he didn't want to find out for certain. There were too many to take on, so escape was the best option.

Wyatt set a course back toward the edge of Near-Fringe space, something he doubted the bounty hunters expected. Now that he closed in on one of the main shipping lanes, the hunters were left with a choice of either completing their kill in front of witnesses—and possibly law enforcement that would view them as dimly as their target— or peeling off and picking up the fight another day.

To Wyatt's relief, the bounty hunters dropped back, then changed their heading and moved out of range. He maneuvered the *Nellie B* next to a large cargo ship, and turned the controls back over to Nellie so she could allow them to hang in the bigger craft's "shadow." Wyatt let out a long breath.

"Not bad."

Wyatt glared at her. "We're still alive. That counts as 'good' in my book."

"What now?"

Wyatt ran a hand back through his dark hair. "We look for another job. Try to put some distance between us and those hunters and lie low."

"You think the bounty hunters will be back?" Beth swiveled to look at him.

"Not until we leave the shipping lanes. They're as vulnerable here as we are. If the Feds show up, it'd be a toss-up which of us they'd go after first."

Now that the shooting was over, Wyatt stopped to take a good look at Beth. She seemed rattled, and by more than just the ambush by the bounty hunters. "Want to talk about it?" He asked.

Beth looked like she was about to decline, then nodded and leaned back in her chair. "I don't even know where to start. Nothing was what it seemed."

"I knew that guy was up to no good," Wyatt retorted. "Can't trust those academic types."

Beth raised an eyebrow. "Watch your mouth." She looked torn between being pissed off and amused. Jealousy flashed through Wyatt, and it must have shown in his eyes because Beth smiled like she had uncovered a secret.

"I didn't mean you; you're a rogue now, not an academic," Wyatt returned with a grin, his eyes a bit mischievous now. He grew serious. "What happened?"

Beth filled him in, from the vision the alien implant in her arm supplied of the firestorm that destroyed the original settlement to the admission that the "research outpost" was really thinly-disguised exile, to the lengths Kalok and Stellar Fed had gone to make sure Daniel and his team remained under surveillance.

"He kept you safe. I'll give him credit for that, so, maybe he's not a total loser," Wyatt replied when Beth finished. He pulled out a flask from his pocket and passed it to her. She took a generous slug and handed it back.

"And they offed the one mole and drugged up the second—after convincing him he's got some kind of condition that makes him pass out and not remember things? Despite all my lingering doubts about university-types, I think I actually like this guy."

"It's bigger than just Keller Station," Beth continued. "From what Daniel told me, there's a whole archipelago of research outposts, archeology digs, and study stations where scientists who know too much or won't stay silent get banished—when they don't just disappear. And I think they've organized more than Daniel let on. I know they're trading some information on RimNet."

"So they've already got one foot in the criminal underworld," Wyatt said, grinning. "Academic outlaws. I'm kinda proud of them."

She ignored him and went on. "I think they're passing along information, providing safe houses for fugitives, and working together. Don't forget; these are researchers who've seen their life's work falsely discredited, who've had their reputations destroyed, and their projects unfounded. Murder has been done for much less cause."

"Never realized you professor-types were so bloodthirsty."

"You have no idea."

Wyatt drummed his fingers on the controls. "So you think they're plotting something?"

Beth frowned. "I don't think they'll be the first ones breaking out the guns if it comes to that. But academics are sneaky. We know how to research and ferret out secrets and things people would rather have stay hidden. We hold grudges like you wouldn't believe. So I'm betting this network—Daniel called it 'the Coalition'—is patiently documenting, waiting for the right time. They won't lead the charge, but they'll be the ones in the background, handing out the ammunition."

"You're scary as fuck sometimes, you know that?" Wyatt said, shaking his head. "So now you've got more dirt on Kalok, with what your little 'hitchhiking friend' showed you," he said with a nod toward the implant in her arm. "Genocide, huh?"

"Sure looked like it," Beth replied, and could not completely repress a shudder. "They never had a chance, never got any warning. And an attack on that scale from orbit—it would have taken warships to defend them." Her eyes flashed, and Wyatt saw the determination in the set of her jaw. "It's not just miners and colonists and work crews. These people had a flourishing colony, and they got wiped off the map because they were in the way."

"We're just salvage rats," Wyatt reminded her. "I am all for being a thorn in Kalok's side—got no love for them or Interplan. But I've been to war," he said, and all humor vanished from his expression. "Having a great idea and a lot of brave people doesn't mean you win. Lots of good people die."

"When I looked up your record," Beth said, "You were decorated for bravery. The newsvid called you a hero."

Wyatt turned to her, eyes shuttered and expression grim. His back stiffened and his jaw set. "I was a fool in a sucker's game. A useful pawn; a weapon. And I found out too late that none of it was what I thought I was fighting for. So if you're looking for a hero to lead your revolution, I'll let you out at the next stop. I paid my dues and got my scars."

"You hate Kalok and Interplan."

Wyatt nodded. "Yep. Made up my mind that I'd get as far away from them as I could, and I did. And I'm all too happy to help your information get into the right hands if it'll bring them down. But I've buried too many friends to go on a damn fool crusade."

"And if you thought you could win?"

"If—and it's a very big 'if'—it ever comes to that. I'll make up my mind when we get there." Wyatt turned back to the main vid screen, purposely looking away from Beth. "So what'll it be? You gonna help me run salvage, or you need to get dropped off somewhere to start your war?"

Beth grinned. "Salvage sounds good to me. And while we're stealing stuff, I'll just keep on documenting what I find."

Wyatt gave a curt nod. "I can live with that."

NELLIE AND THE ship's klaxons roused them from sleep a few hours later.

"Damn, damn, damn." Wyatt stirred to hyper-alertness in seconds and ran to the bridge where he began scanning his readouts, flipping through scan data, and eyeing the panels.

Beth had gone down to the galley to make coffee. "What now?"

Wyatt punched a button. "Nellie, play the message."

"Stand down. Prepare to be boarded or towed. This is your only warning," the recorded message said, and repeated itself, cycling through several of the most common languages in Rim-Fringe space.

"Kalok?" Beth asked, wide-eyed.

Wyatt cursed and dropped back into his seat. "No. And it's not bounty hunters, either. In fact, we're not even what they came for. We were just lucky enough to be in the wrong place at the wrong time."

Beth pressed a cup of hot coffee into his hands. Wyatt's accepted it gratefully and wished for a slug of whiskey in it. "Stellar Fed?"

He shook his head. "No. Pirates. In fact, I don't think the bounty hunters left because they didn't want to be spotted by the other ships. I think they lit out of here because they caught wind somehow that the pirates were coming. Damn."

"What do we do?"

"We don't have much choice. We might not be what the pirates came for, but they won't let us leave. Shit. I'll need to do something about Nellie…"

"You think they want cargo? You already sold what you got off of the *Prince* before you picked me up."

Wyatt gulped his coffee. "Most of it. Wouldn't do to have a completely empty hold. That'd make them tear the ship apart. I always keep some shit, just in case." He eyed the monitor, and Beth could practically read his mind.

"You're thinking about making a run for it."

"Nellie, can you give me a scan of those ships. Let me know what we're up against?"

Wyatt's screen came to life, and unfortunately none of it looked good. Wyatt came to a decision, eyes narrowing as he mentally calculated the distance between the *Nellie B* and the nearest pirate ships. His hands flew over the controls. "Damn," he muttered.

A shot clipped them, bouncing off the shields, but rocking the ship violently.

"Son of a bitch!" Wyatt slammed his fists on the console.

An alarm wailed over the comm system, followed by Nellie passing through the recorded voice. *"Stand down. Prepare to be boarded or towed. Resistance will result in your destruction."*

Wyatt was already out of his seat, running diagnostics, swearing creatively under his breath.

"How bad?" Beth asked. "And what I can I do to help?"

"We're not powerless. They'd rather avoid towing us if possible—too much of a strain on their systems," Wyatt replied. "But until we get to a station or an outpost, we're not going to be able to do any quick starts or hit maximum speed."

"Look," Beth said, and Wyatt turned to follow her gaze. She was watching one of the vid screens that showed the aft monitors. Four of the pirate ships engaged the two bounty hunter craft in battle. They watched the dogfight in silence, trying to keep track of who was winning. It lasted only moments before one of the bounty hunters' ships exploded and the other hung dead, no longer in motion.

Wyatt chewed his lip for a moment, then seemed to come to a decision. He went to the weapons locker and pulled down several blasters, then strapped on his holster. "Go get into one of the hidden bins. I'll hold them off."

"Fuck that," Beth said, shouldering him out of the way to grab several of the weapons for herself. "I spent three hours hiding from Stellar Fed in a secret room on Keller Station. I am not doing that again. Felt like being buried alive."

Wyatt fixed her with a look. "Beth, we don't know anything about these pirates. Some of them are slavers. It won't go well for us…"

"Then they'll be chewing on their own balls with their dicks shoved down their throats," Beth finished, meeting his gaze with an unflinching stare of her own. "No. I'm not hiding. I'd rather go down in a fight."

Wyatt looked like he meant to say something, snapped his mouth shut, and gave a curt nod. "All right then. Grab everything you can carry and at least put on the armored atmo suit. Blaze of glory and all that. Nellie, I'm going to have to put you in safe mode. Can't risk the pirates using you against us."

"Wyatt, what does that do?"

"Protects the A.I. and locks her up tight. I have a code that will wake her. I can even do it remotely, but for the pirates, it will appear that we have the simplest, standard issue automation. Makes the *Nellie B* an absolute bitch to fly. As you might have guessed by the size and stations, she was intended to have a crew of at least four, six preferred."

"Won't they be suspicious?"

"Maybe. But I do have a reputation, and to be honest, I could fly her by myself. It just wouldn't be fun."

The pirates forced the *Nellie B* to land on the out-of-the-way, obsolete space station. They didn't damage the ship, but they fired enough warning shots that there weren't options. Wyatt and Beth prepared for a showdown and stood shoulder to shoulder in the airlock, armed with enough weaponry to take out a dozen men.

The pirates managed to override the outer hatch and as the heavy door slid open, Wyatt saw only a wall of thick smoke. He fired and so did Beth, but in the smoke, they couldn't pick targets. The cloud poured into the *Nellie B* and they heard a metallic clang. Wyatt had just enough time to register the strange ball with lights rolling across the deck at his feet before the blinding flash, the loud bang, and then he screamed in agonizing pain and passed out.

WYATT CAME AROUND slowly. His head throbbed, his throat burned, and his mouth tasted like he had been sick. He still saw rainbow spots before his eyes. Then his sense of smell kicked in and informed him that he had, in fact, thrown up. He sat up with a groan and felt his heart sink as he took in his surroundings.

The small, featureless room held the essentials of a prison cell. Wyatt found a metal tray with standard rations and a container of water set by the door. He pushed off the bed and stumbled to the door, still shaking off the effects of whatever they had used on him.

"Hey! Let me outta here! I demand to talk to the person in charge!" Wyatt hammered on the door, but he heard nothing in response. He stepped back, wondering if the cell was soundproof. "Hey, you! Get me your captain. I've got rights!"

No response came, and Wyatt leaned against the wall and passed a hand over his face. He had no idea how long he had been unconscious, or whether they were still on the space station where he had landed the *Nellie B.* Worse, there was no sign of Beth.

As his mind slowly cleared and the throbbing became bearable, he did a quick triage. His armored suit and helmet were gone, as were his weapons. But he had been left with his boots and jumpsuit, minus his belt and anything that he might have been able to fashion into a weapon. After a careful check, he could see no new injuries or indications that he had been injected or otherwise medicated.

What the hell did they use on me?

His stomach rumbled, and he sniffed cautiously at the food and drink. Wyatt realized that the offering might be drugged, but he also knew that keeping up his strength yielded the best chance for escape.

Although he could see no camera in the room, Wyatt suspected his captors were able to see him since the door opened not long after he had finished eating and had washed up and used the toilet.

Three armed guards stood in the hallway when the door slid open. "You'll come with us," the man in the front said.

Wyatt rose warily. He was still too disoriented to stand a chance of either fighting or fleeing successfully, but it galled him to cooperate without resistance. "Where are we going?"

"Our captain would like to speak with you."

Wyatt debated whether it was a good sign that they did not handcuff him, or whether it merely spoke to his inability to escape. "Where's my partner?" He craned his neck to see if Beth, similarly escorted, might be heading the same way.

"Orders were to bring you to the captain. That's all I know," the man replied.

Wyatt seethed, though the response hardly surprised him. He eyed the guards' weapons, assessing their range and firepower, helpful to know in case he got a break. Then again, since he had no idea where they were, he could run and find himself on a ship between worlds with nowhere to go.

"Where are we?" He asked. The guards ignored him. "Still on that station? Or is this your ship?" He suspected they were aboard the station since the off-white corridors and his cell looked nicer than anything he would have guessed might be on the hard-worn ships the pirates had used to capture them.

They passed no one in the corridors, and Wyatt wondered if the path had been expressly cleared for his transport. He would have expected that kind of protocol in a prison more than on a pirate ship, and seeing it here worried him. *Maybe I've already been transported. Maybe they've turned me in for the bounty, and they're holding me in an off-world jail until Stellar Fed comes to pick me up. But where the hell is Beth?*

At the end of the next corridor, the lead guard opened a door that led to another white-walled, featureless room, furnished only with a table and chairs. Wyatt bet they were bolted to the deck.

"Wait here," the guard said, pushing Wyatt inside before the door slid shut.

Wyatt paced, measuring his prison with footsteps to give him something to pass the time. He had barely made it to the far end of the room when the door opened, and Beth stumbled in.

Beth wheeled and launched herself at the door, clawing at it in fury. "Come back here, you scum-sucking sons of bitches! You *storpp-*

fucking, shit-eating, weasel-screwing bastards!" Her nails found no purchase against the smooth finish of the white metal door, and a moment later, Beth sagged against it, resting her forehead on her arms.

Wyatt hung back, torn between relief and amusement. "Quite impressive. But I'm confused—are the weasels the ones eating the shit or is it the bastards? Because I think it all depends on where you meant to put a comma."

Beth turned, and emotions crossed her features too quickly for Wyatt to interpret. "Where the hell have you been?" she demanded.

Wyatt raised his eyebrows and held up his hands in a placating gesture. "Easy, there. I've been in a cell since I woke up, until they brought me here. No one answered any questions. And by the way, I'll bet anything they're watching and listening to us," he added with a smirk, addressing one of the corners of the ceiling although nothing indicated the placement of a camera or microphone.

Beth closed her eyes and took a deep breath, then pushed the hair out of her face and turned toward Wyatt. "You okay?"

He nodded. "I've been better. My head is pounding, but I can live with it, and I can sort of see around the rainbow burned into my eyes. Bonus, I don't want to heave my guts anymore."

"Yeah. Me, too."

Wyatt's intent gaze silently asked the questions he did not want to put into words. Beth understood and shook her head. "No. I'm all right. Far as I can tell, the only things missing are my atmo suit and weapons."

They worked their way around the room, looking for hidden doors or cabinets, but found nothing. "I can't say I'm impressed with their decor, but at least it's clean," Beth muttered.

Wyatt wished he and Beth had been salvaging together long enough to have worked out a code for situations like this. If they got loose, that would be first on the agenda, he promised himself. He had to remind himself that for all of Beth's spirit, she was a civilian, and an academic, not a soldier. He could fall back on his military training, which had included simulations on surviving as a prisoner of war. He strongly doubted Kalok's off-world orientation had included "how to escape from pirates." Hell, for all Wyatt knew, the pirates were working under the table for Kalok.

That's the good thing about keeping your expectations low. It's hard to be disappointed.

"We might as well sit down and be comfortable," Beth said with bitter humor. "I don't think standing makes much of a protest statement."

Wyatt joined her at the table. They sat in awkward silence, since they dared not say anything of consequence lest it be overheard. "If I'd have known, I'd have brought playing cards," Wyatt cracked. "Wouldn't mind a friendly game of poker."

Beth snorted. "Since when is a card game with you friendly?" The humor in her eyes took the sting out of her retort.

The door slid open, and both Beth and Wyatt jumped up, turning in unison to face the new threat.

"At ease." A blond man in dark fatigues stood in the doorway, with three guards behind him. His outfit looked like military surplus, and Wyatt wondered whether it was seized or stolen. He had a gun holstered on his thigh, but one glance told Wyatt the weapon was the type DNA locked to its owner. Grabbing it would give Wyatt nothing but a cudgel.

"Who are you?" Beth demanded.

The newcomer and his guards filed into the room and the door shut behind them. "I go by Galan. Welcome aboard."

Wyatt glared at him. He took a half step forward, putting himself between Galan and Beth. Beth took a full step and edged him out, shooting Wyatt a sidelong look that spoke volumes.

Galan chuckled. "Sit down. We have a lot to talk about."

For a moment, a silent contest of wills kept them all standing. Finally, Wyatt walked to the table and sat, followed a moment later by Beth and Galan.

"Who are you?" Beth asked, making no effort to hide the edge in her voice.

"Pirates. I thought that might have been clear by the circumstances," Galan replied.

"Why did you shoot the bounty hunters?" Wyatt asked.

"Were they friends of yours? I thought we were doing the universe a favor."

"So scum has a pecking order?" Beth crossed her arms. Wyatt felt silently grateful that she had omitted a repeat of her earlier "weasel" comment.

"Yes. And 'bounty hunter' comes below 'salvage rat' and 'pirate,'" Galan replied. He regarded them for a moment. "I know who you are: Wyatt McCoy and Dr. Elizabeth Parker. You and your ship are rather notorious these days. I imagine that's what attracted those hunters."

Wyatt had plenty of practice bluffing at poker. "Don't know what you're talking about. Plenty of ships out in the dark have the same names. *Nellie B* was my grandmother."

"No doubt sainted and dearly departed," Galan added wryly. "And probably entirely fictitious. And there are so many repurposed Star Force gunships running out in the Dark."

"Watch what you call my grandma," Wyatt shot back. Beth elbowed him in the ribs.

"Supposing you had such 'notorious' guests, why shoot down the bounty hunters?" Beth asked, genuinely curious.

Galan tented his fingers and rested his hands on the table between them. "For one thing, we'd have to split the price on your head, and I don't like to share. Sorry, Wyatt, they're not offering much for you. They just want you dead." The hint of a smile that touched his lips also reached his eyes. "Besides that, I hate bounty hunters. Long story. It's personal."

"It usually is," Wyatt agreed.

"I'm more interested in hearing your side of the story," Galan said. "Here's what the 'official' news has to say. The two of you shot your way out of the old Comstock mine complex after slaughtering the guards who were attempting to apprehend Dr. Parker. Parker convinced ex-military hero, Wyatt McCoy, to join forces with her to escape an official investigation into her alleged corporate espionage. They're speculating she blackmailed you or forced you to help. You both fled to Rum Row, caused a riot that led to significant property losses and several corporate casualties, then resisted arrest, stole a spaceship and escaped—guns blazing—in the company of the infamous Liddy Gang. Did I leave out anything important?"

"Quite a tale," Wyatt said, leaning back in his chair. "I kind of like them, McCoy and Parker. Sounds like the script to a holovid."

"Suppose you ever met them. Would you claim the bounty?" Beth asked. They were dancing around the truth, and they all knew it. It was one thing to suspect and another to have confirmation, especially recorded confirmation. Both Beth and Wyatt intended to spin this out as long as they could before providing that damning information.

"Not if I liked them," Galan replied. "Not if they were the kind I could do business with. The kind of folks doing the right thing for the right reasons."

"And those reasons would be?" Wyatt left his question hanging.

"I told you what the 'official' story was," Galan said, watching both of them as if he were searching for tells that would reveal their game. "Then there's what's being said on RimNet. You're almost famous," he chuckled. "According to the anonymous posts, you've uncovered damning information that Kalok and Interplan can't afford to have made public—and which they'll go to extreme lengths to recover."

"Interesting, if it were true," Wyatt replied, matching Galan's cold smile.

"Neither of you are exactly unknowns," Galan said, lifting his chin a bit. "I've read your service record, McCoy. Impressive. Decorated pilot, medals for bravery under fire, wounded in combat, and a noteworthy number of enemy kills to your credit. A military hero. Certainly a bad public relations move if it gets out you turned on them."

"There's nothing impressive about 'kills,'" Wyatt returned, his voice cold. "Especially in a war of questionable purpose and I was Space Corps, not a Gray for Kalok."

Galan raised an eyebrow. "As if there's a difference. But that's an unpopular sentiment, Mr. McCoy. Most folks think the Rim War was just and necessary."

"Most folks are too dumb to know which end of a skimmer goes forward," Wyatt returned. "Those soldiers and pilots who fought in the war, they just plowed the road for corporate expansion—and profit—under the excuse of fending off threats that were never really there."

"Interesting." Galan turned to Beth. "And you, Dr. Parker. May I call you Beth?"

"No."

"Very well. You had a distinguished career as an academic and author, publications in all the right journals, a position at a noted university, even some corporate consulting to pad out a professor's salary. And then all of a sudden, once you became a paid shill for Kalok, something went very wrong."

Galan leaned forward, keeping eye contact with Beth. "The official version says that you were cheating on your expense reports, stealing from the company. But RimNet is wild with speculation. There's even a version that says you found proof that Kalok might not have been telling the truth about some of its colonization practices."

"Do tell," Beth drawled with a look that dared Galan to make something of it.

"And if you had the chance to talk with these wanted criminals, what would you say?" Wyatt asked, giving nothing away in his expression.

"I'd want to know all the naughty details," Galan replied with a smile.

"So you'd let them go?"

Galan sighed and looked up at the ceiling. "Sadly, no. I'm a businessman, and there are expenses to be covered. Although I might be inclined to find buyers other than those in league with Kalok."

"You rotten bastard," Beth said, beginning to rise from her seat. Wyatt grabbed her arm and yanked her back down.

"Good thing we don't know either of those *wanted criminals*," Wyatt replied with his best innocent smile.

"What kind of 'buyers' are you considering?" Beth glared at Galan and shook off Wyatt's hand on her arm.

"I don't know how much you see of the Fringe aside from supply outposts and maintenance docks and wherever you fence your merchandise. But people come all the way out here to be left alone. They left home for a reason, and usually, that includes reinventing themselves and their past. They don't ever intend to go back; they just want to be left in peace. They've declared their independence, and they're technically outside of Allied space," Galan said, folding his arms on the table.

"What does that have to do with us?" Wyatt challenged.

"Word is getting around that Kalok is thinking of pushing out past the Rim, colonizing new planets, setting up more mines. If that happens, it would certainly affect the Near-Fringe worlds, but if Kalok and Interplan were aggressive enough, even the Far-Fringe wouldn't be safe."

Galan leaned in as if letting them share a secret. "If what the Rim-Net busybodies are saying about you is true, you know things that might put an end to that. Might stop Kalok and Interplan once and for all. That makes you very valuable cargo. Certainly, Kalok has a bounty on you. But so do a few of the players on the Independence front. You've probably heard of some of them, like the Coalition and the Network. There are dozens of smaller ones that have been better at staying hidden. Any of them would give a lot to have you, and what you know, in their pocket."

"Don't we get a say in this?" Beth looked ready to tear Galan apart.

"No."

"Now wait just a minute," Wyatt started.

"I have three potential buyers, all willing to pay me more than Kalok's bounty for you and all of them representing Separatist interests." He checked the chronometer. "They'll be here very soon. Highest bidder gets both of you."

"You can't just *sell* us," Beth sputtered.

"Think of it more as being indentured," Galan replied. "What you make of it is up to you. I assure you all three parties mean you no harm; something you could not say about Stellar Fed or Kalok. They'll hide you, protect you, and probably keep you quite comfortable. And in return, you go on finding the information they need to bring Kalok to its knees."

"You realize that we didn't find that information sitting on our asses locked in a room," Wyatt argued. "What we know we found out by visiting planets, salvaging wrecks, doing our job. Put us in a box, and we're useless."

Galan shrugged. "I understand, but it's now out of my hands. By tonight, someone will have paid good money—quite a lot of it—to acquire you. I'd suggest you make your peace with it."

With that, Galan stood. Beth looked like she meant to move forward, but once more Wyatt kept her beside him with a hand on her forearm, gentle pressure warning her not to make a move that the pirate's well-armed guards would counter. Beth shook Wyatt off angrily and leveled a glare at Galan as the guards closed around him, and they left the room.

"You're going to let him do this?" Beth looked like she might burst or take a swing at someone. Wyatt backed up a step, not wanting to be in her way.

"We're outgunned and outnumbered," Wyatt replied, jabbing a finger toward the ceiling to remind her that they were very likely also under surveillance.

"What about your ship?"

Wyatt's jaw clenched. "It comes with us. We're a package deal. Besides, we won't uncover anything new locked in a room." He cleared his throat. "If we were, in fact, those two fugitives. Which we're not."

Beth rolled her eyes. "So you're okay with this?"

Wyatt's patience ran out. "No. I'm not okay with being captured and sold like cargo. But when there's not a chance in hell of fighting our way out, I'm going to go along with it. At least until something better comes along."

Beth folded her arms and turned aside. Wyatt closed the gap between them, and while Beth glowered at him, she did not move away. "I don't think they mean to hurt us, which is more than I can say for Kalok," he said, dropping his voice. "If Galan's telling the truth, then these groups need us. They're going to want us to be on their side, and that means keeping us reasonably happy."

"As prisoners."

Wyatt shrugged. "Maybe. Maybe not. They don't have an incentive to box us up because we couldn't do what they need us to keep doing. So maybe there's a way to work something out. Create an alliance instead of it being based on having our arms twisted."

"You know details about any of these groups he's talking about? I 've heard them mentioned, but not much more."

Wyatt grimaced. "Some. I've run into them here and there and heard people talking. They keep a pretty low profile since Kalok would love to lock them up. What I've heard is iffy. Some of the groups are pretty hardcore—ready for a shooting war. Most just want to clean up the system and be left alone."

Beth sighed. "So we just wait until we get picked up by our new 'owners?'"

"Guess so." He grinned. "At least we didn't get stuck back in our quarters by ourselves."

GUARDS DELIVERED THEIR dinner, but provided no information. Finally, after what Wyatt guessed to be about four hours, Galan and his bodyguards appeared in the doorway.

"It's settled. I think you'll do well," Galan said.

"Who's the high bidder?" Wyatt asked as more guards entered the room. He and Beth submitted to having their wrists cuffed behind them.

Galan ignored his question. "I figured you'd want your ship. The client agreed to that, although, for obvious reasons, we slaved the controls to their main ship. Tell me, how do you manage to fly that beast?"

"It takes talent. You slaved my ship?" Wyatt's face reddened in anger.

"We've also repaired the damage we found when we captured you. You shouldn't have problems getting to your new home."

Beth and Wyatt exchanged a glance. What had seemed overwhelming when it was just a possibility now felt downright terrifying. Wyatt walked beside Beth, intentionally bumping shoulders in a show of solidarity.

The guards stopped when they reached the main landing bay. A familiar figure waited near the ramp to the *Nellie B.*

"Took you long enough," Miss Liddy said, tapping her toe. "You got everything?"

Wyatt sputtered as he realized she was the winning bidder. "I need my ship, and we want our weapons back."

Liddy gave him a look as if he were daft. "Your ship is behind me, boy. Open your eyes. As for your weapons, Galan assured me his men returned them to the ship already. So if that's all, let's fly. I'll fill you in when we get where we're going."

"I need to…"

"No you don't," Liddy cut him off. "My ship will do the driving. You two just sit back and enjoy the view." She looked to the guards. "Take off those ridiculous cuffs. Wyatt and Beth will behave themselves." Liddy gave them a toothy grin full of promises and threats. "Won't you?"

Wyatt cleared his throat. "As much as we ever do."

Beth elbowed him. "At least for the ride. Then, we need to talk."

"First things first," Liddy replied. "Get your ship ready to go. Time's a wastin'." With that, Liddy turned on her heel and strode back to her shuttle.

Wyatt hurried up the ramp and into the *Nellie B* with Beth close behind him. He had the look of a frantic parent wanting to find reassurance that no harm had come to a beloved child.

"What did they do to you?" he crooned to the ship as he worked the panel to close the ramp. Wyatt noted that their armored suits and weapons were left in a heap on the deck, as the other items they'd had on them.

"You two need some alone time?"

He watched as Beth grabbed her blaster from the stack and headed down the short corridor to her quarters, then returned a few moments later.

"Doesn't look like anything's missing—at least, from my quarters," she reported. "Although someone tossed the place. Not sure what they thought they'd find."

Wyatt raised an eyebrow. "Information." He put a finger to his lips, indicating that he thought someone might have bugged the ship. "*Later*," he mouthed, and headed for the bridge.

To Wyatt's relief, Galan's pirates kept their word. No one tried to interfere when they left. It rankled to have the *Nellie B*'s controls handled by someone else, and Wyatt fretted until he saw enough to be reassured that the arrangement would not cause permanent damage to his ship.

"Did you and Nellie kiss and make up?" Beth teased.

Wyatt scowled. "You don't understand." He patted the control panel. "Don't listen to her," he advised the ship, with a sidelong glare at Beth. He didn't want to risk reactivating the A.I. and hoped Beth figured it out. He couldn't say anything because he had no doubts Liddy was listening.

Beth snorted a laugh and gave Wyatt an amused look. "So now we just get towed to wherever Liddy's going?"

Wyatt shook his head. "Not towed. Slaved." His jaw tightened. "Which means someone got into the *Nellie B's* wiring and controls and rigged her up to be run remotely from Miss Liddy's ship." He looked up, glancing around the cockpit. "I'm not happy about that—you hear me?"

Beth snickered. "Loud as you might be, I don't think she's going to hear you through two bulkheads and open space."

"Oh, I bet she will." Wyatt went to a storage compartment and rummaged around until he pulled out a small contraption. He turned it on and adjusted the controls. A low hum gradually rose to become a shrill whine.

"Looking for ghosts?" Beth snarked.

Wyatt ignored her and walked slowly through the ship, moving the gadget in an arc. He stopped when it shrilled, and examined the compartments, floor panels, and anything easily removable. Each time, he found a tiny concealed transmitter. When he completed a sweep without incident, he put the mics into the trash recycler and hit the button for it to process and compact.

"That should do it," he said, returning the scanner to its place and sitting back in the pilot's chair.

"Why would Liddy want to bug the ship?" Beth asked, more curious than angry.

"She's more of an ally than a friend. I've got no illusions about her 'rescuing' us out of the goodness of her heart," Wyatt replied. "In fact, I won't be surprised if she holds this over our heads. We're going to owe her—and she won't be shy about using that."

"Still, better the enemy you know than the one you don't?"

"Yeah. Although, until now, I've tried very hard to stay out of the politics. Had my fill in the war."

Beth turned in her seat and drew her feet up under her. Without control over the ship or knowledge of where it was heading, neither of them needed to watch the viewscreens too closely.

"I assume you're tracing the course?"

"Yep," Wyatt answered.

Beth was quiet for a few moments as if formulating her question. "What he said about the war, that it wasn't as noble and squeaky clean as they reported to the outside—that was true, right?"

Wyatt looked away, staring at the expanse of stars. The remote piloting mechanism kept them within sight and protective range of Liddy's main ship, but not nearly as close as if they were being towed. "Mostly, or true enough."

"If the separatists rebel against Kalok, do you think your Regiment friends would get involved?"

"Some might," Wyatt replied. "How about your researcher pals? It seems like they've got one foot outside the law as it is."

"For all I know, the researchers may already be in with the separatists. Like I told you, sending people out here and cutting off their research grants, destroying their reputations, and suppressing their findings riles them up."

Wyatt shook his head. "A rather strange reason to join a revolution, but hey, I just pick up abandoned cargo and scrap metal."

"You think Galan will double-cross Liddy—turn us all into Stellar Fed or Kalok?" Beth stretched the kinks out of her shoulders.

"No. Tough for a pirate to claim a bounty on other thieves. If he turns us in, he turns himself in—and I bet he and his boys are wanted in more places for more things than we are. Besides, no one rats on Liddy and lives. She could probably eat Galan and his pirates for lunch and not even notice."

When it became clear that Liddy and her gang were not going to reach their destination soon, Beth dozed in her chair. She woke when Wyatt shook her by the shoulder.

"I think we're heading for that planet," he said, pointing to the viewscreen. "She's changing course, slowing down."

"How do we land, if they've got the controls?"

"That's what I'm about to find out."

Wyatt opened his comm link. "How about letting me land this myself?"

"Don't you trust me, Wyatt?" Liddy replied almost immediately.

"You really need to ask?" He returned, mostly joking. Wyatt was surprised that Liddy had been the one to respond and even more that she'd done so quickly. *Damn, maybe she knows me too well…was waiting for me to ask.*

"We're too close in to turn over control," Liddy said. "Don't worry—as the current owner of the *Nellie B*; I have a vested interest in keeping her in one piece. My boys will take good care of her."

Wyatt growled in response, eyes flashing, fists clenched. "Not a scratch, Liddy."

"Buckle in, Wyatt. You'll be landing soon." The teasing in her voice sounded all too familiar.

Chapter Eight

"Liddy?" Wyatt wasn't sure whether to be relieved or furious as the over-sized goons escorted him and Beth into Liddy's private office. The remarkably tasteful decor took Wyatt by surprise. It could have been the den of any business leader or industry heavyweight. Landscape panels on the walls made it appear as if the office looked out on the best views of a dozen worlds with their high resolution, constantly shifting panoramas. Well-appointed furnishings sourced from across the system gave an impression of refinement and wealth.

Miss Liddy sat behind a heavily inlaid wooden desk that by itself must have cost a fortune, and leaned back in a leather hover-chair of equal expense. A partially empty bottle of good brandy sat to one side of the desk, and Liddy cradled an antique crystal goblet that might have been worth a working man's wages for a year.

"Hello, Wyatt, Beth. Weren't expecting me, were you?" Liddy's triumphant grin made gloating redundant.

"Thanks, I think," Beth said, glancing between Liddy and Wyatt.

"You don't have to thank her," Wyatt growled. "We're going pay for it."

Beth shot him an annoyed glare. "Considering the alternatives, owing Liddy beats what the other guys had in mind for us."

"Are you sure?" Wyatt turned a withering look on Liddy. "All right. Now that we're in your debt, and I'm sure you have a credit value for exactly how much, what do you need us to do to work it off? Can't believe you took grief from other pirates."

Liddy laughed, a deep belly laugh that might have been as close to joy as the pirate leader ever came. "Always know right where I stand with you, Wyatt. I like that. It's a rare thing. And your new partner has manners. That's a nice change." She lingered a beat too long on the word "partner," enough to make implications, and Beth's eyes narrowed.

"Business partner," Beth snapped.

Laughter never left Liddy's eyes. "It's always business, child. Don't ever forget that and you'll be okay. Speaking of which, they didn't hurt you did they, Wyatt?"

"No, Liddy. Other than whatever they used to take us out."

"And I take shit from no one. You should know that. Galan and his crew aren't going to be causing problems for me or anyone else. I don't leave loose ends," Liddy responded; her raspy, whiskey voice making it sound even more final.

"So come on, spill," Wyatt said. "The sooner we know what we owe you, the sooner we can start paying it off. I suppose I owe you for taking out the pirates too."

"Always in a hurry to be on your way," Liddy reproved. "With everyone who's out for your blood, you might think of this as a little vacation. This far out into the Fringe, having people know you belong to me, however, temporarily, will make them think twice about trying to blow you out of the sky. You know I like that… Wyatt McCoy belonging to me…sort of has a nice ring to it. Don't you think, Wyatt?"

"Please, Liddy." Wyatt rubbed his temples. He felt a headache coming on. He bit back the response that immediately came to mind, knowing it would only make things worse—with Liddy and Beth.

Wyatt could feel the weight of Beth's stare. Then again, you'd have to be deaf or a fool not to pick up on Liddy's innuendo and the subtext of the conversation. He hoped Beth would just let it drop because he sure as hell didn't want to explain it.

"Relax," Liddy said, growing serious, although she still seemed to enjoy Wyatt's discomfort. "I have a couple of little jobs for you two. Nothing my boys couldn't handle, but I think you'll do it with a bit more flair and maybe a bit less blood. And consider the pirates a freebie. My contribution to bettering the cosmos."

"I always worry about the 'little' jobs, and nothing is ever free with you, Liddy," Wyatt said with a sidelong glance at Beth. She didn't look nearly as upset as he thought the situation warranted. Then again, she probably felt much safer in Liddy's custody than where they had started out, and he hoped she was right.

You're too used to flying solo, kid, Wyatt chided himself. *If you're gonna have a partner—business or otherwise, gonna have to start looking out for her.*

"The first job is a repo, pure and simple," Liddy said. Wyatt snorted at "pure" but said nothing. "Got a guy who bought a ship off of us and hasn't made the payments."

"A ship you stole in the first place?"

Liddy's eyes narrowed. "A deal's a deal. He still owes me, and he's behind on payments. Won't answer when I call. Hurts my feelings," she drawled. "So that's all I need you to do. Go out to the planet he's squatting on and get him to pay up or take back the ship from his good-for-nothing ass."

"How are we gonna fly two ships back?" Wyatt asked.

Beth cleared her throat and gave him a murderous look. "Two ships, two pilots. No problem."

Wyatt swore. "Great. Just great. Give me a choice between letting you fly the *Nellie B* and fly some hunk of junk we know nothing about? Just shoot me now."

"Don't tempt me," Beth replied. "Doesn't matter to me which ship; pretty sure I can handle either." She leaned back in her chair and met Liddy's gaze. "Just tell us where and when."

Liddy's lips quirked with a smile that might have been approval. "I've already sent the coordinates to the *Nellie B*." She looked to Wyatt. "Part of your debt is for buying that ship back for you. They could have gotten almost as much selling it as they'd have gotten for the two of you."

Wyatt felt his gut tighten at the thought. "Thanks," he croaked. "You mean to say you didn't get your funds returned before you took out the pirates?"

"Of course I did, plus interest. But it took time, resources, and my attention. That's why you aren't indebted to me for life."

Beth turned on Wyatt. "You thank her for saving the ship but not our lives?"

"Priorities, Beth. Priorities."

Beth gave him a look that told him the conversation was far from over, and he decided he was in no hurry for that discussion. "So tell us about the loser whose ship we're stealing," Wyatt replied, resigned to his fate.

He could see a glint in Liddy's eyes that told him she was enjoying this far too much.

"Cade Wallen is a thief, smuggler, and pirate—and bad at all of them," Liddy replied. "He's even tried being a bottom-of-the-barrel henchman and failed. Normally, I wouldn't have thought twice about selling a ship I…inherited…to a guy like Cade, but he had half the asking price in untraceable credits." Liddy gave a what-can-you-do shrug.

"He even made the payments, for a while. But it's been three months, and zilch. He still owes me a third of the price, and it's bad business to let that kind of thing ride. I can't set precedents. He either pays up or returns the ship."

"What makes you think he's still alive if he's that much of a fuck-up?"

"Because I checked on him." Liddy's eyes had gone cold and humorless. "His ship—*my* ship—has been spotted by some of my people, and they've seen him in a few of the seedier outposts, grubbing by selling Dose."

Wyatt raised an eyebrow. "You want us going after a Dose dealer with nothing to lose and take his ship?"

"*My* ship, unless he pays for it."

"Your ship, his gun," Wyatt countered. "Have you ever gone up against someone on Dose?" He shook his head. "Those guys lose it. That stuff blows away any self-preservation, makes them angry and violent as shit, doesn't even let them feel pain until they come down. Worse than fighting a rabid *thanatal*, and twice as mean."

"If it were easy, I'd already have it resolved," Liddy replied. "The problem is, Wallen has holed up on Drega 9. You know it?"

Wyatt frowned. "I know *of* it. I regularly consort with scum, and even I won't go to Drega 9. It's the kind of place scum think is scummy."

"Used to have a mining colony," Beth mused. "Wasn't an Interplan venture, it was an independent group, back when there was such a thing. It didn't last long. No one was sure why, whether Kalok and Interplan ran them out or they just couldn't manage it. Although there were some other theories."

"Save it," Wyatt said. "You can give me all the details on the way. We've got a long flight."

"My boys could go into Drega 9 guns blazing, and take care of Wallen, maybe even get the ship back in one piece," Liddy said. "And in the process, create an 'incident' that might make the official radar, even on Drega 9. I'd like to avoid that."

Beth snorted. "Wait. You're sending us because of Wyatt's diplomatic skills? Have you two actually met?"

Wyatt had the good grace to roll his eyes. "She's got a point, Liddy. That dust-up on Rum Row is more my style."

"And I know damn well you can be stealthy when it's worth it to you," Liddy snapped. "So you go in, get the money or the ship, come back. The condition you leave Wallen in is up to you, but if you kill him, don't leave evidence or witnesses, and preferably not enough of the body to identify. You see something you want to steal from him, go ahead, but it's not going to count against your debt to me. I've got plans for you two," she added with a grin that sent ice to Wyatt's blood.

"Anything else we ought to know before we're hip deep in shit?"

"I don't think you'll see much of Stellar Fed in that area, but don't go out of your way to get your faces on the vid feeds. The types you're likely to run into on Drega 9 make Galan and those pirates we dealt with look like beginners, so watch your backs."

"Go get some rest," Liddy added. "Your quarters—separate quarters—are down that way." She pointed. "Plan to head out tomorrow. Oh, and Wyatt, sometime you'll have to tell me what you did with the *Nellie B*'s A.I. My boys had a devil of a time getting her slaved. Always looking for new tips, you know."

Wyatt could have sworn Liddy hummed to herself as they left her office.

He turned as Beth punched him in the arm. "Let me make this clear. You get us killed on this job, and I will haunt your ass."

"You're the one who sees ghosts, not me. I'll never know."

"I'll throw things at your head. Move your stuff in your cabin. I'll put dents in the *Nellie B*."

Wyatt glared. "You wouldn't dare."

"Dead girls get really pissy. You don't want to find out."

"YOU EVER BEEN out this way?" Beth asked after they had taken off from Liddy's hideout.

"A time or two," Wyatt replied. "You?"

She shook her head. "Wanted to. There are rumors about ruins around here. There was a really old mining settlement on Drega 9."

He gave her a look. "You want to make a side trip?"

Beth grinned. "Can we?"

Wyatt gave an exaggerated sigh. He had been expecting the request from the time she said it used to be an independent mining colony, and he figured it wouldn't hurt to get on Beth's good side. "Yeah. Ought to do it before we go after Wallen. Figure we'll have to make a quick exit after we steal his ship."

"Steal it back," she corrected. "If he doesn't pay off the debt on it."

"Repo it for the person who bought it from the people who probably stole it in the first place," Wyatt clarified.

"You and Liddy have more history than you've shared…" Beth prompted.

"Yeah, none of it good."

"So am I crazy thinking she's hitting on you—or at least baiting you?"

"Crazy? Absolutely. But no, you're not wrong. She just likes freaking me out and keeping me off balance. I can swear to you that I have never, never done anything to encourage it."

"Well… I agree with her that you are sort of pretty. Guess it's good the pirates didn't sell us to the slavers," Beth teased.

"That is not fuckin' funny, Beth." Wyatt didn't like the look she gave him, and he realized he'd have to be very careful. She was too damned smart for her own good.

"Sorry, Wyatt. I didn't mean to upset you."

Wyatt grumbled in response and busied himself looking at the readouts.

They flew in companionable silence for a while, keeping an eye out for any other ships that might show an interest in them. To Wyatt's relief, they saw few other spacecraft.

"So tell me what you know about this colony," Wyatt said after the silence started getting to him.

Beth leaned back and stretched. "The company that planted them, Mining Interests Corporation, or MIC for short, was ahead of its time. This system was even more of a frontier then than it is now, but MIC wanted to stake its claim early on planets and asteroids that looked promising, and it figured that setting up self-sufficient homesteaders would hold their place until it became commercially viable to open the mines."

"So they sent out advance crews?"

Beth frowned. "Yes and no. They sent out teams that had the skills to set up a colony and map out the ore deposits, do some of the preliminary excavation work. But they also picked couples for the work, with the intention that they would be establishing a true colony, not just a beachhead. They intended for there to be families, and that these would be long-term investments."

"And then…"

"The official record gets vague," Beth replied drolly. "There's a lot of conjecture, very few facts. Communication transmissions way out here weren't as good as they are now, so these Far-Fringe colonies were really on their own, with only maybe an occasional cargo ship. No one thought much about not hearing from the colony, because no one was expecting to hear."

"And then someone did check in, and…?"

Beth nodded. "Yep. Everyone was gone, the colony was in ruins, and looked like it had been that way for a while. The official record says 'unknown cause' but the speculation at the time said they ran afoul of an alien culture that didn't like trespassers."

"What do you think?" Wyatt leaned back in the pilot's seat. He kept an eye on the screens, but it was hardly likely he was going to need to do any real work for a while.

"It could be aliens," Beth allowed. "Especially back when they first came to Drega 9, we had explored so little beyond the Rim. People just got a ship, did a geologic survey, and assumed that if they planted their flag, the planet was theirs. Sometimes, they found out that someone else was there first."

"Whatever happened to MIC?"

"They were one of the many small, early firms that got gobbled up as Kalok expanded," Beth replied.

"Do you know what they were trying to mine on Drega 9?"

"*Renium*. The original survey said there was a large deposit, very large. At the time, *renium* didn't have much value. No one had invented the core convertors that use it. That's why MIC wanted to stake its claim to the planet and put off developing the mines. They were gambling, in a sense, that the metal would end up being valuable."

"I thought *renium* was only available in trace amounts." Wyatt frowned. "And it's ungodly expensive. Why didn't Kalok develop Drega 9 if they knew?" He met Beth's gaze.

"According to the official record, the survey that found the *renium* deposits on Drega 9 was later invalidated. Said there was a problem with the scans used on the probe fly-by, that it was just an error in the survey."

"And without a motherlode of *renium*, the price remains sky-high," Wyatt said, shaking his head.

"Not that any of those things could possibly be connected." Beth's voice dripped sarcasm.

Wyatt stared out into the darkness for several moments before he spoke. "Even when we're running away, we keep getting sucked back into this, Beth. I came out here to forget the war, and to stay far away from Kalok. And now…"

"You don't have to do this. I'll fly the repossessed ship back, make a deal with Liddy, and you can go back to salvage."

He gave her a look. "It's too late for that. Kalok's already got me on their hit list. They don't know what I know, so they won't believe that I don't know everything. And Liddy won't let me go that easily."

"Amazingly, I followed that sentence. Your logic is astounding."

"I'm not joking around," Wyatt snapped. "Don't talk to me about walking away. Someone hired fucking bounty hunters, put a price on our heads. Stellar Fed is after us. Do you have any idea of the size of ship I'd have had to steal to rate attention from Stellar Fed?" His voice had risen in tone.

"Then decide whether you're in," Beth shouted back, "and quit bitching about it. Either walk away—I'm sure they'd pay you well if you gave them information on me—or man-up and see this through. Because those are the only options, and all this hand-wringing is going to get us both killed."

She was out of her seat and off the bridge before Wyatt thought of a suitably cutting reply.

"THAT'S IT? THAT'S what all the fuss was about?" Wyatt looked down at the scans as they did a fly-by over the ruins of the Drega 9 colony.

"There wasn't any fuss made," Beth replied. "That's part of the problem."

Wyatt had made sure to bring the *Nellie B* in for a landing while minimizing the likelihood that their presence would show up on any scanners. He had no idea how paranoid the locals were or what early warning systems they might have, but given the nature of Drega 9, he bet people here didn't want to be found. Wyatt didn't want to discover they were on the wrong side of mistaken identity, because he was sure Wallen wouldn't be the only one to have some way to tell when unwelcome visitors came calling. With luck, no one would care even if they did notice a ship landing on an unsettled area of the planet. After all, people on Drega 9 minded their own business.

"What are you looking for?" Wyatt asked as they emerged from the *Nellie B*. The atmosphere was breathable, though the air carried a strange scent and it felt heavy.

"I was hoping the implant might pick something up." Beth headed off through the weathered mounds of stone and rusting metal. Wyatt followed, gun in hand, watchful and worried.

"This looks like what I saw on Keller Station," Beth murmured.

"We don't know if the ruins have been plundered or tampered with over the years," Wyatt replied. "Wallen's not the only one to pick this rock to disappear."

Beth continued to pick her way through the old debris.

"Be careful—ruins are a great place to lie low," Wyatt warned.

Beth ignored him and kept going.

"If anyone's been poking around, it wasn't recently," she said after a few more minutes. "And it doesn't look as if it's been looted for building materials."

Wyatt wandered the silent ruins of the long-abandoned village, eying the crumbling walls and rubble-strewn streets. Whatever had happened here had been violent. Every building had collapsed in on itself or been blown apart. No one could look at what remained and doubt that the colony had come under attack. There was something about the destruction that nudged at the back of his brain telling him this looked familiar. "Anything?" he asked.

Beth shook her head. She stood a short distance from Wyatt, at the intersection of what used to be streets. "Not yet. But looking at the damage, I'd say it all happened at once. None of the rubble seems more weathered than the rest. From the way the metal is twisted and marked, it had to have gotten pretty hot."

"Unlikely they had anything that would have caused that kind of explosion. Even if their power plant blew, it wouldn't take out the whole settlement or have created this much heat—or leveled stone structures."

"Can you tell the angle of the force that did this?" she asked, meeting his gaze.

"That's a lot easier to say when the damage is fresh." Wyatt gestured futilely at the rubble. "It's been years, and we don't know if weather or vandalism moved things around." As he finished speaking, he felt a pang of guilt. He didn't want to admit it, but that nagging familiarity was getting stronger the more he looked around.

"Humor me."

Wyatt didn't like to fall back into what he thought of as "soldier brain." But it really didn't take effort, he just had to stop resisting, and his military training took over. When his life or ship was threatened, and he reacted as he had been trained, his instincts were as good as ever and just as deadly. When the situation went to hell, Wyatt could strategize with the best of them. He'd been top of his class, and real-life experience added knowledge that studying never could.

A pilot knew what an air strike looked like on the ground. It looked like the ruins around him. Wyatt swallowed hard. "They got hit from above, hard."

"How far above?"

"Does it matter?" He turned to Beth, wondering how much she could read in his face. "Whether whoever did this broke atmosphere, or did it from orbit, it ends the same. The people on the ground never had a chance. If the gods exist and were merciful, maybe they never saw it coming."

Beth's stricken expression changed rapidly to a pained gasp. She grabbed her left forearm, and Wyatt could see her eyes glaze over.

"Beth?"

Beth groaned and sank to her knees, clutching her arm against her chest. "Beth?" he repeated, but her green eyes were glassy, blown wide with fear, staring straight through him. Wyatt ran to catch her, and as soon as he made contact easing her to the ground, the vision hit him.

Beth screamed, her head fell back, and her eyes went wide as he was pulled in.

It looked like any other remote settlement, a combination of stone and mortar buildings along with the ever-present pre-fab structures. People talked and laughed as they went about their daily routine. From the angle of the sun, he'd guess it was midday. Then there was an odd thundering sound, and the villagers turned their eyes skyward, shielding from the glare with their hands to their foreheads. The laughter and conversation died, replaced by gasps and frightened chatter. A brilliant lance of light came down and then a loud explosion. The people screamed and ran for cover.

The column of light moved, and the structures in its path exploded or burned to ash. The sound was almost deafening, but Wyatt could still hear the screams. He watched in horror as the vision showed men, women, and children shrieking as their skin charred and clothing went up in flames, their hair lit like macabre candles. Some exploded, others turned to ash instantly. The keening wail sounded like a noise a human shouldn't be able to make; a sound Wyatt had hoped never to hear again.

He let go of Beth and crab-crawled backward until the vision released him, then took a moment to let his head clear and catch his breath.

Beth stopped screaming, and she stared off into the distance as her body continued to shake.

"Beth? Beth, are you with me?" Wyatt asked moving back to put his hand to her neck to check her pulse. No vision overwhelmed him, but her erratic heartbeat worried Wyatt. "Time to get out of here."

Wyatt lifted Beth; she sagged in his grip, her eyes still glassy, but she didn't resist as he pulled her over his shoulder into a rescue carry and headed back to the *Nellie B.*

"Nellie, open up for me." Wyatt held Beth over his shoulder, letting the decontamination process cycle, before entering and taking Beth to her cabin. He gently lay her on the bunk and stretched her out. The shaking had gotten better, now just tremors. She moaned, and her lips moved, and her eyes fluttered as if she were still caught in the vision.

"Nellie, close up and secure the ship," Wyatt called out as he ran to get a med kit. He found it in the locker and was glad he'd restocked before coming to Drega 9. He knelt by Beth and checked her pulse again. She had started sweating and had pulled her knees up in a fetal position. He pulled back the sleeve of her suit and the alien tech glowed a dull fiery orange under her skin. Wyatt couldn't tell if it was still doing something to Beth, but it wasn't sharing anything with him.

Wyatt smoothed the hair out of her eyes and wiped her tears. She wasn't gasping, but her breathing hitched like silent sobs. "We're going to talk about this when you wake up."

He opened the med kit and pulled out the hypo and the tranquilizer. He double-checked the dosage before placing it to Beth's neck and pulling the trigger. Her body relaxed, and she quieted almost immediately. He checked her pulse, which was returning to normal, and now, her breathing was deep and regular. Wyatt opened one of the compartments and grabbed a blanket, carefully tucking it around her.

"I imagine you'll rip me a new one when you wake up, but I couldn't let that go on," Wyatt gave a rueful smile. *Dr. Parker, my life has gotten really complicated since I met you.* He stood up and did one more check. He closed the med kit and took it back, securing it in the compartment before he opened another locker and began searching.

Wyatt pulled out a handheld scanner and checked the battery. "Good to go. Nellie, please extend the ramp; I'm going back out."

Wyatt stopped by Beth's cabin on his way and leaned in to make sure she was still okay. "Don't freak out. I'll be right back. I've got a theory I want to prove." He knew the drugs wouldn't wear off for hours, but if Beth had any awareness, he needed to let her know he wasn't abandoning her.

"Nellie. Please monitor Beth and if she wakes or there are any issues, let me know immediately." Wyatt keyed the airlock and stepped in, already dreading the next few minutes.

"Confirmed," Nellie responded.

He walked back to the ruins, his mood darkening with each step. *Damn the leaders and lowlifes who ordered this strike, damn the power-hungry bastards and greedy sons of bitches who profited from it and damn that alien tech for dragging us into this shithole of a mess.*

Holding the scanner brought back memories, most of them bad. Wyatt had liberated several useful pieces of military issue equipment when he left Star Corps, filing the necessary forms to attest that they had been lost in the line of duty, broken beyond repair, or sucked out a faulty airlock. Wyatt smirked. *Yeah, I always liked that one best.* The items he needed that he couldn't liberate, he'd purchased over the years, often getting better equipment than they used in the Corps.

He watched as the scanner processed, already knowing in his gut what it was likely to show him. The destructive energies of weapons left their power signature in the molecular structure of the rubble and debris left behind, unique as fingerprints and more indelible. The weapons manufacturers, terrorist groups, and even governments had spent fortunes trying to figure out how to hide or falsify that signature, but with no success.

The scanner gave a chirp as it began populating the data. There was a lot of information, but only a couple pieces that mattered to Wyatt: [*Power signature: Burton Weapons Group, registered to Stellar Federation*].

"Son of a bitch," Wyatt murmured. Of course, it proved nothing.

Knowing who manufactured a weapon or the registration of who owned it didn't mean they fired it. Weapons and even entire ships could be hijacked or stolen. The courts had ruled long ago that such details were acceptable as supporting data, but by itself, that information wasn't sufficient evidence to warrant an investigation.

So now what? Am I going to be a hero and join the cause? Because that worked out so well the last time. One more thing he knew that he wished he didn't. There wasn't enough rum in the universe to forget all that was in his head. Knowledge changed a person, with no way to go back to the way it was before. Innocence lost, illusions shattered, trusts broken that could be never be put back good as new.

Wyatt replaced the scanner in the locker; he'd already had Nellie withdraw the ramp and secure the ship. He figured they'd be here a while so had activated the shields and automated defenses.

He keyed the door to Beth's cabin and stepped inside. *Good, still out.* Wyatt sat on the deck next to the bunk. He checked her pulse while chiding himself that he could have just asked Nellie to do it and report to him.

"So, one more piece of evidence. Won't do much for us, but it's sort of impossible to miss the pattern. What do we do about it?" Wyatt didn't expect an answer. Beth would sleep for hours and Nellie would let him know if anything came in range.

Wyatt went to his cabin and grabbed a pillow and blanket. He returned to Beth's cabin and stretched out on the floor beside her bunk, giving her one more glance. *Damn, but she looked so peaceful in sleep. So pretty and almost fragile—misleading, considering the hellcat living under that soft skin.* Wyatt chuckled and closed his eyes.

Wyatt came awake quickly when he sensed Beth moving. He sat up and put his back to the bulkhead, giving himself a little distance.

"Hey," he whispered.

"God, what happened?" Beth rasped as she tried to sit up and thought better of it, laying her head back on the pillow.

"I was hoping you could tell me. You got a vision and then seemed to get stuck there. I had to tranq you."

"You what?" Even with a rasp and some coughing the tone was clear and Wyatt backed up a little more. "Wait…how'd I get here?"

"Carried you."

Beth tried sitting up again, this time successfully as she swung her legs over the side and turned a fiery gaze on Wyatt. She was quiet for a minute, long enough that Wyatt started to squirm.

"You okay?" he asked.

"Yeah, thanks." Beth ran her hands through her hair and gave him a questioning look.

"You aren't going to slug me?"

Beth laughed. "I'm sure that I should. There's probably a long list of things you've done to deserve it, but taking care of me isn't one of them. Thanks, really." Beth pulled her sleeve back, and Wyatt saw that the tech was dormant: no heat, no glow, nothing.

"I have no idea why. It never did that before. The vision kept repeating, over and over."

"I noticed. I saw it. Might as well tell you now. I went back and checked after I got you secured. While it's not legal proof, the blast signature was registered to Stellar Fed. We can assume that means Ka-lok put them up to it, but it also could have been for reasons of their own."

"The colonists were innocents."

"Yeah," Wyatt said as he stared at the deck. "So what do we do about it?"

"Wyatt?" Beth waited until he made eye contact before continuing. "What do you want to do about it?"

"Can't ignore it, but it proves nothing. I'm thinking we keep on going. Look for more tangible proof that we can get to your friends, the Coalition, or someone who can do something with it."

"Agreed. Don't we have a ship we're supposed to reclaim?" Beth asked.

"Yeah, you up to it?"

"I will be by the time you get us there."

Wyatt wasn't about to give Beth the satisfaction of knowing that he had tossed all night with bad dreams, worrying about her as he slept on the deck beside her bunk. He remembered her challenge, to go back to salvage and turn her in. Wyatt hoped she knew he would never consider turning in evidence against her to Kalok and Stellar Fed. That sat wrong with Wyatt in every way, regardless of how complicated his feelings for Beth had become. But whether she knew it or not—and he really hoped she didn't—the whole mess brought up a tangle of emotions Wyatt had wished would stay buried. And the longer he spent with Beth, the deeper she seemed to be dragging him in.

He should have known better. His luck just wasn't that good.

Wyatt had left the war as a decorated hero. He had posed for the pictures, then gone home and burned the ribbons and pawned the medals. Yes, he'd gotten the chance to fly, and been one of the best damn pilots in Star Corps. And when he had gone in, besotted with the chance for adventure and glory, believing in the Cause, it had been so easy to accept what he was told. He trusted in them and their mission.

Only later, when he had seen enough to ask questions, did he realize that so much—maybe all—of it had been lies. Rationalizations. He went from vague uneasiness to insomnia, to nightmares and flashbacks. Wyatt had thought he knew who the enemy was. But eventually, there were too many discrepancies, too many explanations that didn't hold together, too many evasions and half-truths. And even though he wanted to deny what was in front of him with every fiber of his being, even though accepting the truth of it threatened his sanity; in the end, only one conclusion remained.

He and the rest of the men and women from his unit, with whom he had fought and flown and who died for the Cause, had been used. Maybe it wasn't all of Star Corps, maybe it wasn't that pervasive, but he knew for his unit, and the truth was bitter.

Running away helped, at least a little.

Out in the *Nellie B*, Wyatt didn't have to think about the war, or the casualties, the lies, or the profiteering. Didn't have to dwell on the charred bodies and the smoking ruins. And if his salvage targets happened to target old company ships and colonies, well, there wasn't really anyone else to steal from out beyond the Rim. He always made sure to keep a low profile, no splashy takes or salvages, just enough to get by with a few comforts, but not on a scale that would attract the wrong kind of attention.

Until Comstock. Until Beth. He'd liked Beth from the moment she had opened her mouth to trade barbs with him, and pointed a statue at him in lieu of a gun. She was everything he had never realized he wanted, and so totally unlike the women he'd known that he felt like a tongue-tied schoolboy.

And she thought he'd let her fly off in a repossessed ship and take her chances alone.

That wasn't going to happen.

Wyatt had wrestled with the realization that he and Beth were in too deep to get out, at least until they could collect enough information and get it to people better suited to do something with it. Then, maybe, he could talk Beth into going back to salvage, perhaps on the Far-Fringe, where Kalok and Steller Fed didn't bother to patrol.

I've fought one War. I've buried my dead and got the scars to prove it. Isn't that enough? Haven't I already paid the price for a little peace, a little anonymity and maybe someone to go along for the ride?

Wyatt fired up Nellie and looked at the topographical maps to pick the best route. He was sure Wallen would have radar or perimeter warnings, so Wyatt would need every trick he remembered to trigger as few of them as possible.

CADE WALLEN TURNED out to be a sorry son of a bitch with a bad temper and worse judgment. He stood in the doorway of his small, dingy homestead dressed in a stained shirt and grubby pants. His graying hair fell long and greasy to his shoulders, and by his grizzled appearance, it didn't look like shaving had been a priority.

"Get off my land—off the whole damn planet!" he shouted and followed up his order with a few shots that hit just shy of where Wyatt stood, kicking up dirt. Wallen meant to miss him, and the implication clearly conveyed that the next shots would not.

"Not here for you. Just want your ship—or what you owe on it."

"You ain't gettin' my ship! Might as well put a shot between my eyes if you take it—abandon me way out here with no way of leaving."

He had a point, and Wyatt felt for him on that. Losing a ship on a rock like Drega 9 was like being stranded on an island without a boat. He didn't much like what little he knew about Wallen, but he could understand his desperation to hold onto his only lifeline. He watched closely for any of the tell-tale signs of Wallen being pumped up on Dose.

"Can you pay it off?" Wyatt yelled, keeping the fugitive's attention on him while Beth circled around. She had stayed out of sight, so with luck Wallen would assume Wyatt came alone, intending to slave his ship. As if Wyatt would put the *Nellie B* through that kind of indignity. "That's all Liddy cares about. Settle up, and I'll go away and no hard feelings."

Another shot, this one closer, assured Wyatt that hard feelings were going to be a given, no matter how this turned out.

"If I had the money, don't you think I'd have paid off that bitch and kept her from sending her dogs after me?"

Wyatt's eyed narrowed. He had been called far worse in his time, but he didn't much care for Wallen insulting his friends, even if Liddy herself wouldn't have taken offense.

"I think that people get busy. Forget to send payments. Life happens. I don't really want your ship, and neither does she. Give me the money, and we can all go our own way." Wyatt felt a tic beginning beneath one eye. "Customer service" wasn't one of his strong points. In the military, it hadn't been a necessity, and interactions in the salvage business tended to be brief and furtive.

A cold smile curled across Wallen's face. "How about I kill you, and take your ship and sell it back to Liddy? That'll more than cover what I owe her."

Wyatt's finger twitched on the trigger. Not only was that going too far, but he didn't put it past Wallen to do it.

"Not going to happen, loser." Beth's voice pitched low and lethal, came from behind Wallen as her gun pushed through greasy hair to press the muzzle against the hollow between skull and spine.

"Not nice sneaking up on a man," Wallen growled.

Beth snorted. "Good thing you're not one," she replied, bumping her gun against bone. "Now, drop your weapon, get down on your belly, and put your hands out to the side where I can see them."

Wallen threw his gun to the side with a curse and fell to his knees. "I can pay you."

Beth's booted foot gave his ass a shove, and he sprawled on the dirt.

"Don't shoot me! I can pay you. Just…don't take my ship." Stripped of his bravado, Wallen was just an angry, pathetic misfit.

"Start talking," Wyatt replied, cautiously moving closer. Beth brought a knee down on the small of Wallen's back and pushed her blaster between his shoulder blades

"Put your wrists together. Don't try anything. I get fits sometimes, can't control how I twitch," Beth drawled.

Wallen's curses were creative and obscene, but he complied. When his wrists were bound, Beth toed him over. "All right. Payment. You were saying?"

Wyatt watched Beth and felt an odd sense of pride unfurl. After the rough night and restless sleep marred by nightmares, Beth had stepped up without a hitch. Wyatt suspected that Beth would welcome the chance to redirect her anger over what the implant had revealed. Wallen remained oblivious to his heightened peril but had the good sense not to push.

"Been out to those creepy ruins on the other side. Found some good stuff that ought to be worth some credits. You can have it all; just leave me my ship."

Beth and Wyatt exchanged a glance. *Liddy did tell me I could steal little extra if I saw something I liked,* Wyatt thought.

"Show us what you've got, and we'll decide then," Wyatt replied.

Neither of them helped Wallen to his feet, standing to the side while the man managed to get up. He glared at them, then led them into his house.

Wyatt glanced around. The building was standard-issue prefab, the kind he'd seen on one-man outposts and hardscrabble colonies across the Fringe. Cheap, sturdy, and engineered to last for decades, barring a direct asteroid strike—or an assault from warships in orbit.

Wallen wasn't much of a housekeeper, but although cluttered, the house was cleaner than Wyatt expected. Computers, vid screens, and a library cube suggested Wallen might have more interests than stripping his weapons and keeping up the vegetable garden Wyatt had spotted behind the house.

Few personal mementos decorated the shelves, but Wyatt's attention was drawn to a commendation plaque and a faded holovid of a much younger Wallen in uniform receiving a medal from a grinning commanding officer. He looked back at their prisoner and took in the angry, beaten man in front of him.

"Let's see the relics you found," Wyatt said, keeping his voice stern. Beth glanced his way and raised an eyebrow. He shrugged in response and hoped that they could satisfy Liddy without leaving Wallen stranded.

Prefabs like Wallen's generally had only three or four rooms—a sitting and dining area, a small kitchen, and two bedrooms. From the look of it, Wallen lived alone and slept on the couch in the sitting room, which still held a pillow and blanket. He led them past the kitchen toward the two back rooms, now converted to storage.

Wallen glowered, but he took them into a room where crude metal shelves held a motley assortment of found items. "Ain't got much to do except wander," Wallen said. "Came out here intending to see to all my own needs or as much as I could. Grow most of my own vegetables, and I have some goats and chickens out back. What I can't make for myself, I do without, or I get what I need when I go into town."

"Town?" Beth asked.

Drega 9 didn't have any official residents, and most that were on planet weren't the type to set up shops. If Wallen was going off-planet, Drega 9 was remote even by Fringe standards, several day's flight from any stations or other settlements.

"Basker's Moon, mostly," Wallen replied. "Got a trading post there. Nothing fancy, but it has the essentials. I go in a couple of times a year." He looked from Beth to Wyatt. "I don't bother no one out here. I trade with a few of the locals for a lot of the day-to-day stuff."

Trading Dose? Who is he kidding? But…he seems fairly sane. Maybe he's just dealing and not using? Though, I'm not sure that counts as not bothering anyone else, Wyatt thought. Wallen wasn't Regiment, but Wyatt had the uncomfortable sense that their circumstances differed only by a matter of degree. A bad run of luck and he might have found himself in Wallen's shoes. He fought a shiver at the idea of anyone trying to take the *Nellie B* from him.

Wallen stood sullenly by the door to the room while Wyatt and Beth walked down between the shelves. Most of the "relics" were household goods from the former colonists which had survived the cataclysm. They might fetch enough credits to buy Wallen a drink or two, or some supplies he couldn't get in trade, but they wouldn't go far toward his debt to Liddy.

"Wyatt," Beth called quietly. He moved over where she stood and looked down at a short metal rod with a wide, flat end and strange glyphs inscribed on the handle. "It matches my…bracelet."

"Don't touch it; actually, don't touch anything," Wyatt whispered before turning to Wallen. "Where did you find this?" Wallen didn't have to move to know what piece he meant.

"Found that in the mountains, out beyond the ruins. There are some strange rock formations—looks like the rock melted and then got hard again. Damnedest thing. Found a few pieces out there—that's the biggest. You think it's worth something?"

Wyatt nodded. "Yeah, it's a start. Let's take those pieces—they didn't do anything when you touched them, did they?" He carefully picked up the alien artifacts making sure to keep them away from Beth.

Wallen shook his head. "Nope. 'Course, I poked at them with tools before I touched them myself, wondering if they'd turn on. Must be powered down. Bet someone could get them working again," he said, trying to sell them on the pieces' value.

"Maybe so," Beth murmured, moving on to the next bins.

Wyatt had nearly run out of containers when he saw the odd chunk of rock. "How about this?"

"Pretty, ain't it? Found that over by the mountains, too. Looked like whatever made the ruins hit there as well. Whole front side slid down in a big rock pile. But I found that just lying on the ground. Can't figure out what kind of ore that is, but something that shiny ought to be valuable, right?"

Could it be that Wallen didn't know about *renium*? Wyatt wondered. Then again, his ignorance seemed more likely than not. Wallen had likely picked Drega 9 because it was still far off the trade routes, unlikely to attract strangers.

"Got any more of it?" Wyatt asked, trying to sound nonchalant.

Wallen shook his head. "Nope. I looked all around, didn't see more big pieces, just little ones."

"We'll take it, and the odd scrap," Wyatt said. "That should settle you up with Liddy."

Wallen looked warily hopeful. "For real? I mean, that's good. Real good." He looked torn between relief at the possibility of not losing his ship and fear that Beth and Wyatt might figure out his trash wasn't worth the cost of his debt.

"I think I can persuade Liddy to accept this," Wyatt said, not wanting Wallen to think he was getting off easy. "It'll be close, but I think it'll be enough." He paused. "We're doing you a favor, taking your scrap instead of your ship. And I need a favor in return."

"Sure," Wallen said quickly before he closed down his expression to hide his relief. "I mean, it depends."

"You have a way to contact Liddy?"

Wallen nodded.

"Anybody else been by in the last while?"

"Not where I could see them," Wallen replied. "I don't watch the whole planet, but I've got some scanners that tell me if someone gets too close. Maybe you can tell me how you managed to get by them?"

"Just practice and too much time in bad situations. No tech involved. But it's good that you're being careful." Wyatt felt a sense that he owed this guy a little since they shared…history. "If anyone shows up looking for more of those odd pieces from the ruins or any more of those rocks, stay out of their way and let Liddy know."

"You think they will?" Wallen looked uneasy at the idea of having his privacy violated.

"We hope not," Beth said smoothly. "But we don't want you to get robbed. And if you do find more—of either the relics or the rocks—give Liddy the chance to make you an offer before you go to anyone else. I think she'll do right by you."

"Yeah, sure," Wallen replied, surprised anyone would care about the junk. "Just don't tell anyone else where you got them. I don't want strangers poking around."

"We won't say a word to anyone but Liddy," Wyatt swore truthfully.

Wyatt and Beth remained watchful as they finished up with Wallen and headed back to the *Nellie B*, just in case the man changed his mind or decided to double-cross them. When they were onboard without incident, Beth slouched into the co-pilot seat.

"Those alien tech pieces, and the 'melted rocks' he saw—there must have been a colony here, before the miners, who knows how long ago?"

Wyatt nodded. "Could be. Or it was part of the same attack. If they wanted to secure the planet, they might have taken out all signs of habitation. Do we need to secure the 'alien' items in something special or are you okay with me just putting them in one of the hidden compartments? I don't want them messing with your implant."

Beth shrugged. "No way to know unless they do. I'm not touching them. But maybe we can figure out what they are—assuming they aren't just bits and pieces that don't even go together."

"And that rock—"

"I know Liddy said you could steal a little extra, but that counts as robbing a man blind," Beth said, making no attempt to hide her disapproval.

"I saved his life," Wyatt snapped, angry that she had jumped to conclusions. "What would have happened if he'd gone to that trading post with his shiny rock? He might have sold it for a few credits, and then they'd have interrogated him about where he found it—and then he'd be as dead as those colonists." Wyatt shook his head. "It's proof that the *renium* survey data was likely correct. Whoever blew up the colony must have blasted the settlers' excavation site too, to make sure no one took up where they left off."

"The rock alone is worth more than five of his ships. He looked like he could use the money," Beth said, refusing to back down.

"I'll talk to Liddy," Wyatt replied evenly. "The way I see it, Wallen could use a job that doesn't make him leave home or rely on dealing Dose. Suppose Liddy made sure he got regular supplies, so he didn't have to go to the trading post and sell Dose and junk anymore—in exchange for digging around the site."

"You're thinking of starting a black market trade in *renium*? How long do you suppose it would take Kalok to figure out the source?"

"I'm thinking that a few grams at a time, in the right hands, might be just what Worm, the Coalition, and some of their friends might need to fund their activities," Wyatt said with a grin. "Revolutions are expensive."

CHAPTER NINE

"WHAT DO YOU mean, we still owe you?" Wyatt fumed. "The *renium* alone is worth more than Wallen's debt and the ransom you paid the pirates. And besides, you got that money back!"

Liddy tilted her chair and put her boots up on her desk. "Are you reneging, Wyatt? We had a deal." Her eyes narrowed, and the chill in her tone let Beth know Liddy wasn't kidding.

"You want us to spy for you again," Beth said. "It's not about the money."

Liddy gave a lazy, dangerous mile. "It's always about the money, hon. But in this case, information is worth its weight in gold…or *renium.*"

"What is it this time?" Wyatt sighed.

"I want you to do a salvage job for me," Liddy said. "A cargo ship went down on a little world called Logannis. Ever heard of it?"

"Should I?" Wyatt asked.

Liddy shrugged. "No reason. I want you to go get anything you can salvage of the cargo as well as whatever could be resold from the wreck itself, and bring it to me."

"What's the catch?" Beth asked, leaning against the wall. "If it was that easy, you'd have done it by now."

Liddy chuckled. "I like you. You're smart. Maybe you can keep Wyatt on track."

Wyatt glared, but said nothing.

"Truth is, we've had bigger things to chase, and all my crews were busy," Liddy said. "I didn't want to lose the cargo, but I didn't have the right people for the job. Now here you are, owing me some help, and salvage *experts* on top of it."

"Best this side of the Rim," Wyatt muttered.

"Anyone settled on Logannis?" Beth asked. "Research station, homesteaders, criminals?"

"Not as far as I know," Liddy replied. "Never heard there was. Be surprised if there were—it's off the main path—even by Fringe stand-ards."

"And once we're done, that's it," Wyatt clarified. "We've fulfilled our agreement, and we leave, free and clear?"

Liddy gave him a predatory grin. "Always a pleasure doing busi-ness with you, Wyatt—and with your new partner, too. I wouldn't want you to be strangers. Yes, this run clears your debt. But we work well together, Wyatt, and you know it. Even you have to admit that it's nice to have me at your back."

"It is when you're not poking me with the point of a blade. Some-how our 'joint ventures' are never simple."

Liddy let out a burst of laughter. "I really do like you, Wyatt. Some-times, you just need a little incentive to keep you moving."

"Yeah, incentive…let's get this over with," Wyatt said. "Download what you've got to Nellie and we'll leave in the morning."

"I THOUGHT LIDDY said Logannis was uninhabited." Beth frowned as she studied the readings from their fly-by of the planet. As Liddy had briefed them, the world sat far off the trade routes in an unremarkable solar system deep in Fringe space. By Beth's reckoning, the nearest colony of any size lay a week's flight away at normal interstellar speed, and the heavily trafficked space stations and trading outposts were farther than that.

"Maybe there's a research outpost she didn't realize had set up shop," Wyatt said. "From what your friends back on Keller Station said, there's always someone who thinks making a hop to a planet that's a little more remote than the one they're on will get them a better view."

Beth asked Nellie to analyze the data they'd picked up from the fly-by and initial surface scans. Her screen began filling with information. "Looks agricultural. Almost no tech energy signature."

"Homesteaders then," Wyatt postulated. "Squatters, more likely. Although if no one's legally claimed the planet, they aren't exactly trespassing." He stood and moved to the station where she was working and peered over her shoulder. "Any idea how many sentients and how close they are to the wreck?"

"The good news is that there are only about a hundred humanoid life signs," Beth replied. "I'm not counting the livestock."

"That's rather specie-ist of you," Wyatt chided. "Growing up, some of my best friends were cows."

Beth raised an eyebrow. "Really? I would have bet on sheep." She grinned at the glare Wyatt returned.

"The bad news is that they're close enough to the site they can't help but notice when we arrive."

"Shit. Any indication that they're armed?"

"Nellie, please run a scan for weapons' power signatures," Beth asked.

"No power signatures currently detected; however, if weapons are unarmed or deactivated, they will not be detectable."

"Thanks, Nelly. So…inconclusive, but unlikely—at least, not with anything that could hit us in orbit. On the ground—I'm quite sure they've got sidearms, maybe more. If they've got old-fashioned mechanical weapons, those wouldn't register either," Beth said.

"But they can still kill you," Wyatt grumbled an impressively creative string of profanity. "Damn Liddy," he ended his tirade. "This is all her fault. I guarantee she knows a lot more than she shared."

"Maybe not," Beth said, leaning back. "I don't think Wallens is the only guy out there who wants to put distance between himself and his enemies. And if those enemies include the corporations, guilds, or authorities, they have connections all over the Rim. People have been saying they've bought and paid for politicians on all the major planets and space stations. So if you want to get away from the system, you've got to drop off the grid."

"Could they do that?" Wyatt asked. "Is their homestead big enough to be self-sufficient? Because they're long gone from any supply outpost."

Beth looked at the information Nellie had provided and nodded. "If they knew what they were doing when they provisioned, and they've done things right since they set up housekeeping. Yeah, it's possible. Not saying they'd have all the comforts of home. Might be pretty rough, at least by most people's standards. But no worse than the pioneering outposts had it back in the day."

"Huh. Any way to make contact?"

Beth shook her head. "No identification beacon, no repeater message—nothing. Not warning us away, but not putting out the welcome mat, either."

"Nellie, can you determine if there are any radar signatures or scans originating from the planet?"

"Negative, Wyatt," Nellie responded.

"Well, damn." Wyatt grimaced. "Whatcha think? The ship's cargo belonged to Liddy. She's even got a bill of sale. So for once, we're not reclaiming stolen goods—or at least, these have been heavily laundered," he added with a grin. "I'm inclined to put down next to the wreck, keep a sharp eye out for visitors, and do a quick strip down, and get out. If we can do that in a couple of hours, they might be cautious enough that we get in and gone before they get up the nerve to engage with us."

"I like it," Beth said, closing down the screen and stretching. "But take some extra guns, because nothing ever goes that easy for us."

"I'd also suggest we go in full armor suits. They won't stop everything, but if they have weapons we don't know about, it still might save our lives."

"You sure Liddy's people repaired them?"

"Mine was repaired, and I checked it thoroughly. Yours is new, and yes, I trust Liddy's team to do that properly. If she wanted us dead, she'd have never let us leave with the *Nellie B.*"

"I hope you're right," Beth said as she opened the bridge hatch and headed to her cabin. As soon as she pulled on the new armored space suit, it was immediately apparent that it was an upgrade over what they'd salvaged for her. Not only did it fit perfectly, but she also noticed it didn't impede her movement. By the time Beth returned to the bridge, she found Wyatt had already changed and was bringing the ship out of orbit.

Wyatt set the *Nelly B* down for a gentle landing just after dark. It wasn't possible to be stealthy with a Space Corps gunship, but Wyatt did his best. To anyone nearby, the roar of the engines would still be louder than thunder and shake and rattle anything in a notable radius. Beth watched the data feed from Nellie's scans. "All clear," she said and rose from her seat. She grabbed her gun and a few other weapons from the bin near the door and followed Wyatt down the ramp.

"Nellie, secure the ship and set shields," Wyatt said into his mic.

They watched the hatch close and seal, then the ramp withdrew, and the ship took on a somewhat blurry appearance—like looking through a wave of heat.

They headed off in the direction of the wreckage. "That's the *Percheron*," Wyatt said, eyeing the ship. The name seemed fancy for the industrial grade freighter. Thousands of such ships flew the trade routes, unnoticed and uncelebrated, but indispensable to the existence of the space stations, colonies, outposts, and corporations that depended on them.

"Let's get going," Beth said and strode toward the freighter. "The sooner we're gone, the happier I'll be."

Wyatt lifted his arm and activated the portable scanner. "Electrical systems and power systems are down," he said. "It must have hit pretty hard to knock out everything. Those batteries last for years."

Beth shook her head. "If it had hit that hard, there wouldn't be enough left to salvage. Maybe it was already malfunctioning, and that's part of what made it crash."

"Maybe."

They moved closer, weapons ready. The dead ship remained dark and still.

"Son of a bitch," Wyatt muttered when they came around to the other side and found the entry hatch already open. "Either there were survivors, or someone beat us to this."

"Could be both," Beth replied. "Maybe that's why there are no energy readings. She's already been salvaged."

A quick walk through inside the *Percheron* revealed it to be a stripped hulk. The cargo, wiring, usable metal, and salvageable bits were all gone. Even the sections that had plasti-skin walls or coverings had been ripped open to show the bare bulkheads below.

"Looks like the colonists got here before we did," Beth said, wondering how Liddy would take the news. "Do you know what cargo she was carrying? Because if the colony could make use of it, there's probably nothing left to take back to Liddy."

"It sounded like a mixed bag to me," Wyatt said. "All of it contraband, though some items would be hotter than others. Caloran whiskey, fine Talladia tobacco—the real stuff, not the synth replacement—art and sculptures from a dozen different worlds—all of it predigital, and one of a kind."

"Since when is Liddy trading in luxury items?"

"Whatever sells."

"Doesn't sound like it's the kind of a thing a hardscrabble, no-tech squatter outpost might have use for," she replied.

"I imagine they've thrown some mighty fancy parties and thanked whatever gods they worship," Wyatt said. They made another thorough check of the ship but found nothing usable. Even the cushions in the cockpit chairs were gone. Reluctantly, they headed to the open hole on the *Percheron*, to make their way back to the *Nellie B* and figure out their next move.

"It doesn't add up. Though it's kinda funny, thinking about the colonists having themselves a good time on Liddy's whiskey," Wyatt added as they stepped outside.

"The whiskey wasn't as good as I expected."

Wyatt and Beth brought their weapons up, but the sound of other guns coming online and targeting made them freeze.

A man stood with his back to the moon so that his face was in shadow. A dozen other figures stood behind him. "Drop the weapons," the man said. "Nice and slow."

"We were just leaving," Wyatt said.

"Not now, you're not."

Wyatt and Beth exchanged a glance, then carefully placed their weapons on the ground and pushed them away.

"You get here in that ship over there?" the speaker asked.

"Yes and you can damn well keep your hands off her."

The speaker chuckled. "Not yours anymore, son. What comes here, stays here."

The newcomers herded Wyatt and Beth to the village. At this late hour, few onlookers were about to gawk at the strangers. The small group of men steered them into the pub, which was nearly empty of customers.

"Who are you?" The leader asked.

"I'm Beth, he's Wyatt," Beth replied. "Who are you?"

"Zigler," the speaker said. "No hurry for you to learn the other names. Why are you here?"

Wyatt looked Zigler in the eye. "The person who owned the cargo on that wreck hired us to recover it. I can show you the bill of sale. Just give us the goods, and we'll call it square. You can keep the wiring from the ship. Just give us those crates, and we'll forget we ever saw you."

Zigler scratched the back of his head. "Well see there, that's the problem. You have seen us. And you might tell someone."

"You're pretty far out of the trade routes," Beth said. "What made you come all the way out here?"

Zigler turned his attention to her as if trying to figure her out. "We got as far away as we could from everyone. Woulda gone farther, but didn't have the fuel. We don't want to be around when it all comes crashing down."

"When what crashes? The stars?" Wyatt replied incredulously.

Zigler shook his head. "The whole rotten system. It won't last much longer—corrupt to the core. We saw the omens and were willing to heed them. Which is why we take a dim view of outsiders finding out where we are."

Wyatt held up both hands, palms out, in a gesture of appeasement. "We weren't looking for you. If you hadn't kidnapped us, we wouldn't have bothered you. All we want is the cargo—to take to its rightful owner."

"Can't give you that," Zigler replied. "That ship crashed months ago, and we left it alone at first, in case someone came looking. When no one did, well, we figured it had gone so far off course nobody would come after it, and we took everything we could use. We're thrifty like that."

"And the good whiskey didn't motivate you at all, no doubt," Beth muttered.

"We're not thieves," Zigler snapped. "There's such a thing as salvage law."

Wyatt laughed. "If you know your law then you also know that a couple of months means nothing. The cargo and ship are still off limits. Listen, we're not blaming you," he said, doing his best to be conciliatory. "But now that the owner has surfaced, we'd be obliged if you could just return whatever you can and let us go on our way. We won't say a thing about your village."

One of the men behind Zigler gave a disbelieving snort. "Sure you won't."

"If we don't come back, the owner of the cargo will send someone else," Beth said. "They know where the wreck is located—that's how we got here. Only they'll come ready to face an enemy because we didn't return. That immediately tells them you're here and you're dangerous. Let us go, and we'll leave as friends. Friends who don't remember a thing about you."

Another man leaned over to whisper something to Zigler. He had a stocky build, and his cold, dark eyes flickered between Beth and Wyatt as if waiting for them to strike.

"You could be spies," Zigler said when the man finished.

"Yeah, we could be, but we aren't," Beth said. "We've got no love of Kalok or Interplan or Stellar Fed ourselves. Best thing that could happen would be to watch them crash and burn. Are you outlaws? Are they looking for you?"

As soon as she asked the question, Beth cursed her curiosity. The less she and Wyatt knew about these people, the more likely they were to be let go, though that opportunity appeared to be fading, regardless.

"We're not criminals," Zigler snapped. "We just wanted to live out our lives and raise our families safe from the coming cataclysm."

"Weren't you worried about just plunking down on a planet without knowing who owned it?" Wyatt asked. Apparently, he couldn't quite tamp down his curiosity, either. Or maybe, Beth thought, they had both figured they'd have to fight their way out, so they might as well gather some intel while they could.

"We found no other human life here," Zigler replied. "No traces that anyone from the planetary governments had laid claim. So in the homesteading tradition, we took this land for our own."

"No human life," Beth repeated slowly. "Were there…non-humans?" Expansion into new solar systems and onto new planets had a nasty history of ignoring life forms that got there first, especially if they weren't particularly humanoid.

"We found some ruins quite a distance from here, but whoever had lived there was long gone," Zigler said. "That's where we first landed, a place our computer told us could sustain life. When we saw the ruins, we chose a second spot—equally good—but on the other side of the mountains. Just in case."

"How long have you been here?" Wyatt asked. Beth knew the look in his eyes. Wyatt might be fishing for information to find a way out, but he was also a little envious of people who had managed to leave behind the sordid past.

"We've been on this world for nearly five standard years," Zigler said. To Beth and Wyatt's surprise, the man who had whispered to the leader emerged from the pub's kitchen with two plates of food and tankards of odd-smelling ale. Zigler chuckled when he noticed their reaction.

"We may have left civilization behind, but we are not uncivilized," he said, managing a wan smile. "You aren't in danger here."

"You just don't intend to let us leave."

Zigler's expression clouded. "I can't permit a danger to what we've built. But you could be happy here. Safe. You don't want to be out there when the cataclysm happens."

"You don't get it. As my partner explained, your best hope is letting us leave. Because you're guaranteed to be found and likely killed if we don't return," Wyatt said.

Beth could feel the tension. She agreed with Wyatt but thought Zigler might need some time to process, so leaned forward to break the staring match. "Tell me about what you think is going to happen."

Zigler looked confused for a moment at the shift, but his eyes lit up as he directed his attention to her. "I can hear in your voice that you're an educated woman," he said, and Wyatt frowned when the comment did not broaden to include him. "We aren't wild-eyed extremists. Many of those in the colony have university degrees in the sciences and medicine, technology and history. That's how we saw the signs that have foreshadowed every great empire—and what the corporations like Kalok and Interplan have built is, indeed, a modern empire."

"Are you expecting them to fall to an unknown enemy from outside?" Beth probed. "Overextend their resources? Create too high a density and become susceptible to disease and famine?"

Zigler's smile widened. "So you do understand. Good. Very good."

Beth sat back and crossed her arms. "Mr. Zigler. My field of study is space archeology. I do indeed understand your concerns about the expansion of the planetary governments. Wyatt and I share many of those worries. But why do you think that the collapse is imminent right now? To the casual observer, those groups you mentioned would appear to be at the height of their power."

"A small group of criminals might be able to keep their power over a city or a colony for a long time," Zigler replied, "so long as they didn't expand the scope of their operations beyond a size where rules could be enforced and monitored. But the farther the corporations and guilds colonize, the harder it becomes for them to rein in their people and hide what's really going on. We're not the only ones who have left the core worlds and headed for the Fringe to get out while we can."

He paused. "We found each other because we were all researching trends that worried us," Zigler went on. "So we started consulting with one another, and as our research—coming at the problems from different disciplines and methods—all pointed to a common conclusion, we decided that we had to take action in the only way we saw possible—to get our families and our knowledge as far from the collapse as possible and hope we could be the remnant that survived."

Beth paused to eat some of the food they'd offered and found she was hungrier than she thought. "Thank you; this is very good. Perhaps we could work out a trade; I have quite a bit of knowledge about alien technology. If you would show me what you salvaged from the ruins, I might be able to help you make use of it. And it would prove our intent to leave you in peace."

Zigler regarded her for a moment and left the table to speak quietly with two of his supporters. Beth and Wyatt took the opportunity to finish their meals. After a brief but vigorous exchange, he came back and sat down, looking back to Beth. "We'll be glad to show you what we found in the ruins, but I'm still not convinced that we can let you go. Perhaps if we sleep on the matter, we'll all have fresh ideas in the morning."

He looked from Beth to Wyatt. "You're together?"

Before Beth could say anything, Wyatt slipped his arm through hers. "Yes we are," he said smoothly. Partners in every way," he added with a grin and a glance that warned Beth to go along with the charade.

"Then we'll show you to your room," Zigler replied. "Please don't embarrass yourself or us by attempting to escape. I will post guards."

Wyatt and Beth fell silent on the walk to the room. Once they were inside, and the lock clicked ominously behind them, Wyatt stalked to the window, only to note the guards below.

"We're trapped. They can't get the *Nellie B*, but if I have her try to open fire on the village, it's just as likely that we'd be killed or the villagers will shoot us themselves."

Beth slouched into a chair, exhausted. "For now. Zigler doesn't want converts; he just doesn't want to endanger what they've got set up here. They're probably sure we're spies."

"Why would Kalok care about the likes of them?" Wyatt fumed.

Beth tapped her finger against the arm of the chair as she thought. "They wouldn't—if it were only Zigler and his followers. But what if he's right? What if people are packing up and heading as far away from the core as they can? That's bad for Kalok and Interplan—and the planetary governments—because those homesteaders aren't staying inside the Rim. They're going outside the corporations' control, and we already know that some of the Fringe worlds and the colonies out here are feeling kinda forgotten and put upon. It's a dangerous combination."

"You think they're onto something, about some kind of cataclysm?"

Beth thought, then shook her head. "Not in the way he's figuring. Academics run the kind of analysis he's talking about all the time. I'll spare you the details, but while those models have scholarly importance, if they really could predict the future, university professors would all be rich," she added with a smirk.

"What's more likely is that the guilds may also see trends that worry them—like an exodus of people beyond the Rim. So they'll crack down, send out more patrols, get hard-assed about the rules. And that's just like forbidding a teenager to do something," Beth said.

"It makes them want to do it even more," Wyatt added.

"Exactly. So it multiplies, more people want out, the trickle of people heading to the Fringe turns into a stream, and everything the corporations and guilds—and their pocket governments—do to stop it creates more reasons for people to leave."

"And then sooner or later, someone starts shooting, and it goes badly."

Beth nodded. "Yep. And that's where Zigler's right—empires keep making the same mistake and getting the same result."

Wyatt plunked himself down on the room's other chair. A bed sat in the center of the room, with a nightstand and a small desk the only other furnishings. "I figured if he thought we were a couple, he wouldn't split us up," Wyatt said, not meeting Beth's gaze. "Didn't think it was a good idea to be out of sight of each other."

"I figured. And I agree." Beth kept up the tapping as she thought. "I'd like to get him to show us those ruins—or at least, the pieces they brought back. If they're all in some storeroom, maybe you can look for the missing crates, and then if we figure a way out, you'll know where the loot is."

Wyatt leaned forward, resting his elbows on his knees. "The more I think about it, the more I'm sure Liddy set us up."

Beth raised an eyebrow. "She wanted us to get captured by doomsday colonists?"

He shook his head. "No. She wanted us to hear about the homesteaders and the number of people heading for the Fringe. I'm pretty sure she's recruiting us."

"I didn't figure Liddy for the reactionary type. She's too much of a businesswoman to go mushy for causes, however legitimate."

"If Liddy thought that shaking things up would make her money in the long run, she'd back whoever she figured could win," Wyatt replied, running a hand through his hair and rubbing the tense muscles in his neck. "Think about it—the more homesteaders, the more un-sanctioned colonies like this one, and they won't all be good at staying self-sufficient. They'll need trade, eventually. Liddy's people are al-ready out here, and with no love for Stellar Fed. If she bets on the right side in a fight, she wins the trade routes and the loyalty of the colonists. I also don't know all of Liddy's history. While I think greed is more likely, it's possible she's part of the movement."

"Does anyone do the right thing for the right reason anymore?" Beth lamented, pinching the bridge of her nose as she felt a headache coming on.

"Only fools and academics," Wyatt replied, but the trace of fond-ness in his voice softened the comment.

Beth shifted in the chair and let her head fall back. "I want to see those relics. If they're from the same culture as my implant, we might learn something. Maybe some of them can even be activated again."

"Because you had so much fun the last time that thing in your arm met up with a long-lost relative and knocked you cold," Wyatt re-torted.

Beth shrugged. "Nobody said research was fun. Zigler doesn't re-alize that they're already screwed for staying out of sight. I think Kalok is as interested in the alien tech as we are, and won't let anyone get in its way when it comes to collecting the left-behinds. Once they realize the ruins are here, they'll send a group after them—and it'll be just like the last time. Liddy knows about the cargo wreck. And while I don't completely trust her, she's not one to let any of her go-betweens vanish without paybacks. So it's going to come down to choosing sides. We've got to give him a reason to ally with us."

Wyatt and Beth shared the bed, keeping to their own sides. Wyatt seemed to fall asleep immediately, but Beth lay awake for a while, lis-tening to his even breathing, consumed by the thoughts and worries that ran deep and cold in the night.

A sharp knock at the door roused her, and she realized from the light coming through the window that she had slept past dawn.

"Breakfast is ready. Come soon if you want any," a voice called through the door.

Beth poked Wyatt in the shoulder, and he jerked awake. For an instant, his wide eyes held fear, but they shuttered quickly, and he groaned at the early hour. "Farmers need to learn to relax a little," he grumbled, running a hand over his eyes and down over the night's stubble.

"On your feet," Beth said, poking him again in the ribs. "I don't intend to miss breakfast. If we're captives, I want to be well-fed prisoners." She couldn't help but take a second look at her partner in the morning light. The dark stubble accentuated his face, and his thick hair was tousled, adding to the appeal. *Get a grip, Beth*, she told herself. *That man is too handsome for his own good.*

The guards at the door to their room stood aside as Beth and Wyatt headed toward the smell of cured meats, sausage, and fresh bread. A long table held heaping platters of favorite breakfast foods from many worlds. Two empty places remained, with at least twenty other colonists crowded around the table, enthusiastically eating or filling their plates. Beth and Wyatt went unnoticed as they slipped into chairs and helped themselves.

Zigler sat at one end of the table, like a proud papa. A glance that caught their gaze indicated he had seen them, but he made small talk with others and seemed content to ignore them. Beth tried to listen to the conversations around her without being too noticeable. Wyatt did not seem to care about anything but the content of his plate, which he refilled more than once.

To Beth's consternation, the discussions were unremarkable. Everyone else bantered as if they were far more awake than either Beth or Wyatt, exchanging jokes among people who were obviously very well acquainted. The rest of the comments were the day-to-day trivia of seeing to the affairs of the homestead. Beth had to grudgingly admit that while she and Wyatt might be prisoners, none of the others looked to be mistreated or acted as if they wished to be elsewhere.

"Stay," Zigler said when the rest of their tablemates had gone, and both Beth and Wyatt had nearly finished their food. The last couple of colonists caught Zigler's look and cleared out quickly, shutting the door behind them.

Zigler pushed his plate away and wiped his mouth. "I trust you slept well?"

Before Beth could answer, Wyatt laid his hand over hers and flashed his most charming smile. "Quite well. We don't get many chances to enjoy a night in the country."

Zigler returned the smile, but his eyes narrowed warily. "Still haven't made up my mind about you."

"Then spend the day with us," Beth said, jumping in before Wyatt could complicate matters. "Take us to see some of the alien objects you've found. Maybe I can help identify them." She smiled and hoped it looked genuine. "I'd love to see the ruins they came from, too." She hoped that if she proved her academic credentials, some of Zigler's suspicions of her being a spy would be put to rest.

Zigler frowned, and Beth felt certain he would refuse. Then his forehead smoothed, and his face lost its angry expression. She wondered if he had debated the matter with himself before coming to a decision.

"All right," he said. "And since I know it's what you'll be looking for anyway, I'll show you the cargo we unloaded from that wreck, too. As a gesture of goodwill."

"Thank you," Beth said, kicking Wyatt under the table to make sure he didn't cause problems. The innocent look he shot her didn't fool her.

"Come along then," Zigler said, pushing away from the table. "We can talk while we walk."

Zigler peppered them with questions as they headed for the store-house. Beth and Wyatt took turns responding. Both carefully answered the questions, but did not elaborate other than details about Beth's research and prior work. Zigler's interests ran from what they had heard of various political issues in the Rim and beyond, to the availability of new ship technology, to inquiries about Liddy and her gang that they handled with extreme care.

Their answers seemed to satisfy Zigler because he responded with an open, friendly ease that made Beth redouble her wariness. She reminded herself that Zigler held them prisoner, and even well-founded concerns about the volatile Rim politics did not justify holding them against their will.

"Here we are," Zigler said, leading them to a large storehouse. Its walls and rounded roof were constructed of poles holding up a skin of polymer sheeting—cheap, flexible, durable, lightweight, and easy to assemble—a common type of building found across the Rim and Fringe colonies for everything except houses and livestock barns, which were generally made from sturdier rock or wood if it was available.

The storehouse's walls and ceilings kept out the wind and elements while allowing light through—and remaining nearly as tough as the metal hull of the *Nellie B*. Beth and Wyatt followed Zigler into the large open space, neatly filled with rows of crates and cargo containers. "The stuff you want to see is over here," Zigler added, waving for them to follow him.

Beth glanced at the shipping containers as she passed, trying to make out any identifiable logos or handler's marks that might indicate manufacture, origin, or transport. What she saw suggested that the materials had been there for quite some time. If the colony did require outside supplies, those drops were apparently few and far between.

"These are the bins we took off the *Percheron*," Zigler said, laying a hand atop a pile of badly dented and scorched metal cargo boxes. "A lot of stuff in the hold got damaged in the crash. We still took everything, and what was too broken to use got melted down for scrap or repurposed. You don't waste anything, not in a place like this," he added.

Wyatt eyed the crates. Beth could guess his thoughts. There were too many of them, and they looked too heavy for him and Beth to be able to take away without being noticed. Stealing them back wasn't going to work.

"Liddy will understand about the ship, and the breakage," Wyatt said, returning his attention to Zigler. "But they're her goods, bought and paid for." He cleared his throat. "You know as well as I do that the original owner has the rights if they come looking."

"I don't much care about the contents," Zigler admitted. "Not much use to us here, and we don't go to the trading outposts more than we have to. I just don't like letting it be known out there what we've got here—word gets out, and next thing you know, we're beset by thieves and worse."

Wyatt looked ready to argue, but Beth elbowed him, and he shut his mouth. She was determined to make the most of Zigler's relative cooperation to see the ruins and the relics. They could fight about being able to leave later.

"What about the relics?" Beth prompted.

Zigler looked relieved to be spared an argument and nodded. "They're over here. We don't have any archeologists, but anyone who's settled a new world knows better than to muck around with strange alien items. Doesn't go well."

Beth found herself absently rubbing her right hand over her left forearm. Wyatt caught the movement and gave her a look. She gave a nearly imperceptible shake of her head to let him know nothing was wrong.

"Haven't caused us any problems so far," Zigler said, obviously assuming they were following close and listening.

"Have you noticed any activity with the relics?" Beth asked as Zigler removed a worn canvas that covered the pieces. She clasped both hands behind her back and bent over at the waist for a better look, making sure she did not accidentally touch any of the items.

"What kind of activity?" Zigler asked, a note of suspicion in his voice.

Beth shrugged, trying to make the question sound off-handed. Her forearm began to throb, dully at first and then much sharper and insistent. "Sounds, lights, movement—that sort of thing." She hoped her voice gave nothing away. Wyatt had picked up in the shift in her voice and watched her closely without appearing to do so, at least to anyone else.

"They give some of our folks the willies, but we haven't seen them do anything," Zigler replied.

"Then this should be a first." With that, Beth removed her glove and reached out to take hold of a thin metallic case with an odd paddle shape covered with alien runes. She felt the heat build in her arm, even though her suit hid the tell-tale glow. When she touched the case, its markings burst into a bright glow that matched what she saw so often under her own flesh.

"What the…?" Zigler stepped back, eyes wide with fear.

"Don't panic," Wyatt said. He stepped between Beth and Zigler and turned to look at Beth. "Tell me if you want me to share."

"What's it doing?" Zigler demanded, looking at Beth as if she might burst into flames. "What do you mean 'share?'"

"Nothing bad yet," Beth grated between clenched teeth ignoring Zigler's second question. Her eyes lost focus, and she stared at images only she could see.

A small building bustled with activity. Humanoid-appearing men and women regarded a bank of scientific equipment and view screens with concern, moving from one station to another, only pausing to confer in worried tones. Beth realized that this was different than her other visions—less of a stone tape and more like a holovid. The perspective stayed fixed as if it had been recorded, unlike the usual visions which moved and shifted.

One woman appeared to be in command of the room, a nexus everyone else connected to, reporting findings or drawing her over to one screen or another. From the set of the woman's jaw and her furrowed brow, the news was bad.

A man on the other side of the workstation shouted, and the rest came running. Beth found herself edging forward as if she were actually among the tense group of observers. From her vantage point, Beth made the images on several of the screens. At first, she thought it showed the heavens, but when a sequence of pictures flickered across the viewers, she realized she saw a weather map. A satellite map of a giant, brewing storm.

The commander gave curt orders in a language Beth didn't understand, and the others left their posts, rushing away to accomplish the tasks set out for them. The implant did not always give Beth the ability to hear or to translate what she heard, but in this case, she did not need words to know the danger.

Moving from one viewer to the next, the commander toggled something on her collar and talked, though she was alone now in the room. The pictures on the screens changed, and the large blot that represented the storm grew larger, an amorphous, shifting shape that took up most of the viewer.

The commander stared at the screen with a bereft expression, then walked back to the central console and pressed controls. She spoke to a microphone, and her whole body took on a formal posture, head raised, and shoulders back. Beth figured the woman was making an official—possibly final—report or alert to her superiors. Depending on the distance, by the time the transmission arrived, the colony might no longer exist.

She moved to another console and pressed controls that triggered alarm lights, and the way the woman winced, Beth felt and heard the piercing klaxon. The rigid posture left the woman, and her shoulders slumped. She blinked several times as if struggling to keep her emotions in check. Then she returned to the view screens, touched the control on her collar, and took up her monologue, conveying what she saw.

Beth saw what the long-ago alien commander witnessed. The storm moved impossibly fast, and from the shifting colors of the display, Beth guessed that it was picking up both speed and power. *The commander's face held cold resignation, the certainty that she would die at her post. Yet she did not falter, continuing to report, buying the others time with precious information.*

There was a loud crashing sound that made the commander flinch, and her head whipped from side to side, looking for the source of the noise. The building that housed the weather station looked much like the polymer-and-iron sheet warehouse; just another nondescript outpost prefab. As Beth watched, the whole building trembled around the commander, and the images on the screens fizzled to static and then took shape once more. The commander swallowed hard and kept talking, as the viewers struggled to hold the picture. Beth had the sinking feeling that the large, dark red image on the screen hung directly over the commander's location.

Another loud crash and ripping sound and the commander jumped again, startled. Wind whipped at her hair and uniform, in what had seconds ago been a sealed building. Sand and dust obscured the view, and the building's frame wobbled back and forth as pieces of the flexible sheeting tore away, making sails of the remaining construction material.

Viewers toppled as the wind tore apart the building and sent workstations tumbling in a loud roar. The commander held on with both hands to the remaining screen as the wind tried to rip it from her grasp. Her hair swirled in the wind's assault, and from her wide-legged stance, the storm's violence threatened to take her off her feet. The cords stood out in her neck as she screamed her last bits of precious information to those on the other end of the link, trying to be heard over the cacophony.

Something forced her attention skyward, even as the storm winds tore the screen from her hands. Beth glimpsed a large, dark shape seconds before it struck the commander and swept her away, and then the vision vanished.

When Beth came back to herself, she sat on the floor of the colony's storeroom, a distance from the table with its troublesome alien relics. The piece of equipment remained clutched in her hand, but its markings, like those on her arm, had gone dark. Zigler watched her from several feet away. His pallor and wide, frightened eyes suggested that her vision had put on quite a show. Wyatt was with her, his eyes wide with concern.

"You all right?" Wyatt asked, both hands on her shoulders to steady her. "You took a little side trip there for a few minutes."

"They got hit with a bad storm," Beth said when she could find her voice again.

"Who?" Zigler asked.

Beth shifted to look up at him over Wyatt's shoulder. "It's a long story, but I have an implant that lets me…link…to some alien technology. My bet is that this was some type of recording device. In this case, the outpost that was on this planet got hit with a really bad windstorm. I don't know how widespread the damage was, but it killed the woman I saw in the recording."

Zigler swore under his breath, frowning. "Seems like there's some important information you've been keeping to yourselves," he said.

Wyatt stood, putting himself between Beth and Zigler. "I doubt you've bared your soul to us, either. That device is need-to-know only," he added, making it sound official. "Instead of feeling left out because we didn't tell you all our secrets, maybe you should focus on whether there's a threat to your colony."

"What kind of threat?" Zigler shifted as if he expected a fight.

"A natural one," Beth replied, hating how shaky her voice sounded. "Your people haven't been here all that long, and I doubt anyone collected more than the bare minimum of data on this world because no one cared. You probably liked it that way. Less data, fewer people who might come poking around." As she caught her breath after the vision, her tone grew calmer, more professional and commanding.

"Which means you don't have a lot of weather data, do you?" Wyatt asked.

Zigler's silence provided all the answer they needed.

"I don't know whether that storm I saw was a one-time freak thing or part of a natural cycle—and neither do you," Beth continued, reaching out a hand for Wyatt to help her up. She dusted herself off and raised her chin in challenge. "I'd like to go see the ruins. Maybe I can tell what happened to the original colony—and try to keep it from happening to your people."

"How would that tell you anything? You expect to find more recording devices?" Zigler's tone suggested that Beth's reaction to an unseen threat had rattled him. "How do I know you're not just making this all up?"

Wyatt shrugged. "You don't. We could all just sit on our thumbs and wait to see what happens. But I can tell you that when Beth's implant has shown her things in the past, they've always been right. And when she gets a vision, it's because there's something important or some kind of danger. So personally, I want to see what she finds out at the ruins, so we don't all die like the last folks who lived here."

Zigler's expression made it clear that he was not fully convinced.

He touched his hand to his ear, activating a comm link. "You got anything strange on the scanners?" Zigler listened to the reply and nodded. "All right. Keep an eye on it. I want to know right away if it moves, got that?"

He disconnected and looked at Beth and Wyatt. "Bill says they've picked up something, but they're not sure what. The last time we scrambled because of a strange image, it ended up being a flock of some weird bird-things migrating."

"What's worse? Battening down for a killer storm and finding out it's only a flock of bird-things or assuming it's just a migration and getting scoured off the face of the planet?" Wyatt asked pleasantly.

Zigler glowered. "All right. Suit yourselves—it's quite a ways from here back to the ruins. Bring that thing along," he added, with a nod toward the sleek case still gripped in Beth's hand. "Just in case it turns back on again."

Wyatt looked up at the sky when they emerged from the storage building. "If you've got weather-tracking abilities, maybe it would be good to have them turned on, and people watching all the time."

Zigler slanted a look his way. "You think that just because she might have seen something that happened hundreds—maybe thousands—of years ago, it means the same thing is going to happen now?"

"I have no clue, but do you want to take the chance?"

As far as Beth could tell, the images she usually saw, thanks to the alien tech that hitched a ride on her arm, were just energy impressions, "stone tape" vibrations without sentience or personality. Yet their appearance had served as a warning or emerged to provide helpful information too many times for her to brush off the timing of the images as mere coincidence. While she felt grateful for the help, she distrusted anything she did not understand, and that included the freeloader under her skin. Still, if she got another vision at the ruins, then it meant they really were in danger.

"STOP THAT."

Beth looked up and frowned at Wyatt. "What?"

He rolled his eyes. "You've been fidgeting since we left the compound. Stop. It won't get us there any faster, and it's driving me nuts." Wyatt said playfully.

She grinned. "Sounds like a great reason to keep going." Her smile faded. "I'm nervous."

"You don't say," Wyatt drawled.

"Not helping." Beth turned to look out the window of the craft that skimmed across the planet's surface. "It's just got me on edge. Zigler admitted they didn't do exhaustive research before his whole clan…cult…family…moved here."

"Very few colonists do," Wyatt replied. "Even now, it's more of a wing-and-a-prayer kind of thing, especially for people who are willing to trade off the possibility of getting killed sometime and the certainty of getting killed now."

"Still," Beth said. "It seems so…reckless."

"You know, 'reckless' disappeared off our rear sensors about the time we blasted off of the Comstock," Wyatt said. "Or were you commenting because you know it when you see it?"

Despite her mood, Beth chuckled. "Point taken. And everything I learned in school told me people were just as reckless when it came to exploring new continents, long before they ever got to the stars."

"It's a gift," Wyatt said with a shrug. "One of those double-edged ones, but still—keeps life from getting too boring."

"I hope I'm wrong," Beth said quietly, surprised at how easily Wyatt could make her laugh. "I hope there's no connection, just an insight into what happened to another set of colonists a long time ago." She turned to Wyatt. "Because if it wasn't a fluke and might happen again, I don't think the colony was built to withstand the kind of storm I saw."

When they reached the ruins, Zigler's pilot set the craft down a distance away, earning Beth's approving smile. "We aren't archeologists, but we're not totally ignorant, either," he said as they debarked. "We knew enough to take care with how things were excavated, for history's sake and because collectors pay more for that sort of thing, assuming we ever sold the pieces."

Whatever his motives, Beth was grateful that the site had not been wrecked by careless digging. Beth paused on a slight rise, overlooking the excavations. From there, they could see the foundations of the buildings and in some cases, the way the walls had crumbled.

"If the culture that built the outpost used prefab materials like your storage building, there's little chance anything survived except as debris," Beth said, shielding her eyes against the suns. "So the actual settled area could have been much larger than where you've found ruins."

They slipped and slid their way down the hill, followed by a tumble of loose dirt and gravel, until they came to the first foundation outline.

"Looks like they built some structures from native stone and mud. Maybe they were too far out from the home world to supply, or maybe no one came looking for them," Beth said.

"We've done the same," Zigler said from behind. "Our ships could only carry so much, and with marriages and new children, we've grown. Needed more room."

Beth nodded and hunkered down for a good look at the ruins. Then she straightened, and moved from one foundation to another, before climbing a pile of rocks. When she climbed back down, her mouth set in a grim line.

"From the way the rock lies, I'd say the buildings were blown over."

"Stone walls?" Zigler countered, raising his eyebrows.

Beth nodded. "Look at how the debris fans out from one side. If the roofs had collapsed, the debris would be in the center. If they just fell down on their own over time, the pattern wouldn't be uniform. I also don't see unusual soot deposits, which tells me it wasn't a catastrophic fire."

"You think a windstorm wiped out a whole settlement?"

"Stranger things have happened," she replied. Beth glanced to Wyatt. "I'm going to try it," she said.

"Beth, if we need to convince him, maybe you should…"

"Yeah." Beth pulled off her gloves and slid them into the pouch at her belt then held out her hand to Zigler.

"Sometimes Beth can share the vision, but you have to be touching her. Brace yourself. It can be disorienting. I'll stand watch," Wyatt said.

Beth saw Wyatt watching her closely, and she took comfort in knowing he was ready to step in quickly if things went wrong. She knelt next to a well-preserved chunk of wall, continuing to hold Zigler's hand and placed her other hand on the foundation stone. She felt her implant flair to life under her suit.

"Holy shit!" Zigler exclaimed.

Beth and Zigler saw people who matched the appearance of the aliens she had seen in her previous vision. Hominid, humanoid, with a sallow skin tone and large, wide-set eyes. Not a race she could identify, though admittedly the farther out from the Fringe, the more unknowns. She realized that these might be the people who created the tech that now lived under her skin. She wondered what their home world looked like, how different their capital and major cities might appear from this remote outpost town. No matter that a civilization could send ships out to the stars, on its remotest outposts, it all came back to wood and stone, mud and water.

She found herself standing on a busy street corner, as people and hover vehicles rushed past her. They seemed at ease, going about their normal routines, without the frightened, wary look of people expecting calamity. Beth glanced at the sky overhead. Clouds hid the suns, but at least at the moment, it did not have the look of a sudden storm.

Beth returned her attention to the street level. As she had guessed, some of the buildings used high tech materials, and sections or entire structures had been prefabricated. Smaller secondary buildings and those more toward the outskirts had been built from stone, wood, and bricks the same strange color as the alien dirt on the hillsides.

She wished the vision would allow her to climb the stairway in a building for a better view, but nothing around her had substance. From a better vantage point, she might have been able to make sense of what remained in the ruins, placing it in a larger context. Beth forced herself to focus on what was going on around her. Presumably, the vision showed her what she saw for a reason. Back on the research station, she had seen the obliteration of an academic colony by orbiting warships. Now, she feared she might glimpse the worst that nature could do.

The vision froze and skipped like a bad video feed, and Beth had the feeling she was seeing a time lapse. *The suns changed position overhead, and the shadows lengthened. The wind picked up, gradually at first, and passers-by pulled their clothing close around them, averting their faces to keep the grit out of their eyes. Perhaps it had grown colder as well, she guessed from the tight-lipped expressions on the faces of those around her.*

The wind grew stronger, lifting debris from the sidewalk and street, churning in dust devils that swirled at the entrances to side streets. Beth shivered in sympathy, although she could not feel the chill. *Gusts of wind tore through the streets, their power magnified in the enclosed space, strong enough to force the pedestrians to lean hard into them to avoid being blown off their feet.*

The sky overhead had grown threateningly dark with green-gray clouds and savage bursts of lightning. Traffic thinned, and walkers sought shelter, as others glanced warily up and then doubled their pace. Beth wanted to scream at them to seek cover, to get below ground and stay there, but she knew they were only reflections and that their fate was already sealed.

As the sun set, the winds picked up again, gale force so that no one dared try to walk outside. Shutters and signs tore loose and spun away, along with anything else not firmly attached. Beth was grateful to be unaffected as pieces of building materials tore from their moorings and swept like scythe blades in the wind.

Beth's work as an archeologist had taken her to many climates, and she had survived severe weather on more than one occasion. She had taken shelter during blizzards and sandstorms, hurricanes and typhoons, meteor showers and gas eruptions. Once or twice, she had even escaped civil violence, with bombs and weapons going off around her. Nothing prepared her for the sights that unfolded now.

The sky had turned an unholy green-yellow, as the clouds overhead roiled and churned. The streets were deserted, and the winds buffeted the vehicles left parked along the sides, turning them over or tossing them end-over-end like children's toys. The pre-fabricated buildings shook and groaned. Lightweight, quick to assemble and adaptable, they had not been designed for extreme weather. They were the first to disintegrate under the relentless wind. The storm tore the buildings apart, drowning out the screams of those inside, flinging their bodies into the street and against the walls that were still standing, or just bearing their corpses away in its fury.

Even the more solidly built structures could not withstand the force. Roofing shingles tore away first, and then a monstrous gust tumbled the bricks and stones, ripping apart the soft, defenseless bodies inside until the wind stank of blood and droplets soaked the ruins.

In minutes, the destruction was over. The vibrant town Beth had glimpsed now lay in rubble, its residents battered by the winds or crushed beneath the fallen walls. She wondered if they had tracking systems, and if so, why they failed. Or had the storm come up so quickly advance warning would have been too brief to make a difference? And if it happened once, could it happen again?

The vision receded, leaving Beth and Zigler still standing amid the ruins. Wiping away tears with the back of her hand, Beth released Zigler. He stepped away and shook his head. They stood in silence for a moment as they struggled to regain their composure

"A huge storm came out of nowhere and killed them," Beth said to Wyatt, shaking her hair back from her face as she took a deep breath and tried to push the disturbing images from her mind. "It only took a few minutes, and everything was gone."

Wyatt glanced at Zigler. "You'd better get your people to—" The buzz of Zigler's communication link cut off the rest of Wyatt's sentence.

"What do you have," Zigler snapped at the person on the other end of the link. He still looked stunned from the vision. For all that he had argued against Beth's concerns, he seemed worried now. "Where? Well, fire on them, dammit. What do you mean?" He listened as the caller replied in a voice loud enough for Wyatt and Beth to pick up on the agitation even if they couldn't make out the words.

"I don't care!" Zigler thundered. "Keep them from landing. We'll be back as quickly as I can get there."

"Trouble?" Wyatt asked, cocking an eyebrow.

"Got two unregistered ships—probably thieves—in orbit. Can't figure out what they'd want here unless you led them to us," he said and glared at Wyatt.

"No one followed us," Wyatt replied. "Give us some credit— we're professionals." He frowned. "Anything else about the ships?" Beth knew that look on Wyatt's face; it meant trouble.

"The ships are a little bigger than yours, modified Class 4. No insignia, no call signals, no broadcast license."

"Those aren't thieves," Wyatt said, paling. "Those are press gangs. Slavers. They haven't come to steal your belongings. They want your people. We need to get back there now."

CHAPTER TEN

"SLAVERS?" ZIGLER ASKED as he struggled to keep up with Wyatt's pace. "What are press gangs?"

Wyatt didn't slow. "You wanted to be out in the Far-Fringe, away from Stellar Fed and Kalok. Can't blame you for that. But you're not the only ones who don't like having the law looking over their shoulders. You wanted peace and quiet. Other folks who come out this far want to do what they do without getting caught. Like slavers."

"Who's buying the slaves?" Beth asked, keeping up with him easily. Zigler looked flushed and out of breath, but he did not complain, and the look on his face conveyed his worry. They reached the skimmer, and Zigler quickly powered her up.

"Lots of people, unfortunately," Wyatt replied as they buckled in. "Everyone keeps forgetting that just because planets aren't part of Kalok or Interplan or the Stellar Federation, they still have people on them. They've got their own laws, or they bank on being out of reach of any law. Plenty of mines and factories and cargo ships out there need workers and don't much want to pay them. Press gangs make good money supplying warm bodies. Little colony like this, not much in the way of defenses, looks like easy pickings."

"Not my colony," Zigler said as he spun the craft around and headed back to their base.

"Then we'd better get back there, and I'm hoping you've got some firepower, or your people are in big trouble."

Tense silence filled the flight back. Zigler received updates, but those communications were short and to the point since no one knew whether the press gangs were listening. "You can? How far out is it?" Zigler wiped a hand over his face as he listened.

"All right. Start moving everyone and everything into the caves," Zigler replied. "Make sure they know it isn't a drill. Don't count on anything being left topside." The link squawked with a vocal protest. "Yes, I know they won't like it. Too bad." Zigler pinched the bridge of his nose and tipped his head back as if fighting a headache. "Now quit wasting time talking to me and get going!"

He shut off the link. Wyatt noted that Zigler had a white-knuckle grip on the controls. "A storm too?"

"As if the slavers weren't enough," Zigler spat.

"What kind of defenses do you have?" Wyatt asked, leaning back in his chair. "Anything that can hit a ship in orbit?"

Zigler gave him a sidelong glare. "We're farmers, not a military base. We've got handheld weapons—blasters and old-style projectile. The energy guns shoot farther, but they're terrible to recharge with the equipment we've got. The projectile guns don't have the range, but they don't need a recharge, and we can make our own ammo."

"Do you have anything that flies up in the air and goes boom?" Wyatt rephrased his question, straining for patience.

"Fireworks," Zigler said, and Wyatt looked at him with surprise. Zigler shrugged. "They were part of the cargo on the *Percheron*."

"It's a start," Wyatt said, thinking that Liddy wouldn't miss them. "What else?"

"Not exactly what you asked for, but we've got one low-atmo flyer rigged to spread feed or fertilizer over the crops," Zigler went on. "If we filled it with dirt, it could put up a big cloud, hide what's going on below for a bit."

"If your dirt has the right minerals in it that might even fuzz the slavers' readings," Beth added, and Wyatt knew from her expression she was hoping he was on to something.

"Okay, that's good. How far are the caves from the village?"

Zigler grinned. "Not far. Right under us. Been using them for storage and they've got underground water in them, so they're like an emergency cistern."

Wyatt nodded. "Better. How far away are the coming storms?"

Zigler's grin faltered. "Not far enough. We've got a couple of hours—maybe less."

"Can your people get me a visual of the press gang ships?" Wyatt asked.

Zigler spoke into his link, and grainy photos came up on the skimmer's vid screen. Wyatt studied them intently, chewing on his lip. He triggered his bio-comm. "Nellie, please scan inbound ships and send data to my comm unit. Activate defenses and power up."

Zigler gave a questioning look to Wyatt. "Nellie?"

"My ship," Wyatt responded absently while he looked at the data then up at the skimmer's screen again. "Those ships aren't just modified, they're heavily bastardized," he said. "The slavers put their money into their engines and their front shielding. Engines for a quick getaway, and front shielding so they can fend off attacks by anything non-military and still land. They don't put as much into the rear shielding because they don't intend to leave anyone alive behind to shoot at them on the way out."

"What good does that do us?" Zigler's tense expression told him that despite their differences, the man was hoping Wyatt saw a solution.

"If you can distract their attention long enough for us to get our ship up, I can come behind them and do some damage," Wyatt replied.

"We might not be able to hold both of them off head-to-head, but my guns will put some nice holes in those engines if I can get them before they see us coming."

"How do I know you won't just leave?" Zigler asked, eyes narrowing.

"I'm a man of my word."

"Maybe Beth stays with us until you come back."

Beth crossed her arms. "You want our help? We go together. That's the deal. It will take both of us to bring them down."

Zigler didn't look happy about it, but he finally nodded. "All right. But I keep that damn cargo until you get back."

"Fine with me; more weight cuts down on maneuverability," Wyatt said. "But when this is over, assuming we're not all dead, we get the cargo, then Beth and I leave."

"You holding us for ransom?"

Wyatt shook his head. "Just stating my terms. Do we have a deal?"

"Yes, dammit. You'd be too big of a pain in the ass to keep anyhow."

Wyatt grinned. "Now we've got an understanding."

In just the time it had taken to come back from the ruins, the residents had made good progress moving children, livestock, supplies, and belongings into the caves. The colonists formed human chains, passing items from hand to hand to cover the distance quickly. Others shuttled wagons from buildings farther out, trying to save as much as they could before the storms came.

"Get that duster filled with dirt and ready to fly," Zigler ordered, and two men ran to comply. "You two—find those fireworks and set them up. Nothing fires until I give the order."

The link squawked again, and Zigler's brows drew together. "All right," he said into the mic, "it's going to be close." He turned to Wyatt and Beth. "Best do what you're going to do. The storm's getting closer, and the chatter we're picking up from the ships overhead sounds like they intend to get in and out before the storm hits."

"Get your distraction going," Wyatt said with a wolfish smile. "It's time to have some fun."

Zigler ran toward the fireworks and the duster ships.

Wyatt triggered his comm. "Open up for us Nellie, Beth and I are coming on board."

Beth hurried to match Wyatt's pace toward the *Nellie B.* "You're serious, you think this is fun?" she said as she strode up the ramp and through the outer hatch opening before her.

"Yep."

"You mean to take on those two slaver ships?"

"Chalk it up to an old grudge."

Once on the bridge, they dropped into their seats and started verifying that the *Nellie B* was ready. They heard the clangs and thumps as the ship sealed and withdrew the ramp and the thrusters heated.

"Old grudge? There are two of them and one of us, and they've sized this up as easy pickings, so they aren't going to give up quickly."

Wyatt's hands moved across the familiar controls as he spoke. "That's where you're wrong. Slavers and press gangs are cowards. They grab drunks and homeless people and snatch up farmers because they can't fight back. So we're going to make this 'easy' job very expensive. If they're smart, they'll turn tail and run. But, given that they haven't spotted or taken our ship into account, I'm not wagering on strong intelligence. They're relying on scans, not visuals."

"And what if they don't run?"

Wyatt shrugged. "Then we have some *real* fun." He waited until the fireworks began to explode and the dusters sent up their heavy cloud of dirt before lifting off, taking the *Nellie B* in the opposite direction, hoping the slavers' attention would be on the strange spectacle.

"Hang on, and handle the aft guns; Nellie will give you targeting information," he said as the ship tore free of the atmosphere and looped into position, coming in hot.

The first slaver ship took the brunt of the hits, and Wyatt let out a howl of glee as their shots ripped up the engines. Beth's grin turned feral as Wyatt dove and dipped, evading the second press gang ship as it belatedly realized the colonists had a defender.

"Shit, those are some damned big guns for that ship," Wyatt muttered, taking a hard roll to evade shots that were too close for comfort. The first ship lacked maneuverability, but its forward guns still posed a danger if Wyatt crossed their line of fire. He knew the ships had been modified, but weapons like that didn't come cheap.

"Now what?"

"Look for an opening and shoot them," Wyatt replied, coming out of the roll firing, then making a steep dive as he tried to get behind the less damaged of the press gang ships. The *Nellie B's* klaxons screamed as sensors registered hits.

"Nellie, report!" Wyatt called out.

"Damage to shielding, some sensor arrays inoperable. Currently, not life-threatening," her voice responded.

"So, nothing serious—yet," Beth said looking at the data rolling across the sidebar of her targeting screen. "Let's keep it that way."

"Fine by me." Wyatt set his jaw and fired a barrage at the front ship, then swung round to strafe the side of the rear craft. Tendrils of atmosphere snaked from the breaks in the ship's hull. Wyatt skimmed above the ship and then underneath, loosing another volley of fire. He knew the other slave ship dared not shoot while so close to their companion, but they had shifted position to get a good shot as soon as Wyatt came into range.

"They're waiting," Beth warned, taking the chance to send more shots into the damaged craft, which now moved erratically with debris floating in its wake. Wyatt knew they both wanted to see the slave ships destroyed, even if they hadn't said it out loud.

"Then they're going to be disappointed." Wyatt slung the *Nellie B* around and fired his thrusters, close enough that the force of his exhaust nudged the derelict craft toward its companion. The other ship failed to get out of the way.

"Fire at will," Wyatt growled, rolling the *Nellie B* onto her back, so the guns had a good shot at the remaining slave ship's underside, and Beth's aim held true. The ship sped clear, dodging their return fire as the sensors registered another hit.

"Nice flying," she said, though her expression suggested that some of the maneuvers had gone hard on her stomach.

"Nice shooting," he replied, as he pulled the *Nellie B* back and waited. The derelict ship had hit the prow of the second ship broadside. The craft appeared to be stuck together, though the less damaged one unloaded its guns into the wreck in a vain attempt to knock it clear.

Wyatt moved in for the kill, coming up behind the slavers and taking out the maneuvering ship's engines with a few well-placed, close-range shots. Explosions lit the surface of the second craft. The tangled ships hung in space, drifting slowly toward the planet as gravity caught them until they burned up or crashed.

"They're done," Wyatt announced, pulling the *Nellie B* out to a safe distance and leaning back with a satisfied sigh. "I got their transmitters, so no one will be riding to the rescue."

"Can't think of a better way to send slavers packing to the afterlife." Wyatt watched the ships for another minute, waiting for the questions he knew Beth was dying to ask.

"Old grudge?"

Wyatt looked out the vid screen for a while without answering. "Yeah. Couple of years ago. Ran into slavers at one of the dodgier space stations," he replied, his voice flat. "I got away. Some of my friends didn't." He took a deep breath. "Played hide and seek with press gangs on some other jobs. Nothing I could do about them then except to stay out of their way, but they took good people, and no one seemed to care."

"These won't take any more good people," Beth replied.

Wyatt met her gaze. "Damn straight." He touched the controls, bringing them into position to return to the colony.

"You meant it? We're going back?" Beth stared at him. "Wyatt— they weren't going to let us go."

"We still need that cargo if we're going to pay Liddy off," Wyatt reminded her. "And Zigler already agreed. Besides, we can't just leave them to that storm. We'll need to make sure the *Nellie B* stays clear, but I can't just let them die if we could have helped." He nodded toward the screen as Nellie supplied images of the encroaching storm and Beth caught her breath as she realized what she saw.

A huge, roiling storm front shrouded the area where the colony had been not long before. Wyatt read the sensor report, lips pressed together at the grim data. "I hope like fuck they got below, because that's no normal storm."

"No, it isn't," Beth agreed and shivered. Wyatt guessed she remembered the visions, and it was too easy to transpose that outcome onto Zigler's stubborn little settlement.

"We can't land in that," she remarked.

Wyatt shook his head. "So we'll ride it out, and then go down for a look. Get Liddy's cargo, and give them whatever assistance we can. Maybe we can send back help."

"You think Zigler would allow that?"

Wyatt frowned. "I think your visions scared him," he replied. "I got the feeling he wants what's best for his people. Might not agree with him on what that is, but I don't think he's a maniac."

Beth's gave a weak smile. "No, just an academic."

The storm passed as quickly as it came, but Wyatt waited before heading down, just in case it shifted its path. When the storm finally dissipated, he set a return course. Their scanners revealed the damage long before they had visual confirmation.

"Shit," Wyatt murmured, as Beth cursed under her breath.

Zigler's settlement was gone.

They set the *Nellie B* down near where they had been before, but closer to the cave entrances. Wyatt and Beth emerged warily, well-armed in case his read of Zigler proved wrong. They'd scanned the area thoroughly to make sure the storm didn't carry anything unexpected or, worse, leave something nasty in its wake. Nellie had cleared it but recommended they wear helmets just in case.

Nothing stirred. After the destruction wrought by the winds, it felt wrong for the air to be so utterly still. Their suits confirmed that the air was good.

"You think they made it?" Beth murmured, her voice through the suit sounding oddly metallic.

"Hope so. Scanners couldn't get a good fix below ground. Let's go make sure they didn't get trapped somehow."

They made their way carefully across the fresh ruins that looked so much like those from long ago. There was no trace of pole and polymer sheet structures, while the footprint of stone and brick buildings remained, along with toppled piles of debris and mounds of dirt carried and dropped by the winds. Eerie silence replaced the lively sounds of the settlers and the noise of their frantic preparations for catastrophe.

Beth eyed the land with a professional's appraisal. "Over here," she said, heading off and leaving Wyatt to follow her. "I'm betting that the cave entrances would have come up in this direction."

Wyatt and Beth stood in the wreckage of what had been one of the main gathering halls. Bits of construction materials littered the ground as well as dented and damaged possessions that had not been essential enough to take below.

"All that work, for nothing," Wyatt said, kicking at a teapot. It clanged against the stones, too loud in the silence.

"I wonder how many times something like this happens, and no one ever hears about it?" Beth eyed the ridge behind the settlement, looking for a clue to the colonists' whereabouts. "It's not the fault of the colonists—it's not like anyone can keep telescopes trained on every planet in the galaxy. Who would have recorded the data and how would it have been shared? Not the aliens—they died. This far out, it took a while before anyone decided to set down roots here again."

"And they would have died, too, if you hadn't warned them."

Beth shrugged, and Wyatt could see she was still ambivalent about the implant and its visions. "I guess. Or they would have been taken by the slavers. Going to be easier for them to watch for the storms than for press gangs."

"If you want safety, don't go to the frontier." Wyatt paused as his boots struck a metal panel buried in the dirt. He brought his heel down and heard a hollow sound. Wyatt grinned and met Beth's gaze, then hammered his mag boot down several more times in a rhythm that no one would mistake for natural.

Two sharp bangs came in response. Wyatt stamped his foot again twice, then started to brush away the dirt that covered the metal door. Beth knelt next to him and helped dig out the panel. The metal door lifted, the remaining dirt falling aside. Zigler and another man pushed the door the rest of the way open and squinted into the bright daylight. They looked weary, sweaty, and dirty.

One by one, the surviving colonists climbed up from the caves. Down below, Wyatt heard voices, footsteps, and the sounds of pets and livestock echoing in the dimly lit caverns.

"You got below all right?" Wyatt asked as Zigler turned to help others from the caves.

"Most of us." Zigler looked away. "I told them to let things be, to get to cover. Some of the folks tried to bring one more load, and the storm just came in so fast." His voice caught.

Beth and Wyatt watched the colonists as they emerged to find their settlement scoured from the surface of the planet. Homes, crops, barns, everything gone.

Some collapsed and burst into tears. Others clutched the person nearest them. A few stood perfectly still, pale and silent, staring in utter shock.

"What will you do now?" Beth asked.

Wyatt looked around for some way to be of help. In normal circumstances, it would have been easy to give the survivors a cup of water, a chair or a blanket. All those comforts were still in the caves. Only the harsh reality of destruction awaited topside.

"I hoped you might be able to send some supply ships our way," Zigler replied. "We've got enough down in the caves to tide us over for a while. We'd put emergency rations and supplies down there before we ever knew about the storms, figuring this planet might hold a surprise or two. We can get by for a while, but it'd be a whole lot more comfortable if we could buy some supplies to move things along quicker." He paused, then looked up sharply. "We can pay. Just so you know."

"Never doubted it," Wyatt replied. "I'll call some people I trust, get you what you need." He had planned to do that anyhow if Zigler had been too stubborn to ask. Wyatt looked at the devastated faces of the colonists as they veered between shock that they had survived and grief for all that had been lost.

"We got that damn cargo of yours down below," Zigler said, not bothering to look back at Wyatt and Beth. "In case you did come back. So you can take it—on one condition?"

Wyatt stilled, giving him a wary look. "What?"

"Send word to Miss Liddy. Tell her that if the rebellion that's a' brewin' needs a waystation, we'll do what we can to help."

"I thought you didn't want to be part of anything out there," Beth replied with a vague gesture toward the sky and the stars beyond.

"A man can change his mind," Zigler said, with an expression that dared her to argue.

"Absolutely right," Wyatt agreed, hoping Zigler wouldn't change his mind again about letting them leave with the cargo. "Come on, Beth. We've got a delivery to make."

Chapter Eleven

"Shit, damn!" Wyatt growled, slewing the *Nellie B* to dodge gunfire.

Beth handled the aft and side guns, while Wyatt let Nellie handle the forward port canons and he put his concentration into keeping them alive. Nellie was good but too predictable for dogfight maneuvers.

Should have known those press gang ships were too few to have been out here on their own. The slaver mothership was the size of a cargo vessel, with bays to hold the smaller craft used to make stealth strikes to unwary planets. From the way the larger ship moved, its engines had been heavily modified, a necessity for making a quick exit.

"We can't fight, not like this. If we hadn't taken damage…" Wyatt made the repairs he could manage before they left Zigler's colony, but the patches would only get them as far as the next outpost. He might not like to admit it, but the scuffle with the press gang ships had done some harm, even if he and Beth had ultimately gained the upper hand.

"I don't think we get a choice." Beth's voice took on the strained note that told him she was holding it together out of sheer anger at their attackers.

"Keep shooting. I'll figure it out." The mothership likely knew the *Nellie B* had taken out the two smaller ships, so the slavers would be looking for revenge, and a damaged *Nellie B* couldn't outrun them. Wyatt already knew they'd be screwed in a straight fight. No nearby outposts or space stations offered easy refuge.

"Let's see how bad they want to get us," Wyatt muttered, putting on a burst of speed even as he steered an erratic course to miss the majority of the slavers' shots. The *Nellie B* shook and groaned as the shields protested the hits he couldn't dodge, and warning alerts updated him on the damage he didn't dare pause to fix.

Their course required the mothership to come around, costing them seconds of delay. Wyatt pressed for all the speed he could safely ask of the *Nellie B*, and a little bit more. Zigler's outpost had been in Far-Fringe territory, outside of the main trade routes. Still, plenty of cargo vessels and other spacecraft traveled this area. "I'm going to try to get us into the shipping lanes; they can't afford to keep up this assault with all those witnesses."

"I hope you're right," Beth replied. They'd gotten ahead of the press gang mothership, and for the moment, the attack broke off. She glanced up at the sensors. "They're still behind us, and closing."

"Need a few more seconds," Wyatt said between gritted teeth.

A hard jolt slammed him against his restraining harness as the slaver ship got in a strike, and a new klaxon joined the others. The *Nellie B* pitched and rolled as Wyatt did his damnedest to make them hard to hit. Shots flashed past a sensor, blindingly bright.

"No, no, no! I've gotta see!" Wyatt shouted, cursing as he dodged to compensate. Sure, he could put the ship on autopilot, but Nellie's evasive maneuvers were no match for the second-to-second calculations and inspirations of a seasoned pilot when it came to a hot fight. So he needed to see, and he wondered as first one screen then another blinked on and off, momentarily overloaded, whether the slavers were intentionally trying to get him to wreck.

If so, they didn't know who they were up against. Wyatt McCoy wasn't ready to give up yet.

"Almost there," he muttered and pushed the *Nellie B* for every last bit of speed she could muster. He heard the engines strain. A shot clipped them, and the ship lurched, throwing them painfully against their harnesses. Wyatt kept a death grip on his controls, eyes fixed on a streaming glow that grew brighter the closer they got.

"Yes!" He shouted as the *Nellie B* shot up into a stream of vagabond ships of every size and configuration. Warning lights flashed and voices shouted insults in a variety of languages over the comm, cursing them for disrupting traffic and narrowly avoiding collisions with almost a dozen craft. Wyatt slowed and leveled off as the torrent of abuse poured from the comm. He grinned and answered silently with an obscene gesture.

"I don't care what they call me, as long as that damned ganger ship doesn't follow," he said, anxiously scanning his readouts.

"I don't see them," Beth replied, doing the same on her side. She kept her weapon controls hot, just in case, but as they matched the speed of the traffic around them; neither could see either the mothership or the smaller craft.

After a cautious wait, Wyatt finally unbuckled and rose, silencing alarms and warning bells as he moved around the cockpit, sparing an anxious glance at the diagnostic report the ship's internal scans was already compiling.

"That was closer than I'd have liked," he said and ran a hand over the stubble on his chin. "Nellie, please do a complete diagnostic and damage assessment."

"What now?" Beth asked.

Wyatt didn't answer right away. He waited until he had read and re-read the data Nellie streamed to his console, while Beth kept a lookout for trouble. Then he disappeared to scout some of the damage for himself. Finally, he trotted back and plunked down into his chair.

"Well, it could be worse. We're not completely screwed."

"Good to hear," Beth said, flashing a fake perky smile. "Now, how bad is it?"

Wyatt winced as if the damage to the *Nellie B* were his own physical injury. "I pushed her hard to get us into traffic. That didn't do good things, on top of the damage we'd already taken. We won't get up to top speed again without repairs. Don't have enough fuel to get back to Liddy, either. Jump engines are still off-line. Some of the systems will auto repair, but that takes time."

"So…" Beth let the word drag out.

"If I reckon right, there's a mechanic near here who's Regiment, out on Huck's Folly," Wyatt said, asking Nellie to pull up star charts and paging through them with a flick of his fingers. "There's an out-post there, too—black market, but they sell the genuine articles, not cheap fakes—so any parts or supplies we buy should be safe enough."

"Will *we* be safe enough?" Beth asked, swiveling to look at him.

"Safer than here," Wyatt added, refusing to meet her gaze. "John's Regiment—he won't give us up to anyone. If he's anything like he used to be, he's got a network that can get us whatever we need—and they hear everything worth hearing."

Beth frowned, watching him in silence for a while. "You're torn about the Regiment." She didn't make it a question.

Wyatt grimaced, shrugging as if he could physically evade the question. "John's a good guy. He'll take care of us."

"That wasn't what I asked." Beth leaned forward, resting her elbows on her knees. "Everything I've heard about the Coalition tells me it's full of people like me—academics, scholars, researchers, scientists—who found out something inconvenient or caught on to secrets they weren't supposed to uncover. I'm fascinated. I want to find them—not just because they might have information we need about Kalok, but because they sound like my kind of people."

"Which I'm not?" Wyatt said.

"I think we've established that you and I make a fine salvage team," Beth replied. "But I doubt we'll share the same taste in books." She folded one leg under her in the chair and shifted so that she could see Wyatt's face. "My point is, why do you keep your distance from the Regiment when you've got so much in common? I'd think they'd be people who felt like home, no matter where you went."

Wyatt stared at the vid screen for a long while in silence before he answered. "That's the problem. They do." He turned to meet her gaze with an aggressive intensity. "Not everyone wants to go home."

To Wyatt's relief, Beth let the matter drop. For now. He had no doubt that she'd resume her questions later. It was what made her a damn fine researcher. And while he wasn't in a mood to care and share, the longer he worked with Beth, the less he minded her knowing a little more about his background, just as he became more curious about hers. *Not going to be able to hide much, if I keep dragging her into every Regiment port in the Fringe.*

HUCK'S FOLLY HAD just enough atmosphere, gravity, and arable land to make it sustainably habitable, but not enough of anything to make a man rich. Wyatt didn't know what disillusioned cynic named the world, but the bitter moniker stuck, and the planet seemed to attract those who held disappointment at bay with low expectations.

"Bit of a dust bowl, isn't it?" Beth mused, wrapping a scarf around her hair to keep it from tangling in the wind.

"No one comes out here looking for gardens," Wyatt returned. He had already connected with John, so they were expected. The conversation had been warm enough to make Wyatt comfortable setting down for repairs, but not enthusiastic. Then again, he'd never known John to get too excited about anything, good or bad. He slipped a gun into his belt under his jacket, and escorted Beth off the *Nellie B.* This time; they had to forego the armored suits. Wyatt didn't think it would go over well with John and he didn't want to trigger any unpleasant memories.

"Wyatt! You're a long way from the Rim!" John Bellant stood a little taller than Wyatt and bulkier overall; not fat, just hard muscle and a lot of it. His black hair had some gray around the temples, and his tanned face showed fine lines around his eyes, but otherwise, the years had gone easy on him.

"I'm just passing through. You live here, so what does that say about you?" Wyatt returned with a friendly shoulder punch. He stepped back. "John, this is my business partner, Beth. Beth, this is John, the best damn mechanic in the Regiment."

John's smile broadened, as wide and genuine as Wyatt remembered. "Maybe I should deny that, but I've never liked to lie," he joked. "Why don't you show me what you did to the old girl this time, and I'll give you a reasonably exorbitant price for fixing it."

Beth fell in step beside Wyatt as they walked back to the *Nellie B*. Wyatt knew Beth's silence meant she had gone into what he thought of as "researcher mode," and she would hold her questions until later. Oddly enough, knowing that she was judging John for herself and watching for details made him feel more comfortable reconnecting with his old acquaintance. Time could change a man, and although Wyatt didn't like to think that about John, he'd been disappointed before.

"Shit, Wyatt, what did you get yourself into?" John made a slow circle around the *Nellie B*. He looked at the carbon scoring, the places where the press gang ships' weapons had torn into the outer hull, and let out a low whistle. "Fighting your own private war?" He raised an eyebrow.

Wyatt shrugged. "Why change now?"

John smirked at the comment, and Wyatt knew from Beth's eyes that she read a long, unspoken shared history wrapped in few words. She'd probably get it out of him eventually, and he only hoped that when she did, she'd still stick around. Tempting fate and looting salvage wrecks was unexpectedly more fun with company.

"We ran a job for Miss Liddy and got to a colony world just ahead of a bad storm and a press gang," Wyatt replied. "Fought the slavers off only to run into the mothership, and we did the only thing we could—ran like the Feds were after us."

"And are they?" John didn't look up as he asked the question.

"Maybe. Would it matter?" Wyatt's chin rose defensively.

John shook his head, still examining the damage. "No. We're Regiment. Fuck the Feds. Just had to ask, that's all."

"How bad?" Wyatt asked, shoving his hands in his pockets nervously, partly worried about the price, and partly because of the old memories seeing one of his old squadron dredged up, assuring a rough night's rest.

John named a price. Wyatt nodded and tried not to wince. He knew John wasn't gouging, but it would wipe out a chunk of his reserve cash.

"Do it," Wyatt replied. "We need some supplies, too. That outpost still here?"

John nodded. "Sure is. I can loan you a speeder to get there. Take your time; you've given me a nice challenge here," he said, thumping his hand against the *Nellie B's* hull. "It'll take me a few days to put this right. I got a spare room in the back you're welcome to, 'cuz I don't think you'll want to stay on the ship with me banging around at all hours. You can clean up, and I've got a med kit. Looks like you got thrown around a bit."

Wyatt opened his mouth to protest that they weren't a couple, but Beth just smiled. "Thank you," she replied. "That's gracious of you."

"Hold on. You tell Nellie I'd be muckin' around in her innards? Last time, she nearly fried me."

"Not to worry. Yes, she knows, and I put her on standby."

"Standby? Shit. She only goes off-line when she wants to; you know that, don't you?" John said with a serious look.

"You're safe, honest. We'll get cleaned up and head in for some supplies."

John laughed and jerked a thumb toward a beat-up land craft parked next to his shop. "You won't have trouble finding the outpost—go west, and there's nothing else between here and there. Come back before too late, and I'll take you to the roadhouse—it's a Regiment gathering place. Good food, decent whiskey, and plenty of scuttlebutt."

"Count on it," Wyatt said, knowing his smile didn't completely reach his eyes. "Let me unload a box or two from the cargo hold for us to sell off, and we'll get out of your hair." Other than the crates that had to go back to Liddy, they didn't have much. Just what they'd left as a ruse. Fortunately, they'd had several successful runs, even with the close calls, and Liddy had given them a good cut of what their last job brought in. Once they delivered Liddy's cargo, Wyatt resolved to work a few more jobs to build up their reserves; insurrectionists, and Stellar Fed be damned.

Beth didn't say anything until after they'd cleaned up and were in the speeder heading for the outpost. "You think we'll get decent money for that?" She asked.

"It's good salvage, and some of the pieces are hard to find," Wyatt replied. "Probably not top price like we'd have gotten on Rum Row, but we're unlikely to end up in prison, so there's that."

"You're not too excited about going to the roadhouse."

Wyatt saw nothing to be gained by lying. "I'm loyal to the Regiment and the guys I served with mean a lot to me. But I didn't mind leaving the Corps behind, and I don't like thinking about the war."

"They say you were a hero." Beth's voice was quiet.

Wyatt turned. "Don't believe everything you hear."

"I don't. So I did my own research when I was back on Keller Station. Medals, commendations. Same for the rest of your squadron."

"Did it also tell you how many Regiment folks we lose every year by their own hand?" Wyatt asked, with an intensity in his eyes that made Beth back up a step. "Did you read the part where we drink too much or can't sleep a full night or end up on the wrong side of the law?"

"Wyatt, I'm—"

"Don't say you're sorry!" Wyatt snapped. "I was proud of my service until I realized companies like Kalok were calling the shots. How Interplan operates. They have a stranglehold, and I helped them keep it. Coming back from the fight messes you up enough. Finding out it was all a pack of lies makes it worse." He turned away and stalked off toward the marketplace, not bothering to see if Beth kept up.

After a brisk few blocks, Wyatt slowed, then stopped. He turned back to Beth and managed a chagrined smile. "I'm sorry. It's just, being back around John and thinking about meeting up with more Regiment folks, it makes the past a little too close."

"Apology accepted," Beth said with a grin. "Come on. Let's get the supplies so we can be done in time for dinner. I don't know about you, but I'm starving."

The marketplace sprawled across a mix of tables, wagons, and sheds that served as shops. Booths filled with goods of dubious legality from across the Fringe and the Rim enticed buyers, and the sellers called out with promises of special bargains. Beth took the lead, with Wyatt following a half-step behind to watch her back.

She certainly knew how to work this crowd, he thought. She joked with the merchants, switching between languages, and restrained herself from drawing a knife when the banter became flirtatious, turning their interest—and their underestimation of her skills—to her advantage. Wyatt hung back, appraising the crowd.

"…been worse lately," a passer-by noted to his companion.

"…what do you expect? Hardly an accident," the speaker's friend replied.

Frowning, Wyatt listened more closely to the buzz of conversation around him. He had picked up key phrases in the languages heard most near the Rim, but his only fluency lay in cursing. He'd have to leave it to Beth to eavesdrop on anyone not speaking Common, or the patois of borrowed words favored by fences, snitches, and thieves throughout Far Space.

"…getting bolder, because they know nobody's going to do anything about it."

"…you know who's behind it, which is why it isn't going to stop."

Beth moved on to another merchant's table, handing the purchases back for Wyatt to carry. Despite the good deals, he might have balked at that, but the bits and pieces of information he kept picking up made it well worth some dented pride. That, and the significant amount of money Beth was saving with her shrewd bargaining and outrageous flattery.

"…the bombings. You know what people are saying."

"…I'm telling you, those are false flag attacks. And we all know who benefits if they have to step in and take over."

"Are you ready?" Beth roused Wyatt from his concentration. She looked bemused and a little perplexed. "You know, bodyguards aren't supposed to daydream on the job."

Wyatt shook off his intent focus and gave a rueful chuckle. "Well, that's what you get for going with cheap help." He steered her away from the merchants and a few feet away from the press of the crowd. "Something's up. Everyone's talking, but no one's giving details—"

"Because everyone else already knows what happened," Beth finished. "Yeah, I heard bits and pieces too, but I couldn't focus on that and barter."

"I did a little better, but maybe we can get more of the story at the roadhouse tonight."

"So you decided to go?" Beth asked.

"If you go along with me. Figure you can be the one to eavesdrop and pick up what's happening."

They headed back to John's shop and followed the noise of his machinery to find him in his coveralls at work on the *Nellie B*. When he spotted them, he turned off his tools, took off his protective gear, and headed over to greet them. "Find what you needed in the market?"

"This is what we could carry. The rest is getting delivered here. Beth worked her magic and got us some good deals. How's it going? Nellie give you any grief?"

John grinned. "She's a fine lady. I've got some work ahead of me, but it's coming along. I should be able to get you out of here pretty close to when I promised. And she's left me in peace, but thanks for asking."

"That's great," Wyatt said, surprised at the flush of relief that ran through him. "Dinner soon?"

John wiped his forearm across his sweaty brow. "Yeah. Let me get cleaned up and we can head over to the roadhouse."

"I heard some things in the market I need to understand," Wyatt said. "Sounds like there's trouble brewing."

John's expression darkened. "There's always trouble brewing. Let's talk at the roadhouse. I'll tell you what I know—and I'm sure we'll find some folks there who can fill in the gaps."

While John got ready, Wyatt made his own examination of the repairs and the remaining damage. Beth busied herself at one of the consoles, picking up what she could from the news services and boards. She turned to greet Wyatt when he came on board.

"There's a lot of chatter on the underground channels the folks on Keller Station showed me," Beth said. "Just like what you heard in the market—it's like coming in on a conversation in the middle. Everyone else knows the whole story, and I'm just getting the punchline. But from what I can make out, the dissident networks like the Coalition are really worried—more than usual—that Kalok's about to make a big move. Exactly what that move is, that's the part I'm missing. But it's buzzing out there about how far into Fringe space to go, how to stay off the grid. It's a panic."

Wyatt plopped down in the pilot's chair and looked absently at the darkened screens. "You think it's more than just another conspiracy theory?"

Beth shrugged. "No way to tell without more details, but people don't pull up stakes and head off to the unsettled reaches on a whim."

"Might explain why we ran into so many craft in the shipping lane out here—although that saved our asses with the press gangs," Wyatt mused.

"About that. I tapped into one of the uncensored news feeds the Coalition favors. Apparently, there've been a lot of disappearances lately," Beth replied. "Small passenger carriers going missing without a trace. Not the ones with the big commercial lines, the small cheap ships people who can't afford a comfortable ticket squeeze into to get where they're going."

"People who wouldn't be missed as easily."

Beth nodded. "Yeah. And there've been reports of small colonies and outposts going silent—nobody can raise them on comms. People are worried."

"I'm sure the press gang we ran into isn't the only one working out here."

"Uh huh. And the rest of the news is just as disturbing. The free colonies near the Rim have always been pretty vocal about their independence from Kalok and Interplan. There've been rumors about Kalok getting handsy, wanting to expand its territory. The free colonies protested. And lately, some of the protests are turning violent."

"One of the people I heard in the market mentioned a bombing. You think it might be related?"

"Could be," Beth said. "And that doesn't bode well. Because either the free planets have a problem with anarchists, or someone is making an effort to cause problems."

A chirp on Wyatt's comm signaled that John was ready. Wyatt stood and stretched. "Too many questions, not enough answers. Let's see what John can tell us—and what we hear from the rest of the Regiment."

The smell of roasted meat and decent beer greeted them when they followed John into The Last Ditch roadhouse. From the greeting called out by the bartender and the men and women at the tables, he was a regular. John led Beth and Wyatt to the bar, then left to make the rounds of the room, trading jokes, clapping shoulders, and shaking hands.

Wyatt glanced around, relieved that none of the faces looked more than vaguely familiar. He had questions for John, but no desire to relive old times with anyone else. Then again, Regiment members this far out on the Fringe probably shared his aversion to playing by the rules. He reminded himself that the Regiment included those who served before and after his time, so membership alone didn't guarantee recognition. Still, just being here made the past press too insistently against the present, and he would be happy to be on their way once repairs were finished.

By the time John returned, Wyatt and Beth had drinks, and John led them to a relatively quiet table near the back. They made small talk as they placed their order, and Wyatt tried not to fidget. John looked up at him. "Still as twitchy as ever, I see," he said. "All right. Spit it out. You're making me nervous just watching you try not to bring it up."

Wyatt clasped his hands and leaned on his elbows. "There was talk in the market about a bombing—and maybe a false flag attack. And I got the impression we weren't the only ones who might have run into press gangs."

John let out a long breath and ran his hands back through his hair. "You know right where to find the shit to step in, don't you, Burner? Just like always." They fell silent as the server brought their food, and John leaned back.

"Word on the street is that Kalok and Interplan want to expand beyond the Rim."

"The worlds just beyond the Rim have been pretty vocal about not wanting any part of that," Beth said. She turned her attention to the plate and tucked in.

John nodded. "Yep. It's been a big, loud argument for years now. But it's gotten worse lately since it seems like Kalok means to make a move soon. So there have been demonstrations, protests, speeches, on the out-worlds. Peaceful, at first. But lately, there's been trouble. Violence. Riots. Bombs."

"And people think Kalok's behind it?"

John shrugged. "It would work in their favor if the governments were destabilized. Then Kalok and Interplan could swoop in and take them over 'for their own good.'"

Beth muttered a curse. "Yeah, that sounds like them."

"And the press gangs?"

John knocked back his drink and ordered another. "There've always been slavers that prey on vulnerable ships and isolated colonies. It's a risk of being out in the Big Black Beyond. But the reports of the press gangs have ticked up lately—except not in the official news."

"So either they're rumors, or someone doesn't want the information getting out?" Wyatt asked.

"Yeah. Some of the Regiment guys who hang out here went to check stories. They found abandoned outposts and signs of a struggle. Ships that showed up adrift and empty."

"The stories are true?" Beth asked finishing the last of her meal.

"Seems like it," John replied. "My friends with connections to some of the dissident groups like the Network think Kalok's behind the slavers. Cheap labor to expand their mining operations."

"Shit," Wyatt muttered. "You think they're right?" Even as he asked, the likelihood of it being so settled into his stomach like a rock.

"I'd put my money on it," Beth replied. "It fits with what we're hearing elsewhere." She looked at John. "Ever hear of a group called the Coalition?"

"Renegade academics, isn't it?" He asked.

She nodded.

"I've heard the name. Folks in my circles are more likely to favor the Network, and the more radical ones drift toward Phage. Why?"

Beth glanced at Wyatt, who nodded assent. She gave John an abbreviated and somewhat edited version of what they knew, skirting around who else had been involved and how they came to know some of the details. When she finished, he ordered another round of drinks.

"Where the fuck do we run to stay out of this shit storm?" John asked, looking suddenly tired and worn. "I came out here figuring that we were so far away from everyone else that by the time Kalok cared about the Fringe worlds, I'd be dead and gone." He shook his head. "I did my fighting. Wanted to be done with it and just be left alone."

"Except that what we did helped Kalok get a tighter grip on our nuts than it had before," Wyatt said, sipping his drink.

"You think I don't know that?" John's voice was loud enough a few of the other patrons turned to look. He dropped his head and closed his eyes. "I know," he said, much more quietly. "I hear the talk, about where our duty lies. Can't get away from it if you spend enough time here, with the Regiment folks. Ain't no use going elsewhere; this is where I belong."

"What's the general opinion, among the regulars?" Wyatt asked.

John met his gaze. "They think there's a fight coming. That Kalok and Interplan intend to seize the worlds beyond the Rim—hell, maybe all the way to the Near-Fringe—and that they won't take no for an answer."

"Can they do that? Stellar Fed—" Beth started.

"Stellar Fed exists to crack down on the likes of you and me. Kalok and Interplan can buy off the people necessary to have the Feds stay on the sidelines."

"Not all the out-Rim worlds are little research colonies," Beth said. "There are established worlds that have their own history, that aren't colonies or settlements—and the biggest of those have armies."

"And not a one of them could stand against what Kalok and Interplan can bring against them." John shook his head. "No. We can't win this with another war like the one we fought," he said, looking at Wyatt. "We go up against them head-on, we get crushed. But I don't think that's the plan."

"There's a plan?" Beth asked.

"More like an idea that keeps going round and round," John replied. "Decentralized strikes. Kalok can fight a single massed flotilla. But thousands of individual, independent strikes with no central organization, no core group to crack or infiltrate? It's like water on rock or those blood-sucking flies on Rone 24 that could drain a fellow dry in an hour, one bite at a time."

Beth flashed a feral smile. "I like it."

Wyatt looked away, pensive. "Sounds like a lot of casualties to me. Don't forget, we swatted hundreds of those flies and thought nothing of it."

John fixed him with a look. "People don't come out to the Far-Fringe or the out-Rim for fun. We came for independence, or to start over, or to dodge a warrant. Kalok might be focused on the established worlds. And I'll grant you; they'll be a thorn in the side for expansion. But us," he said, with a gesture that took in the roadhouse's customers and far beyond, to the thousands of sparsely inhabited worlds beyond the Rim, "we've got nothing to lose. And I guarantee you, when the shit hits the rotors, we'll fight with everything we've got, and make them damn sorry they tried to take what's ours."

Chapter Twelve

"Cargo delivered, Liddy is happy, and our debt's paid off," Wyatt said a few days later as the *Nellie B* lifted off from the abandoned moon base Liddy and her gang had temporarily claimed for their own.

"So were we right?" Beth wondered. "Did Liddy know more than she told us? You met with her long enough."

"She knew about the settlers for sure and even agreed to make certain the right people helped them get back on their feet. So yeah, I think it was to get us pulled farther into the 'movement,' or whatever they call it. Still, don't know if she's in it for money or the cause though."

"Hey, at least Zigler and his people might get some help. And let's face it, we're already in deep whether we chose to be or not."

"Yeah, so now what? Ready to do some salvage runs and build up our account?"

"I want to track down the contact Daniel gave me for the Coalition," Beth said. "If we're going to be neck-deep in rebellion, I trust the Coalition more than I do Phage or the Network."

"Because they're academics?" Wyatt asked skeptically.

"Maybe, but mostly because they sound a little saner than the alternatives. Or at least I'm thinking they've thought it through. And I'm still not completely convinced we shouldn't turn tail and run as far into the Fringe as we can."

"I like that idea better," Wyatt admitted. "But I have the feeling Kalok will push its way out there, sooner than we'd like to think unless something puts a stop to the expansion and their methods."

"Which is why I'd like to hear what the Coalition has to say," Beth replied. "Phage is taking credit for the riots on the Rim worlds, and that worries me. They're poking at Kalok, trying to make them take action. More people are going to get killed. And the Network seems to focus on the non-aligned governments, which is all well and good, but it's not going to do anything for the outposts and the research stations and the homesteaders."

"Have you heard more from your friends on Keller Station?" Wyatt asked.

"No, nothing, and that worries me. I've tried regular channels and secure, encrypted, and downright illegal ones, and I don't get anything except an automated message." Beth pushed her hair behind her ear. "But the message includes one of the code words they gave me for the Coalition."

Wyatt leaned back in his seat. "So you think something happened to run them off, and they're steering anyone who was in the know to the Coalition?"

"That's exactly what I think. And I hope that the worst that happened was someone did run them off," she fretted. "Because we've both seen what Kalok does when they don't want loose ends."

Wyatt rubbed his neck. "All right. Do you have the coordinates?" He plugged in the numbers, and they headed out away from Liddy's base.

The jump would have been quite a distance from Keller Station, but from Liddy's place, it wasn't so bad—still longer than he'd like.

The farther the jump, the more time they spent in-between and the more likely they'd need a jump pack or have to use cryo. Wyatt turned to Beth as Nellie's estimates scrolled on his screen.

"So, drugs, cryo, or a few hours of the worst hell you've ever experienced," Wyatt asked. He watched Beth as she thought about it, clearly not liking any of the choices. Being able to travel tremendous distances through a tunnel in the folds of space was a miracle. But what it did to the human body could only be considered torture. For civilians, it was just assumed they'd 'take a nap' in cryo. It was a time-proven, safe way to travel the Dark, but that was when there weren't enemies at every turn trying to kill you. He wondered if she'd ever had to use the jump packs.

"Drugs."

"You sure? There's no shame in using cryo."

"Yes."

Wyatt got up and left the bridge, returning a few minutes later with a couple of med-packs. "I picked up some from Liddy's team that are formulated for your size. What I had was too strong for you, and my half-packs, too weak." He ripped open a pack and pulled out the hypo.

"Wait, what are you going to do?"

"I'll use a half-pack. A reduced dosage for my size and metabolism. It will still hurt like a mother, but it will be bearable, and I'll come out of it much faster."

"Okay." Beth leaned her head back, exposing her neck. Wyatt placed the hypo to her skin and hit the trigger. It made a small *woosh*, and Beth's eyes fluttered.

"Good night Princess. Nellie prepare for jump." Wyatt opened a second med-pack, put it to his neck and triggered.

"Jump commencing in four, three, two…" Nellie's voice whispered as Wyatt felt the world going dim.

Wyatt woke to excruciating pain. His training kicked in, and he began his breathing exercises before he opened his eyes. No matter how many jumps he made, this part was still hell. Yes, he could survive it, but it certainly wasn't something he'd choose. No sane man would.

But the thought of dropping out into a trap and blowing up was a worse option.

He managed to open his eyes and bring the screens into focus. They were almost through. All the external feeds were dark. At the entrance to the wormhole, there were bright swirls of light. But in-between, it was pitch black. No light, no stars, nothing, just an endless void.

"Nearing jump exit," Nellie's voice sounded odd and distant. None of the senses worked quite right during jump and many pilots had made grave errors trying to react to what they thought was reality in-between.

Wyatt swallowed the bile in his throat as the lurch of the drop sent another wave of pain. He closed his eyes and tried to stay calm and let it pass. Nellie sounded the alarm to indicate they were back in normal space. In theory it was to wake him up; in reality, it felt like a sharp spike through his head.

"I'm awake Nellie," he muttered. "Scan for hostiles."

"No ships detected in immediate range. Expanding scan."

"Nellie, please continue course to the coordinates programmed. Alert us if you detect any ships on our path."

Wyatt looked over at Beth; she was still out from the drugs. He put on some music and laid his head back. Doing a jump always took a toll, but a few minutes without threats or problems and he'd be good as new.

It would take several hours to reach their destination. One of the challenges with doing a jump was having to rely on navigation satellites, beacons, and detailed astronomical mapping. Out in the Fringe and beyond the most populated areas of space, helpful navigation satellites didn't exist, so pilots had to choose destination points to come out of jump reasonably far from any planets, stars, or shipping lanes. If not, the risk was high for coming out of jump on top of something already occupying the same space. Which made for a very abrupt end to the trip.

Wyatt let the music relax him and turned to look at Beth. She looked very peaceful in sleep, and he again thought about how pretty she was. Her features were delicate and her fair skin contrasted with the silky dark hair and lashes. He briefly wondered what it would be like to kiss her. Would her lips feel as soft as they looked? *Shit Wyatt! Get ahold of yourself and quit perving on your partner. She probably already thinks you're a low-life, don't give her evidence to support it.* Wyatt closed his eyes and focused on the music.

Beth woke up gradually, and Wyatt waited until she seemed coherent before filling her in on what he'd found at the site of the coordinates they had followed.

"I don't understand," Beth said. They'd arrived at the destination only to find a defunct satellite in shaky orbit around a barren moon of an uninhabited planet. "This can't be right."

Wyatt started to answer when Nellie picked up a streamed message.

"We're receiving an incoming tight-beam message. Nellie, put it on the speaker."

"Hello, friend," a recorded voice greeted them. "It's good to see you."

"We're being scanned," Wyatt said quietly, watching as Nellie reported what her sensors were picking up to his screen. "It's coming from the satellite." There was a long pause, and then the message continued when the scan appeared to have stopped.

"Looks like we know the same people. The rest of the family would love to meet you. Here's where to go." A new set of coordinates followed. The voice went silent; then the message began to repeat.

"They're not taking chances," Beth said as Wyatt eased them away from the satellite and back toward open space. "Want to bet that scan goes to someone who checks out the ship registry and decides what kind of welcome we get at the next stop?"

"Yeah, I think that's exactly what's going on. So you still want to go?"

Beth nodded. "Let's see what happens."

The second coordinates brought them to another obsolete satellite, this one orbiting a lifeless, abandoned mining planet. Fortunately, this trip did not require another jump, just several uninteresting days of travel. A signal hailed them as they came in range.

"Welcome back," the voice said. "Our mutual friends say you're all right. We'd like you to meet the family, but they're shy. So we'll give you coordinates, and when you reach a certain point, the family will let you know the rest of the directions." The message repeated once, then fell silent.

"Paranoid bastards," Wyatt muttered.

"Do you blame them?"

Wyatt gave Nellie the coordinates and looked at the star map she supplied of their destination.

"I wish we knew what happened to the Keller Station folks. If they left on their own, that's one thing. If Kalok realized they had connections with the Coalition and killed them, these messages could be a set-up."

"I thought of that," Beth agreed. "But the only way to check would be to go back to the station, and even then we wouldn't know for sure. If it's empty, they could have fled, or Kalok could have nabbed the lot of them and just not blown the place up to cover the disappearances."

"Great," Wyatt muttered. "And if Kalok is on to the Keller folks, they'd be watching anyone who came by—if they didn't already know we'd been there." He hesitated for a few seconds, then confirmed the flight path to Nellie. "Might as well see this through."

The next hop required more travel time and a short jump. Beth still opted for drugs, so she got some extra rest. They spent the days doing needed maintenance for the *Nellie B,* talked, ate, and napped, both deep in their own thoughts.

Beth looked up as they worked together to clean out and organize the ship's storage lockers and cargo hold.

"How far do you want to go with all this?" Beth asked.

"I've been asking myself the same question. And if you'd have asked me before we met up on Comstock, I probably would have washed my hands of the whole thing and run the other direction." Wyatt scratched at the stubble on his cheek. "But I know things now that I didn't know then. And the way I see it, I've got some responsibility for how things are since I fought in that war to give Kalok the power it's got now."

"That wasn't your fault—"

"Maybe. Maybe not. Feels like it, even if I didn't know the truth at the time," Wyatt said and hated how tired he sounded. "I'm not a fan of suicide missions. If this Coalition turns out to be a bunch of grouchy academics with no clue how to run a revolution, I say we get out and keep going."

"And if they're legit?" Beth asked quietly.

Wyatt shrugged. "Then we hear them out. See what the plan is, and how we fit in and take it from there."

A night's sleep and a day of puttering around the ship left both Beth and Wyatt edgy by the time they reached the coordinates.

"Seriously?" Wyatt yelled at Nellie. "This is where they brought us?" He punched his fist into the padding of his chair and swore at the empty darkness in front of them.

"Maybe there was a mistake—"

Nellie interrupted Beth and announced another message coming in.

"This had better be good," Wyatt growled. "Making us fly around in circles…"

"Almost there, friends," the recorded voice greeted them. "Had to make sure you were who you said you were, and that you didn't bring any uninvited guests with you, if you know what I mean."

"We're being scanned again," Wyatt muttered, looking at the data Nellie sent him. "Whoever these people are, they're not taking any chances."

"Sloppy revolutionaries don't live long," Beth observed. "That's probably a good sign."

"The coordinates have been sent," the voice resumed. "Set your ship down and remain onboard. Keep your ship's guns powered down, nice and friendly-like. We'll send someone to meet you." After a single repeat, the voice silenced.

"Last chance to turn back," Wyatt said with a glance toward Beth.

"If it's a trap, they're going to a lot of trouble when they could have shot us out of the Dark at the first satellite."

Wyatt nodded. "That occurred to me."

"And it sounds like they know who we are—or want us to think that," Beth reasoned. "If they do know, then we're already screwed if it's a trap. So we might as well go see what happens."

"Might as well," he said, authorizing the new flight path. "Not like we were doing anything less illegal."

Wyatt spent the travel time seeing to routine maintenance and diagnostics, making sure the *Nellie B* stayed fit to fight or flee. Beth looked up when he returned to the cockpit.

"Did you notice anything about the latest coordinates?" She asked.

Wyatt frowned. "They're about halfway between the Rim and the Fringe. Not as close as Keller Station, but not as far away from the Rim as I'd like to be."

"Aren't we supposed to be out of the main shipping lanes?" Beth asked, watching as the scanners tracked the positions of traffic around them.

"Yep. I swear it's as bad as the *erinium* rush when they found that vein of ore on Norral 12," Wyatt replied. "Anyone with a tub that can fly seems to have headed out."

"Somehow, I don't think it's an ore rush this time," Beth observed.

"Wyatt, we are receiving a distress call," Nellie announced.

"Put it through."

A voice crackled over the comm. "If you're out there and you can hear me, we need help! This is CR-2639587. Engine trouble; need a tow. I've got my family with me. Please, help! Mayday!"

Wyatt swore under his breath, and his fingers flew across the controls. Within a few minutes, the ship's sensors had identified the source of the distress call. Wyatt's eyes narrowed as the information scrolled across the screen.

"Damn, it's a legitimate call."

"You don't think it's a trap? Could be pirates. Or thieves," Beth warned.

"If so, they're dumb as rocks. That ship's lucky it made it this far. Engine is shit, and the internal systems look like they're held together with a prayer. And Nellie's scans confirm, there's a genetically-linked group with a man, a woman, and several children."

"Pirates have families, too."

Wyatt glared at her. "Do you see any other ship hovering around to swoop in and grab us if we help out? I don't."

"Just making sure you think before you get all heroic."

Wyatt reached for the comm. "Attention CR-2639587. Signal received. We will tow you to the next outpost. Secure your ship, and prepare to be towed." He switched off the link.

"The next outpost—the one with the Coalition contact?"

Wyatt shrugged. "It's still a working station. Been there for a while, so they can't be just Coalition. And from there, the crap ship can get a mechanic or buy a ticket for a slow boat home."

Beth leaned over and gave him a quick kiss on the top of his head. "You just can't resist being a hero, can you?" She left the cockpit before he thought of a suitable reply.

THE TRIP TO the outpost took longer with another ship in tow. As far as Beth could see, the *Nellie B* was the only craft out of all those on the busy vector that took the time to stop. As much as Wyatt could get on her last nerves, stopping to help in the middle of joining a resistance movement was exactly the reason she had decided to stick around and explore their partnership.

"Any more communications from them?" Beth asked.

He watched as she settled into the co-pilot seat with a hot cup of coffee. Wordlessly, she passed him a second cup

"Yeah, they kept thanking us so much I finally had to ask them to keep it silent. The link is still open though."

"Hey, it's nice to be appreciated," she said. "Bet you've done a lot of stuff, and no one bothered to say thanks."

"That's not the point." He could feel the heat going to his face and hoped she didn't notice.

Nellie interrupted. "A new communication coming through."

The comm crackled. "Mayday! Cargo Ship ST89724, en route to Kalok Mine #3492. We've got a situation on board. Mayday!" A strange scuttling sound of metal on metal rang in the background.

"Oh gods," the speaker said, voice thick with fear. "We can't hold out long. They're coming. Please, if you can hear this—"

In the background, alarm klaxons screamed a warning. The squeal of wrenching metal and that scrabbling sound, louder now, drowned out everything but the screams.

Wyatt and Beth watched Nellie's screens as the ship on the sensors she identified as the source gave a puff of icy atmosphere into the void, and the comm went silent.

"Cargo ship ST89724, respond!" Wyatt radioed back. Static answered him.

Beth took over the scans. "Hull breach. Massive decompression, loss of atmosphere." She looked up. "They're dead."

"Fuck!" Wyatt slammed his fist down on the console.

"What's going on?" A hesitant voice asked from the open line to the ship they were towing.

"Nothing that affects you," Beth replied, with a glance toward Wyatt that warned him to stay quiet. "Just an accident with another craft out in the shipping lanes. Hold tight. We'll be in port soon." She clicked off the comm.

Wyatt looked so tense he was nearly vibrating. "That shouldn't have happened," he said thickly.

"You don't know what was going on," Beth replied. "Maybe they had a containment breach. Or a malfunction—"

"There's something about the recording," Wyatt said, and he replayed the last, desperate cries for help and shivered as he heard the sounds again. "Did you hear that?"

"What?"

"The metallic scuffling sound. I know I've heard it before."

Beth shook her head. "It could be anything, even a faulty air handler. You don't—"

"Oh, gods. I know that sound." He turned to Beth, eyes wide with remembered terror. "Do you remember, when you visited Keller Station, and I went on that salvage run without you?"

"You didn't say much—"

"The cargo hold had some broken crates from Kalok. They were all empty. Mack and I loaded up the *Nellie B* with the other stuff—"

"Mack?"

Wyatt looked away. "He was a robot, but not the usual…he had swagger."

"What happened?"

Wyatt's gaze remained fixed on the vid screen. "Something activated the Kalok bots; I think that was what busted out of the crates. They came after us. Nearly killed me. Nasty things. Mack and I almost got out, but they swarmed. He pushed me through the hatch, and jammed the lock and then…they got him." His cheeks flushed at the catch in his voice, and he glanced at the beach hat that hung in a place of honor above his station.

"You think that's what happened to the cargo ship?" Beth asked gently.

Wyatt nodded. "Yeah. That noise…not the kind of thing you forget."

Beth swore. "So why did they have Kalok bots on their cargo ship?"

Wyatt adjusted the course and added as much speed as he dared. "I don't know. But once we get to the outpost, that's what I intend to ask your Coalition friends."

They put into port and managed to detach themselves from the disabled ship's grateful family only after accepting effusive thanks that left Beth blushing and Wyatt uncomfortable with the attention. As soon as they were docked, they'd received an encrypted message from their "friends." They secured the *Nellie B* and headed for the rendezvous point included in the message.

Wyatt and Beth wound through crowds of people from dozens of planets and races that hurried through the outpost's corridors. They stayed alert for anyone who looked like they might be following them, but to Wyatt's relief, no one seemed to pay any attention.

"You sure you made contact?" Ever since the explosion on the mysterious freighter, he'd felt tense. He didn't like leaving his armored atmo suit behind and was suspicious that part of the instructions required street clothing.

"I'm sure," Beth said.

Wyatt knew he'd asked a version of the same question half a dozen times. But he still felt naked and exposed.

Beth said she'd come through this outpost several times on her way to academic conferences or archeology digs, though at the time she hadn't known about the Coalition. Fortunately, she remembered the basics of its layout and had a vague memory of the bar where the encrypted message had indicated they meet. That gave Wyatt a little comfort.

He fervently hoped they weren't being set up. Beth opened the door, and Wyatt stayed close on her heels.

He'd been in worse places. The Star Rider bar smelled like spice and smoke, dimly lit and relatively uncrowded for the time of day. He watched as Beth took out a scarf from her bag and tied it around her neck, their signal the anonymous contact had designated.

Wyatt and Beth found a booth where they could see both the entrance and the kitchen door and ordered food. Beth also asked for the "Keller Fizz," a drink that wasn't on the menu and which they'd already decided was a code for the bartender.

Wyatt kept his eye on the barkeep as the server relayed the order, but the man behind the bar didn't look their way and never left his station.

"I changed your order to-go." A slim woman slipped up next to Beth's side of the table.

Wyatt looked for the indicators the contact had specified: a ring with a bright red stone and a scarf tied around her throat. Beth turned and caught his eye, giving him a nod.

"That's good. We're hungry," Beth said, feeling like the heroine of a drama-vid reciting the coded response.

"The air's bad in here. I can get you a better table," the woman said.

Beth gave Wyatt a nod, and they rose, following the contact. The server handed the woman two packaged meals, which she passed back to them. Beth smelled the food and Wyatt heard her sigh.

He had to agree. He was happy they got to keep their dinners. Whatever else came out of the meeting, a good meal would be a treat.

The woman led them to a back room that looked like it usually held overflow boxes for the kitchen. She gestured toward the chairs that seemed out of place among the boxes and crates. They sat, and Beth opened her box immediately.

Wyatt couldn't help but smile as Beth balanced the container on her knees. *Guess she's not about to let revolution or conspiracies keep her from a well-deserved dinner,* he thought.

"So you're Beth. I've heard a lot about you. Mutual friends and all that."

"And you're Katherine—or at least that's what you want to be called," Beth said.

Katherine turned to regard Wyatt. "Wyatt McCoy. Your reputation precedes you."

"Please, don't let that get in the way."

Katherine smirked in response and sat across from them. "Pardon my manners. Go ahead and eat. I didn't want you out in the main section any longer than necessary. Things are getting…tense."

"What do you know about the cargo ship that blew up a few cycles ago?" Wyatt asked, his mouth full of food.

"How did you—"

"We saw it happen. Wow, this is good." Beth replied and wiped a bit of broth from her chin.

Wyatt had to agree the food was excellent and while the *Nellie B*'s food processors were completely adequate, better than average, nothing beat a meal made from non-synthesized ingredients.

"It's the fourth cargo ship to go like that in six months," Katherine said.

"That was no accident," Wyatt said. "I'm pretty sure I know what caused the decompression."

Katherine's expression sharpened. "How is that?"

"Because I'm the one who got away."

Katherine took a deep breath. "Then we really need to talk." When neither Beth nor Wyatt jumped in to fill the silence, Katherine cleared her throat. "So…the cargo ship—*Valiant Voyager*—was a scamper." Wyatt and Beth, both knew the term. It was what spacers called the independently owned ships that ran cargo for less than the going rate. They skirted the law and were unsurprisingly popular with shippers despite repeated efforts to regulate them.

"They picked up jobs for some of the more far-flung Kalok mines," Katherine continued. "In each case, the mine ended up having an 'accident' after the scamper ships were already on their way, filled with cargo. All four ships had an incident en route. One crashed, one blew up, two had explosive decompression—killed the crew, and the cargo was declared a loss."

"That's a lie," Wyatt said. "Decompression wouldn't affect most cargo. It could be salvaged. Someone's cheating insurance."

"You have no idea," Katherine replied. "It's bigger than that. Leaving the question as to whether or not what happened to the mining colonies was actually 'accidental,' the cargo had been purchased by Kalok before the scamper ships left port. Then mid-voyage, it wasn't needed anymore."

Beth felt a chill go down her spine. "The cargo was expensive?"

Katherine nodded. "So if the ship was recalled, Kalok would still have to pay for the cargo, even if it wasn't needed."

"Unless it was lost in transit," Wyatt supplied in a flat voice.

"You said you thought you knew what happened?" Katherine asked.

Wyatt nodded and told the whole, painful story about Mack and the salvage run. "The sounds in the background on the distress call, they sounded like the noise those Kalok bots made," Wyatt said and didn't even try to hide his shudder. "What if—"

"What if Kalok included bots in every shipment?" Beth said quietly, as if speaking their suspicions aloud made it worse. "So that if they wanted to abort the delivery and not have to pay for it, they could activate the bots—"

"And boom," Wyatt said with quiet certainty. "Gone."

Katherine nodded. "I'm afraid that's very much what it looks like."

"Shit," Wyatt swore under his breath.

Katherine turned her attention to Beth. "Why did you get in touch with us?"

"Because I—we—know what's going on," Beth replied. "And we want to see if there's a way to stop more people from getting hurt. I was also worried I couldn't get through to the people I knew on Keller Station."

She and Wyatt had already agreed not to tell everything they knew. Exposing Beth's ability with the alien implant put her at risk. Too many people on both sides might be tempted to snatch a resource with that kind of power. Or just try to remove the implant for themselves.

"What do you propose?" Katherine asked. "This isn't an academic exercise. You're already in some trouble." She gave a wan smile. "Yes, I checked your file. But if you throw in with the Coalition, Stellar Fed won't have to make up reasons to hunt you; as a possible anarchist, it makes it easier for them. This isn't a romp."

Wyatt moved to answer, but Beth stilled him with a hand on his arm. "I know that Kalok's been killing the skeleton crews and clean-up gangs on their mines. I know that Interplan has sent ships against alien colonies on worlds they wanted to acquire, against Allied colonists if they got in the way, too. And now my people on Keller Station are missing," she hissed. "So spare me your condescension. We know what it is and we want to help. Stellar Fed has already decided I'm a threat and want me dead; joining the Coalition won't change that."

Katherine smiled. "All right, then. You're just in time. It's about to get real interesting out here."

Chapter Thirteen

"There's got to be a way Kalok is activating the bots remotely," Wyatt said as Katherine finished their quick tour of the outpost. Wyatt tried to remember the basic layout, an old habit based on the need to find a quick exit. When Katherine opened the door to her office, a man looked up, waiting for them.

Wyatt drew his blaster before he registered the face. "It's Worm," Beth said, just as Wyatt recognized the fugitive programmer.

"Worm's been working with us since Liddy found him safe passage," Katherine said with a smug smile. She moved to sit behind her desk, and Worm edged closer, keeping a close eye on Wyatt until he put his gun back and no longer looked ready for a fight. "So yes, we knew a lot more about you than we admitted."

"How much of the Outpost is Coalition?" Beth asked, claiming one of the two guest chairs. That left Wyatt with the chair stacked high with boxes. He thought about knocking them over and decided it would best to play nice. Katherine nodded approval as he carefully moved the boxes to the floor and took a seat.

"We're a small settlement on one of the very few truly usable land masses on the planet," Katherine said. "As far as the surveys have revealed, between the terrain, the weather, the lousy soil, and the lack of resources, no one has any reason to want to make a grab for what's left. Until now, that's meant people leave us alone, content to stop for repairs and supplies and move on. There are about a thousand permanent residents, give or take a few with every ship that comes and goes. Two hundred of those are Coalition."

"We've been here long enough to have eyes and ears in all the right places," Worm picked up, looking pleased with their surprise. "Our people are part of all the critical functions, and the Outpost commander is a sympathizer."

"So do you have people monitoring communications—not just in and out of the Outpost, but within a range?" Wyatt asked. "Because something triggered those bots on the cargo ship, and I'm betting it was a code that Kalok transmitted. If your scans picked up the activation code, maybe you could hack a way to de-activate."

"Maybe." Worm's eyebrows drew together as he thought. "A lot of ships out there, all chattering at the same time. Gonna be a shit ton of work to parse out a blip of communication to one particular craft."

"It's not the first time Kalok's done this," Wyatt returned, refusing to let the idea go. "They'll do it again. If you can isolate the code, figure out how to turn them off—"

"They could come up with another code," Worm argued.

Wyatt shook his head. "Do you think it would be easy to reprogram all the bots they've got out there remotely? Could they even do it?"

Worm pondered for a moment. "Maybe, maybe not. It would take time. And pushing out a broadcast like that, we'd hear it—"

"And change it all over again," Beth said, her eyes lighting up. "We could tie Kalok up in knots over this."

A small, vengeful smile touched Worm's lips. "All right. I accept the challenge." He thought for a moment. "It would help a lot to have one of those Kalok bots to dissect."

"I know where we can get one—neutered, of course," Wyatt replied.

"Oh, no. Oh, hell no!" Beth retorted. "If you think—"

"You don't have to come with me," Wyatt said with a shrug. "I can go by myself. I made it out in one piece when you were on Keller Station."

Beth glowered. "You want to go salvage one of those drifters, don't you?"

"Seems logical," Wyatt replied. "It would prove our theory about what caused their damage, and if we go in with the right weapons, I can fry one and bring it back for Worm to dissect."

"What's to keep it from transmitting our coordinates?" Katherine asked, looking intrigued but wary.

Wyatt looked to Worm. "Can you build a Black Box?"

"What's that?" Beth asked.

"It's a secure way to transport a seized object during a reconnaissance mission," Wyatt replied. "Especially when you aren't sure how dangerous it is. Pretty much a lead box with a few extra bells and whistles to cut off a tracking signal. And limit the blast if the thing explodes."

Worm nodded. "I can do that. How big?"

Wyatt gave him approximate dimensions, as well as gestures to indicate size. Worm looked to Katherine. "If we transport the bot in a Black Box, it can't transmit. And if I unbox it in the interrogation room, it's still cut off from everything. That room is basically a person-sized Black Box." He gave Wyatt a look. "You just have to make sure the damn thing doesn't activate while I'm working on it."

Wyatt held up his hands in appeasement. "Trust me. I've got a big stake in not letting that happen."

"All right," Beth agreed. "I'll go. But we need weapons, jammers—something that gives us an advantage."

"If you can tell me what you need, my team can come up with a couple of prototypes," Worm offered. Wyatt and Beth followed him back to his office and spent the next hour taking down specifications.

"Give us a day, and we can modify existing equipment for you, give you something good enough to get on and off one of those derelict ships," Worm said when they finished. "We'll have the Black Box by then, too. You can consider it a test run—we'll take what we learn from your use in the field and make better weapons for the next time."

"All right," Wyatt agreed, glancing to Beth for her nod of agreement. "We'll track a couple of likely ships and have the coordinates ready to go."

"In the meantime," Worm said, "I'll get some coders working on the activation and shutdown code problem. We've got people with Kalok backgrounds, so we can get a head start and then validate when you bring one of the bots back for us to experiment on."

"Works for us," Wyatt assured him. "Can't think of anything I'd rather see vivisected."

TWO DAYS LATER, Wyatt and Beth took off from the Outpost, with the *Nellie B* locked onto coordinates for one of the drifting ships. A wheeled lead box sat in the cargo bay, and several modified welding guns hung in the weapons locker, next to a crate of experimental jammers.

"We're still taking a big risk. You do realize that, don't you, Wyatt?" Beth said as she watched the stars go by.

"Yes, I realize it. I fought these things, remember? Facing them again isn't my idea of a good time." Wyatt knew Beth would figure his sharp tone as a cover for his nerves. "On the other hand, if we can cripple one of the bots and take it back for Worm to study, that's huge. And if the cargo on some of the closest drifters isn't damaged, we might even recoup some costs. We need to make a little money, revolution or not."

The *Wayfarer* was a small Class D cargo runner, long past its prime. Wyatt didn't know how long it had been drifting, but from the scratched and dented outer skin, it looked like the ship had seen better days, even before the final accident. Wyatt and Nellie debated the best approach to manage a docking since the *Wayfarer*'s systems were offline. None of the options were desirable, but some were marginally safer than others. When they finally reached agreement, Wyatt sat back with a scowl.

"You do realize you just spent half an hour arguing with a computer," Beth observed.

"Shut your mouth. You'll hurt her feelings," Wyatt replied with a mischievous grin. "Don't listen to that kind of talk, Nellie, girl." Beth rolled her eyes.

"You two need to get a room?"

Wyatt slapped a hand to his chest melodramatically. "Ours is more of a spiritual connection."

"Oh for fuck's sake, cut the crap!" Beth protested. "Are we going in or not?"

Wyatt chuckled as he got out of the pilot's chair. "Soon as Nellie gets us connected and works out the airlock code, we're in. Get your atmo suit and gear up." He turned back to the console. "Nellie, while we're onboard, scan for chatter. Not just whether someone's coming our way, but if you pick up anything about the Outpost, the Network, any of the resistance groups, I want to know about it."

"Of course, Wyatt," Nellie replied.

The *Wayfarer*'s interior was as dilapidated as its outer shell. "I bet they were beyond thrilled to get a Kalok load of cargo," Beth said as they made their way through the corridors. "Looks like they needed every credit."

"Which Kalok undoubtedly knew," Wyatt replied. "Probably went looking for family-run rigs that no one would kick up a fuss over if they went missing, and that needed the money so bad they'd overlook any irregularities." Legitimate big shippers scanned crates to avoid accidentally carrying contraband and probably would have refused to load the bots. Small ships desperate for work couldn't afford to be choosy.

Nellie had connected them to an airlock by the cargo bay, so they didn't have far to go before the evidence of the *Wayfarer*'s last days became apparent. "Carbon scoring," Beth pointed out, noting blast marks on a bulkhead that also bore deep gouges.

"Cover me while I see if there's anything here worth salvaging," Wyatt said. The ripped-open Kalok crates were easy to spot, telling him they could expect at least three bots to be somewhere onboard. The rest of the cargo appeared to be intact, mostly supplies of use on any outpost. The merchandise might not be exotic, but it would fetch a fair price anywhere on the Fringe.

Beth kept watch on the corridors as Wyatt used a hover cart to ferry two loads into the *Nellie B.* When he returned the second time, he had the Black Box on the cart, which he parked right beside the airlock.

"Let's find a bot and get out of here," Wyatt grumbled. The silent ship made him nervous. A truly dead ship was a tomb, and could easily become one for an unwary salvager.

They moved like a recon team, a formation Wyatt had taught Beth during their downtime. She might not have had military training, but her instincts were good, and she learned quickly. Wyatt couldn't imagine a better partner, and he trusted only a handful of his Regiment buddies as much as he did Beth.

"Did you hear something?" Beth murmured as they made their way down the corridor, methodically checking every cabin as they passed. The faint sound of metal skittering against metal carried through the silent ship.

"Yeah. They're here, and they're waking up," Wyatt replied. He and Beth both carried a bag full of jammers set for a range of frequencies since they had no way of knowing if all of Kalok's bots had the same settings.

"Looks like you were right about what happened," Beth said with a nod toward the body of one of the *Wayfarer*'s crew that lay against the bulkhead. Even with the corpse frozen from the lack of atmosphere, the bloody gashes that had killed the man were impossible to overlook.

"I hate being right about some things."

They walked until they came to the corridor intersection. "Let's set up here," Wyatt said. "I don't want to go any deeper than we have to." Beth covered him as he affixed a variety of jammers to the bulkheads, including the upper and lower decks, creating a trap zone in the center of the intersection. Wyatt also prepared a fallback in the nearest cabin that would protect them within a circle of jammers should the bots somehow come from behind them.

"You're still going to be bait?" Beth asked, her opinion of the plan clear in her voice.

"Yep. These bots are killers. They probably woke up as soon as they read our vital signs. You know the drill. I lure them in, and you activate the jammers."

Wyatt didn't like the plan any better than Beth did, but it still beat going looking for the bots and being ambushed in a part of the ship that might be more difficult to defend and farther from the cargo bay and the *Nellie B.* The less distance he had to cover with the incapacitated bot in tow before sealing it into the lead box, the better.

The skittering noise sounded closer, coming from two directions and overhead. Beth set off a chain of jammers to keep their retreat clear, all the way back to the cargo bay. Wyatt stood in the center of the intersection, surrounded by more jammers that had not yet been activated. Beth had the bastardized blaster/welder weapon in one hand, and the jammer controls in the other. Wyatt had his weapon ready, although he planned not to shoot until the bot was trapped within the circle of jammers.

The metal-on-metal scrape grew louder. "Incoming!" Wyatt yelled as he spotted one of the Kalok bots scrambling down the corridor on the left, making for him at top speed.

"Wyatt! Behind you!" Beth's voice was urgent but not panicked.

"Shit," Wyatt muttered, not needing to turn to know he had two bots closing on him. Right on cue, the third bot came into view on the ceiling of the corridor directly in front of him.

"Get out of there, Wyatt!"

"Not yet."

"We didn't plan on three of them!"

"Not going to be different on any other ship," Wyatt grated. It took every ounce of courage he possessed to stand his ground. The *skritch* of metallic legs against the decking made his gut clench, and he could feel sweat dripping down his back inside his suit.

"Wyatt—"

"Be ready!" He snapped as the bots drew closer. Wyatt kept an eye on those sharp metal feet. They could not only pierce flesh, but they could rip his suit to shreds. The atmo suit could seal a small puncture, but a gash would leave him exposed to the elements. He'd be dead before the bot could tear him apart.

The bots matched each other's speed to narrow the gap like a pack of hunting dogs, cornering their prey. Wyatt felt his heartbeat spike, and he knew he was holding his breath. He'd always trusted his reflexes and his gut, and thus far, it had kept him alive. Now, he knew he was cutting it fine.

The bot on the ceiling reached the circle a fraction of a second before the others. As it fell, Wyatt shifted, tensing. If he leaped to safety too soon, the other bots might not be trapped inside the circle. Hesitate a second too long, and the bot might jump outside the jammer trap and endanger Beth.

The two remaining bots scrambled for the circle. Wyatt dove toward Beth. "Now!" He shouted, twisting in mid-air to evade the jabbing, slicing robo-feet that had slashed the *Wayfarer*'s crew to ribbons. Something caught at the edge of his pant leg. He felt searing cold, momentary pain, and then the suit resealed, leaving him gasping.

The frequency jammers lit up, and their high-pitched wail reverberated from the bulkheads, answered by the chatter of the trapped bots within the circle. Wyatt hit the deck, and Beth started shooting. He forced himself to get to his feet, ignoring the pain in his leg and opened fire. The bots squawked and shrieked, but they were trapped inside the ring of jammers. The blaster-welders could pass through the invisible frequency barrier, so Beth and Wyatt aimed for the bot's vulnerable areas, the joints that articulated the deadly metal legs, and that joined the legs to the bulbous bodies.

"It's not working!" Beth yelled above the whine of the jammers and the drone of the blaster-welders.

"They're tough," Wyatt shouted back. "Just don't hit the bulkheads!"

The bots moved constantly within the jammer circle, making it hard to get a direct hit on their joints. Beth severed the leg off one bot, and Wyatt sheared off two from another, making it list and wobble. The remaining bot hesitated, uncertain whether to rip apart their fallen comrades or keep hurling itself against the jammer barrier.

"Try to leave the body intact on the last one," Wyatt reminded her. "We only need to take one back."

Their atmo suit helmets darkened in response to the bright glare of the blaster-welders. The sealed suits also shielded them from the acrid smell of burning wiring and circuits that Wyatt remembered too well from his previous fight.

Beth kept on the crippled bot until she had blown off a third leg, and the bot collapsed, unable to support its own weight. The other bots were missing a few legs as well, their movements growing more random and uncoordinated as the shots scrambled their wiring and the jammers affected their programming. Beth scored a kill shot through the robotic eye of one of the Kalok spiders, and the bot went down and remained motionless.

Wyatt focused on the least damaged bot, which had slowed its frantic attack, tripping over its fallen companion. That gave Wyatt a chance to aim, and he made his shots count against the trapped bot. A few minutes more, and only one bot was still twitching.

"Get the net," Wyatt said, keeping his weapon trained on the last bot. Beth returned with a net made from a mix of metals Worm had assured them was strong enough to tow a spaceship. Wyatt still didn't trust that the bot couldn't slice through, so after he and Beth carefully prodded the damaged bot into the net, he tossed one of the jammers in with it.

Beth grabbed most of the jammers, leaving four still active in case the bots weren't quite as defunct as they appeared. Wyatt hauled the remaining bot in the net, careful to maintain distance to avoid the tips of the razor-sharp metal feet. When they reached the airlock, Wyatt heaved the net—jammer, bot and all—into the lead box and slammed down the lid, locking it securely.

"Let's get out of here. We got everything we came for."

Beth cast a glance back toward the ruined ship. "We don't even know who they were."

"They were cargo haulers. They knew the risks. Say all the prayers for them that you want, but we need to leave."

Beth glared at him, but followed. "What about the ship?"

Wyatt didn't answer until they were back on board the *Nellie B*, out of decontamination, and with their dangerous cargo stowed inside a force field containment area. "Nellie. Uncouple and get us out of blast range, then open fire."

"Why—"

"Because if Kalok comes looking for their bots, we don't want anyone to know that we've figured out a weakness. Let them think they're invincible until we're ready to fight back in a big way."

Beth eyed the lead box and the glowing force field around it. "Think it'll hold?"

Wyatt shrugged. "It's the best I've got, and that box isn't going to be easy to get out of, even for a bot. Plus, I had Nellie add a little upgrade." He paused when they reached the door. "Nellie. Begin jammer sequence." The familiar squeal filled the bay. Wyatt grinned. "She can play it anywhere on the ship. Broadcast it in an atmosphere, too. That bot isn't going anywhere onboard Nellie."

Beth returned his smile, and they stripped out of their suits and returned them to the lockers before heading up to the bridge. She watched him limp toward the controls and frowned. "You're hurt."

"I'll live."

"Can't fight with a bum leg," she countered. "Drop the pants and sit down. A few minutes won't hurt."

Wyatt sighed, knowing he had already lost this round and did as he was told.

Beth grabbed the med kit and then methodically cleaned, sterilized, and sealed up the wound while Wyatt grumbled.

"Better?"

"Yeah. I guess so. Thanks." Wyatt growled, not willing to admit how nice it was to have a partner, someone to watch his back, who actually cared whether he got hurt. That line of thinking was dangerous, so he shifted his thoughts back to business as he pulled himself back together.

"Nellie. Report scans. What did I miss?" Wyatt asked as he strapped in.

"Very little of importance," the AI replied. "I've run relevancy filters on all of the transmissions I was able to intercept. There's one I think you need to hear."

"Play it."

The transmission sounded faint, partly garbled, and Wyatt guessed it had been at the edge of Nellie's intercept range. Bursts of static drowned out some of the words. "…think there's trouble…last report said they're getting bold…send a package…" The rest were coordinates that Wyatt recognized at once.

"Fuck. We need to get back. Those coordinates—they're too close to the Outpost for comfort."

WYATT AND BETH touched down at the Outpost, having flown as fast as the *Nellie B* could travel. Even so, the trip to the *Wayfarer* and back had taken two days. "I hope Worm and his hacker buddies made good use of their time," Wyatt said. "Because I think we're going to need whatever they've come up with."

"The bot's in the box," he called out to a tech who jogged toward the ship. "Take it to Worm. We need to see Katherine. Now."

Wyatt and Beth hustled through the corridors, jostling their way past slower pedestrians. When they reached the main office, a guard blocked their way. "You can't go in there."

"The hell we can't. I've got intel Katherine needs to hear. Tell her Wyatt and Beth are here. Tell her now."

The guard gave him a dubious look, but he toggled his comm link, listened to the voice on his earbud, and then glowered as the orders came in Wyatt's favor. Wyatt tried hard not to smirk as the guard stepped aside to let them enter.

Katherine rose from her desk. "What's so important—"

"We got the bot," Beth reported.

"And Nellie intercepted a transmission," Wyatt interrupted. "Someone gave the coordinates of the outer system. I think you've got a mole—and I think we're about to get company."

Katherine looked like she was about to add something to the conversation, when the loud blare of a klaxon sounded, deafening in the confines of the small office. Monitors burst into life around the room, and Worm dove for a desk on the other side that had been hidden in the shadows, covered with vid screens and keyboards.

Katherine touched the earpiece that tied into her comm link. Even from a distance, Wyatt heard the person on the other end shouting.

"Where? Can you contain it?" Katherine swore as the answer came back negative. "Drop the fire doors. Get everyone out of the affected areas." More shouting and Katherine closed her eyes like she was trying hard not to shout back. "We're working on it. Yes, I know—I *know*. Just get everyone the fuck away from there, and we'll come up with something. Now!"

Wyatt leaned forward. "Is that—"

"Bots," Katherine replied. "Cargo bay four. Already killed five people."

"Maybe it's not just the cargo ships anymore," Beth said, horrified as the obvious conclusion dawned on her. "Salvagers, pirates, smugglers, even legal traders moving those bots unknowingly for Kalok. There's been time to send cargo all over the quadrant, out beyond the Rim—"

"Right now, I've got people dying," Katherine snapped. "So save the conspiracy theories for later. I need to know how to stop those damn bots."

"I can help," Wyatt replied, standing. He turned to Beth and Worm. "Your haystack just got closer. Forget tracing the communication to the cargo ship. If the bots activated here—"

"Then we got a code too," Worm finished for him. "I'm on it."

Beth stood. "We're the only ones who've fought them and survived," she said, turning to Wyatt. "I'm coming with you."

Wyatt shook his head. "You're good with patterns and codes. Help Worm. We stand a much better shot of surviving this if we can turn them off, especially now that we've got the bot from the *Wayfarer*. Fighting them is going to get a lot of people killed, but I can hold them off and buy you time."

"We made some more jammers, and rigged up a few more blaster-welders," Worm volunteered. "Not hardly enough, but some. They're down at the cargo bay."

Beth looked like she wanted to argue, but instead she clamped her lips tight and gave a curt nod. "Be careful," she said, leaning forward quickly and giving him a kiss on the cheek.

Wyatt wondered if she could see the fear in his eyes. He gave a gentle touch to her arm as his hand drifted down to squeeze her hand. Their eyes met for just an instant. "You too," he said and darted forward. Katherine came around the desk and hustled Wyatt toward the door.

"Come on," she said. "Tell me everything you know about taking these things down."

Wyatt jogged beside Katherine. "Where are we going? You don't want to run into those things in a hallway. We could really use the stuff from the *Nellie B* because my gun won't do shit to stop them." *Damn, I wish I had my suit too.*

"In here." Katherine stopped in front of a door and pulled him inside. The outpost's command center buzzed with tension as half a dozen men and women monitored video feeds and the constant influx of reports from earpieces.

"Shit," Wyatt muttered, with a cold, sinking feeling as the feeds confirm his fear, that the bots were the same design he faced on the *Merchant Prince* and the *Wayfarer*, the same things that murdered Mack.

"That what you fought before?" Katherine asked, and everyone in the command center turned to look at him.

Wyatt swallowed and nodded. "Yeah." He tamped down the fear and turned to the others. "Guns don't make much of a dent, at least mine didn't and mine's heavy-duty beyond legal," he said, as their gaze dropped to the weapon in the holster on his thigh. "The blaster-welders are better, but they still take multiple shots. The high-intensity jammers Worm made can help us trap them. Beyond that…we improvise," he said.

"I already sent someone to your ship to grab what they could," Katherine said.

"Good. Also, they don't like electricity," Wyatt continued. "And they're damned fast. So we need arc welders, anything that throws a bolt of electricity without frying the person holding it. And hover carts, loaders, something you can ride down a corridor sparking their ugly tin asses. Plasma torches might work, but they'd have to be powerful."

He turned to Katherine. "If they just woke up, can we contain them? Do you have a way to…I don't know…electrify the floors or walls and keep them bottled up? Mess with the gravity? As smart as they are, they're still bots."

Katherine shook her head. "The outpost's built to keep something like that from happening. Everything insulated, coated…even if we could figure out a way, it wouldn't be fast."

"Then we'd better hope Worm and Beth come up with a code," Wyatt said. "Because containing them is going to be rough." He frowned, thinking of something. "Can you confine everyone to quarters? Tell them to go in and lock the door and don't come out?"

"If those things could rip apart a cargo ship, how's a door going to stop them?" One of the command techs asked.

"I think the cargo ship depressurizing was an accident," Wyatt said, voicing his suspicions. "The bots on the *Prince* could have killed the crew—and me—by opening up the hull, but they didn't. Think about it. If the bots rip the hull, the ship's worth nothing but scrap. If the bots kill the people but don't do major damage to the craft, Kalok's solved its problem and keeps an asset."

"How'd you get away?" One of the techs asked. He was a thin young man who looked to be barely out of his teens, with lank dark hair and a skeptical expression.

"A friend and I fought as hard as we could with weapons and arc welders," Wyatt replied, letting his voice go flat and cold. "But there were just too many of them. My friend pushed me through an airlock into my ship and then jammed the controls so the things couldn't get to me. He died." Wyatt's expression dared the man—or any of them— to say something. Wisely, they didn't. "On the *Wayfarer*, we went in prepared and set a trap. It was still a tough fight and it's too late for that here.

"Beth and I barely got away from the *Wayfarer* with the new weapons Worm rigged up for us. So if you've got ideas, I'm all for it." When no one spoke up, he continued. "If everyone locks themselves into rooms, the bots might get through the door, or they might not, but it won't be quick. And it'll keep people a lot safer than trying to run or fight. They seemed to be drawn by activity."

"Enough talking," Katherine ordered. "What do we have we can work with?"

"I've got Bay Two gathering the loaders and hover carts, and everything from the welding bay that's portable," a tech replied.

"Get down there," Katherine said, glancing at Wyatt. "You're the only one who knows what we're really up against. I'll have the weapons from the *Nellie B* brought there." Katherine started speaking into her comm, giving orders.

"I'll get him there," a dark-haired man cut in. He glanced at Wyatt. "Name's Anselm."

"Let's get going, Anselm," Wyatt replied, heading for the door. He grabbed one of the blaster-welders and passed another to Anselm. Only four more hung on the wall. Not nearly enough.

"Give three of those to the guards, and keep one here to hold them off," Wyatt said with a nod toward the guns.

"Try not to get killed," Katherine said behind them.

"No promises," Wyatt said. Anselm paled. "Come on. Show me the way."

Anselm took off, and Wyatt trailed a few steps behind, drawing his gun for all the good it would do. "This is the shortest way, and—" Anselm broke off at the sound of whining machinery and clattering metal.

"Detour," Wyatt ordered, nearly skidding past the turn when Anselm changed course to avoid bots in the main corridor. The second route proved to be blocked as well, though gunfire and shouts made it clear the bots met with active resistance.

"Let's try this." Anselm unlatched the panel over a maintenance door and started up the metal ladder that would take them into the ductwork catwalks. Cursing under his breath, Wyatt followed, replacing the panel, though the narrow access ladder was far too small for any of the bots to follow. At least, none of the ones he had seen on the *Prince*. The idea that the bots might come in a variety of sizes, small bots able to wriggle into tight spaces like this, made his gut clench. Claustrophobia was bad enough, but there would be no room to fight in the access tube. He kept climbing, and resolutely refused to picture how such a battle would go.

"So far, so good," Anselm said as they crawled through the mechanical shaft. They were in the walls and ceiling of the outpost now, and Wyatt heard the battle on the other side. He kept his gaze on the soles of Anselm's boots as they maneuvered through the tube, but he listened intently to the sounds of the fight just a steel panel's thickness away.

The sudden clatter of metal on metal provided only seconds of warning. "Get out of the way!" Wyatt yelled, shoving Anselm forward and pulling back himself as something large and heavy hit the wall hard, denting into the space where Anselm had been seconds before. A sharp, mechanical arm punctured the inner bulkhead, then ripped free.

Wyatt ignored the thudding of his heart as he forced himself to scramble past the rip in the wall, praying that the bot didn't decide to fish around to see what it could catch. Luckily, from the sound of the fight on the other side, the bot had plenty of opponents to keep its mind off any movement it might have picked up from the maintenance tubes.

"How much farther?" Wyatt whispered, unwilling to give away their position any more than their movements, body heat, and vital signs might already betray to the mechanical monsters.

"Almost there," Anselm said, but Wyatt noted that the man crawled faster now and kept as far to the inside of the shaft as he possibly could. Wyatt did the same.

By the time they dropped through the ceiling into the second cargo bay, Wyatt's knees were raw and bruised, his shoulders were tight from crawling, and the muscles in his neck felt like his head would snap off from the angle he'd had to keep in the tube. He and Anselm stared into the business end of a dozen guns, and Wyatt raised his hands in appeasement, as the sweat dripped down his temples and his heart thudded in his chest.

"It's just us. Came from the command center. Got a few ideas about how to play bloody havoc with those bots," Wyatt said, not daring to breathe until the others lowered their guns.

"We got what the boss asked for," a woman with short blond hair said and jerked her thumb toward equipment massed near the cargo bay doors.

All kinds of welding machinery sat next to hover carts and lifters, along with the specialized weapons Worm had given them for the recon mission, but what caught Wyatt's eye were two metal exoskeletons. "Hello, beautiful," he said, walking up to one of the mechanical steel frames.

"That's Dora," a man said, catching up with him before Wyatt could touch the suit. "And the other is Denny." At Wyatt's quizzical look, the guy just shrugged. "The names just stuck."

"A trained operator can lift over a thousand pounds wearing one of these suits," the blonde added, striding up to Dora with a proprietary glint in her eye. "Reckon they can punch about that hard, too."

"I like the idea," Wyatt replied. "But what about all the soft squishy parts in the middle?"

Dora's operator grinned. "We've got body armor suits to protect us from hazardous materials. Let's see what these babies can do."

Screams from outside the cargo bay door ramped up the urgency of their mission. "Right," Wyatt said. "We need to get those welders lashed onto the carts. The bots can run up walls, stick to ceilings, and jump as high as your head. Put a team on each cart, two with metal poles, one with the welders. Another team can take the last of those jammers and put them on the main corridor. It might at least slow them down. Let's go, folks. Time's wasting." *Damn, wish I hadn't left that shit on the* Wayfarer. *Too late now.*

In minutes, Dora and Denny's operators were suited up, and the carts and loaders with their crews waited at the door to roll out. Wyatt was in the first hover cart, forcing down the memories of the fight aboard the *Prince* and trying not to be ill.

"Only ram them as a last resort," Wyatt yelled as the doors opened. "Their legs are sharp!"

"We'll do the ramming for you," Dora's operator said, as she and Denny waded out into the corridor first, where three of the bots awaited them.

Dora moved left, while Denny right, leaving the bot in the center for Wyatt and his crew. Dora's operator came out swinging, and each hit of the robotic fists left deep dents in the bot's bulbous midsection. Denny moved faster than Wyatt would have thought the heavy exoskeleton could go. They were built for strength, not for speed, but Denny's operator knew his equipment, and he forced the bot back, delivering a hammering with the mechanical arms that would have had the robot skittering away except for the heavy steel boot Denny planted on one of its jointed feet, keeping it in place.

The bot tugged and twisted, as Denny kept the hits coming. With the snap and creak of breaking metal, the bot ripped away from its trapped leg. Denny delivered a merciless blow to its "head" with both mechanized fists, sending the damaged bot staggering away, unbalanced without its missing leg, sparks and flames shooting out of the exposed shell.

Wyatt had happily relinquished wielding the arc welder to one of the bay mechanics, who had suited up with an insulated apron and gloves, his face protected with a welder's helmet. Two other bay workers stood one on either side of the cart, each holding a long steel pole. Wyatt let out a whoop as he steered the craft straight for the bot in the center, shouting even louder at the crack and snap of the welder's electric arc and the tang of ozone in the air. The arc struck the bot in that sweet spot Wyatt had identified the hard way, the place where its control unit joined with its body.

The bot trembled, then came at them again. Steel poles kept the welder out of range of those deadly sharp legs, fending off the attack until the sizzling bolt snapped out once more, hitting the optical unit this time and sending the blinded bot stumbling backward, right into Denny's reach.

Two steel fists collided with the damaged bot, crushing the core. It struck out with its long, jointed legs, slashing at anything in reach, as the last of its power bled away. The sharp-clawed legs skittered harmlessly against Denny's metal exoskeleton but opened a bloody gash across the driver's armor suit exposing his all-too-human legs.

Denny's operator swore, then gave the dead bot a solid kick that sent it screeching down the corridor like a metallic game ball. "I'll live," he answered the unspoken question. "Let's go hunting."

Voices in their earpieces guided the unlikely flotilla as it poured from Cargo Bay Two. Dora went with Wyatt's group, while Denny split off with a second team, and a third group took two extra welders to make up for the lack of steel muscle. All the while, Wyatt wondered how Beth and Worm fared with their hacking, fearing that their first salvo had been lucky and that the fights to come were not at all certain to go their way. Beth and Worm needed to hurry.

Wyatt had a bad feeling that they were running out of luck.

He hated being right.

Dora came around the corner hard and fast, alerted to the presence of the bots by the sound of fighting and the smell of blood. She caught the nearest bot with a kick that sent it spinning, but the bot on the ceiling crashed down on her, overbalancing the exoskeleton and taking them both to the floor.

"Get it off her!" Wyatt shouted, driving the hover cart right for the bot, with the metal poles angled like javelins to knock the robot clear.

Dora's operator fought hard, even stuck on her back by the weight of the mechanical suit. She punched and kicked, and the blows rang out as metal hammered against metal. But the slender, strong legs stabbed down like daggers, looking for weak points in the body armor, for joints and seams where their knife-sharp tips could slide through to soft skin and vulnerable organs.

"I can't use the arc!" the welder yelled. "She's too close."

"Then hang on!" Wyatt rammed the bot, lifting up just enough to skim the hovercraft over top of Dora, slamming its full weight into the robot and dragging it away from Dora.

"Can you get up?" he yelled back, trying to figure out whether the blood on the bot's legs belonged to Dora's operator.

"Not fast, but keep them off me, and I can handle it," she answered, and as Wyatt spared a glance behind them, he saw thin steel rods extend from the shoulders, hips, and knees of the exoskeleton, slowly pushing Dora upright.

"Cover her!" Wyatt yelled back to the hover cart where Anselm had the controls. Anselm grinned and snapped a salute.

Wyatt couldn't spare the attention to watch behind him; too many bots crowded the corridor in front. His welder knocked two of the creatures loose from the ceiling with his arc, and in the seconds of free-fall, when the bots were vulnerable, the jousters had their guns in hand, getting in blasts that hit the vulnerable control unit heads. A second glare and sizzle of the arc caught the bots when they were still reeling, filling the corridor with the smell of frying circuitry. Wyatt rammed the craft forward, and the jousters used that momentum to drive their steel lances into the robots' vulnerable joints, and a final hit with the welder's electrical arc left the bots smoking ruins.

"It's too damn narrow; we can't get enough of our people in here," Wyatt shouted. "Anselm, up and over!"

With that warning to his crew and the team behind them, Wyatt lifted the hover cart farther off the floor, sailing over the top of three bots to come down on the other side, trapping them between his crew and Anselm's, with Dora engaging two more bots that had come up behind them.

Wyatt heard chatter on his earpiece, but he couldn't afford the distraction of listening. He sent up another prayer to gods he didn't believe in that Beth and Worm would figure out the code soon, and threw himself into the fight.

They weren't the first to encounter the bots in this corridor. Splashes of fresh red blood painted the walls and slicked the floor, and Wyatt tried not to look too closely at the savaged bodies of the fallen outpost crew or the blood-spatter drying on the bots that swarmed the hallway.

Katherine's estimate on the number of Kalok bots loosed by the transmission seemed woefully low. Despite those they had already put out of commission, six more remained. Wyatt gathered from the chatter on the link that the other two teams had their hands full as well. If Beth and Worm couldn't figure out how to shut down the bots, the fight would be over and running would be the only choice.

Bots closed in from both sides. The welder could only strike one at a time, and the jousters were equally limited. Wyatt did his best to steer the hover cart, but it had already far exceeded its original purpose as a mechanical beast of burden, not designed for precision maneuvering and definitely not for close-quarters deathmatches.

A cry of pain behind them alerted Wyatt just in time to see one of the crew from Anselm's cart topple off the edge, taking his steel pole with him, his chest ripped open from a bot's sharp feet. Farther down the corridor, Dora defended their flank, holding off another bot to keep it from joining the two already assailing Anselm's beleaguered team.

Wyatt's welder tech lashed out again and again with insane courage, pushing his arc generator far past its intended use, holding off one bot and then another, long enough for the jousters to rain down more blows or stab at vulnerable joints. Wyatt rammed the nearest bot with the edge of the cart, knowing that the move carried the risk of throwing off one of his team even as it put the heft of the craft to work for them.

A bot came up from under the cart and slashed one sharpened leg across Wyatt's shins, cutting deep and making him curse harder. The thin, deep cut across barely-padded bone hurt like a mother, but there would be worse coming if he let down his guard, so Wyatt gritted his teeth and kept a hand at the helm.

They were all bloodied and ragged by this point, forearms and thighs cut and bleeding, and for one of Wyatt's crew, a deep slash across the back where a bot got too close before the other jouster pushed it clear. Dora brought one mechanical boot down hard on the control unit of a damaged bot, kicking it savagely into its companion before lunging after the remaining, lopsided robot as if it were the prize in a desperate scrimmage.

Blood stained Dora's exoskeleton and Wyatt desperately hoped not all of it was her drivers. His attention snapped forward as his right-hand jouster seemed to fly off the edge of the cart, jerked sideways with a bot's leg impaling his chest. Warm blood sprayed over the cart, dousing them all with gore and the screaming ended as two of the bots swarmed over their fresh kill.

With a savage growl, Wyatt drove the craft into the bots as they vivisected the still-twitching crewman, scattering them like bowling pins. He went after the bots, and his crew howled a battle cry as they took their vengeance. The welder lashed first one bot and then another with bright, crackling whips of raw power, scorching metal, and scrambling circuits. The jouster jumped from her perch, racing in to hammer the bots with lengths of pipe, sweeping the steel rods at the joints of the thin, dangerous legs.

"Get out of the way!" Wyatt warned, and the jouster threw herself back on board. Wyatt raised the craft by a few feet, then slammed down on the damaged bots, once, then twice more. The beleaguered hover cart whined in protest, its straining propulsion unit nearing its end.

Four bots left. Down the corridor, Dora remained on her feet and fighting, but the exoskeleton moved slower, its blows erratic, and one mechanical arm hung uselessly by her side, vital wiring ripped or cut by the bots' sharp claws. Wyatt's crew was down a man, and the welder's machine was sputtering and wheezing. Anselm's cart had also lost a jouster, and the remaining man bled from so many gashes Wyatt was surprised he was still on his feet. Wyatt's wounds throbbed, and he felt light-headed with exertion and blood loss.

He had survived a war and years of dangerous salvage work to die on a Fringe outpost in a corridor with a bunch of drone bots.

"Fuck that," Wyatt muttered, ramming two of the remaining bots with the cart at full speed. He barely kept hold of the controls, and the welder had to grab onto his machine to avoid being thrown over it as the jouster slid wildly across the tilting platform, scrabbling for a hand-hold.

Wyatt felt a burst of primitive satisfaction as the edge of the cart sheared off the control unit of one bot and the corner drove deep into the body of the second, opening up its sturdy metal shell. The welder snapped a blue-white arc at the vulnerable components as his machine sputtered its last.

Wyatt turned, a victory cry on his lips, only to see Anselm go rigid as a thin, sharp metal leg lanced through his back and out his chest, holding him upright as his body shuddered and blood dripped from his lips. Behind them, Dora stumbled. The exoskeleton wobbled, and then came crashing down atop one of the remaining bots and lay still.

Wild with grief and anger, Wyatt and the remaining crews leaped from their damaged crafts, circling around the last bot. He pulled out his plasma torch and held it in one hand, with his blaster on the other.

Pain and the knowledge of impending death made them fearless, as they hammered on the creature's metal skin and stabbed at it with plasma blades, steel poles, and the severed sharp legs of its mangled comrades.

The bot listed, going down under the onslaught of blows, but Wyatt's elation was short-lived as the sound of skittering metal feet sounded just past where Dora lay unmoving across the wreckage of another bot.

Wyatt and the others exchanged a glance, then drew themselves up, weapons ready, to make a final stand.

Four fresh bots scrabbled into view, and Wyatt knew he and the others were royally screwed. They stood shoulder to shoulder, a line across the corridor, daring the bots to do their worst.

The bots swarmed toward them, then froze. One of the mechanical killers hung from the ceiling and suddenly dropped like a stone, landing on its back and making no move to right itself. The others stayed motionless, legs lifted mid-stride, as the light faded from their mechanical eyes.

"It's about damn time," Wyatt murmured, as close to a prayer of gratitude as he would ever get, wondering if Beth and Worm had any inkling of just how fine they had cut the odds.

The surviving station crew moved warily around the deactivated bots. Denny took his frustration out on two of the robots, smashing them to bits with his powerful exoskeleton. Wyatt sighed as he saw Anselm's bloody corpse and the bodies of their other comrades, along with Dora's fallen warrior.

"Let's load the bodies on the carts and take them back with us," Wyatt said. "And then we'll come back and take those fucking bots apart bolt by bolt."

Chapter Fourteen

"It worked!" Beth's eyes were alight with triumph as Wyatt returned to the command center. Worm managed to appear somewhat interested, a change from his usual sullen self.

Wyatt managed a grim, grateful smile. "You saved our asses. We wouldn't have made it without the shut-down." The blood spattering his clothing testified to the fact that many of their fellow fighters did not.

Beth seemed to realize the reason for his somber mood and went to stand beside him. "Close?"

He nodded, averting his gaze. He didn't want Beth to see the grief in his eyes. "Yeah. Good people died. But it would have been worse without you guys figuring out the code, so don't let me rain on your parade."

Beth returned the peck on the cheek he had given before the battle. "I've never been much for parades." She squeezed his arm.

"We've still got the matter of the remaining Kalok bots," Katherine said, bringing their attention back to the here and now. "I'm not willing to keep them here, and I doubt anyone else wants to, either."

"Pushing them out an airlock won't work, even if we weren't on a planet," Wyatt replied. "It wouldn't destroy them. They'd just become floating parasites."

"Reprogramming them as a group won't work, for the same reason it will be difficult—if not impossible—for Kalok to remotely revise their code," Worm added. "So that leaves us two options—destroy them, or manually rewire them to defend what they initially tried to attack."

Wyatt met Katherine's gaze and smiled as he realized she was thinking the same thing.

"I like that," Katherine said, and Worm looked surprised to find his suggestion accepted. "How hard will it be to rewire them—and assure that they can't be made to turn on us?"

"Not too difficult," Worm replied. "We'll need to hard code the defensive instructions, so they can't be re-written even if Kalok does figure out how to try to re-activate them. The one from the *Wayfarer* was pretty beat up, but we have more specimens now. Give me a day or so."

"Get working on it," Wyatt said.

"They're vicious sons of bitches, so if we hand out the instructions to the rest of the Coalition, or to everyone who hates Kalok, there's a chance they could still be used against people who don't deserve it," Beth cautioned.

Katherine nodded. "That's true of any weapon. But it might put a crimp in Kalok's plans, and it makes use of assets that would otherwise go to waste. Do it," she told Worm.

"What's your end game?" Wyatt asked, and Katherine frowned as she looked at him. "I mean, what does the Coalition want when it's all over? Sovereignty? You want to be the new Interplan? Or is loosening Kalok's hold enough—and if so, how long is that going to last before some other big bad moves in and wants to play?"

"Maybe the out-Rim and the Fringe will stay frontier forever," Katherine replied, squaring her shoulders. "Probably not, if history is any guide. But you two, of all people, know how Kalok and Interplan work, how many people die to secure their claim and make their money. And it's got to stop. The cover-ups, the murders, leaving people to die, the bots. No, all the little backwater worlds probably won't be able to stay independent, but if they have to get absorbed into something bigger, then there's got to be a better way for it to happen."

"That doesn't say much about the 'how' to stop them," Beth pressed. "Kalok's pretty clear on 'how' to continue their expansion. So you're going to have to do better than that."

"The 'how' is exposing Kalok to all of the unallied planets who are thinking of throwing in their lot with Interplan or giving up their mining rights to Kalok," Worm said, taking a step between Katherine and Beth. "If enough people know the truth, Kalok won't be able to cover it up anymore. People will be watching, expecting it. And the unallied worlds will be able to put pressure on for changes."

"And if they don't?" Wyatt asked.

Katherine shrugged. "Then we keep exposing what Kalok does, make it expensive for them to do it."

Wyatt shook his head. "You've got more faith in the system than I do."

Katherine managed a wry smile. "I have faith in people to do the right thing more often than the wrong thing."

"You're a better person than I am," Wyatt replied.

Beth bumped his elbow. "No, she's not." Wyatt shrugged uncomfortably and did not look up.

TWO DAYS PASSED and the tension rose. Worm and his team worked on the code and rewiring the bots. Katherine let Wyatt and Beth know that new intercepted chatter from the Coalition listening posts warned of ship movements and rumors about police cruisers mobilizing. Whenever Wyatt had a spare moment, he sent updates to his contacts in the Regiment, warning them about the coming storm.

"Do you think they'll help?" Beth asked.

Wyatt sighed. "Maybe a few, but most of them? I can't blame them if they don't. They came out here to get away from Kalok, not take on another battle."

"They might surprise you."

"Surprises aren't usually a good thing," Wyatt warned her.

Beth stretched out on her side of the bed. "Worm still doesn't have the codes all figured out."

"We've still got time," Wyatt said, pacing their quarters after they had finished a nearly twenty-four-hour shift pitching in wherever needed. "The cruisers can't drop out of the wormholes just anywhere. No navigation satellites and beacons out here past the Fringe. So they've got to come through at a known point and fly in normal space—and that's going to buy us some time."

"That's why Katherine triggered the evacuations for the non-essentials," Beth replied. "Let's hope those cruisers aren't faster than you think."

They only slept a few hours before returning to the war room. From the haggard faces and many cups of stimulant, Wyatt knew they weren't the only ones pushing their limits.

"Katherine—you need to see this." One of the Coalition members watching the vid screens beckoned urgently. "It's from the relays," she explained, more for Wyatt and Beth. "A feed that jumps among dozens of satellites throughout the space between the Rim and the Far-Fringe. I think we've got trouble in Sector 429."

"Show me," Katherine replied, her voice cool and unruffled.

The woman touched the screen, and a sequence of images from several points near the Rim's edge showed dozens of Kalok and Interplan security corsairs gliding through the darkness.

"What the fuck are those?" Wyatt demanded.

"Exactly what they look like," Katherine replied. "Muscle."

"They aren't warships," Beth protested.

"They don't have to be," the woman who called them over said, with an expression that warred between fear and professionalism.

"Those police ships still out-gun everything except the biggest pirate frigates or the navies of the unallied planets."

"Can you track their course? Are they heading for specific stations or settlements?" Beth asked, frowning as the collage of images continued.

"It looks like they're closing on the main shipping corridors," the analyst replied.

"A lot of people are fleeing the Rim for parts unknown. That's a threat to Kalok. If they start firing, there's going to be a bloodbath," Beth commented.

"How far away are they from here?" Wyatt asked.

The tech shrugged. "A couple of cycles, depending on speed. Maybe half a standard day, or a little less."

Wyatt leaned closer to the screen. "Do those police corsairs carry smaller craft?"

The woman shook her head. "No. But each one has twenty gun ports."

"You have the specs?" Wyatt asked.

Worm shouldered his way closer. "Of course." The analyst stepped aside, and Worm accessed the database, replacing the satellite feeds with the schematics for the security vessels.

Wyatt studied the schematics. "The weapon mounts—where's the blind spot?"

Worm looked at him quizzically. "Blind spot?"

"Yeah. Mounted guns have an area they can't hit because they would have to shoot through their own ship to get to it. Can you run a simulation—estimate the firing range and blind spot for all the guns on one police corsairs?"

Worm grinned. "Yeah. Give me a couple of minutes."

"You've got an idea?" Katherine asked.

"I'm sure as shit not going to sit still and get shot," Wyatt replied. "If they're going to shoot at me, I want to be moving—and shooting back."

Beth pulled Wyatt aside as Worm worked his keyboard magic.

"What do you have in mind?"

"Have you ever seen small birds gang up on a much bigger bird of prey?"

Beth looked puzzled, "I think I know what you're talking about. Tell me more."

"When a predator bird enters their territory, the little birds work together and harass the predator until it leaves."

Beth met his gaze. "That's crazy."

"It works."

"It works for little birds. But the large birds aren't—"

"The predator could kill any one of them easily. But it can't kill five or ten or twenty of them at the same time," Wyatt said, intent with the rush of a good idea.

"Got it!" Worm announced. By now, all of the analysts had shifted positions to be able to see what was on Worm's screen as well as monitor their own.

Wyatt, Beth, and Katherine leaned in as the simulation ran the fan-shaped reach projections of each of the corsair's weapons.

"Slower," Wyatt ordered. Worm obliged.

"There!" Wyatt said, pointing. Worm froze the screen. A narrow area above and toward the rear of the craft had no overlap from the projections.

"Forward," Wyatt said, and Worm started the montage again, moving frame by frame.

"Freeze!" Wyatt's finger outlined two more areas where the weapons' coverage was sparser than elsewhere.

"Attack points," Wyatt said, turning back to Katherine. "Weak spots where their weapons don't completely cover them."

Katherine shook her head. "The Coalition doesn't have any ships that could take on those corsairs. None of the resistance groups do. We've spent years trying to stay out of their way, to avoid going head to head."

Wyatt nodded, impatient to get his point across. "You don't need warships or even corsairs. My *Nellie B* could take out any one of those gun ports by herself." He gave a wicked grin.

Katherine processed the thought for a moment without giving anything away in her expression. "The pilots would have to be crazy to try it."

"Desperate people do crazy things," Wyatt replied.

"We can send out the overlay Worm did to the rest of the Coalition," Beth said, catching some of Wyatt's mad enthusiasm. "Put out the call to join us."

"Not just to the Coalition," Wyatt said. "Get it out to everyone. The Network. Phage. Hell, the Regiment."

Katherine frowned. "It's like declaring war on Kalok."

Wyatt shook his head. "No, Kalok's declaring war by moving gunships against the craft in the shipping lanes, civilian and commercial vessels. Every treaty in the Allied Worlds says so. Kalok isn't a recognized security force or the navy of a member government. It's a rogue entity."

"There will be retribution," Katherine warned.

"So what…we just let them shoot down enough of the ships in the lanes that they all give up and turn back and accept Kalok's shackles?" Wyatt argued. "We force them back now, with all the planets watching, and Kalok can't hide what they're doing anymore. Someone will make them account for it because the evidence will shame the governments backing them."

"Nice idea, but who's going to lead the charge?" Katherine asked. "You're crazy enough to do it, but one ship won't be enough."

"I've got some friends who might be interested," Wyatt said with a grin. "Let me see what I can do."

"LIDDY'S IN," WYATT announced when Beth brought dinner for both of them back to the room. "And she promised to spread the word."

"That's good, right?"

Wyatt grinned as he reached for a sandwich. The food synthesizers at the Outpost specialized in the comfort foods from the main worlds, and Wyatt could tell from the delicious aromas that his meal was done perfectly. "Yeah, that's good. I've got messages out to everyone—in code, of course. Assuming the encryption and scrambler relay work right. We'll have to see who shows up."

"Any word from your Regiment friends?" She asked, sitting down beside him. Beth looked as tired as he felt, since they had both been pulling double shifts helping out wherever needed.

"No. And I don't—" He frowned as a message came in. "Well, son of a bitch!"

"What?" She crowded closer to see his screen.

"*Riding vapors.*" The screen said.

"I don't understand."

Wyatt stared at the message, still in shock. "It's Space Corp slang. When you lift off in atmosphere, there can be vapor trails. When we all lift off together, following each other, that's 'riding vapors.'"

"Meaning?"

Wyatt could not contain his glee. "They're in. And if John and Codger are in, there'll be others, too." He let out a whoop.

Beth grinned. "That's good news. I told you they'd join up."

Wyatt shook his head. "No, you don't understand. I never thought…this isn't like them. It's too big a risk, and it's still technically treason…that hits bone, Beth. We—Regiment—are loyal. That's what caused the problem in the first place, because what we thought we were loyal to turned out to be a lie. Even so, after all that, we ran as far as we could instead of trying to burn the system down because it would have been disloyal."

"You changed your mind," she said quietly, taking Wyatt's hand.

"Not right away. And it took seeing all the betrayals up close and personal—not just abstract ideas—for it to click in my brain. By going against what Kalok and Interplan are doing, I'm still being loyal to what I thought I was fighting for in the service. Not that any of that would matter if we got caught."

"Kalok's not Space Corps, and neither is Interplan," she reminded him.

"No, they just own it." He looked at the screen again. "This is…a big fuckin' deal."

"They wouldn't do it for just anyone," Beth pointed out. Wyatt stilled as the impact of her words sank in. "They trust you. All joking about 'Burner' aside, they respect your judgment. *That* is a big fuckin' deal."

"We could get our asses kicked. This could be one of those rebellions that ends up being a footnote in history."

"Not trying to overthrow anyone," Beth replied. "Just pushing back against two corporations that have overstepped. Trying to make them back off. Letting them know we're on to what they're doing."

"It could still go all kinds of wrong."

Beth nodded. "It could. But even then, it's a shot across the bow for them. Kalok and Interplan aren't used to anyone standing up to their power. Just making the information public changes the game."

Wyatt smiled. "Maybe you should have been military. You're pretty good at strategy."

Beth made a dismissive noise. "Please. The military can only kill you. A good academic with a grudge can ruin your career and reputation and leave you alive amid the wreckage to suffer the humiliation. A shooting war is refreshingly transparent."

"You're scary sometimes."

He did not miss the glint in her eyes or the danger in her smile. "That's what makes us such a good team," Beth said.

"FIRE AT WILL!" Wyatt ordered, and angled the *Nellie B* down for a strafing run, leading his misfit squadron by example. He put out the call, and friends answered—his own and those of the pilots who heeded the summons. The Regiment turned out like he hoped they would, hungry for vengeance long overdue. Liddy's gang showed up too; they were spoiling for a fight as well.

Beth took to her role as gunner like she had been born to it, steady-handed and unflappable. Given her wolfish grin when the *Nellie B's* guns hit their target, Wyatt wondered if she might not be enjoying her work too much.

"Two down!" She crowed, and in the next few seconds took out another mount that tried to fire at the edge of its range. Beth's shot had no such limitations, and the offending weapon rig went up in a burst of smoke.

"Incoming!" Wyatt yelled into his comm. His ragtag squadron included two of Liddy's ships, three old comrades from the Regiment, and four craft owned by pilots who had heard about the "mad birds" and decided to throw in their lots.

One of the Interplan corsairs had changed course and vector, rising out of its former trajectory to menace the smaller, faster craft that were taking potshots at the corsair and two other police vessels.

"Scramble!" Wyatt ordered. "Make it random, hit the weak points. Pattern's gonna get you killed, so don't repeat."

Easier said than done, he thought, since human brains didn't do "random" particularly well. Computers could randomize, but brains liked patterns and order, which other computers could lock onto and hit. Much as Wyatt loved seat-of-the-pants flying, he turned the controls over to Nellie for the next few runs, and let out a sigh of relief as shots streaked past, narrowly missing them.

Small, illegal, unregistered ships dodged and wove like gnats on a hot day, taking potshots at the larger corsairs and streaking away. A few hulks hung dead in space, a reminder not to get cocky. But none of these pilots had stayed alive this long playing it safe, and for the first time in a long while, Wyatt felt the swell of pride in his chest at being part of something bigger than himself, something that he could trust.

"Watch your flank!" Wyatt cautioned, taking control back from the computer, and brought the *Nellie B* in so close to the police cruiser on the next run that Beth could not stifle a gasp, though her surprise did not affect her aim.

"You're really suited to a life of crime, you know." Wyatt flashed Beth a grin.

"What else can I do? My tenure bid is shot to hell," she replied, squeezing the trigger and sending a burst of covering fire to shield one of the Regiment ships as it made good on its run to take out two more of the corsair's gun ports.

"You'd think they'd get the message and head home," Wyatt remarked, bringing the *Nellie B* around in a tight loop to make another pass.

"How're we holding up?" Beth never looked up from her screen, but she didn't have to. The wailing klaxons and Nellie's reports made it impossible to ignore the fact that they had taken damage.

"Manageable, so far," Wyatt said tightly, shooting between two corsairs and dancing around the reports of their guns, as Beth targeted the ports. He rolled the *Nellie B* and evaded the worst of the return fire, grimacing as enemy shots clipped a rear panel. Yet another warning alarm sounded. A glance at the data Nellie was streaming to his console told him they weren't dead yet, and he forced himself to ignore the shrieking alerts and focus on the battle in front of him.

The corsairs were the size of mid-range cargo ships, but sleeker and faster, though they lacked the sheer power of the slower craft for long-range trips. They were never intended for true combat, built to patrol shipping lanes for pirates or escort valuable cargo to its destination, or perhaps stay in orbit above a mine or colony plagued by undesirable trespassers. By comparison, while the *Nellie B* wasn't the newest, she was still a gunship.

All around the *Nellie B*, small ships bedeviled the corsairs. Most of the craft, like Wyatt's ship, had been heavily modified, far beyond the standards on their—often falsified—registrations. Compared to true warships, the police corsairs were fast and nimble, but against the small craft and their wild pilots, they couldn't compete.

The floating hulks of the ships blown apart by the corsairs served as a reminder about the stakes of the game. Precious time elapsed as Wyatt and Katherine gathered their forces, and ships were readied for battle. By the time the outlaws closed in on their targets, the Kalok corsairs had left a trail of wreckage and death in their wake.

"That's the last of the gun mounts on the port side," Beth said. "Good for drop off."

"Deploying payload," Wyatt announced over the comm to the

other renegade ships. He brought the *Nellie B* in low and tight, then maneuvered into position just above the corsair, matching its speed. The *Nellie B's* hatch opened, and five reprogrammed Kalok bots tumbled out as Wyatt activated their new orders.

Instead of rolling off the hull of the corsair, the bots' sharp, magnetic, metal legs dug in, clawing deep into the police cruiser's outer skin. He shuddered as he realized just how close a call he had on board the *Merchant Prince*, sending up a grateful "thank you" to Mack wherever good robots go when they die. These bots looked like they would make short work of the corsair, which immediately broke off from its course and went into a series of rolls and loops to shake off the metal parasites, with no luck.

"It's working!" Beth yelled excitedly. "The bots—they're working!"

Once Worm and Beth had figured out how to reprogram the robots, they had sent the details out to their allies, along with the plan to turn those bots into weapons. Now, the *Nellie B's* sensors reported multiple ships dropping off their payloads of subverted bots, which tore into their former masters' ships enthusiastically.

"Trouble—incoming!" Wyatt had mere seconds' notice to veer off as a battered corsair rose out of the fight below them to block their path. Swearing loudly at the near miss, Wyatt fought to bring the *Nellie B* back on course, only to find the damaged police cruiser gaining speed and moving toward a knot of small craft that had been trying to stay out of the way.

"Those ships aren't even fighting," Beth said, anger clear in her voice.

"The corsair won't make it home in that state," Wyatt said tightly. "Guns are down, hull's been compromised, and they're leaking atmosphere. It's gonna ram those ships and take them out with it."

"We've got a strip right up the middle if you want to take your shot," Beth called out.

"I'm on it." Wyatt set his jaw and brought the *Nellie B* around. Beth had learned quick to aim for the top banks of guns, and once those were knocked out, the corsair was vulnerable to an attack from above that none of the side guns could prevent.

"This one's for Comstock," Wyatt muttered as he lined up his target and opened fire.

The *Nellie B's* cannons ripped a gaping wound down the spine of the corsair, from bow to stern. Wyatt looped around, and came at the corsair head-on, guns firing, aiming right for the ship's bridge.

Frozen mist drifted clear from the hull breaches, and the last salvo took out its command center, leaving it adrift. Wyatt made another pass, aiming for a vulnerable area near the engines, difficult to hit when the ship was under full power with its guns firing. He loosed another barrage and veered off a second later, kicking up acceleration to get them out of the way as the shots triggered a series of explosions inside the corsair and it blew apart, sending debris flying.

"That was a mercy kill," Beth said when she could speak after a maneuver that had her struggling to control her stomach.

"If they had been willing to limp home in peace, I would have let them go," Wyatt said quietly, staring out at the bits and pieces of the corsair that gyred across the Dark. "Then they went after those damaged civilian ships, and after that, they were dead in space. Shitty way to die, even if they were Kalok." Adrift, damaged, rudderless, the corsair would have drifted until its food ran out and the life support systems failed, dooming the crew to a slow, painful death.

"The fight seems to be winding down," Beth observed, and Wyatt brought the *Nellie B* around and took in the reports scrolling across the screens. He had no way to know how the battle had gone at other points along the shipping lanes, but in their sector, the outlaws managed a rout. Three corsair hulks hung lifeless and silent, ripped open by guns and bots. Two more signaled surrender, their guns destroyed and hulls badly damaged. On the edge of his sensors, four other cruisers retreated, heading back to base, defeated.

"You gonna let them go?" Beth leaned back in her chair.

Wyatt shrugged. "I can live with them going back, neutered, proof that we aren't going to let Kalok get what it wants without a fight."

"There'll be paybacks."

"And there won't be if we blow them up?"

"You know what they say, 'dead men tell no tales.'"

Wyatt let out a sigh and rubbed his temples, fighting off a headache. "They've got to make their way back, humiliated, proof to anyone with sensors that we whipped their asses. Not a navy, not gunboats—a bunch of outlaws. Even Kalok can't keep word of that from spreading. I'm sure they already reported back. Not like we could keep this a secret, survivors or not."

The comm crackled. Wyatt had Nellie put it through to the speaker when he saw Liddy calling.

"Nice work," she said. Smoke curled in the cockpit of her ship, and klaxons blared just far enough distant for her voice to carry above them. "You did good." She leaned away to give orders to a crewman who dared to interrupt, and came back into the picture.

"We aren't sticking around," she added. "Dropping back to the Far-Fringe. I'll send you coordinates on a secure channel. You might want to join us. I heard what your bounty is up to, and damn, but it's enough to tell you who your true friends are. You know, there aren't many ex-Space Corps gunships out there fighting for the resistance. Maybe not the best choice to remain anonymous."

"Yeah, but she's mine. We'll be careful," Wyatt assured her. "And I'm sure we'll see you out there."

"I'll be looking for you at the bar," Liddy said. "Got some jobs for you, and a couple of good fences for your regular cargo."

"Will do," Wyatt promised. "Just give us a little time to clean up here."

He switched off his link with Liddy and listened for several minutes to the chatter on the line. The outlaw squadron members peeled away with raucous jokes and bawdy punchlines, as the pilots went back to their boltholes. Traffic in the shipping lane routed around the wrecks, and larger ships took the damaged craft in tow, many heading for the Outpost for repairs.

"How bad's the damage?" Beth asked, taking in the alarms and warning screens that seemed to flash from every inch of the cockpit.

"She's had worse," Wyatt said with pride, running a hand across the controls lovingly. "We've got fuel, and I can patch us up enough myself to get well and gone from here before we need a real mechanic."

"Looks like a salvage rat's paradise out there to me," Beth said, with a nod toward the graveyard of drifting ships.

"My thought exactly," Wyatt replied, grinning in anticipation. "We can quick-strip the electronics and weapons, and what the Coalition and the Outpost don't want will find plenty of buyers Far-Fringe, especially now."

After the Coalition secured the survivors, Beth and Wyatt scavenged the dead ships until the Nellie B's hold was full, and sent out distress signals for the few civilian ships that were too damaged to get far on their own power.

"You know we've only barely touched what's out here for the taking," Wyatt said with a wistful note in his voice as he looked out at the drifting craft.

"Can't be helped. You know Kalok and Stellar Fed will be here soon. This has to be a smash and grab," Beth replied. "It's too bad the Coalition had to evacuate, but I guess it was better than the alternative."

"We did our part. It was nice to be appreciated, but think it's time to move on. Before we get more company."

"I know some nice abandoned colonies that are ripe for picking," Beth said.

"Sounds good to me. First, we need to sell off this cargo."

"And the Coalition?" She asked, reaching out to silence the alarms if they weren't imminently in danger of decompression. The pinched look on her face suggested she shared his headache.

"We made some friends, and we're in too far to back out now, I'm sure we'll be hearing from them again once they get settled," Wyatt said, setting coordinates and leaving the battlefield behind them. "Besides, that bounty Liddy warned us about tells me Kalok thinks we're even more of a threat than we were before."

"You think Liddy'll turn us in?" Beth asked, moving into the pilot's seat as Wyatt got up to tend to repairs.

Wyatt chuckled. "No, But I'm not planning to test her, either. Seems to me she's spent enough time and energy maneuvering us here, that this is where she wants us. But being the stubborn bastard that I am, we'll play this our way, and the Regiment, the Coalition, and everyone else is going to have to deal with it." He glanced at Beth, gauging her reaction. "More than you bargained for?"

Beth grinned. "I knew you were an outlaw when I came onboard. I got exactly what I bargained for." She adjusted the music, switching from Wyatt's playlist to her own and enjoying the way he flinched in response. "We've got a lot of salvage runs waiting for us. Time's a' wastin',"

"What? This auditory punishment is my reward?"

"Nah, that comes later. I just like keeping you on your toes. If you're nice, I may share."

"Thanks. So look at the list of possible runs and tell me what looks interesting," Wyatt said, stifling a smile. "Revolutions don't come cheap."